I0726718

THE

DREAMING

COMING SOON

BY
JEFFREY BAILEY

Legends of the Makers:

The Awakening
The Ascension

THE DREAMING

LEGENDS OF THE MAKERS: BOOK ONE

JEFFREY BAILEY

Phase Publishing, LLC

Seattle

If you purchased this book without a cover, you should be aware that this book is stolen property. It was reported as "unsold and destroyed" to the publisher, and neither the author nor the publisher has received any payment for this "stripped" book.

Text copyright © 2016 by Jeffrey Bailey
Cover art copyright © 2016 by Phase Publishing, LLC

All rights reserved. Published by Phase Publishing, LLC. No part of this book may be reproduced or transmitted in any form, or by any means, electronic or mechanical, including photocopying or recording or by any information storage and retrieval system, without written permission from the publisher.

Phase Publishing, LLC first paperback edition
October 2016

ISBN 978-1-943048-16-8
Library of Congress Control Number 2016957767
Cataloging-in-Publication Data on file.

ACKNOWLEDGMENTS

To all the friends and family who supported and encouraged me to keep up with my writing.

To my mother, who provided ongoing enthusiasm and excitement, constantly asking for the next chapter.

To my wonderful test readers, who collectively reassured me that this was a story worth telling.

And most especially to my brother, who started me on this writing journey with a shared story, and who may, someday, have a chance to finish it.

This is a work of fiction. Any resemblance to actual persons, living or dead, or actual events is purely coincidental. The views and opinions expressed in this novel are not necessarily those of the author or the publishing company.

CHAPTER ONE

Flowers.

There were flowers appearing on the sidewalk. They were not growing from the cracks, but from the firm, solid concrete. And there, just behind them, grass was also beginning to appear, covering the sidewalk in a lush, green blanket.

The young man smiled as he watched the flowers grow rapidly. He glanced ahead of him and saw where they were beginning under the feet of a pretty young lady walking ahead of him. She must be having a daydream, he thought to himself.

After a few more moments, the lady ahead of him began to change, her form changing to that of a little girl. Her clothes changed as well. Her light grey coat changing to a bright pink jacket. Her hair lengthened and became a mass of unruly blond curls. The girl began skipping down the sidewalk, flowers growing under her feet and lush grass flowing right behind them. Ah, so not just a daydream then, he thought. It was a memory. Those were always more vivid.

He smiled again as he thought about just how common things like that had become. A quick glance to the side gave him the sight of a man in a business suit, an impossibly beautiful woman on his arm in a bright red form-fitting dress and what must be at least six-inch heels.

The young man chuckled softly as the woman moved with inhuman grace, keeping up with the pace of the crowd easily, even in the imposing heels. Now that's a daydream, he mused with another smile.

A quick glance around him showed other daydreams as well. A young boy was consuming a veritable mountain of sweets, an old man flickered back and forth between his current form and what was likely his much younger self, and a mother with four children that had sprouted eight arms trying to deal with all of them.

They weren't real of course, more's the pity, he thought. Life would be quite a bit easier if everything people dreamed became real, but the Dreaming only brought the illusion of a daydream to life for all to see.

He chuckled to himself as he remembered how awkward it was for the first few months. Everyone's dreams and fantasies out in the open for all to see. It had become very difficult to keep a secret anymore, as the first hint of a fantasy or daydream activated the Dreaming and brought that daydream to illusionary life.

Strangely enough, it didn't seem to affect normal nighttime dreams. Nor were focused thoughts projected. Though he had heard that the brief daydreams that many people indulged in right before they went to sleep often did appear. Much to the consternation of a wife who suddenly saw another woman in their bed, or a husband who found himself underwater in a coral reef, or the poor spouse of a fantasy reader who ended up looking into the face of a dragon, just as they were drifting off to sleep.

It had been a difficult adjustment for the first few months as most people learned to control their thoughts to a degree none of them had ever imagined. Things still slipped out of course, like the woman in the red dress on the arm of the businessman. But for the most part, people had learned to control their flights of fancy.

It had been five years since the Dreaming hit. At least, that's what everyone called it, the Dreaming. He wondered idly if it had any relation to the dreaming that the aboriginal Australians talked about. That was probably the most confusing thing about the Dreaming. No one seemed to know where it had come from.

There were lots of theories of course. Some said it was a super-weapon gone wrong. Others said it was caused by aliens. Some thought it was the land of faerie returned to earth. There were more theories about the origin of the Dreaming than there were magazines and newspapers to print them all. But whatever it was, it had changed life on Earth dramatically.

As he continued down the sidewalk toward the subway entrance, he continued to reminisce about what life was like just five short years ago. Politics was one area that was hit hard by the Dreaming. He remembered when everyone just wanted to know what a politician was really thinking; when they were telling the truth and when they were lying. Well that question had been answered very quickly for everyone.

The young man laughed out loud at the irony of it. The Dreaming had hit right in the middle of the elections. With a half-dozen politicians debating on national television, all of a sudden every secret dream and fantasy they had while the other candidate was talking had been brought to life. And since the illusions caused by the Dreaming could be seen by everyone, the entire country knew what each candidate thought about when their mind wandered, and it was a revelation.

In the chaos that followed, the people actually rose up and said no. It was a grand thing, he thought. Just like that old movie with the guy who inherited a bunch of money and decided to use it to get people to vote "None of the Above".

Almost overnight, nearly every political candidate both running and incumbent was stripped from office by mobs of people so disgusted by what they had seen that they had to take action. Unfortunately, the aftermath of that mass impeachment left a power vacuum that was difficult to fill. Thankfully, many of the more local leaders were able to stay in place and help their people to weather the storm. Things were still chaotic on the national level, but the individual cities were holding up fairly well.

Several of the big city mayors, and a surprising number of business leaders, had stepped up to fill the void and kept things running on the local level. With greater or lesser success depending on the city, he thought wryly. But the country had not collapsed, almost everyone was still going about their lives as normal. Or as normal as they could with their every flighty daydream suddenly brought to life.

The young man quickly glanced around as he started down the steps toward the subway station. He was slightly surprised that no one was looking at him. People still tended to stare when they saw someone's daydream manifest, and he had been reminiscing quite a bit in the last few minutes.

Shaking his head, he marveled again at the unpredictability of the Dreaming. Unbeknownst to many, there were a small, select few people whose daydreams did not become an illusionary reality around them. They could think and daydream with impunity, and no one knew the difference.

It was such a rare phenomenon that no one had really studied it yet, though the young man had an idea as to why that was, and why he was one of the select few whose dreams did not appear like a holographic movie projection.

His thoughts were interrupted as he reached the turnstile for the subway. Realizing he had forgotten to pull out his transit card, he fumbled for a moment digging it out. Trying to ignore the grumbling of the people behind him who suddenly had to stop and wait for him, he got his card out, swiped it, and continued into the station.

As he went to put the card back in his wallet, he absent-mindedly rubbed off a bit of dirt on the front of it. He was a monthly card holder, so he had a full photo ID on the card itself. 'Garrett Castlemain', the card read in thick, block text.

Garrett squinted at the photo, trying to see if there was dirt there as well. The photo showed a man in his early thirties. Short, brown hair topped a strong face, the pointed chin and aristocratic nose showing some kind of Eastern European background. Thick eyebrows atop somewhat narrow eyes gave him a brooding appearance. At least, in the smile-less government issued photo. Deciding the card was clean enough, he slipped it back into his wallet and continued on to the subway.

He pressed forward through the crowd, moving

toward the platform. His broad-shouldered frame and a fraction under six feet in height made him larger than most of the crowd, a fact he tried hard not to exploit when he was in a hurry.

Idly, he noticed that the pretty lady ahead of him was no longer a child and was again a full adult with a grey coat and short, blond hair. Glancing around quickly, he noticed that the businessman no longer had a woman on his arm, though the harried mother had apparently sprouted even more arms. It really was too bad all those extra arms weren't real, he thought. At least, not for her.

Again his train of thought was interrupted, this time by an actual train. He could hear the sound of the subway coming down the tracks toward the station. The crowd pushed forward, preparing to quickly enter the subway as it stopped.

From the side, he heard a loud clacking sound. He didn't recognize it, but it sounded a bit like something mechanical being ratcheted. A second later came a sound he did recognize, the sound of machine gun fire.

His head whipped around, trying to find the shooter as people screamed and started to scramble in every direction. There, about ten feet behind him next to the tiled column.

The man was wearing a dirty sweater and jeans, with worn, ragged shoes and a torn trench coat. The only things new about him was a shiny new machine gun, and of all things a ridiculous-looking clown mask. Seriously, he thought, are we back in the 1980's?

Without warning, the man's face turned toward him and he started firing again. Diving for cover, the young man cursed his drifting mind and resolved to pay more attention the next time he was being shot at.

Rolling to his knees behind a pillar, he turned at the sound of a scream. The woman in the grey jacket with the happy childhood stood frozen on the platform. The evilly grinning face of the clown mask was looking right at her.

The young man cursed under his breath as he saw the barrel of the gun swinging in her direction. Leaping out from behind his cover, he dove at the woman, knocking her to the ground as a spray of bullets slammed over their heads. Clutching her tightly, he rolled them both across the ground until they were behind another column. I bet she wishes those dreams of hers were real, he thought to himself. Fortunately for her, for some people they are…

The young man felt his consciousness fading as the feeling of metal plates sliding over his body engulfed him. His last thought before everything went black was to wonder where the metal for the armor came from.

The powerful knight assessed the situation in an instant. The woman lying behind the column next to him and the sound of a weapon being discharged seemed to indicate that young Garrett had saved her. That was good. He was a good lad if a tad inexperienced. But now was not the time for inexperience.

Rising quickly, he jostled the shield on his left arm, making sure it was secure. It always was. Lifting the visor of his helm, he risked a glance around the tiled column. There was a poor looking fellow with a demonic face waving some sort of weapon around. It was discharging projectiles randomly. Pulling his head back, he listened and heard the sounds of injured people all around him.

Commoners, he thought. They always complicated things. No matter, he knew what must be done. Reaching down, he grabbed a piece of tile that had been knocked off the column he stood behind. Snapping his visor back down, he charged out from behind the column.

Hurtling the rock to the left of the attacker, he smiled grimly as he heard it crack against the far wall. The attacker was distracted and turned toward the sound, just as he expected. The attacker released another volley toward the sound as the knight charged forward, leading with his massive shield.

Unfortunately, the sound of hundreds of pounds of armored knight was enough to catch the attacker's attention again. Redoubling his speed, the knight continued to charge, knowing he would not reach the attacker in time.

He was right. The demon-headed man released another volley at the knight. The knight felt the impact of each projectile as they slammed into his shield. The knight allowed himself another grim smile as each was deflected off of the shield without penetrating, the angle of the shield allowing the force to be turned, rather than taking the full brunt of it.

The hail of projectiles halted as the demon-headed man realized his danger, but it was too late. Three hundred pounds of fully armored knight shield-slammed the attacker with the force of a freight train. Faintly, the knight heard a voice in his head saying something about mass and velocity, but shrugged it off as he watched the attacker fly backward to slam against the wall with the resounding crack of breaking bone.

Walking quickly toward the broken body, the knight wasted no time. He drew his broadsword and in a single swipe removed the demonic head from the tattered and broken body. Nodding in satisfaction, the knight reached around behind himself to grab the edge of his cloak. Pulling the cloth around, he quickly wiped his blade clean before re-sheathing it.

Turning, he looked out toward the crowd. Most of them were on the floor and many were wounded. There was little he could do for them, so he walked back to where the woman in the grey jacket still lay huddled behind the pillar. Extending his hand to help her rise, he spoke.

"Are you all right?" he asked, his voice deep and booming, resonating in his helmet. Tentatively, she nodded as she took his gauntleted hand.

"Yes, thank you," she replied, looking at the same time awed and confused. "Who are you?" she asked.

"I am Peter, Knight of the Tower," he replied with an air of pride.

"How did you get here?" she asked, her voice moving more toward confusion.

Just as he was about to answer his head snapped up as he heard the authoritative sounds of law enforcement. It never changes, the knight thought to himself, law enforcement sounded the same no matter where you were.

"Stay here," Peter said as he ducked around the column. A voice in his head told him that there was a group of children off to one side. With a grunt of acknowledgment, he began to move in that direction. With clenched teeth, he fought down the instant of panic he always felt whenever his armor began to fade. His stride became faster as his legs became shorter. The knight shook his head as his consciousness began to fade. He hoped the child would be all right on his own.

The child rounded the corner just in time to run into another young boy. The boy was a little bit bigger than he was, wearing a green rain slicker, and he was crying. Bawling actually, in pure abject fear. The child's lip began to quiver as he saw three other children crying nearby, huddled around a woman who was laying on the ground. The entire scene became too much for him and he too burst into tears.

As the police swept the subway platform, they found the five bawling children standing around a woman who had been shot in the shoulder. The officer with the stripes on his sleeve grabbed the radio on his shoulder and barked something about wounded and children.

Within moments, paramedics had arrived. Two of them gathered the children and guided them to one side while the other two looked at the woman. One of them had brought a long board that they slid under the woman. With a quick heave they picked her up and began carrying her toward the stairs.

With that, the children began to bawl even louder. One of the men tried to calm them, saying that their mother would be all right and that they were going to take the children to her soon. Slowly the children's cries calmed somewhat. They still cried, but it was softer now. As they began to calm they started looking around. The young boy in the green rain slicker looked over at the new child.

"Who are you?" he asked.

"I'm Justin," the child replied, his voice still shaking with tears.

"Did you lose your mommy too?" the boy asked.

"No, I'm just lost and alone," Justin replied looking worriedly at the adults. Thankfully they were all distracted talking to other adults.

"Where are your mommy and daddy?" the boy asked with concern.

"I don't know. I'm all alone. Can I stay here with you?" Justin asked, his lip starting to quiver again.

"Sure, I'm Sam," the boy replied, "and this is Ben, Doe, and Ada," he said, pointing to each of the other children.

"Hi," Justin said timidly, waving to each of them. The other children waved back but didn't seem interested in talking, they just watched the stairs where their mother had been taken out.

The children all lapsed into silence as they watched the police and paramedics moving around the subway station. The two adults stayed with them, but didn't interact. They spent most of their time talking to other adults who came and left regularly. After what seemed like forever, other adults arrived, a man and a woman, who came over to them.

"Hello, children," the woman said, kneeling down in front of them. The children mumbled back uncertainly. The woman smiled at them, trying to be friendly.

"We're going to take you to see your mother," she said. "She's all right, and waiting to see you." With that, both Doe and Ada looked up with hopeful expressions.

Sam and Ben still seemed a bit wary, but wanted to get out of this frantic place.

"Please come with us," the man said, his voice soft with a subtle accent. Quietly, the five children followed the pair back up the stairs and onto the street. They all climbed into a large van, tussling a little bit as they each tried to get the seat they wanted.

"Buckle up," the woman said brightly, and the children quickly obeyed. Justin thought this was a bit strange, but thought that they must be eager to see their mother. Pulling out into traffic, the van began the trip to the hospital.

Justin sat quietly, looking out the window. He could hear the voices in his head. They were arguing… again. Justin figured they were worried about him, but there wasn't really anything they could do. Justin was here, and that's the way it was. Justin didn't mind, he liked being out.

Garrett didn't let him out much, he was always so busy. So Justin really liked it when he got the chance to see the outside. Not that he didn't like his room. It was large and had lots of toys, and the adults didn't seem to mind playing with him, but he still liked to get outside every now and then.

The trip to the hospital was quick. Apparently the subway station was only a couple of miles away from the hospital. Justin liked the bright lights and the billboards though, everything was so bright out here.

The van pulled into the hospital near the emergency room, and the children scrambled to climb out. They were herded into the ER and down the halls, finally arriving at a small, white room with a sliding glass door in front of it. As the children walked in, Justin hung back a bit. Sure enough, the man and woman entered the room first and the children pushed their way in beside them. Waving good bye to his new friends, even though they didn't see him do so, Justin turned and walked down a different hallway.

It was important to be nice, Justin thought, even if they didn't know it. Sean always said that. It was important to be nice. So Justin was nice. Almost all the time. The only time he wasn't nice was when he thought people weren't being nice to him. That's what Peter said, that when people are mean to you, that's when you should stop being nice. Sean didn't like that. They often argued about it when they thought he couldn't hear them.

Justin passed another room like the one the other kids went into, with a sliding glass door on the front. He stepped inside and saw that it was empty. The voices in his head were getting louder. They were telling him it was time to go back. Justin didn't want to go back, but he was still trying to be nice, and do what he was supposed to do. With a little wave to the bright happy world, he closed his eyes.

Garrett opened his eyes again inside an emergency room. The small admitting room was thankfully empty. He quickly checked himself over. All here, he thought, as he went through his mental tally. He was always all there when he came back. He never ceased to have that instant of panic though when the others took over his body. And the moment of wondering if he would come all the way back when he returned. Straightening his shoulders, he stepped out of the room and walked briskly to the exit.

As he left the hospital, he sighed to himself. There was no way the subway station was going to be operational again tonight, he thought. I'll have to catch a cab. Thankfully, there were several cabs parked in front of the hospital. Sliding into one, he told the driver his address, and sat back in the seat. Yes, the Dreaming had certainly changed things, he thought ruefully, but nothing had changed as much as he and those like him had changed.

CHAPTER TWO

Garrett awoke the next morning with a sore shoulder. *Well that's what I get for playing hero,* he thought, walking into the bathroom. He glanced at the mirror as he walked in, slightly surprised as always at what he saw.

Unlike what many movies and TV shows tried to portray, he didn't see all the other personalities in the mirror that he heard in his head. He didn't have to. All he had to do was to close his eyes and look inward and their faces became crystal clear to him. He didn't choose to do that very often, hearing their voices like a buzzing drone in the back of his head all the time was plenty, he didn't need to see them too.

Glancing again at the mirror he saw only himself. His wide-shouldered frame still held most of the trim of youth, though a closer examination told him he needed to cut back on the double cheeseburgers. His short brown hair was a bit thinner than he remembered. His father had also gone bald at a fairly young age, so that was to be expected, he supposed. His eyes were bright and cheerful, his best feature, he had been told.

Something odd caught his eye, however. Looking

closer, into his eyes in the mirror, he saw the tiny flecks of gold around the iris that told him that Derrick was near the surface.

Well, that could complicate things, he thought as he stepped into the shower. Derrick didn't demand a lot of time, thankfully, but when he did he was very difficult to ignore. Garrett scrubbed quickly, and ran a bit of shampoo in his hair. His eyes closed as he engaged in the "lather, rinse, repeat" prescribed by the directions on the shampoo bottle. Closing his physical eyes, though, often opened his mental ones. He was very quickly aware of Derrick standing there next to him.

The cave walls of his mental world gave him a dark grey background. The torchlight on the cave walls really made Derrick creepy looking, Garrett thought idly to himself.

"I need to feed," Derrick said, his richly Romanian accent thick and smooth.

"Yeah, I know," Garrett replied with a sigh. Vaguely, he was aware of his body continuing the lathering of his hair as his eyes took in the mental world his mind had created.

He sat in a large, stone chair in the middle of a circular cave, the outer wall covered in doors. Each of those doors led to a room which belonged to each of the other minds inhabiting his head. The doors were plain, rounded at the top and squared off at the bottom, much like you would see in a movie rendition of an interior castle door. Between each set of doors was a brightly lit torch that to his knowledge never went out. Leaving the room well lit, despite its size.

He had never bothered to count the doors, though there were more than three dozen lining the walls. He did know however, that most of them were locked. Only a half dozen or so unlocked and led to the rooms of the minds he knew about. Who knows what lurks in the other doors, Garrett thought with a slight shiver. He certainly didn't want to find out.

"I need to feed," Derrick said again, sounding slightly impatient.

"Yeah, I know," Garrett said again, looking at the other man standing beside the stone chair.

Derrick was a bit shorter than he was, probably five nine, or something like that. His hair was jet black and long, brushing against his shoulders whenever Derrick turned his head. His eyes were bright green, with a solid gold ring around his iris. The gold always seemed to get brighter when Derrick was hungry, he thought.

Derrick had a long face, with a pointed chin and aristocratic nose. His attire however, was straight out of a B-rate horror flick. A tuxedo cut in a style that hadn't been popular in centuries adorned his slim frame, and the dark cloak trimmed in red set off the style nicely.

"I 'vant to suck your blood," Garrett said sarcastically, making a face. Derrick's eyes narrowed.

"I have been very patient with you, boy," Derrick replied, his voice lowering menacingly, "but my patience is not without its limits."

"Could you be more cliché?" Garrett replied, unimpressed. A large grin split the thin man's face, showing the hint of the fangs that would help him in his feeding.

"Of course," Derrick replied, his voice brightening, "but that would annoy that idiot Peter, who would then make things uncomfortable for me."

"Fine," Garrett said, more annoyed at the cheer than

the menace. "I'll try to find some time for you in the next few days."

"Garrett, you know better than that," Derrick replied with a frown, "I try to be patient, and do not come to you with my needs until they are pressing. Tonight, tomorrow at the latest, I will need to feed. You are aware of the consequences if I don't." Garrett sighed again.

"Fine, I'll see what I can do." Then he opened his eyes, sighed again, and quickly finished his shower.

Heading to the closet to find some clothes, he struggled to suppress the frustration at the constant demands on his body. He wished, not for the first time, that he was alone in his own head. Trying to deal with the constant demands of a half dozen different people was exhausting to say the least.

Grabbing jeans and a t-shirt that read 'I used to have superpowers, but my therapist took them away', he decided that he had better get some grocery shopping done today. Ugh, he hated grocery shopping. And it didn't help that everyone had different tastes; meat for Peter, vegetables for Sean, sweets for Justin, wine for Derrick. And none of them liked what the others ate. The five-year-old was actually the least picky of the lot! As long as he got dessert at the end, he would clean his plate.

Oh well, it actually meant they were probably all getting a balanced diet, he just had to eat in courses. Though to be fair, most of the time they didn't really bother him about it, they let him get on with the messy business of everyday life. They just jumped out when they needed or wanted something.

Grabbing a light jacket, he headed out of his apartment and down to the bus stop. He waited for about fifteen minutes, staring silently ahead, his mind caught up in listening to Peter and Sean's latest argument about the need for violence.

Well, if you could call it an argument. Sean didn't really argue, he just talked very calmly and logically. He stated the facts and then his opinions, and sometimes his opinions as facts calling it a logical conclusion.

Peter argued. He loved to fight. Any kind of fighting; physical, mental, verbal, he loved it all. He was made for combat. And he never backed down, he never gave up, and he never quit until his opponent surrendered. Or in Sean's case, walked away calmly after making a final, salient point.

Peter often wondered what it was like for other people like him. People with more than one personality. Dissociative Identity Disorder or DID, as they called it in the books. Or rather The Book, the DSM4-CM, the holy book that told people what mental deficiency you had.

Garrett sighed. He supposed he was being a bit too hard on them. Most counselors and social workers were good people who were trying to do the best they could to help people. Garrett just got annoyed when he felt like he was being classified. Put into a tiny box, by what felt like tiny minds trying to explain the infinite complexities of the human psyche. Or, thanks to the Dreaming, the partially human psyche.

Garrett knew that other people with DID also switched, and that since the Dreaming, they also changed their physical form with their personality. Garrett was a bit different however. Most people with multiple personalities had all human personalities. Sure, they may look, talk, and act different than the original personality, but they were all human. Garrett's alters however, were not human.

Well, Justin was still human, he supposed. But Sean, Peter, and Derrick were most definitely not. That had really been a shock to him, Garrett remembered. Because not only did they take on the appearance of their personality, they actually retained the attire, and abilities of their personality.

The first time he shifted, after the Dreaming, had been on his way home. He had heard a muffled scream from an alleyway. Garrett hadn't wanted to get involved, and had started to pass by, but Peter was having none of it. He had forced Garrett out of the way and had charged down the alley, as heavy, armored plates enclosed his body. That had been the real shock, the feeling of the armor closing in around him.

Peter had charged down the alley and found two men and a half naked girl. One backhand to the girl's face from the man struggling on top of her had convinced him of what was going on. So naturally, he backhanded the man right back. With a metal gauntlet. And the strength of a mythical hero out of some fantasy movie. The man didn't just fall off of her, he was knocked twenty feet into the air to slam against a brick wall, and slide down in a perfect example of Hollywood stunt violence. Only this wasn't Hollywood, and the man didn't get back up again.

The other man, however, did respond. With a gun. Peter took four rounds to the chest. Then he lifted the visor on his great helm, and laughed at the man. That's all, just stood there and laughed off four bullets to his heavily armor-plated chest.

It was about that time that the dispassionate voice of

Sean had broken in and mentioned that the armor must not be made of conventional metals, since a bullet at close range could penetrate most metals of the medieval era.

Peter took two large steps forward, and drawing the sword hanging at his hip, swung it upward at an angle from left to right. Sean then commented about surgical sharpness and the density of alloys, because the sword didn't stop when it impacted the man in his side just under his ribcage. It didn't slow as it cleaved him up through his ribs and collarbone. It didn't stop until it was aloft, straight in the air, pointed perfectly upward at the sky.

Garrett remembered throwing up then. It was one thing to watch a gory movie, or read a book. It was quite another to witness it first-hand. Thankfully though, he was still on the inside of the mind when it happened, or Peter might have been very upset. The sword whistled back down again as Peter grabbed his cloak, quickly wiped the sword clean, and resheathed it.

About that time, the surprised man fell over. In two parts. Garrett had vomited again, and was shocked that the woman still on the ground wasn't doing the same. Instead she had looked up at Peter in horror. Peter reached his hand down to help her to stand and she had scrambled away from him, screaming again. Peter had started to become angry, but thankfully Derrick was quicker.

Derrick had pushed his way to the surface, heavy armor plates becoming elegant evening wear. In an instant he had caught the woman's gaze and mesmerized her just like in those campy vampire flicks. But somehow it worked for him, and the woman quickly calmed and took his outstretched hand. Pulling her to her feet Derrick smiled a satisfied smile.

"My dear lady," he said, his Romanian accent also belonging in a campy vampire flick. "You seem to have torn your dress in your fall. Here, take my cloak."

With the soul of gentlemanly courtesy, he had whipped off the dark, red-lined cloak and wrapped it about her shoulders.

"Now, you have had a nasty tumble," Derrick said, his eyes still locked with the girl's. "You are going to go straight home now, take a long, luxurious bath, and sleep very deeply tonight. You will awaken tomorrow, peaceful and refreshed, with no memory of tonight other than having had too much wine, having a nice bath, and going to bed early." He then turned her shoulders and pushed her gently toward the entryway to the alley.

"And now," Derrick said idly, "I am thirsty." Inside the mind, Peter strode forward angrily, and Derrick held up a mental hand. "No," Derrick said, "I am entitled this, after saving you from your own impulsiveness." Then, wrapping his arrogance around him like the cloak he had just gifted, he went off to hunt.

Garrett didn't remember much about what happened next. Derrick had worked hard that night to keep all of them out so that he could hunt and feed. Garrett knew he had found a willing woman, that they had gone back to her apartment, and that Derrick had come home the next morning smiling like a cat in the cream. Garrett hadn't asked, he hadn't wanted to know. But every couple of weeks since then, Derrick had approached him, letting him know that he needed to feed again.

He was so surprised the first time Derrick had asked, he actually went to Sean to see if the request was legitimate. Sean had theorized that if the physical manifestations of their personalities were real, then the needs of those personalities would be real as well. So he acquiesced, and every couple of weeks Derrick got a night out.

He and Derrick had quite a row about that the next day, though. Garrett had asked him how he could be so careless as to leave his cloak with the strange woman. Derrick had protested that he had assumed it would return with him when he went back inside. Especially since he was always wearing it when he came out again.

Fortunately, Sean had proposed a test to see what would stay outside and what went back inside with them. After a series of tests, they had determined that anything that one of them brought out with them, would return inside with them when they switched again.

Garrett had been thankful that there would be no evidence of Derrick's intervention, but he was still irritated at Derrick's carelessness. Considering none of them had known that until Sean proposed the tests, Derrick's actions were extremely careless.

Garrett's reverie was broken as the bus pulled up and the small line of people trudged on. Briefly, he saw a glimpse of a thick chain linking each of the passengers together as the boarded. Apparently someone in the line was feeling a little trapped. Garrett just shook his head and climbed the steps. Finding a seat, he stared out the window, lost in thought again.

It really wasn't fair, he thought, that everyone else got to experience their cool daydreams. He, however, had to keep a very tight leash on his mental partners, or it could be civil war inside. His therapist had called it concurrent splits. Which he supposed meant that each set of personalities broke off in pairs, to complement each other. Or contain each other, in the case of Peter and Derrick. Peter was immune from mesmerization, and had a strength that was equal to that of the vampire. So they tried to keep each other out of trouble, with greater or lesser success. Then he heard a familiar voice inside his head, and sighed as he closed his eyes.

"I truly do need to feed," Derrick said, a hint of impatience in his voice. "You could permit it now, and be back home in time to watch your television programs."

"No, I wouldn't," Garrett replied, equally as annoyed. "If I let you out now you won't be home till the sun comes up. And since the sun only came up three hours ago, that means I would lose an entire day."

"Garrett," Derrick began, "it must be tonight, within the next few hours." Garrett started to sigh again, then looked more closely at Derrick's face. He was always lean, but today it was lean almost to the point of being gaunt. And the gold in his eyes had expanded to cover half of the iris.

"Okay, tonight is yours. But I need the day. Give me till sundown and the rest of the evening is yours."

"Very well," Derrick said, and turned to walk back to the door leading to his room.

Opening his eyes, Garrett saw his stop coming up and pulled the cord to let the driver know. Glancing around, he saw the back of the bus had become a thick forest, and he could just see the tip of a unicorn horn peeking out from behind a tree.

Scanning the bus briefly, he saw a small child gazing

out the window, as her mother tapped away on a smart phone. Well, I guess that's one way to keep from daydreaming, Garrett thought wryly. Keep your attention buried in something else. He felt for the kid though, and hoped her daydream was a happy one.

The bus stopped and he exited from the rear door. Stepping down onto the sidewalk, he watched a couple pass him by. The wife was talking animatedly, and unhappily by the look of it. The husband was trying hard not to react, but he kept flashing into images of a broken down laborer carrying a giant stone block on his back. Thankfully, the wife was too caught up in her apparent rant to notice, and they moved on down the sidewalk.

It's all about control, he thought again. Those without mental control will not survive very well in this new world. He rounded the corner heading toward the grocery store, walking quickly to get out of the cold. Thankfully, the store had a warm air vent blowing just inside the vestibule, and he straightened from the slump he hadn't realized he was in.

"Hmm, perhaps I should have worn a thicker coat," he said idly.

"Perhaps you should," came a familiar voice from behind him. Turning quickly, he broke into a grin.

"Ann! How are you? I haven't seen you in two weeks! How was your trip?" Garrett exclaimed, happily opening his arms for a hug. The short, grandmotherly lady smiled back as she stepped into his arms, hugging him back enthusiastically.

"Oh, it was wonderful! I got to see all of my nieces, and even attended a dance recital choreographed by the oldest. They're all growing up so fast!" she laughed, stepping back. He noticed that she too was only wearing a light jacket, and smiled again.

"Hmm, it looks like I'm not the only one who needs a thicker coat. Aren't you cold?" Garrett said jokingly.

"No," Ann replied with a chuckle. "Doran sees to that." Garrett remembered Doran from their one brief encounter in group therapy. Doran was a sasquatch. And a mute sasquatch at that, which made group therapy a bit hard for him.

"Ah, and how is the big guy?" he asked.

"Oh, he doesn't come out much," she replied, tapping her head, "but he is taking care of the littles so that makes him happy."

Garrett had a brief mental image of a nine foot, hairy sasquatch sitting in a nursery, playing with a large bunch of elementary age kids. The thought brought another smile to his face. Garrett wrapped his arm around her shoulders and they walked into the store together.

"And how are yours doing?" she asked politely.

"Oh the usual; arguing, bickering, fighting, and getting me into trouble," Garrett said, suppressing a sigh.

Ann's eyes narrowed briefly, her eyes glinting with a fierce intelligence that was all too often missed by those who just saw her as a sweet little grandmother.

"The kind of trouble that ends up in a lone gunman being crushed, almost every bone in their body broken, and his head three feet away from his body? The kind of trouble that saves young maidens then disappears like smoke?" she asked cannily. Garrett was shocked for a moment, then laughed.

"Yeah, that kind. You sure don't miss much, do you? How did you even know about that?" he asked, curious.

"You know, you really should watch the news more

often," she replied, shaking her head. "They were reporting on the incident on every major channel last night. Then when you said trouble, it wasn't hard to put two and two together and figure out it was you and yours."

"Um, yeah. I did kind of forget that it might hit the news." Garrett said sheepishly.

"Well you'd best be more careful with your forgetting," Ann said, stopping to look up at him. "I worry about you Garrett, and that lot of misfits in your head. I would hate it if anything happened to you." Garrett turned, wrapping her in another hug.

"Thank you. Ann. That means a lot to me. Especially from someone who understands what it's like." Ann chuckled in his arms and pulled back slightly.

"Oh, I understand all right. Greybeard was trying to make a potion of flight last night and nearly burned my kitchen down!"

"And how is the old wizard? Still trying to cook up spells in bottles then?" Garrett laughed.

"Oh yes," Ann replied, "and still as annoyed as ever that his potions only seem to work on this body, and not on anyone else."

Garrett shook his head ruefully. They were still trying to figure out all of the rules on how this personality thing worked with the Dreaming. So far, they had concluded that effects that altered the environment, such as greater strength, or throwing a fireball, worked relatively well. But things that were meant to affect an individual only worked on the individual who created it. So Greybeard, who was a wizard alter of Ann's, could throw a respectable ball of fire that would burn what it hit, but could not craft a potion that would work on anyone but

Ann's body.

Interestingly, it didn't seem to matter which of Ann's alters was up, the potion would work on any of them. Garrett hadn't mustered the courage to try one of the potions himself, to see if they worked on other people with DID. He was curious though, and he probably would eventually.

"Well, I had better get my shopping done, so I can get home before my favorite show comes on." Ann smiled and gave him another quick hug.

"Thanks, Ann," Garrett replied with a smile, thankful that he had run into her.

She always made him feel less alone, less of a freak. With her bevy of alters, she knew exactly how he felt. Grabbing a basket, he turned back into the store to finish his shopping when he heard the all too familiar sound of a metal bolt being ratcheted back.

CHAPTER THREE

Oh, not again, he thought angrily. Turning around, he witnessed the now familiar sight of a man in ragged clothes with a garish clown mask holding some kind of automatic weapon.

Before he could react, the man began to fire into the crowded store. Before the bullets could hit, however, a pale blue light appeared between the shooter and the crowd. The bullets struck the light and fell as though all of their inertia had been stolen.

The man looked around wildly, trying to find the source of the light. Both the clown-faced man and Garrett saw him at the same time. A tall, thin, old man standing at the end of one of the isles. He was dressed in a grey robe, with the traditional pointed hat and gnarled staff one would expect from a fantasy wizard.

The shooter paused for a moment in shock, then swung the weapon toward the old man. With a grim smile, the old wizard just stood there and stared directly at the clown mask. As the gunman finished turning the weapon toward the old man, he suddenly yelped in pain and dropped the gun on the floor!

Garrett watched as the gun began to glow, first a dull

red, then brighter until it glowed like a foundry, the plastic of the buttstock melting into a puddle. Just then Sean's voice echoed urgently in his head reminding him of what happens when bullets get too hot. Garrett was already changing as he leapt toward the gun.

His clothes changed to evening wear, his fingers lengthened, and his body became even thinner as he picked up speed to superhuman levels. Grabbing the edges of his cloak Derrick used it to grab the red-hot gun and moving faster than the human eye could see, he pointed it toward the ceiling. Not an instant too soon apparently as the magazine exploded, bullets and shrapnel flying in every direction.

Holding the gun, Derrick took the full brunt of the blast, knocking him backwards into a display of baked beans. Cans rolled everywhere as Derrick hit the ground on the other side of the display.

He suppressed a grunt of pain as he looked down and saw the tattered shreds of his shirt and tuxedo jacket. Reaching up, he tore the shirt open to reveal the ragged flesh underneath. With another groan of pain, he lay still and concentrated on healing the mortal wound. Or what would have been a mortal wound on a mortal, Derrick thought to himself with a flicker of amusement.

The shooter, meanwhile, had pulled another handgun from somewhere on his person and had begun firing randomly at people. Thankfully he wasn't a very good shot and most of the bystanders had managed to find cover.

Derrick glanced over at the wizard in time to see his hands moving as he muttered under his breath. Suddenly he made a throwing motion and a tiny pea of flame flew from his hands. Expanding rapidly, it became a four-foot raging fireball that streaked toward the clown-faced gunman.

The gunman had just enough time to scream before it engulfed him. The fire was so hot that death was nearly instantaneous. Oddly, nothing else seemed to catch fire, and there was no smoke, so the smoke alarms hadn't gone off either.

Derrick stood up, the wounds on his chest now fading into pink scars, which also faded. He walked over to the remains of the clown masked attacker and shook his head. There was almost nothing left of the body. The fire had been swift and hotter than he could even imagine, though he could hear Sean in his head attempting to calculate the probable temperature. There was nothing left but a charred skeleton and some ash.

The doors to the store opened, and Derrick looked up in time to see some of the patrons running out and away from the store. The breeze from the open door stirred some of the ash and a glint caught Derrick's eye. Glancing down he saw the gleam of metal in the ash of the remains.

Reaching his hand into the ashes he picked up a tiny knife, the remains of a sheath falling away. It was a very small knife, less than two inches, though it was almost an inch wide. The strange thing about it though, was the clown face that had been etched into the blade itself.

His head snapped up at the sound of a wailing scream. His eyes quickly latched onto a woman, wailing as she crouched over the prone body of a young teenage girl. Quickly walking over to them, he saw that the girl had been shot in the upper chest. He wasn't sure if it had hit a vital organ, but it was bleeding profusely. He guessed she had only minutes left. Looking over at the wizard he gestured him over. Moving well for a man of his apparent years he strode over to see the girl.

"She is beyond my help," the old man said imperiously.

"It is not your help I desire," Derrick replied, his voice dark with anger. "Give me the beast."

"I will not be ordered about…" he began, but Derrick's hand snapped out, grabbing him by the throat.

"Do as I say, or I shall kill you where you stand," Derrick replied, his accent thickening as he felt his fangs begin to extend. "You know you cannot match my speed, and you would be dead before you could utter a single syllable."

The old man's eyes widened and he nodded slightly. Closing his eyes, he began to change. Derrick quickly released him as his body began to grow. Swelling to over nine feet, and sprouting long dark brown fur the sasquatch was an imposing sight. It wasn't the height that made him seem enormous, though. It was the nearly six-foot span of the shoulders.

Doran looked down at Derrick and slowly blinked his large, brown eyes. Garrett always thought that they looked a bit sad, but Derrick only thought they showed a depth of intelligence one would not expect from a nine-foot furry monster. Blinking again slowly, Doran frowned slightly, pointed at Derrick, and tapped his head near his eyes.

"I know!" Derrick replied, still angry. "That's why I need you. I need you to fix her before I lose control and eat her!" he growled, pointing at the wounded girl.

Doran nodded and knelt down. At that moment, the wailing woman, whom Derrick assumed was the mother, saw the nine-foot behemoth kneeling down next to her daughter. Letting out a primal scream of fear, the woman threw herself over the body of her daughter, trying to protect her.

With an exasperated growl Derrick grabbed the woman by the arms and lifted her bodily into the air. Staring into her eyes he caught her mind with his.

"Shut up, woman!" he growled at her. Instantly, the screaming stopped. "Good, now stand over there by the bread and be silent until we are through." He set her down on her feet, and without another sound she turned and walked over to the bread aisle. Turning around, she stared at her daughter and the giant, furred monster, but remained silent.

Turning to Doran, he gestured for him to proceed. The gentle giant leaned over the girl and held out his massive hands, palms down. Slowly he passed them over the wound in the girl's chest. Derrick could see, once the hands had passed, the wound slowly closing. The bullet pushed its way to the surface and fell out as the wound finished knitting back together again.

The process had taken perhaps sixty seconds, but the blood was gone from everything except her clothing and Derrick could see that the wound was completely healed. Not even a scar to remember it by, he thought wryly. Slowly he breathed a sigh of relief. He could no longer smell the fresh blood and managed to push his hunger back down for the moment.

The girl's eyes fluttered, then opened. Derrick could see an instant of panic in her eyes as she saw the great, furry giant leaning over her. Thankfully, she was still young enough to look twice, and saw the gentle twinkle in Doran's big brown eyes.

Calming, she smiled up at the sasquatch. A small smile curved the great lips and he offered a gigantic furry hand to help her up. Taking it with a smile, she stood, and with a grin wrapped her arms around his neck in a big hug. With infinite tenderness, the great arms wrapped around her, one massive hand covering her entire back. They hugged for a minute before the girl pulled away.

"Thank you," she said timidly, giving Doran another smile.

Then her eyes widened, and she turned around to see her mother standing next to the bread stand. Racing over to her, the girl wrapped her mother in a tight embrace. The instant they touched, the woman's voice returned and she cried unbelieving tears, her heart-wrenching sobs echoing loudly in the warehouse-like ceiling of the large store.

"Come, my powerful friend," Derrick said to the sasquatch. "It is time for us to go." Nodding, the gentle giant stood and started to walk toward the door. "But perhaps less conspicuously." Derrick added with a small smile. Nodding sadly, the gentle giant closed his eyes and began to shrink down again. Once again becoming a short, grandmotherly lady.

"Come, my lady, it is time for us to depart," Derrick said offering her his arm.

"It is indeed," Ann replied, wiping her mouth absently. "But shouldn't you be less conspicuous as well?"

"I cannot switch now," he replied gently.

"Oh my," she said looking into his eyes. "Yes, I can see why. Come on, then."

Derrick closed his eyes, and only moved when he felt her taking his arm. Opening them again, he saw she was leading him out of the store. Glancing down at the tatters of his shirt and jacket, he stumbled slightly. Ann turned to take another look at him, following his gaze to the torn clothing. Turning, she reached out and grabbed a dark blue jacket that had been left in a shopping cart; abandoned when patrons began fleeing the store.

A brief flicker of indecision crossed her face as though she was struggling with a question. Faintly, he heard a voice in his head, saying something about discretion likely being more important than personal property. Apparently coming to the same conclusion, she handed it to Derrick. He reluctantly removed his cloak and dropped it behind a row of carts before putting the jacket on, zipping it up to the neck.

Just before they reached the entrance Ann stopped, looking up at Derrick in concern.

"Wait, it's still daylight. Can you go out in the sun?" Ann inquired, a note of worry in her voice. Derrick smiled slightly, before responding.

"Of course, my dear. I am not one of those weak-willed, vulnerable vampires from your cinema." Derrick chuckled softly. "I am of the line of Vlad Tepes, the great Vlad the Impaler. Or as you may know him, Count Dracula. I am not harmed by, nor am I fearful of, the sun. I do lose some of my more exotic abilities, but that is the extent of it." Derrick grinned down at her, a hint of his old rakish humor in his eyes. "You really should read the book, my dear. I think you would quite enjoy it."

Despite his reassurances, Derrick seemed to whither and diminish as they moved into the bright sunlight. Fortunately, they turned the corner just in time to see a bus pulling up to the stop. Without bothering to check which bus it was or where it was going, the pair climbed aboard. Ann pulled some change out of her purse, paying for both fares, and they made their way to an empty seat near the back of the bus.

Derrick looked around, as they walked down the center aisle. The bus was almost empty, the only other passengers were a woman and her young son, and an elderly lady in the front of the bus.

"I need to…" Derrick began.

"Yes, I know dear," Ann interrupted. "We will find someone for you."

"Too late," he replied, his voice strained. "No fun." Smiling wanly at her, his fangs now obvious against his lips.

"As long as it's not too late for safety, then we should be all right," she replied firmly.

"I'll try," he whispered, his thick accent making him difficult to understand.

"Can't Peter help you?" she asked, concern filling her eyes. Derrick barely held back a snarl.

"No, Peter can contain me. Not help me," Derrick replied, trying to contain his anger. "And when I am released it will be worse; much worse."

"How did it get to be so bad this time?" Ann asked. "Didn't Garrett know you needed to feed?"

"It was the fight, the healing. I used too much blood healing myself. And I was too close already… too close." His voice fading as he closed his eyes, trying to maintain control.

The pair traveled that way for several minutes before Derrick heard the bell cord, ringing the driver that they wanted to disembark. He felt Ann's hand at his elbow indicating he should follow her.

Derrick's eyes remained closed as they stood and she guided him to the door in the back of the bus. As the bus pulled away, Derrick opened his gold-shot eyes and looked around.

"Where?" he asked softly.

"A jolly little Irish Pub I saw about a block back," Ann replied, taking his arm. Silently, Derrick nodded and they began walking. As they approached the pub, Derrick's arm began to tremble, and Ann looked up at him with concern.

"Can you do this?" she asked quietly.

"I will do what I must," Derrick replied, straightening. He let go of her arm, and without looking back strode into the pub. After several minutes, a young couple left the pub and started walking toward the parking area in the back.

After a moment, Derrick exited the pub as well and slowly followed them. His movements were cautious and tightly controlled as he made his way over to the car that the couple had just entered. Derrick paused at the door of the car, his will reaching out and taking control over theirs.

The woman stepped out of the car again and got into the back seat. Derrick opened the door on the other side and joined her. Tenderly, Derrick brushed the woman's dark brown hair back from her neck and then drew her into his arms, to feed.

After a few minutes, Derrick released the woman and climbed back out of the car. Standing next to the driver's window he paused for a moment, then turned and walked back toward Ann. His gait was light and his posture straight and confident. A smile crossed his lips as he approached her.

"What was the bit with the husband?" Ann inquired.

"Instructions, my dear lady. His lovely wife has taken ill, which is why they left the pub early. He will take her home and put her to bed with some hot soup. After a couple of days, she will feel much better." A rakish grin crossed his face, though thankfully without fangs this time.

"I'm not entirely sure how I feel about helping you feed on a human like that," Ann said, slightly cross at his joviality.

"Garrett has the same problem," Derrick replied, still smiling. "However, if we do it my way, no one is seriously harmed. No lives are lost, and I continue to remain a productive member of society."

"And just how do you contribute to society?" Ann asked, her voice softening again.

"Why, I save innocent people from strange fellows in masks of course," Derrick responded, his grin widening. Ann chuckled softly and shook her head.

"All right then, have it your way," she said with a touch of amusement. "Will you be all right on your own? I'm afraid I must be going now."

"I will indeed, dear lady," Derrick said, taking her hand and gently kissing the back of it. "Thank you, for your timely assistance." Ann smiled again, shaking her head and turned to head back to the bus stop. Derrick watched her go before acknowledging the voices in his head, and closing his eyes.

"You should not have fed in broad daylight on a

woman who was not seeking your attentions," Peter's deeply booming voice echoed in his head. As Derrick focused on the world inside, he saw the grey walls of the cave and the dozens of rounded doors, all tightly closed and locked.

"A matter of necessity," Derrick replied, his eastern European accent growing thicker with annoyance.

"That is not an excuse," Peter said angrily.

"But it can be a reason," stated another voice, "and a compelling one."

"Thank you, Sean," Derrick said, nodding to the pointy-eared man walking up to them.

"There is no need to thank me," Sean replied reasonably. "The effects of your hunger when taken past the point of control have been well documented. As this is not a desirable circumstance, your efforts to avoid it while maintaining a level of decorum are appreciated."

"It is unacceptable for him to force his attentions on a woman, regardless of the circumstance!" Peter exclaimed, his fingers clenching on the helmet in his hand, and his face going red with anger.

"It is illogical to deal in absolutes in a situation with this many variables," Sean replied turning toward the huge, armored knight.

"It is unacceptable!" Peter boomed, rounding on Sean.

With a small smile, Derrick slowly backed away from the conflict. He gave a silent nod of thanks to the pointy-eared man for distracting the armored lout. Quietly making his way to one of the large doors he knocked politely.

"Yes?" Garrett's voice said as he opened the door.

"It is time for me to discretely exit," Derrick said

with a small smile.

Garrett nodded and stepped out of his room, striding toward the center of the chamber. His gait hitched as he saw Peter and Sean near the stone chair. He continued forward with a sigh however, braving the verbal battle to take control of the body again.

Derrick chuckled again softly, then turned to his own door in the line. Opening the door, he took a moment to brace himself, then stepped inside.

Opening his eyes, Garrett looked around. No one seemed to be paying any attention to him. He frowned to himself, remembering that he had been out for groceries when all of this took place. He sighed again. That grocery store wouldn't be open again for some time. He would have to find another one.

As he walked down the street, his mind wandered to the two gunman he had now seen. Both had been wearing worn and tattered clothing, both had possessed very new and powerful weapons, and both had been wearing those ridiculous rubber clown masks. Honestly, they looked like some of the disposable henchmen of some comic book supervillain.

He supposed he should pay closer attention to the news, as Ann suggested. He just didn't care about all of the petty little squabbles, and bad news that always seemed to show on the regular news channels. He got enough bad news in his own life. More bad news was not required. Reaching a main thoroughfare, he flagged down a cab and got inside.

"56th street grocery, please," he said to the driver.

The driver nodded and pulled back into traffic. Garrett's mind started to wander again when he heard the cabbie's voice talking to him.

"Quite a week we're having, right?" the cabbie said, trying to strike up a conversation. Garrett made a noncommittal sound, not wanting to get drawn into a conversation with a man he did not know.

"I mean twelve gunmen in two days, is just crazy right?" the cabbie asked. "And what's with all the crazy clown masks? Some kind of clown death cult or something? It's just crazy right?"

"Wait, what did you say?" Garrett asked, suddenly far more alert.

"The clown masks are just crazy! I mean, none of them stopped till they were dead, so they couldn't have been hiding their identity or anything. So why the masks?" The cabbie became more energetic now that he thought Garrett was talking to him.

Twelve random attacks in two days, each a lone gunman, each wearing a clown mask, and each not stopping until they were dead. The description sounded familiar, and Garrett racked his brain to try to remember where he had heard it before. Idly, he was aware of the cabbie continuing his conversation, but he had stopped paying attention. He just had to remember where he had heard the story before.

"Take me to the police station," Garrett demanded, as he suddenly remembered where he had heard the story before.

"What?" the driver replied, pausing his tirade and turning slightly.

"Take me to the police station, now," Garrett stated angrily.

"You got it," the driver said, settling back in his seat.

Garrett's mind whirled with the possibilities. The story was from a comic book. An old costumed hero comic, where the hero had a crazy clown as an enemy, and the clown was trying to wear the hero down before confronting him.

They spent the rest of the ride in silence as Garrett tried to remember the details of the comic. They arrived at the police station and Garrett hurriedly paid the driver. Telling the driver to keep the change as he got out, Garrett strode toward the doors.

Standing in front of the entryway for a moment, Garrett took a deep breath, steeling himself for this encounter. He knew it would not be easy convincing a cynical police officer that there was a connection between these attackers and an old comic book, but he had to try. Taking another deep breath, he opened the door and stepped inside.

CHAPTER FOUR

It was pandemonium.

Officers were moving around the large room with a sense of great urgency. Garrett noticed that many of them had their weapons unholstered and that most were facing a door at the back of the room. Garrett presumed that's where the lockup would be, but didn't understand why that area would be causing so much panic. Glancing around, he noticed that there were bullet holes in the metal detector just inside the doorway, and a splash of blood on the wall behind it.

He stepped quickly out of the doorway and along the wall. He saw more bullet holes decorating the walls of the large open room in irregular patterns. The desks and chairs were also askew, and some of the desks looked like they had been overturned. Though oddly enough, they did not look like they were overturned in the same direction. Looking quickly behind him, he noticed bullet holes in that wall as well, meaning shots had also been fired in this direction.

"Hey!" An officer yelled, noticing him. "Get out, now!" Garrett watched as a tall, stocky officer quickly approached him. A sergeant, judging by the stripes on his sleeve.

"What's going on?" Garrett asked.

"We have an active shooter in the building, get out now!" the sergeant barked again. For a moment, the wall on the left side disappeared as the image of a large tank rolled through before fading away again. Faintly, Garrett heard a voice in his head saying someone in the room must have been former military. Especially since the tank was an M1A1, painted in desert camo like those that were sent to fight in Operation Desert Storm.

Realizing that no one was going to listen to him until the current crisis was resolved, Garrett decided that he needed to lend a hand. In the space of a blink he had looked inward, and asked Sean if he could knock on Derrick's door and ask for both of their assistance. Opening his eyes again he looked at the angry sergeant.

"Yes, sir," he replied, and made his way for the doors, while keeping the sergeant in his peripheral vision.

Just before he reached the door, the rapid staccato of shots being fired echoed through the large room. The sergeant turned to look toward the back for just a moment, but that moment was all they needed. Taking a quick step backward out of the sunlight from the doors, they shifted rapidly.

Freshly fed and at full power, Derrick smiled mischievously as he dissipated into his mist form. The windowless station proving to be just as effective as nighttime, he dispersed into a thin mist, floating gently up to the ceiling. By the time the sergeant turned around again, it looked like Garrett had gone back out the door after hearing the shots. With a soft grunt the sergeant waded back into the room, to speak with a man in plain clothes.

Still in mist form, Derrick glided across the ceiling to the doorway that was sparking all the fervor. Thinning to the limits of his capacity, to help prevent the watchful officers from seeing him, he glided down and through the crack in the top of the door.

The lockup area was larger than he had expected, painted all in white, including the bars of the cells. Four large, open cells ran along the two side walls, separated by a somewhat narrow hallway. The first cell was empty, but the one across the hall contained the bodies of at least three former prisoners. Derrick looked wistfully at the blood pooling in the room for an instant, but returned his attention quickly to the far end of the lockup area.

As they had feared, at the end of the hallway was a man in shabby clothes and a clown mask, with a brand new automatic weapon moving wildly around the room. Faintly, Derrick heard a voice in his head saying that it looked as though the man couldn't find something he wanted.

All of a sudden, the masked shooter looked over at the entry door. His body's frenetic movements slowing as he watched the nearly transparent mist moving across the ceiling. The barrel of his rifle swept up and in a moment he unleashed a lengthy spray of bullets through the gathering mist. Amateur, Derrick thought as he continued to glide across the ceiling toward the clown-faced gunman.

The gunman, however, followed the movements of the mist, his hand twitching as though he wanted to pull the trigger again. Seeing that the clown was now calm and collected disturbed Derrick. It was as if the shooter knew that he would have to take corporeal form again to do anything else. That implied a level of knowledge about the vampire that a random killer should not have. Derrick continued, however, reaching the back wall and moving down toward the floor, the gunman's rifle never leaving its misty target.

Just as he had reached the floor, the entry door burst open, spilling officers in riot gear into the narrow hallway between the cells. The clown-faced man turned, ready to open fire on the intruders. In that instant, Derrick coalesced back into his physical form, and crouched behind the shooter. Rising rapidly, he shifted again, his ears and eyebrows pointing as his face changed.

As his utilitarian grey shirt and pants molded around him, Sean calculated the rate of rotation for the shooter, the speed of entry for the three officers that had made it through the entry door, and the rapidity of his own ascent into a vertical position, and estimated that their plan could indeed be put into action prior to any weapons discharge. Garrett's plan was quite logical, Sean thought to himself, if a bit simplistic.

As he rose to his full height, however, he detected a flaw in Garrett's plan. Sean was one hundred and eighty five point four centimeters in height, while Sean calculated that the shooter was only one hundred and sixty eight centimeters in height. This meant as Sean reached his full height that everything from his eyes upward would be visible to the incoming officers over the clown mask. That was unfortunate.

As his hand moved to precisely the correct position along the man's neck and closed with tremendous strength, Sean alerted Derrick that his assistance would again be required for a clandestine exit.

Sean followed the limp body down, as the man was rendered unconscious by the precise pressure on his vagus nerve caused by the pinching hand. As they neared the floor and Sean calculated that the duration of the pressure had been enough to immobilize him for at least five minutes and fifteen seconds, Sean allowed Derrick to again resume control. Derrick immediately shifted into mist form, dissipating as quickly as possible to avoid being seen.

As he moved his incorporeal form into the shadows of one of the cells he heard the officers yelling. Derrick was amused as he watched the stocky sergeant from before, push out from behind the officers in riot gear to quickly roll and cuff the shooter. He then ripped the clown mask off and tossed it behind him for one of the detectives to collect.

Patting him down quickly but thoroughly, the sergeant also found a tiny knife identical to the one Derrick had found on the shooter in the grocery store. Holding it up for another detective to collect, he then grabbed the gunman by the back of his collar and belt, and in an impressive feat of strength, picked him up and carried him into the empty cell at the front of the lockup area. Derrick was surprised, and slightly disappointed that the stocky sergeant didn't throw the man into the cell, but instead placed him relatively gently on one of the benches riveted to the wall of the cell.

Locking the door behind him, the sergeant turned

and opened the entry door to the lockup. Derrick could hear yelling in the other room. Someone, presumably the captain, was yelling and demanding an explanation as to what just happened.

Mentally chuckling to himself, Derrick slowly made his way across the ceiling, toward the entry door. By the time he had moved through the crack in the door and into the main room of the station, he could hear ambulance sirens whining in the distance. The captain was still yelling, but now it was in his office at the three officers in riot gear that had been the first ones through the doorway. Demanding explanations, no doubt, Derrick thought, as though anything they said to the captain could explain him.

Reaching the far wall again, Derrick found an out of the way corner and solidified back into corporeal form. Shifting quickly, he once again allowed Garrett to take control.

Garrett took in the scene in the police station again, and realized he wasn't going to get anywhere with them today. With a small sigh, he slipped back out the main doors and into the sunlight. Flagging down another taxi, he again gave directions to the grocery. He didn't remember shopping, though he walked out of the store with a full cart. His mind was on the shooters, and the comic book he remembered them from. If only he could remember what happened next in the comic…

The darkness surrounded him, enveloped him, enfolded him. He floated blissfully along in sweet silence. He could neither see, nor hear, nor feel. He could not smell, or taste, or sense anything around him. He was alone. Totally, blissfully alone. For what seemed like an eternity, he floated in darkened silence when suddenly, jarringly, that changed.

The lid to the sensory deprivation chamber opened to reveal the craggy face of one of his men. He didn't know the man's name, nor did he care to know. All he knew was that his peaceful silence had been broken.

Calmly, he sat up, and in one smooth motion reached over to the man's hip, pulled out the pistol holstered there, lifted his arm and shot the man under the chin. The report echoed loudly in the room as the high-caliber handgun removed the back of the man's head and transferred it to the far wall. The impact was enough to lift the man slightly backward off his feet, so that the man fell straight back, still standing as though in the middle of a trust fall. Well, he trusted that the man would fall anyway, so he dropped the pistol over the side of the tank and stood up.

The soft clearing of a throat had him turning quickly, only to reveal one of his more familiar minions. His eyes narrowed in understanding. This was the man who actually ordered his chamber opened. The other was simply a scapegoat for his wrath. It was a clever ploy. A bit too clever. This man understood him a little too well. He would probably have to kill the man soon, he thought to himself. The thought brought a smile to his face. He noted that the man relaxed slightly at the sight of his smile. Perhaps the man didn't understand him after all.

"Sir," the man began, "he has been sighted." Instantly he froze, focusing on the man so intently that the man shifted uncomfortably, standing against the wall. "He took down two of our shock troops, and we believe was responsible for the capture of a third."

"Capture?" he replied, his voice slightly raspy and higher pitched than one would expect from such a tall, lanky frame. "There were to be no captures. Each of them was instructed to die." His eyes narrowed, wondering if this man was to blame for the failure. He then wondered if he cared, or if it even mattered whether or not there was a reason to kill the man, or if he should just do it for the fun of it.

"Yes, sir," the man replied, becoming even more nervous. "Apparently our man made it into the holding cells of a police station, but collapsed just as the officers burst into the room."

"Straight down?" he asked. "As though his marionette strings had been cut?"

"Yes, sir," the man replied again. Screaming with rage, he leapt out of the tank and grabbed the man by the throat. Lifting the man off his feet, he shoved upward and smashed the man's head against the low ceiling.

"That damned pointy-eared alien did it! I told them to be wary! I told them not to let anyone stand behind them! I told them to die!"

With each sentence, he lifted the man up again smashing the now broken head against the ceiling. Releasing the body suddenly he allowed it to drop to the floor, noting with satisfaction that now this side of the room had a matching red stain against the white walls.

Wiping his face with his bloody hand, he growled.

"Very well, then we shall simply have to make sure our loyal trooper dies before they can get any information." Striding out of the small room, he yelled at the first man he could see. "Bring me some C4, a clown mask, some duct tape, and a two-bit hooker!" Without a word the man ran off. Suddenly, his head snapped to the side in time to see another one of the idiots looking away hurriedly. "What's the matter?!" he screamed at the man, "Never seen a naked albino with purple hair before?! Or are you just amazed that the rug matches?!"

"No, sir!" the man yelled, trying to hold a rigid posture. Stalking over to the man, he got right in his face.

"Do you know what I hate most?" he asked in a voice so soft that only the now trembling man could hear him.

"No, sir," the man replied.

His voice dropped even lower as he answered, "Liars."

The man's eyes had just enough time to widen before his hand slammed through the man's chest, taking the man's heart and ripping it out the other side. A look of shock crossed the man's face for a few moments before the widened eyes began to glaze over.

Pulling his arm back out of the man's chest, still clutching the heart, he turned to see the first man running back with a satchel under one arm and a dragging a girl with the other. A smile again spread across his face as the running man saw the grisly sight and slowed before approaching.

"Excellent," he stated happily. Stepping forward, he thrust the heart toward the man, forcing him to release the girl to catch it. "You just became a suicide bomber. Go blow up the station, starting with the cells." The man's eyes widened, but looking down at the bloody heart simply nodded slightly. Turning ink black eyes toward the girl, his smile widened. "Hmm, I've never raped a hooker in a sensory deprivation chamber before. I guess you get to be my first!"

With that, he grabbed the girl's arm with his still-bloody hand and dragged the girl toward the small room he had just vacated. The girl's struggles were subdued, staring transfixed at the heart still in the man's hand.

"Go!" he yelled as he finished dragging her into the room. "Go, and die gloriously!" With a maniacal laugh, he slammed the door shut.

The unsettling laughter continued for a few more moments before cutting off suddenly. The man looked down at the heart, dripping blood on the floor, then back at the door. Slowly setting the heart down on the floor, the man sighed and began pulling C4 out of the satchel.

CHAPTER FIVE

Garrett awoke late the next morning and rolled over with a groan. It was Sunday, the day all the good boys and girls frolicked off to church. And all the bad girls and boys like him went to group therapy. He sighed heavily as he rolled out of bed. Shuffling slowly into the kitchen, he felt a tug on his pants leg. He looked down, surprised to see that no one was there. A small smile touched his lips as he felt it again and closed his eyes.

"Garrett?" came the voice of young Justin.

"Yes, Justin?" he replied.

"May I have chocolate frosted sugar bombs with marshmallow bits for breakfast?" Garrett chuckled to himself at the old Calvin and Hobbes reference.

Justin didn't understand many of the Calvin comics, but he remembered most of the ones he did understand. For that very reason Garrett had purchased several boxes of Chocolate Lucky Charms, which were the closest cereal he could find to the legendary sugar bombs.

"Yes, you may," Garrett replied with a smile, rising from the stone chair.

"Yay!" Justin cheered as he raced over to the chair and sat down.

Opening his eyes, Justin looked down at his Spiderman pajamas, grinned, and raced to the kitchen. He said an enthusiastic thank you in his head to Garrett as he opened the lower cabinet next to the fridge and pulled out the sugar bombs. He knew they weren't the really real sugar bombs, but he was thankful that Garrett took the time to find them for him. Taking his special bowl and spoon from the same cupboard, he opened the fridge and pulled out the milk.

"Got to take the small one," Justin said to himself, reaching for the smaller half-gallon jug of milk. He had tried the full gallon one once, and made such a mess Garrett decided that he should have his own milk jug.

Setting the bowl, spoon, cereal and milk on the floor, Justin sat down next to it and carefully poured the cereal into the bowl. Setting the box down, he picked up the milk. With a look of intense concentration, he took the lid off of the milk and picked it up. Being very gentle not to spill any of it, he poured the milk into the bowl of cereal. He frowned when a little bit splashed onto his Spiderman pajamas, but at least it didn't hit the floor. Setting the milk back down, he replaced the cap and stood up again. He quickly put away the milk and the box of cereal, then turned to stare at the over-full bowl of cereal and milk.

"Rats," he said to himself, "too full again!" With a look of grim determination on his face, he gingerly picked up the bowl and started to move, inch by inch out of the kitchen and into the living room. His pace was agonizingly slow, and he kept wanting to lean down and nibble just one of the chocolate bits on top, but shook his head each time. "Nope, not gonna spill this time!" After what seemed like a whole hour, he finally reached the coffee table and delicately set his bowl down.

Grinning with pleasure he jumped up to grab the TV remote… and bumped into the coffee table, spilling cereal and milk all over the top of the table. His eyes welled up with tears of helpless frustration, ready to have himself a good cry, when he heard a voice behind him.

"What is the matter, my young friend?" Justin closed his eyes and turned in the stone chair to see Derrick standing next to him.

"I was trying so hard," Justin began, the hint of a sob starting in his voice. "I tried so hard not to spill and now I have!"

"I see," Derrick replied, his thick accent light and inquisitive, "So you are then preparing to cry over spilled milk?" The corner of Derrick's mouth twitched upward with suppressed mirth.

Justin froze for a moment trying to understand, then he remembered one of the characters in his cartoons saying that line. That it was no use crying over spilled milk.

All of a sudden his tears turned to giggles, and Derrick's mouth split in a wide grin. Justin had never understood why Peter yelled at Derrick so much. Derrick had always been nice to him. Justin jumped off of the stone chair and raced around to give Derrick's leg a big hug. The supposed dark lord of the night smiled softly and reached down to gently stroke the boy's head.

"Thanks, Derrick," Justin said, pulling back.

"You are welcome, my young friend," Derrick replied, scooping him up and placing him back on the stone chair again. "I believe that a towel might be in order. I'm certain there is one in the kitchen."

With a final smile, Justin opened his eyes. He glanced again at the spill, then raced into the kitchen to grab a towel. In a matter of moments, the spill was cleaned up, the spilled cereal eaten, and the towheaded boy was seated on the floor with the remote.

Pushing the power button, Justin saw that the TV was set to a news channel. He heard a quick snippet about a police station being blown up before he found the channel button and started flipping over to the cartoon channel. Rats, it was the stupid cartoon about a sea sponge and his starfish friend. Garrett hated it when he watched that show.

Justin didn't really care one way or the other. He didn't understand a lot of the humor in that show. Besides, he preferred action cartoons, heroes battling with villains, swinging from webs, and smashing buildings. Those were much more exciting.

Flipping again, he finally found one he liked. It was about a wandering samurai that stopped wandering because he found a girl he liked and then made a bunch of friends. There was a kid who was trying to learn how to be a swordsman, and a tall guy with a really big sword that yelled a lot. Especially after the samurai cut his big sword in half and he had to punch everyone instead. It was all in Japanese, so he didn't understand any of the words, but he really liked the swords, and the way the samurai was always trying to protect people.

It reminded him a little bit of Peter. Peter always tried to protect people. Peter had a cool sword too, though his was thick and straight, whereas the samurai in his show had a thin, curved sword.

Justin settled in, happily watching his cartoons while he ate. Once his samurai show ended, it changed to a show with a guy that looked a little like Derrick, except he wore a red suit with a broad brimmed hat and used a gun which he always pulled back with fanged teeth. After that, he flipped back to the other channel just in time to catch his favorite big green hero and watch him smash everything in sight. Justin lost track of how many shows he watched after that.

Garrett sat in the recliner in his room of the cave reading a book. It was one he had already read, of course. That was how books entered the library of his mind. He read them, and they were recorded here, for him to pick up and enjoy again.

He supposed it was the same for others, though they probably experienced it more as memories of their imaginary ventures into literature. But since when he read a book he really did experience it, they were more like memories of reality to him. And so they were here. All of them. Every book he had ever read. There were hundreds of them. Some old and musty, some new and crisp. Garrett had been a voracious reader as a child. Being a loner nerd can do that to you.

Though he had slowed down to only fifty or sixty books a year once he became an adult, he remembered with fondness the summers at the library. He would go once a week and bring home ten to fifteen books at a time. Then head out on the bus again the next week to swap them out for ten to fifteen more. He remembered happy summers where the only time he left his room was to eat, use the bathroom, and go to the library for more books.

In fact, one of the worst punishments his father could give him as a child was to tell him to put his book down and go out and play. He had hated that. Coincidentally, it always seemed to occur when he was at a particularly climactic part of the novel.

Suddenly, it occurred to him that quite a bit of time had passed and Justin had not come back inside to get him. Time sometimes flowed differently in his head than in the real world, but Garrett was fairly certain quite a bit of time had passed out there as well.

Putting the book back on the enormous shelf, Garrett opened the huge round-topped door and stepped into the main chamber. Walking around, he saw that Justin was still on the stone chair. Stepping up close, he tapped on the boy's shoulder. After a moment, Justin's eyes opened.

"Hey, Garrett!" Justin exclaimed happily.

"Hey, Small Fry," Garrett replied. "What time is it?" Justin paused for a moment, blinking. Then a look of panic crossed his face.

"Umm, two thirty?" the boy replied hesitantly.

"Two thirty?!" Garrett shouted in surprise. "We're going to be late!"

"I'm sorry Garrett, I didn't mean to make us late. I forgot to look at the clock. I was watching this new show with a cat man, and his other cat man and woman friends. And they were fighting a dog man, and a lizard man, and a bird man, and a mummy!"

"It's okay Justin, but I need to take control now. I've got to hurry if we're going to be there by three."

Justin just nodded and jumped down. Running for his room he yelled back at Garrett. Probably another apology, he thought wryly. He would have to check on Justin later, to make sure it wasn't overblowing the guilt thing again. The little guy had a tendency to do that on occasion.

Sitting on the stone chair and opening his eyes, Garrett picked up the empty cereal bowl, turned off the TV and went into the kitchen. He rinsed the bowl quickly before putting on his shoes and a ball cap and heading out the door.

The hallway of his apartment building had become a cobblestone road, but Garrett ignored it as he locked his door and headed in the direction of the stairs. Thankfully, the image of the road ended before he bumped into the far wall. Turning quickly, he took the stairs two at a time. Dangerous, he knew, but he was in a hurry.

In moments he was out on the street and hailing a cab. He was forced to smile, however, as a large black hearse pulled up to the curb, with a taxi sign fading in and out of view on top of it. Opening the back door, he slid onto what looked like plush leather seating, but was in fact old, worn cloth with several unseen tears in it. He gave the driver directions and tried to ignore the coffin that kept fading in and out of the back of the grim vehicle.

After a couple of harrowing, near-miss accidents, the hearse was again a yellow taxi cab, and Garrett was paying the driver, thankful the ride was over. Looking up at the uncompromisingly sharp edges of the new social services building, he sighed heavily.

"Sad again already?" came a familiar voice. A small smile tugged at his lips as he turned to regard his friend.

"Again, still, what's the difference?" Garrett replied with a wry smile.

"Oh now, talk like that will get you picked first for sharing time," Ann chuckled as she took his arm and walked inside with him.

"Oh, goody!" Garrett exclaimed with mock enthusiasm.

"Come now. It's not that bad. It's certainly a lot more fun going to group therapy since the Dreaming hit. Now at least we can talk to everyone without forgetting which alter is up for which person." Ann smiled happily at him.

"Always a silver lining with you, isn't it Ann?" Garrett replied with a chuckle.

"Ooh, I like silver lining. It looks so good with black don't you think?" Pausing for a moment, she flashed her black jacket at him which, sure enough, had silver trim.

Garrett threw back his head and laughed a deep belly laugh. After a moment, Ann started laughing as well. As the laugh died down to a chuckle, Garrett shook his head.

"Thanks Ann, I needed that. You always seem to keep me from taking life too seriously. Thank you for that," Garrett said with a warm smile.

"My pleasure," Ann responded with a grin and a mock curtsey. Chuckling again, Garrett extended his arm to her, and they walked into the large conference room together.

There were already two people seated at the table when they entered. Katie, a plump middle aged lady with a service dog lying next to her; and Phil, a mountain of a man with a shaved head, biker tattoos and a leather vest with "Ride or Die" embroidered on it.

Garrett and Ann took their seats at the small conference table and looked around. Just then, a slender woman with large, round glasses burst into the room, practically humming with energy.

"All right, it looks like we're almost all here. Where is Susan?" she asked as she took her place at the head of the table.

"Not here yet," came the rumbling bass of Phil's voice.

"Well, I think we can give her another minute before we get started," the woman said briskly.

"Whatever you say, Miss Ruby," Phil's voice rumbled again.

"So, while we wait for her, how is everyone doing this week?" Ruby asked brightly.

"Well, I killed three people," Garrett replied flippantly. Ruby froze solid for a moment before looking over at Garrett.

"Garrett," Ruby began, "you know perfectly well that you cannot go around saying things like that. I have a duty to report certain actions and murder is one of them."

"Oh Garrett is just exaggerating," Ann said, patting Garrett's hand. "He only killed two of them, I killed the other one."

"ANN!" Ruby yelled in shock. "You can't say things like that!"

"Besides," Ann continued as though she hadn't heard Ruby, "it wasn't murder, it was self-defense. And it wasn't even Garrett that did it. It was some of the others." Garrett sighed unhappily.

"Oh fine, I didn't really kill two of them. I only killed one of them. The other, Sean knocked unconscious for the police to apprehend." Garrett grumped, folding his arms in front of him.

"What are you…" Ruby began, when suddenly the doors to the conference room burst open and a tall, stocky woman with two long, blond braids burst into the room.

"Sorry for late!" she exclaimed quickly taking a seat, her thick, Slavic accent blurring the words together slightly. "What happens?"

"Glad you could join us, Susan." Ruby replied, with a greater measure of calm than Garrett had expected. "We were just discussing the week's activities."

"Yes, we were just taking score on how many people we've killed in the last week. Garrett and I are tied one and one. Though perhaps he should get an extra half a point for knocking a man unconscious for the police?" Ann interjected brightly.

"Ann," Ruby said with a sigh, "you know I have to report that kind of thing."

"Wait," Susan said looking confused, "No understand joke. You are for killing people?"

"No, all four of us didn't kill people," Ann explained, "Just Garrett and I." Ruby hung her head for a moment.

"All right, all right. Just so I can make sure I am filling out the police report correctly, how exactly did you kill these people?" Ruby said, with her head still hanging down.

"Fireball," Ann replied.

"Sword," Garrett added.

"I see," Ruby sighed again before looking up. "Perhaps you'd better take it from the top.

"Well, it had to do with those clown people," Ann began.

"Subway," Garrett interrupted. "The shooter in the subway. Peter got to him with his sword. Probably saved a dozen lives or more."

"And Greybeard got the one in the grocery store," Ann beamed. "Cooked him up with a little magic fire!"

"Sword," Ruby said pointing at Garrett. "Fireball," she finished pointing at Ann. Throwing up her hands in frustration she sighed heavily. "Fine! I won't tell anyone about it. I can't tell anyone about it, because no one will believe me! There is no police precedent for turning into a magic fireball-wielding wizard and cooking a bad guy." She turned to Garrett, "Now sword they would believe, but not a beheading! And they would want to know about the sword, and where it went, and then we would run into the 'it went nowhere' problem! So fine, you win! I won't tell anyone, except my cat when I get home!" With that, she slumped back into her chair and folded her arms in frustration. After a moment, Ann turned to Phil and smiled sweetly.

"So Phil, would you like to start the session off today?"

An hour later, Garrett and Ann walked arm in arm out of the social services building to catch a cab home.

"That wasn't very nice, you know," Garrett said, looking down at his friend.

"What wasn't?" Ann asked sweetly.

"You know what," Garrett replied, bumping into her. "Baiting Ruby like that."

"You started it," Ann answered, bumping back.

"Yeah, but I was being flippant, and she could have blown it off as me being rude. You went into enough detail that she knew it was true, but couldn't do anything about it," Garrett said, with a touch of accusation in his voice.

"I know," Ann said not sounding at all apologetic, "I wanted to make sure you were safe, though. You might have said too much for her to ignore, and too little for her to realize it was beyond her ability to report. You could have gotten yourself into some serious trouble, you know."

"Wait," Garrett said pausing his walk, "you did that for me? To push her past her ability to report it, so I wouldn't get in trouble?"

"Of course," Ann said with a shrug. "What are friends for?" Garrett shook his head, grinned, and leaned down to kiss the top of her head.

"Thanks Ann, you're the best," Garrett said, leaning into her in lieu of a hug.

"So are you, sweetie," Ann replied, leaning back into him with a smile. Garrett flagged down a cab and they rode most of the way home together in comfortable silence.

His face was serene as he sat on his gilded throne and looked out over his little minions. So ready, so eager, so willing to die. Like a sheltered virgin during the wedding night. They didn't know what was in store, but they were ready to do it anyway. They were well trained at least.

Not one of them moved as he sat there and stared at them. Row upon row of black-clad peons, waiting for him. For his word. And on the eve of his greatest triumph, he was withholding it from them. He wanted to see if someone broke. Someone, anyone, in the front, the back, the middle, he didn't care. He just wanted someone to break. It had been six hours already and everyone was still standing. It was starting to annoy him, actually.

He almost broke himself, just for the joy of killing someone. But no, he wouldn't break. He was stronger than any of these peons. Not that he felt he had to prove it to them. He didn't. He didn't have to prove anything to these worthless minions. Only to Him. He was the only one that mattered. He had to break Him at any cost. Only then would it end. Only then could he be free. So he didn't break. He waited; silent, serene, sociopathic.

Then he heard it. A tiny sound in the silence. A whimper. A smile curved his lips, someone was about to break. There! A movement, in the middle row! As he watched, a black-clad figure began to waver and finally to slump down to the floor. With a hideous scream, he leapt up to stand on the seat of his throne and point at the failure.

"TRAITOR!" he screamed at the crowd. "I said no one could move, NO ONE! That man is a traitor! I command you all to kill him! Tear him limb from limb! I want to hold his bloody heart in my hand before I count to ten!"

The crowd surged, turning on the hapless person on the floor. In an instant, they changed from an apparently disciplined group to a rabid mob. Dozens of them grabbed hold of the man and pulled. Clothing flew from the body, ripped off in their quest to dismember their victim.

"ONE!" he screeched, and grinned as the crowd

became even more bloodthirsty. Knives came out of sheaths and blood sprayed as the crowd tore into the man.

"TWO!" he cackled, as the sound of bone shattering echoed in the chamber.

"THREE!" he exclaimed as the mob became even more frenzied.

"FOUR!" he yelled at the distinctive cracking of a ribcage.

"FIVE!" he screamed, reveling in the carnage.

"SIX!" he exulted, watching them work themselves up into even more wild abandon.

"SEVEN!" he roared as one arm thrust triumphantly into the air, its prize clutched tightly.

"EIGHT!" The crowd surged as the victor pressed forward.

"NINE!" Hundreds of eyes turned to follow the victorious peon pushing through the crowd to present the bloody heart to him.

Taking the bloody heart in his hands he looked down at the rabid mob. They had worked themselves up to a killing frenzy in seconds. They were ready. Grinning, he thrust the bloody heart into the air, laughing in pleasure at the cries and screams coming from his mob.

"Now is the time!" he cried out, still holding the blood prize aloft. "Now is the time to strike, to maim, and to kill! Go out, tiny creatures! Go out and wreak thy havoc!"

Cackling maniacally, he watched as they turned as one body and surged for the exit. He couldn't wait to see how He dealt with this one. The lone gunmen were the introduction, the mob was the warmup, and next the climax! He couldn't wait!

CHAPTER SIX

Garrett awoke early on Monday and rolled out of bed. Another day, another chance to earn a living. Though thankfully as a freelance writer, that didn't include a dreary nine to five grind. It did, however, include a morning run.

Slipping quickly into his sweats, he tucked his door key into his shoe and walked out into the living room. Picking up a stopwatch that rested on the entry table he clicked the button to start the timer, then set it back down. With a smile, he quickly exited his door, locking it on the way out, and headed for the stairs.

Garrett took the steps quickly but safely, lifting his knees as he hit every step. He warmed up on the way down. Upon reaching the bottom landing, he took a few minutes to stretch properly before leaving the apartment building at a light jog. He jogged for about a block before picking up the pace into a full run.

Garrett liked to run. He wasn't usually a very physical guy, but the steady rhythm of his feet on the pavement and the feeling of the air blowing through his hair always helped to clear his mind. Block after block rolled by with nothing but the sound of his shoes slapping against the cement.

Glancing up, he saw he had reached 56th street. He'd run almost two miles already. With a grin he picked up the pace a bit. By the time he'd reached 78th he was breathing hard. Pushing himself even harder, he sprinted the last half mile, his stride finally breaking as he reached 100th street.

Garrett bent over, holding his knees as he took great, gulping breaths. Four miles. Not too shabby, he thought, smiling to himself. Feeling a tap on his mental shoulder, he smiled again and closed his eyes.

"Yes Peter, it's your turn now," Garrett replied in response to the tap.

"Thank you." Peter's powerful voice echoed in the cave as Garrett stood and walked around the stone chair.

Sitting quickly, Peter opened his eyes and looked out over the barren landscape of the city, jostling the shield on his left arm to ensure it was secure. It always was. Sliding the shield off of his arm, he secured it to his back.

Briskly, he turned toward Garrett's home and began to move. More than a walk, but less than a run, Peter moved in an easy, loping stride. To an experienced historian, the lack of rattling and clanking from a man running in plate mail armor would have come as a shock. But to Peter that was normal. His armor had been crafted by the finest smiths in all the kingdoms, fitted perfectly to his frame and buckled on tightly. The fabulous armor barely moved at all on its own.

Picking up the pace, his massive ground-eating stride propelled him down the empty sidewalks at a pace that would be the envy of many professional runners. And the fact that he could do it in plate mail would confirm the existence of mythical heroes to every geek and fantasy gamer who saw him. Fortunately, there was no one out that would see him this early in the morning. Garrett got up early enough to see to that.

Glancing up, Peter saw the sign that read 38th street. With a roar of triumph, he surged ahead at a breakneck pace that no one would believe even if they could see it. The speed, the power, the sheer magnitude of his massive six foot six, three-hundred-pound frame charging down the street in a hundred pounds of plate mail armor made him laugh at the feel of it. He felt unstoppable. Though it was good that he wasn't, otherwise this run might end badly for him. The tiniest of smiles touched his lips as he prepared to finish his run.

Reaching back over his shoulder he pulled his shield off his back and slid it back onto his left arm. Then with a final leap, he dove forward leading with his shield. He hit the ground shield first and used his momentum to turn his landing into a right shoulder roll. As his hips cleared the roll his free hand was at his waist drawing his massive broadsword. Finishing the roll, he surged to his feet, his sword leading in a brutal thrust that would have spelled doom for any creature smaller than an elephant.

However, the cat sitting on the banister a bare inch away from the razor-sharp tip of the mighty blade appeared to be unconcerned. Looking lazily over toward Peter it leaned over and licked the tip of the blade, as if to show just how unconcerned it really was. Then with a flick of its head, it turned and hopped down, walking slowly away.

With a snort of disgust at the antics of the tiny creature, Peter sheathed his sword and finished walking up to the apartment. Shaking his head in frustration at the time restrictions placed upon him, Peter closed his eyes.

"I say again Garrett; I protest the unreasonable demands placed upon my time in the world. I must train more than simply half of a candle-mark each day if I am to retain my skills!" Peter announced as he stood up from the stone chair.

"Dude, no you won't," Garrett replied with a sigh. He knew they'd had this argument before, and they would have it again, probably tomorrow. "You are a mythical hero of legend. Straight out of some fantasy role playing game where the fully armored characters can run for six hours straight and then fight a bloody dragon, and never get winded. Your skills can't deteriorate."

"Perhaps that is so, but I need more time to practice my art!" Peter exclaimed loudly.

"All right, I'll see what I can do, but not today!" Garrett replied, sitting on the stone chair.

Garrett opened his eyes, looking up at the plain brick face of his apartment building and reached for the door. As he pulled his key out of his shoe, he heard a strange sound coming from down the street. Taking a couple of steps back down from the landing he looked down the street in shock.

A group of perhaps two dozen individuals dressed all in black with faces painted in a variety of clown colors and expressions, were methodically making their way down the street. Smashing windows, kicking in doors, they seemed hell-bent on doing as much damage as possible. Garrett watched in horror as they dragged a young woman kicking and screaming out of her apartment. As they threw her to the ground, the lead assailant began to kick her in the ribs.

In the blink of an eye, Peter was there, throwing Garrett bodily off of the stone chair and taking control. Peter didn't wait for the steel plates to form around him before he began his charge at the gang. With a roar of rage, he drew his mighty sword and rushed the group. So fast was his charge that the leader of the gang had barely lifted his head before he found it separated from his body by a single swipe from the armored warrior.

The rest of the group fared little better, scattering in all different directions to avoid the onslaught of the enraged knight. Two more fell to his blade before the rest managed to get out of range. Two of them stepped forward however, brandishing some form of club. One looked like a thin metal club with some kind of lettering painted on it. The other looked more like an unforged steel rod, but with a strange malformed bit at the end that looked something like a wedge.

Peter set himself, prepared for their charge, when suddenly he heard a loud clang of metal on metal behind him. Turning swiftly, he saw a third man with a thick iron bar that was curved at the end so that it looked like a farmer's hoe. The man dropped the weapon and looked at the knight in shock. Peter grinned broadly as he realized that the man had hit him in the back with the weapon, apparently not realizing that not only was Peter's back covered in armor, but that his shield was still strapped to his back as well.

With a single step forward, Peter backhanded the unfortunate assailant, launching him into the crowd which had begun to return. Peter chuckled as he saw them stay at a distance they foolishly thought was beyond his range. They apparently had no idea what his range actually was. Oh well, they would learn as soon as he dealt with the two fighters with odd clubs.

Peter turned back again to see the two men already charging him. With another roar, Peter stepped forward into the charge of the man with the malformed stick. Grabbing the down-swinging arm with his left hand, he swung his sword upward, severing the arm at the shoulder joint. Using his momentum to spin, he dropped the severed arm as his left elbow went backwards and into the chest of the now one-armed man.

Using the force of the impact, he shot his left arm forward again to catch the other metal club on his bracer. The metal club rang with the impact and Peter was irritated to note that some of the paint from the club had rubbed off on his bracer.

Stepping forward, he thrust his sword, impaling the man just under the sternum, the force of the blow lifting him off of his feet and into the air. Peter held him there for a moment, lifted completely over his head, impaled on his sword while he glanced around at the men's companions.

The first glimmer of concern flashed through his mind as he realized that none of the man's black-clad, painted companions appeared at all worried, scared, or disgusted at the sight. In fact, they seemed to be getting more excited with each blow.

Faintly, Peter heard a voice in his head commenting about berserkers; warriors who became stronger and stronger the more blood was spilled. Very well then, Peter thought, reaching behind him and taking his shield from his back. He slipped it on his left arm quickly as several members of the crowd lifted projectile weapons, similar to the one Peter had seen on the man in the subway.

Quickly he lifted his shield to deflect them when he heard the same metallic sound behind him. He grunted as his shield began taking blows from the powerful projectiles, his head turning rapidly to see two more men preparing to fire behind him.

Leaping to his left he dove forward into one of the attackers, allowing the bullets from the other two in front to pass by where he had been standing a moment earlier and into the fighters behind him. Shield slamming the attacker on the left and knocking him backward, the knight slashed out to his right with his sword in an upward arc. His sword caught the weapon of one of the other shooters and shattered it, the broken pieces flying upwards.

Pivoting on his right foot, he turned toward the man he had just disarmed, swinging his shield parallel to the ground at neck height. The bottom edge of the large shield caught the man in the throat, crushing his windpipe. The man dropped to his knees and Peter brought his knee up to the man's face as he rushed past him to the third shooter on that side.

Thrusting forward with his sword, Peter was shocked when the man swung his own weapon in an arc to deflect the broadsword. This one has some skill, he thought to himself as he stepped again, slamming his shield forward.

Peter felt the impact of the shield striking the man, but when he pulled it back to look he saw the third shooter coming out of a crouch to land on his feet a few yards away. Peter was again surprised. The man had apparently jumped off of the ground in order to absorb the force of the blow and allow it to push him backward, instead of knocking him down.

Peter laughed. Finally, an opponent worth fighting in this forsaken land! Charging forward, he executed a series of precise slashes and thrusts, ever more impressed that his opponent continued to evade them. After several near misses, the man suddenly dropped down into a crouch and stepped forward. Peter suddenly felt a searing pain under his arm. The man had drawn a small dagger and, striking upward, he had managed to land a blow just under Peter's extended arm at the exposed portion of his armor between the plates. Peter almost dropped his sword as a numbing shock shot down his arm. Looking to retaliate, Peter kicked at the man, but a well-timed somersault to the side put him out of reach.

Peter flexed his fingers around the hilt of his sword a few times. He had underestimated this opponent. Assuming everyone was weak and helpless here, he had let his guard down and over-extended his thrust. He would not make the same mistake again.

Bashing the flat of his blade against his shield to indicate his readiness to proceed, he stepped forward, extending his shield arm as if to shield bash again, noting the man also stepping back to avoid it. Peter twisted his arm so that the shield flipped outward until it was horizontal, the bottom edge catching the man under the chin and knocking him off of his feet.

The man landed hard, the knife clattering out of his hand and across the ground. Peter glanced at it quickly to make sure it was out of reach of his opponent. As he looked at the blade, Peter noticed a small demonic-looking face had been etched into the blade. The visage was gruesome, much like the demon-headed man he had killed in the tunnel the other day, with the powerful projectile weapon.

As the man rose, Peter heard grumbling from the rest of the group. They would not stand this duel for much longer. Either way, it would be over soon. Peter allowed the man to stand and set himself before charging forward again, his sword slicing upwards as if to cleave the man from hip to shoulder.

It missed as Peter expected that it would, and he used the momentum to spin himself around, now leading with his shield to bash into the man. Again, the man managed to dodge backwards, but now he was off balance, as Peter reversed the spin into a rapid pivot that brought his broadsword around once more in a lightning-fast thrust.

He took the man right through the chest, a perfect strike between the ribs. Peter looked into the man's eyes and nodded in respect to his defeated foe. Then he withdrew his sword and turned back to the crowd.

As he suspected, they had become restless, but agitated again at the sight of new blood. Slamming his sword against his shield again, he prepared for their next onslaught.

A tiny whimper caused him to glance down and see

that his fight had taken him near the girl whose abduction had initiated this fight. He felt rather than saw the projectile that was thrown at him.

Dropping his sword, he caught the round object, intending to throw it back again. Unfortunately, he did not have the opportunity as the metal ball exploded in his hand.

Peter felt himself being lifted off of the ground his shield flying away. He had a few moments to marvel at his own foolishness for not being prepared for the weapons of this culture before slamming into the ground and rolling backwards. Metal plates clanged as they hit the concrete and Peter felt more than one buckle break under the strain of the impact.

Finally, he came to a stop. His body ached and he had the impulse to lay there for a moment and assess the damage. However, he was still in combat and therefore didn't waste a moment before rolling over and getting to his feet.

As he stood, he felt his right shoulder plate fall off, the buckles snapped and leather torn. Glancing down at his hand he realized that the metal plates of his gauntlet had been bent and he could no longer close his right hand. Momentarily, he wondered if the hand itself had been damaged.

Damage to the gorget around his neck prevented him from being able to turn his head all the way to the right. Unwilling to allow his opponents such an advantage, he reached up and removed his helmet. As he dropped the helmet to the ground, his eyes lifted and beheld a sight that caused him to freeze.

The woman… she had not been protected by steel plates. She had taken the full brunt of the explosion, since she had been standing right beside him. As he beheld her ruined body, rage began to well up in him. Suddenly, a black cloak obscured his vision. His rage had summoned the master of their shared rage. Peter caught a quick glimpse of Derrick, his figures bestial and his eyes glowing red with fury before losing control of the body.

Even with the red haze of the blood rage clouding over his vision, Derrick still took in the situation in a heartbeat. Seeing the lovely young girl, her body broken for nothing but sport, filled him with a blood anger he had not experienced in many years.

The foolish men paused as they saw his most bestial form exposed. His fangs already extended, his features shifted, almost bordering on the demonic. His skin withered to a dark craggy grey as thick bony ridges grew where his eyebrows used to be. His nostrils extended, growing upwards while his nose flattened against his face.

The vampiric ears also grew, becoming large and pointed. Not quite the ears of a bat, but some unholy blend of bat and human. Growing in size, his fine evening wear tore and fell off of his body to reveal the same grey craggy skin, dark, black fur cascading down his shoulders and back.

The eyes however, are what truly captured their attention. Twin glowing, blood red eyes could be seen from under the thick brow ridge, with the rage and fury of hundreds of years behind them.

Derrick allowed them one pulse of fear at his hideous

form before launching into them. Claws tore, fangs ripped, and blood was shed on the cold street. Unlike Peter, Derrick did not give them a chance at an honorable fight. He killed, and maimed, and fed. One broken body blending into another as he made his way with superhuman speed through the crowd.

After watching a dozen of their companions fall in a matter of moments, Derrick felt another pulse of fear from them, and the men broke, running in all directions trying to escape. But the blood rage had been unleashed, and Derrick had no intention of allowing any of them to leave alive. Again and again he killed, until he was covered in the blood of his victims. For that's what they had become. Not fighters challenging a warrior, but victims of a primal rage, and an endless thirst.

As Derrick glut his thirst, he began to slow. Each death slower and more painful than the last. He was slipping, the rage beginning to take full control. He was losing his humanity to a wash of blood, death, and pain.

As he held the last of the black-clad men over his head, he found that he could not close his fingers around the man's throat. The rage welled up inside of him and he strained to crush the life out of the insect who would kill innocents. But again something stopped him. A flicker. Derrick paused as he saw his hand flicker again, as though armor plates were forming and disappearing around his hand. Again he strained, putting all of his rage into the death of the man held in the air, but he could not close it.

Closing his eyes, he snarled in fury at the armored knight standing next to the stone chair. Still in a rage, he lashed out with a clawed hand which rang against the steel breastplate without leaving a mark.

"Derrick, that is enough," Peter said, his voice deep and sorrowful.

Derrick's only answer was a snarl. Leaping out of the chair, Derrick grabbed onto Peter's shoulders, trying to tear the steel gorget around his neck away with his teeth. "Derrick, you cannot bring her back, she is dead." Peter said softly, his hands grasping the enraged vampire and pushing him back. "And you cannot defeat me. That is my purpose. To be powerful enough to stop you from going too far. To be strong enough, and hard enough that you cannot kill me. So while you contain the rage, I can contain you. You know this. That is why we were split in pairs. I was designed to be able to stop you."

At the sound of the deep bass voice rumbling over the words, completely calm and soft, Derrick's movements began to slow. Standing on his own feet, Derrick took a step backwards. His face had returned to normal, though his eyes were still full of anger and hate as he glared at the knight.

"I curse you!" Derrick hissed. "I curse you, knight. I curse that you alone can contain me. I curse that you will not allow me the vengeance that woman deserves. I curse your foolish honor and pride that allowed them to live long enough to kill her. I curse you, knight! Though I know I cannot destroy you, I will scream my rage into the maelstrom and grow stronger. And one day… one day we shall see who is truly stronger." Turning sharply on his heel, he strode quickly toward the large wooden door of his room and slamming it open, stepped inside.

Peter sighed softly. Derrick was right. He had allowed himself to become too caught up in the battle to remember that he had charged in to protect, not to fight. His heart broke at the knowledge that he had not been enough. For all his strength, for all his skill, he had not been enough to save the girl. Peter sighed again as he sat on the stone chair and opened his eyes.

The man was still held in the air, not realizing how much had happened inside of the knight's mind in the space of the few heartbeats the man had experienced. Still holding the man by his neck he walked over to the severed arm of his first opponent and extracted the odd-looking club from his hand.

Setting the man down next to a lamp post, he took the man's arms and wrapped them around the pole. Moving to the other side, he put the man's wrists together and then bent the club around his wrists. Realizing there were too many awake now for him to change back to Garrett safely he turned and started to walk away.

"A golf club?" the man wrapped around the lamp post asked. "You are going to restrain me with a golf club?"

"If the land of Golf is so weak that its clubs can be bent, then yes I will restrain you with one of the clubs of the land of Golf." Peter answered without turning, "And unless you want to see our fanged friend again, I suggest you stay there." Peter nodded in satisfaction at the slight whimper he heard and strode away down the street.

CHAPTER SEVEN

It was almost two in the afternoon before Garrett was able to make his way back to his apartment. It wasn't just a matter of Peter finding a place where Garrett could change back. The police had been doing their investigation for most of the day, and he didn't want to have to explain his whereabouts to them.

Trudging back to his apartment, he could still see the remnants of the crime scene personnel taking final measurements and preparing for the city cleanup crew. The crime scene area they had taped off was enormous. It covered the entire road for almost a half block. There was a little walking path taped off for residents to be able to leave their homes but other than that, it was still completely blocked off.

Garrett figured they had probably already canvassed the surrounding buildings asking if anyone saw anything. He hoped he was late enough that they had finished with that part of the investigation. He honestly didn't know what he would say.

"Why no officer, I didn't hear any gunfire. A grenade you say? How odd that I didn't hear it." Garrett mumbled to himself as he fished out his key and quickly went inside. Stepping into his apartment, he heard the sound of his cell phone voicemail. Hooking his house key on the hook next to the door, he walked into his bedroom and grabbed the phone.

He walked back into the living room as he scrolled through his messages to find out who had called him. It was Ann. Looking down, he realized the stopwatch on the table was still running. Clicking it off again, he gave a sarcastic chuckle.

"Ten hours and thirty-two minutes, a new record." Garrett said to himself. Quickly punching in the voicemail password, he brought the phone to his ear.

"Garrett, it's Ann. Where are you? I heard on the news about the attackers and the ones that were slaughtered near your apartment. Be careful Garrett, please! That group was not the only one loose in the city this morning. Every other group though was taken down by teams of policemen and SWAT teams. Only the group in your area turned up dead before any of the police had arrived. The news said they had wounds like a pack of wild animals had attacked, which would have been bad enough, except they found one alive! Tied to a lamp post with a bent golf club! Now, I know perfectly well who fights like an animal when cornered and who has the strength to bend a golf club like a twist tie! So I'm telling you to be careful. You've been present at four incidents now, and if anyone figures that out, you could be in some real trouble! So call me when you get this message, okay? I want to hear that you're all right."

Garrett couldn't decide if he wanted to chuckle or sigh. He appreciated that Ann cared and worried about him, but at the same time, he was very tired and all he wanted to do was to go back to bed for a few hours. He sighed as friendship won out and he hit the redial button.

"Garrett, there you are!" Ann answered almost immediately.

"Yeah, I'm here. It's okay, I'm all right." Garrett responded, trying not to sigh again.

"Well, of course you're all right. How are Derrick and Peter?" Ann said with a note of worry in her voice.

"They're fine too, Ann." Garrett replied ruefully, "Peter got a little banged up, but he's unkillable, I think, so he's fine. Derrick shut himself in his room and hasn't been seen since, so he'll be okay too."

"Well that's good to hear." Ann said in her most motherly tone. "And what about you, Garrett? Why did it take you so long to call me back?"

"Dodging cops, mostly," Garrett said with a chuckle.

"What?!" Ann exclaimed worriedly.

"It's okay, Ann," Garrett said quickly, "I meant staying away from my place until the police had finished questioning everyone."

"Oh, all right then," Ann replied in a much calmer tone.

"I really am okay, Ann," Garrett said softly. "I know you're worried, but I'm all right. And as far as I know, no one has made the connection between me and the four incidents. It helps that I left the scene each time as a different person."

"Oh, right," Ann said, "Now I remember. Though I don't think you ever told me what you were doing at the police station. At least I assume that was you. Taking down a masked shooter without being seen, in the middle of a police station?"

"Yeah, that was me." Garrett answered.

"I thought I remembered you said you knocked one out for the police, though I didn't realize it was in the police station itself until I saw the newscast," Ann explained, "but you didn't ever tell me why you were there."

"Well, I had a strange thought, about the shooters," Garrett replied. "I thought I remembered a story, in an old superhero comic, where his crazy clown enemy does the same thing. So I thought I would tell them. I figured they wouldn't believe me, but I figured I had to try. But another shooter was there, and they were so busy with him, that I knew no one would listen to me about it."

"So you didn't tell anyone about your thought?" Ann asked.

"Not till just now," Garrett said lightly.

"Well have you tried to research it?" Ann inquired.

"I've been a little busy Ann," Garrett replied with a note of frustration. "I went from there to therapy yesterday, then to a gang attack and raging vampire this morning. I haven't exactly had time to do any research."

"Okay, I understand. I just wanted to offer to help." Ann said softly.

"Oh," Garrett replied, a bit embarrassed. "Sure, I would like that."

"Good!" Ann replied sounding far more cheerful. "Should we start tomorrow? At the library?"

"No, I don't think the library will have anything like this. We should hit a comic shop and ask some of the comic enthusiasts about the storyline. See if anyone else remembers it," Garrett said. "You want to meet me at the comic shop Nerdy Comics, around ten o'clock tomorrow?"

"I'll be there!" Ann replied brightly.

"Thanks Ann, see you then." Garrett replied with a smile.

"See you tomorrow," she responded. "Bye."

Garrett chuckled as he hung up the phone and slipped it into his pocket. Sitting down at his computer, he decided to spend a bit of time browsing for stories with crazy clowns, just in case he stumbled across the one he was looking for.

Four hours later, Garrett shut off his computer with a big sigh. Well, he now felt that he knew more about crazy, murderous clowns than he ever wanted to know. He had searched comics, TV shows, movies, cartoons, everything, but he still couldn't seem to find the story he was looking for.

Standing up, Garrett stretched, stiff from sitting at his computer for so long. Walking into the kitchen, he decided that Justin had been very well behaved lately and deserved some time up. Glancing at the clock, he saw that it was already seven in the evening. Pulling out a bag of dinosaur-shaped chicken nuggets from the freezer, he popped them into the microwave and closed his eyes.

Standing up from the stone chair, Garrett paused for a moment to marvel that although he had been sitting in that chair for close to twelve hours, he didn't feel stiff and sore like he did when sitting for too long in the outside world.

Chuckling to himself, he walked over to Justin's room and knocked. Garrett grinned at the sound of stamping feet, knowing that Justin was running to the door. In a moment, it was flung open to reveal the towheaded boy.

"Hey, Small Fry, you want to have some time up to watch your samurai show tonight?" Garrett asked with a smile.

"Sure!" Justin answered with a grin. "Hang on!" And with that he slammed the door in Garrett's face.

Garrett froze for a moment trying to decide if Justin was angry or just in a hurry. He remembered the smile though, so he chalked it up to five-year-old enthusiasm. After a few more moments Justin again opened the door and came out.

"So what were you doing in there that you had to go back for?" Garrett asked with a smile.

"Spilling milk," Justin replied happily.

"Wait… spilling milk?" Garrett asked, confused.

"Yup!" he replied proudly.

"And why were you spilling milk?" Garrett asked cautiously.

"Can't tell you." Justin said with a note of finality in his voice.

"Well, okay then. Just make sure you clean it up." Garrett said, trying to sound parental.

"It's okay," Justin replied, "I'll make sure it's cleaned up." With that, Justin raced over to the stone chair and opened his eyes.

He looked quickly around the kitchen just as the microwave dinged. With a grin, he raced over to his cupboard and pulled out a cup. Setting it carefully on the floor, he opened the fridge and pulled out his half-gallon of milk.

Sitting down on the floor, he carefully opened the milk and poured himself half a glass. Jumping up and putting the milk away, he carefully carried his milk out to the coffee table and set it down.

Justin smiled to himself as he looked at the milk. Derrick really was awfully funny, he thought to himself. He was glad Derrick reminded him not to cry over spilled milk, and he really hoped that the milk he spilled under Derrick's door would remind him of that. Derrick had been awfully sad today.

Justin could sometimes hear through the door that adjoined their rooms, the sound of things breaking. And sometimes Derrick howling. Not like a wolf howl, more like a howl you would make when you stub your toe on the couch.

Justin had been thinking all day about what he could do to cheer up Derrick. Finally, it came to him. Derrick had told him not to cry over spilled milk, so maybe if Derrick saw the spilled milk, he would remember not to cry.

Justin turned and raced back into the kitchen. Grabbing a paper towel, he opened the microwave and pulled out the hot plate full of nuggets. Justin grinned as he raced back to the coffee table with his prize.

Setting it down quickly, he went to grab the remote when he felt a tap on his shoulder. He closed his eyes to see Garrett standing next to him.

"Okay, you've got one hour, Small Fry. At eight o'clock I want you to come get me, okay?" Garrett said, still smiling.

"Okay!" Just said with a grin and opened his eyes again. Grabbing the remote, he turned on the TV and flipped to his favorite streaming channel. Loading up his profile, he clicked on the first show and sat down to his dinner.

As he reached for his glass of milk, he smiled again.

Yup, he really hoped the spilled milk would help cheer Derrick up again.

Garrett woke up at his usual run time, rolled over, turned off his alarm, swung his legs out of bed, and froze. As he sat there, his legs dangling off the side of the bed, he realized that it might not be safe to run for a few days. Ann had told him that there were several groups of black-clad, clown-faced gangs walking the streets yesterday, and there was no guarantee they had all been caught. With a sigh of irritation, Garrett rose and began his morning routine.

Within a few minutes, he was wandering into the kitchen, toweling his head dry and wondering what was left to eat in his fridge. Glancing over at the empty sink, he smiled as he realized that Justin had remembered to put his plate and cup in the dishwasher.

He really was a good kid, Garrett thought to himself. He still wondered about the whole spilled milk thing, but he was sure that Sean would let him know if something was wrong.

Garrett marveled again at the complexity of the human mind. He had known quite a few people over the years with multiple personalities. Some were simple, some were complex, some were very strange, and some completely defied explanation.

Take his own mind, for example. Garrett was a Gemini, and somehow when his mind was splitting personalities it apparently took that concept to the extreme. Each one of his alternate personalities came in pairs. The completely logical, pointy-eared alien and the completely emotional child. The monstrous, blood-drinking vampire and the mythical hero of legend capable of containing him.

He had idly wondered about himself on various occasions. After all, there were five of them total that he knew of, since he didn't have an opposite. He supposed it was probably because he was the first. The original personality that the others had split from. Still it was interesting to think about.

He really had it pretty easy, come to think of it. Most of his friends had far more than five to deal with. He knew Ann had well over a hundred, and he was pretty sure Katie had at least double that many. Though many of Katie's weren't human. In fact, many of them were not even bipedal.

Katie actually had alternate personalities that were animals. Small animals mostly, at least that's all he'd ever seen. He wondered if she had anything bigger, something predatory perhaps. Susan's weren't human either, though they were humanoid. All of Susan's alters took the forms of shadows. Misty, indistinct, wavering with any breeze that wafted through the room. And they didn't really talk, they just moaned a lot.

The one he felt the worst for though was Phil. Great big biker dude, and he had nothing but tiny fairies and pixies as his alters.

Not that anyone outside of the very small subset of clinical psychiatrists who dealt with people like them would believe that. Try to tell someone that a man could have an alternate personality of a rabbit, or a tiny fairy, and they would think that you were crazy. Most people just didn't understand how far the mind would go to protect itself.

Garrett couldn't think of any better way to protect yourself as a child from violence and abuse than to go unnoticed. And that's what their alters were for. To help them go completely unnoticed, totally ignored, totally safe from abuse.

Still, he didn't envy Katie and the others the therapy it would take to convince a rabbit to reintegrate with a chipmunk, or a two-ounce pixie to integrate with a two-hundred-and-fifty pound biker. And that's what every one of those know-it-all therapists wanted you to do. Reintegrate the personalities back together again and become a functional member of society.

Right. Like that was going to happen. Garrett felt he was doing quite well at being a functional member of society just like he was, and had no intention of trying to force personalities, who were designed to be each other's opposite, to join back together again.

Suddenly, Garrett heard a sound from his living room that sounded like a roar. He raced around the corner only to be confronted with the head of a gigantic tyrannosaurus rex poking through his living room floor. Freezing in his tracks he had a single moment of sheer panic before realizing it was just a daydream.

Garrett chuckled to himself. The boy downstairs must be reading his dinosaur books again. Quite the vivid imagination on that one. Garrett hoped he would be able to pursue his dinosaur dreams in the real world. The boy certainly seemed enthralled by them.

He closed his eyes momentarily to see if Justin was nearby. Justin loved to see the dino-dreams of the boy downstairs. He said they were more real-looking than the dinosaurs that moved back and forth in the museum.

Unfortunately, Justin was nowhere to be seen.

Garrett opened his eyes, smiled at the dinosaur in his living room, and walked back into the kitchen to find some breakfast.

Two hours later, he was exiting his apartment and heading down the stairs. At the sound of pounding feet behind him, he wisely stopped at a landing and moved aside. Sure enough, not three seconds later two very energetic boys came racing around the corner.

Garrett shook his head as the stairwell suddenly became a water slide. He chuckled to himself as the first boy leapt down the slide butt first, only to fall through the illusionary slide and crash into the very real stairs beneath it.

The trailing boy laughed as he jumped over his fallen adversary, ignored the slide and raced down the stairs. Within moments, the first boy had jumped up, rubbed his tailbone, and taken off after the prankster. With a final smile, Garrett resumed his own trek down the stairs and headed off to the bus stop.

Those were the ones to watch out for, Garrett thought as he waited for his bus. The ones who had already figured out how to use the Dreaming intentionally. Those who could do it at will, and not just by accident. Those were the ones who would become very powerful, very quickly. It was a whole new level of deception, and he was quite certain that every organization, from the federal government on down, had figured that out already.

His mind was still wandering as he boarded the bus that would take him to Nerdy Comics. As he gazed out the window, he speculated idly about what new organizations and secret divisions the federal government was no doubt already creating. Secret organizations dedicated to utilizing the Dreaming as a weapon. Studying it, learning how to manipulate it in every possible way.

Garrett frowned as he wondered how long it would take them to learn about those like him; to realize that people with multiple personalities could change form and become someone else. He thought back to every spy movie he had ever seen and shook his head. It was a whole new world all right. And it was only a matter of time before they found out about him. About all of them.

Garrett stared off into the distance as his thoughts grew darker and darker, until finally he pulled the bell cord to signal the driver to stop. Disembarking, he looked up, his brow furrowed as he spotted the sign to Nerdy Comics. Suddenly he heard a voice behind him.

"My goodness, aren't you ever happy?!" Ann exclaimed loudly.

"And aren't you ever going to get tired of coming up behind people?" Garrett asked, a smile returning to his face as he turned around.

"Nope! Never!" Ann grinned impishly. "And I've got ways of making it happen too!"

"I'll just bet you do," Garrett laughed as he wrapped her in a big hug. "Thanks for helping Ann, I really appreciate it."

"Of course! It's the least I can do. I have to fill the time somehow; we don't have group again until tomorrow." Ann said cheerfully. Garrett froze.

"Group tomorrow?" he asked slowly.

"Of course. It's Tuesday today isn't it?" Ann asked surprised.

"Dang, I suppose it is," Garrett said, and then sighed

loudly.

"Then group isn't until tomorrow," she said with a smile. Seeing the pained expression on his face, Ann just laughed. "Oh don't worry about it," she said consolingly. "I really don't think Ruby will ask if you killed anyone else in the last three days. And if she doesn't ask, you won't have to lie to her." Garrett just sighed again and turned toward the doors of the shop. Ann took his arm and they walked in together. "Now you said it was a superhero story, right?" Ann asked brightly.

"Kind of. It was more about the clown villain, but yeah, I think it was in a hero comic." Garrett replied.

"Okay, so where are the superhero comics?" Ann asked. Garrett simply pointed and they walked down the aisles toward the Action Hero Comics section.

As Garrett turned the corner into that section however, he froze, his heart beating rapidly. Standing there in front of him, bending over a man in a red hoodie that was huddled in the corner, was another clown-faced gang.

CHAPTER EIGHT

Garrett's heart raced and he could feel the pounding in his head that indicated Peter was on his way. Blinking rapidly, he braced himself for the rapid change he knew was coming. Suddenly he felt himself being yanked backwards.

"Garrett, no!" Ann yelled as she pulled his shoulder with surprising strength, causing him to lose his balance and crash backwards onto the floor. Ann stepped across him, straddling his waist and looked him straight in his eyes. "They aren't real!" she stated firmly, never breaking eye contact. "They are coming from the mind of that man in red. They aren't real," she repeated, trying to forestall the knight's advance.

Blinking rapidly again, Garrett looked over at the gang of thugs, and for a brief instant saw them flicker. Garrett let out the breath he hadn't realized he was holding, blinking more slowly he looked around. As he looked again over at the corner the thugs flickered again, along with the man in the red hoodie.

In that moment, he saw the man, but he was standing up and staring at the cover of a comic book, no doubt remembering his own experience with the events of yesterday.

"Okay Ann, okay." Garrett said, waiting for her to step aside.

"All right, you just make sure that big lummox doesn't come out and wreck the place!" Ann said firmly.

"It's okay Ann, he won't. It's just me now." Garrett replied gently.

"Fine," she said curtly as she moved to the side allowing Garrett to regain his feet.

Garrett slowly stood still, looking intently at the images of the thugs. Taking a slow step forward, he came face to face with one of them trying to see if he could recognize anything. After a moment, he shook his head. Nothing.

Just as he was about to turn away, he noticed something in the hands of one of the black-clad men, a small knife. Leaning over to get a better look he noticed the same etching of a clown's face on the blade. It was just like the other lone shooters, and just like the man Peter had fought the day before.

As he leaned in closer, the gang suddenly disappeared. Glancing up quickly he saw that the man had broken out of his daydream and was peering down at him suspiciously.

"I'm sorry, I was just looking at that odd knife one of the men was holding. I didn't mean to intrude," Garrett said as he rose.

"It's okay," the man replied, "I was just thinking about something." He held up the comic book he had been looking at. The cover art was that of a young man, huddled in the corner of an alley surrounded by a group of men, each brandishing a weapon of some kind.

"Ah," Garrett nodded, "I can certainly see why that

would make you think of those guys." Garrett paused for a moment. "I'm sorry, I don't mean to pry, but those were awfully vivid images for a daydream. Did you actually see one of the gangs yesterday?" The man looked away for a moment.

"Yeah, I did." He was silent for a few moments before he continued. "I was over on Union, heading to work when I saw them coming. They seemed to be breaking things indiscriminately. Most everyone stayed out of their way, but one woman… her high heel broke and she fell. They didn't seem to be in any hurry, but it was shocking how fast they reached her. One of them pulled out a small knife and they…" The man turned back to the bookshelf to regain control of himself. "She didn't last long… thankfully." The man in the red hoodie said softly. "Now they haunt my dreams, sleeping and awake." Garrett looked around as the gang flickered in and out again with the man's recollection.

"I'm sorry, I didn't mean to bring up something so painful for you," Garrett said with concern.

"It's okay, it was less painful for me than her. But I will remember her face until the day I die." The man closed his eyes for a moment, and Garrett saw the image of a woman in her mid-twenties, with long brown hair and a twinkle in her eye as she smiled. Then the image flickered and he saw, for the briefest of instants, the same woman's heart-shaped face twisted in a spasm of pain and fear.

"I'm sorry," the man said again as he turned and hurried out of the bookstore. Garrett must have made some motion to follow him, as he felt Ann's hand on his arm.

"Let him go," Ann said gently. "He has to deal with

this in his own way. Nothing that you or I could say will help him at this point."

"I know, you're right," Garrett replied with a sigh.

"You saw her smile?" Ann asked. Garrett just nodded. "She wasn't just some random woman. He knew her… he loved her. It's hard to come back from that." Ann shook her head before continuing. "So what could you do if you caught up with him? Recommend a good therapist?" Ann said with a gentle smile to soften the sting of the retort. Garrett snorted, then shook his head.

"No, you're right. There's not much we can do now, other than try to find out who they are, and why they are killing people," Garrett replied turning back to the shelves.

He quickly thumbed through the comics in front of him, but they were the wrong ones. The hero was in a brightly colored costume standing in the sunlight. He was looking for a hero in a dark or black costume, standing at night, in kind of a gothic looking city.

"Don't remember the name of the exact comic, but look for ones with a darker cover. Black-clad, caped hero, crazy clown adversary." Garrett said without turning around.

"You got it," Ann replied, turning to her own stack of comics and beginning to thumb through them. After two hours, the pair had compiled almost fifty comics with a black caped and cowled hero and a crazy clown villain.

"So I don't know about you," Ann began, "but I don't think I can afford to buy fifty comic books."

"No, you're right. We can't afford this many. And we don't have time to read them all while standing here, either." Garrett replied sadly.

"All right, so what if we buy five of them?" Ann asked.

"So give ourselves a ten percent chance of finding the right one, out of the less than five percent chance we already have since we only have fifty and not a thousand comics?" Garrett asked wryly. "Remind me not to take you to Vegas."

"Oh, fine!" Ann said with mock severity. "So, now what?"

"Well, I guess I flip through these and see if anything jogs my memory." Garrett answered with a sigh.

"Can I help narrow things down?" Ann asked cheerfully.

"I suppose you could flip through pages and see if you can find a picture of a guy in a clown mask shooting a gun into a crowd. Make sure it's a clown mask and not a clown face, the clown-faced guy is the leader. The others are just henchmen." Garrett answered, staring at the large pile of comics. With a sigh, he picked one up and started flipping through it.

An hour and a half later, Ann put the final comic back on the shelf with a sigh.

"No luck here," Ann said sadly.

"It's all right. It was a long shot anyway," Garrett replied smiling at her. "Thanks for coming down here and looking with me. I appreciate it." Garrett leaned over and gave Ann a tight side hug.

"Any time," Ann grinned as she hugged him back. The pair meandered to the door, with Garrett's arm still around Ann's shoulders. He walked her over to the bus stop, and gave her another quick hug.

"I'm going to walk for a bit, try to clear my head,"

Garrett said, looking off down the street. "You be safe Ann. Keep your inner ones close, just in case."

"I will. You be careful too Garrett," Ann replied, staring intently at his face. "I'll see you tomorrow then." Garrett seemed to start in surprise.

"Tomorrow?" he asked.

"Yes, tomorrow," Ann answered patiently. "Tomorrow is Wednesday; we have group tomorrow."

"Oh right! I forgot." Garrett replied with a wink and a smile.

"Ha! Erased it from your memory more likely." Ann quipped, grinning at him. Garrett's only answer was a shrug as he grinned at her and started off down the road.

Garrett barely paid attention to where he was going as his mind whirled with questions. Who were the clown men? Why were they randomly killing people? What was the connection between the lone shooters and the gangs of murderous thugs? What were the knives and what did they mean?

As he continued to walk, Garrett felt a tap on his mental shoulder. He closed his eyes for a moment and saw Derrick standing next to him. Garrett's surprise was so great he stopped dead in his tracks both outside and inside his head.

"Derrick, are you okay?" Garrett asked with genuine concern.

"I am… better," Derrick replied, his accent thick with lingering emotion.

"What happened?" Garrett pressed. "I thought you were going to be in your room for days. You've never come out of your rage that quickly before." A breath of a smile crossed Derrick's face.

"I had to come out of my rage sooner. I needed to

clean up some spilled milk." Derrick answered in all seriousness.

"Wait, what?" Garrett fumbled, confused. "Spilled milk?"

"Yes," Derrick's serious face relaxing slightly, "I had to clean up the milk, so I could not afford to rage or cry out in anger any longer." Garrett however, was even more confused.

"How would the need to clean up a spill help you to calm down? Usually that makes people upset?"

"Indeed," Derrick's smooth voice intoned. "However it was not the milk that calmed me, it was the memory."

"Hang on, are you talking about the milk that Justin spilled the other day?" Garrett asked, starting to catch on.

"Indeed," Derrick's replied with a tiny chuckle. "Who else would have the temerity to pour milk under the door to my room?"

"Huh," Garrett replied, dumbfounded. "The little scamp."

"Quite," Derrick responded. "That, however, is not why I came to you now."

"Right," Garrett straightened in the stone chair as he shook his head slightly to clear it. "What's up?"

"I have been paying attention to your activities this afternoon, and I have something you might be interested in," Derrick began, as he pulled a small cloth-wrapped bundle out of his dinner jacket. "I acquired this at the grocery the other day, when Greybeard burned the unfortunate shooter to a cinder."

"Unfortunate?" Garrett queried.

"Indeed, he was most unfortunate to have been

burned alive. A most terrifying way to die, I assure you," Derrick answered with a small smile.

"Oh? How would you know?" Garrett asked, but received only silence as a reply. He unwrapped the bundle gingerly to reveal the blade of one of the etched knives. The hilt had been burned away but the blade was still completely intact, including the etched clown face on one side.

"I shall leave it in your nightstand drawer by morning," Derrick assured him as Garrett's gaze shot up in surprise.

"Thank you!" Garrett said in shock. "With this I can try to hunt down who etched these knives, how many there were, who he sold them to, the works!" Garrett paused mid-cheer, however, as a new thought struck him. "But wait, how can you leave it? Won't it disappear when you go back inside again?" Garrett asked.

"No," Derrick replied. "It did not originate inside. I took it from the body of the man that Greybeard killed. It came from outside, it will remain outside."

"Hang on, how did you take it inside then?" Garrett asked, dumbfounded.

"I do not know," Derrick replied. "I simply had it in my pocket when we shifted. I discovered later that it was still in my pocket even though I was no longer in control of the body."

"Then how do you know it will stay if you leave it on the nightstand?" Garrett asked suspiciously. Derrick signed in exasperation.

"I do not. I surmised that it would remain since that's where it came from," Derrick answered with a slight growl.

"Okay, okay," Garrett said placatingly. "We'll try it

and see, okay?"

"Very well. Then I shall leave the investigation in your capable hands," Derrick said a bit too mildly as he took back the knife and re-wrapped it. Slipping the package back into his jacket, he turned and strode back to his room. Garrett shook his head again and opened his eyes.

Looking around, he realized he had walked all the way from 50th to 98th avenue. Well, I suppose if I don't get my run in each day, I'll get my exercise walking, Garrett thought to himself. Turning right, he began the trek up the hillside toward the city park, thinking he could cut across and be home in half the time.

Ten blocks later, he reached the edge of the park. Glancing up at the sky, he guessed he had about an hour of daylight left before it started to get dark again. Shaking his head at Ann's admonition, he set off on one of the trails that crossed the mile-wide park.

As he walked, he continued to search his memory for any clue as to where he had read that comic book. He knew there was some sort of correlation between the storyline in the comic and the events that had been happening in the last week. If only he could remember, he might be able to predict what would happen next.

He was so caught up in his thoughts that he almost tripped over a young couple lying on a blanket and kissing. Fortunately, they were too caught up in each other to notice him, and he quietly made his way past with a smile.

As he entered the forested area of the park he paused, closed his eyes, and enjoyed a moment of just feeling the wind and the trees and the air around him. He liked to do that whenever he entered the shade of a large group of trees. It made him feel calmer, more at peace with himself. Garrett didn't know why he felt so connected to the trees, only that they made him feel better.

After another moment, and after a deep breath, he opened his eyes again and continued down the path. He had almost reached the other side, when he heard voices off to one side. Curious, he made his way off of the path and over a slight rise. As he crested the hill he saw a group of people standing around a large bonfire. They were all in robes and were chanting something Garrett couldn't make out.

Suddenly, all together, they turned toward the setting sun and raised their arms. A shock of adrenaline hit as he saw the small knives in each of their hands. He quickly ducked behind a tree to catch his breath. Peeking out, he saw the group turn to the south, toward him. Looking closely at the group he could see that several of their robes looked homemade and most wore necklaces. As the group turned to the east he crept out for a closer look.

He froze as the group all turned outward, just as he hit an open patch between the trees. Garrett stood stock still for a moment, before he got a good look at the necklace worn by the closest of the group. He heaved a sigh of relief as he smiled slightly. It was a pentagram.

This must be a Wiccan coven, he thought. They were about as far from murderous thugs as you could get. After all, it's really hard to justify a brutal murder when you hold the belief that everything you do comes back on you threefold. He waved slightly at the group, then smiled as one of them waved back before focusing on their ritual again.

Turning, he started to make his way back over the hill when he heard it. The sound he had heard so many times before, and hoped to never hear again. The sound of gunfire echoed in the close confines of the trees.

Garrett turned just in time to see another gang of black-clad, clown-faced men walk out of the tree line, automatic weapons firing into the group of unarmed worshipers. For an instant he stood in stunned shock, that the peaceful serenity of this wooded park and the gentle faith of the nature worshipers had been torn apart with such reckless violence. He felt the anger welling up in him as he cried out.

"NO!" he yelled, foolishly forgetting every movie he had ever watched where a protagonist yells out and only succeeds in gaining the attention of the antagonist. And just like the movies, all eyes shot over to him, some with fear, some with gleeful malice.

Suddenly remembering his movie hero responses, Garrett flung himself down to the ground just as a spray of bullets riddled the trees behind him. He rolled to the side, then crawled, trying to get behind one of the larger trees. He rolled again rapidly as another spray of bullets struck the ground, this time striking the ground and trees to his left. Oh great, he thought, they're on all sides.

Finally managing to get behind one of the larger trees he closed his eyes briefly to enlist the aid of his more durable mental companions. He was shocked to see that it wasn't Peter or Derrick who stood beside his chair, but Sean.

"Sean, what are you doing?" Garrett gasped. "Where's Peter?"

"Garrett, I have analyzed the situation and determined that I am the most logical choice to meet the current threat. These adversaries are using ranged weapons, making Peter an impractical choice. Further, I do not believe that Derrick is fully recovered from his earlier breakdown, and would not advise him entering into a combat situation again so soon," Sean said, his voice calm and measured.

"Umm, last I checked, you aren't bulletproof," Garrett said with concern.

"I am not armored against ranged ballistics, however I do have superior firepower," Sean gestured toward a black case hanging like a satchel over one shoulder. Garrett blinked, then realized Sean was referring not to the black case, but to what looked like a laser gun strapped to his hip.

"Okay, then. If you're sure about this," Garrett acquiesced reluctantly.

"I have calculated my probability of success to be ninety-seven point two six three to one," Sean replied confidently as he took Garrett's place on the stone chair. Garrett simply nodded and stepped back.

Sean opened his eyes, glancing quickly at the trees in front of where he was sitting to ensure that there were no assailants in that direction. Nodding to himself, he pulled the black case around in front of him and opened the scanning device.

After a few moments, the device readout displayed that there were twenty-four total humanoids still in a vertical position within a one-hundred-meter radius. Taking a careful look at the readout, he smoothly drew the sleek pistol from his belt, rolled to his left around the tree and fired three precise shots before rolling back behind the tree.

The bright red beam of focused, polarized light lanced out, striking each of the three targets in less than a breath. Each of them was knocked off their feet, smoke rising from a large burn mark in their chest.

Sean had used the lowest setting, so there was a chance that they had survived the encounter. Unfortunately for the men, their partners seemed to be even less inclined than Sean to check the status of their health.

Glancing down at the scanner again, he saw that there were now twenty-one total humanoids in a vertical position. Excellent. He paused for a count of fifteen while the attackers released the expected return volley of firepower at his position. Now came the difficult part. Taking a deep breath center himself in preparation, he engaged the enemy.

CHAPTER NINE

Sean exploded into motion, rocking himself forward into a crouch, then leaping from behind his cover at a twenty-five-degree angle, in a display of grace and strength that would make a leopard proud. Dropping his arms until his hands touched the ground he turned the leap into a right-shoulder roll taking him behind a new tree.

After waiting for the expected volley of return fire Sean glanced at his scanner again. They were clumping up defensively. Excellent. That would make his next maneuver more effective.

Taking another glance at his scanner in order to track relative movement, Sean leaned slightly to his right and pointed the pistol behind him over his right shoulder. Leaning quickly, he fired four more shots while watching the scanner readout.

He allowed himself to raise a single eyebrow slightly in satisfaction as four of the indicators on his display changed to show that all four of his shots had been successful. Seventeen remaining, time to increase the complexity of his maneuvers.

As he had calculated, after seeing the effectiveness of

his last volley of shots, the assailants began to spread out again. Time to change tactics. Holstering his pistol, Sean rose and faced the tree.

Calculating distance, force, wind speed, and friction coefficients, Sean dropped downward, then leapt straight up into the air and caught a branch that was four point three seven meters above the ground. Swinging slightly for momentum, he flexed the core muscles in his stomach and wrapped his torso around the branch, using the momentum to move himself into a pushup position. From there, he quickly got his feet under him and looked up at another branch.

This branch was an easy three point nine two meters up. He quickly ascended through the branches of the tree. Upon attaining an altitude of twenty-six point four five seven meters, he paused to look at his scanner. The indicators showed that the seventeen remaining antagonists had begun circling the tree in a wide arc. Excellent, that position should do nicely.

Taking careful aim, he fired one quick burst at a tree branch above the heads of two of the black-clad individuals. He noted the branch breaking and falling down to strike both of them as he turned and began to run along the branch toward the edge of the tree.

Again calculating wind speed, velocity, friction, and tensile strength of the branch he was running on, he quickly reached the end of the structurally sound portion of the branch and leapt forward toward a neighboring tree.

He lost ten point three seven meters in altitude as he descended toward his chosen branch on the neighboring tree, but that was of course anticipated. As he hit the branch, he turned the landing into a forward roll along the branch that ended with him at the trunk of the tree.

Jumping across to another branch on the same tree, he pivoted to his left and with one smooth motion drew his pistol and fired three shots downward into the canopy. He was rewarded with two groans and one shout of pain. Three more out of commission.

As he glanced again at his scanner, his lips had a barely perceptible twitch. A less informed individual might have interpreted the flexing of the muscles around his mouth as irritation, however since he did not display such emotions, there was no such interpretation. Quickly calculating his variables Sean realized that there was only one efficient course of action at this stage of the battle.

Striding quickly from branch to branch he traversed the trunk of the tree in rapid order. Gathering his strength, he again began to run down the length of a branch. However, this time his target was not another tree branch.

Quickly calculating the tensile strength of this much larger branch, he continued to run until reaching the end of the structurally sound portion of the limb. From which point, he jumped out into the air toward two more of the assailants.

The remaining sixteen point zero eight seven meters was a bit far to fall even for him, but thankfully each of them intercepted a blow from one of his descending feet, thus reducing his velocity significantly and allowing him to turn the fall into a forward roll. His roll took him three point four meters forward, and allowed him to attain a half-kneeling position with one knee on the ground and the other foot planted beside it. Which was the perfect firing position to drop three more of the masked gunmen. Seven remaining. Perfect.

Scooping up a machine gun in his free hand, Sean fired two short bursts and then one long burst from the weapon into the air. That should make them think their friends have me cornered, Sean thought to himself as he moved quickly behind a clump of bushes.

Two more men burst into the area just as anticipated, and Sean took them down easily with another pair of precise shots. The five remaining fighters would be more careful than these latest two.

Sean holstered his pistol again and opened his scanner to see where the remaining five were located. As the screen pictured where each of the men were, Sean rose quickly and started to turn, only to hear a voice from behind him.

"Gotcha, pointy-ears." The voice was gruff, and Sean knew it was one of the attackers. "Now really slow like, take that pistol out of its holster and place it on the ground." Sean, still unable to see the man, had no choice but to comply. Leaning over, he gently placed his shiny pistol on the ground next to his feet. "Now kick it," the man said with a hint of smugness. Sean hesitated; he didn't like to abuse well-functioning equipment. "Kick it now, or you get a bullet through your brain," the voice said sternly. Sean's facial muscles twitched ever so slightly again as he wedged a toe under the firearm, and flipped it up into the air to land in a large berry patch.

"Now that wasn't very smart," the man said as the laser pistol landed. Pressing the barrel to the back of Sean's head, he barked, "Now kneel down!"

Sean however, was doing calculations. Now that the man had revealed his physical distance by touching the barrel to the back of Sean's head, and his angle relative to Sean by what portion of the barrel touched first, Sean knew exactly where and how to move.

Faintly, Sean heard a voice in his head stating that firearms had a certain range of efficacy. If an attacker maintained that range they were safe from hand to hand attacks. However, if they were to move within that range, their effectiveness dropped dramatically.

Sean patiently counted to three before the man touched the gun barrel to his head again. Instantly, Sean exploded into motion. He bent his knees dropping his head below the barrel of the rifle while simultaneously pivoting on his left foot. Upon completion of the pivot, he shot upward again, his left hand grabbing the barrel and pointing it up and away from him as he rose. Using his momentum to take a large step forward, and still holding onto the barrel of the gun, Sean snapped his hand forward in an open palm strike directly to the man's chest.

What was a simple breakaway maneuver by an ordinary human became a devastating attack by the pointy-eared alien. The man was lifted off his feet and flung backwards by the force of the palm strike, his back and then head hitting a nearby tree before he crumpled to the ground. And then there were four, Sean thought to himself.

Dropping the rifle, he knelt down and reached his arm into the berry patch to retrieve his own weapon. Ignoring the green blood welling up in the small scratches caused by the thorns, he quickly holstered his weapon and began to move toward the clearing again, checking his scanner as he went.

The four had taken up defensive positions at each corner of the clearing. That would make it more difficult to remove them. Entrenched positions, crisscrossing fields of fire, and enough distance they could cover each other without being so close they were vulnerable to melee attack.

Calculating quickly, Sean turned up the intensity of his pistol and reached down to find a suitable rock. Quickly discarding several he finally found one of the right kind of mineral. Something with a low refraction index and a more lattice-structured molecular pattern. Yes, this rock would do nicely, he thought.

Taking up a position behind some thick shrubbery for concealment, Sean threw the stone in a high arc toward the middle of the four men's positions. At precisely the right instant, he fired his pistol in a long, continuous beam at the falling stone. Sean knew his calculations had to be accurate to within one hundredth of a second for this to work, but he was confident it would be successful. It was.

A half second before the stone would have struck the earth, the low refraction index of the stone allowed it to absorb so much heat from the beam that it exploded in a shower of dust and shards. Additionally, with the lattice structured molecular pattern, when it did explode into shards, those shards were large, thin and shot outward like a stone buzz saw.

Taking a grim appraisal of his work, Sean walked back into the clearing to see if any of the worshipers had survived. It took little more than a glance to confirm that none of them had survived the initial attack by the clown-faced men. Taking one last glance at his scanner to ensure that there were no more assailants he had missed, he walked back over the hill, holstered his weapon and closed his eyes. Garrett still stood by the stone chair, waiting for Sean's report.

"Although I was unable to rescue any of the Wiccan practitioners, I was able to eliminate all twenty four of the aggressors." Sean reported calmly.

"Are they all dead?" Garrett asked quietly.

"I did not verify their vital signs, however if any did survive they are sufficiently incapacitated to no longer be a threat for quite some time," Sean replied, rising from the chair. "You may now resume your journey." Garrett nodded as he moved to sit down.

"Sean," Garrett called out. Sean paused without turning. "Thank you." Sean simply nodded his acknowledgment as he proceeded back to his own room again.

Garrett opened his eyes and glanced around. Although he could not see the clearing where the worshipers had been gunned down, he didn't think he would ever be able to get the image of their broken and torn bodies out of his mind. His therapist was going to have a field day with this one.

This had to stop, he thought angrily. I need to recruit some help. And with that frustrated thought he continued his trek across the park and back home again.

Garrett awoke early the next morning, briefly considering going for a run before discarding the idea and sitting down in front of his computer instead. He was just about to start research on his next writing gig, when he remembered what Derrick was supposed to leave on his nightstand. Jumping up, he nearly tripped over his own feet in his haste to retrieve the package. Sure enough, the cloth wrapped bundle was there.

Gently unwrapping the cloth, he saw in a moment that this was the same kind of blade that he noticed on each of the other attackers. The hilt was gone, completely burned away by the heat of the fire, but the blade itself remained clear and the clown-faced etching stood out against the steel.

The clown was a twisted caricature of a clown however. It wasn't the bright happy face of a circus clown, but more like the dark angry face of a clown from a popular horror movie. The eyes though… Garrett shivered slightly. The eyes were not that of an angry killer, they showed a visage that was completely insane.

Even as he shivered at the sight, he had to admire the artist who had etched it into the blade. It was masterfully done, capturing the complete lack of humanity in the eyes staring at him from the gleaming steel.

Taking the blade over to his computer, Garrett hopped online and searched for places that did metal etching in the city. He growled a bit in frustration when fifty-two listings popped up within the city. He really needed to narrow it down somehow. He tried several variants of the search, starting with blade etching, and high-quality etching. Unfortunately, he was only able to lower the possible number down to forty-nine. The other three only did industrial work. That was still too many to handle on his own. He was going to need some help.

Fortunately for him, it was Wednesday. The day he got to see the few people he actually trusted… a bunch of mentally disturbed people who heard voices in their heads. Garrett shook his head at the thought. Those that seemed to be the craziest were often the sanest in his opinion. Garrett quickly got dressed, printed out the list of etching shops, and after rewrapping the knife, jogged out to catch the bus.

Garrett arrived at the social services building quite a bit earlier than he had expected. One of his connections had reached the bus stop early and he was able to ride an earlier bus, which was nice. Usually it was the other way around. Looking around, he saw that the building wasn't unlocked yet, so he took a seat next to a stone pillar and closed his eyes.

After a few minutes, he heard the door of a car close, and a woman's voice talking softly. Garrett opened his eyes and saw a pretty young woman with a shock of curly red hair walking away from a taxi cab. She walked past him without noticing and approached the large double doors. She pulled on them gently, only to discover that they were still locked. Garrett smiled as he stood and walked over to her.

"They don't unlock the doors until a quarter to ten," Garrett said as he came up behind her.

"Eep!" she squealed, jumping into the air. She whirled around, her eyes wide as dinner plates as she looked at him. Garrett stepped back a step, surprised at her reaction. "Who are you?!" she demanded in a thick Irish brogue.

"I'm Garrett," he replied, trying to smile disarmingly. His smile faded a bit though as she completely relaxed upon hearing his name.

"Oh, it's you," she said with a smile of her own. Garrett's brow furrowed in confusion.

"Have we met?" he asked suspiciously.

"No, not yet," she replied, still smiling. "But I've

heard so much about you! I'm Molly," she said, extending her hand. He took her hand slowly, surprised at how soft and smooth her hands were.

"Good to meet you, Molly," he answered, trying to be polite, while furiously trying to figure out where she might have known him from. The girl laughed, sensing his confusion.

"It's okay," she assured him, her brogue light and lilting. "I'm one of Ann's alters. We've just never met before."

"Oh!" Garrett replied nonplussed. "How come I've never met you before?" If she was shocked at his blunt question she didn't show it.

"Because Ann likes to surprise you so much," Molly giggled.

"Oh!" Garrett replied again. "That's what she meant by having her ways of sneaking up on me!" Garrett began laughing as well. "Well, I suppose that makes sense. So why are you up now, then?"

"I've found that most people are nicer to a pretty girl than a grandmotherly lady," Molly replied, her brogue becoming thicker as her voice became more serious.

"Really?" Garrett said surprised. "But Ann is a sweetheart, like everyone's beloved grandmother who bakes cookies and gives great hugs."

"Of course," Molly replied seriously, "but not everyone responds well to their grandmother. Whereas most men will respond favorably to a pretty young lady. You would be shocked at how many taxi drivers tell me not to worry about paying when I smile at them and bat my eyes." Molly demonstrated, batting her long eyelashes prettily at him. Garrett just chuckled again and shook his head.

"I suppose that's true," he said ruefully, "but it's really their loss, Ann is a wonderful lady." Molly grinned at him.

"And that is why she likes you so much!" she replied. Garrett grinned at her and extended his hand again.

"Well it is good to finally meet you then, Molly," Garrett said, "Though you'll have to tell Ann she needs a new cover girl if she wants to surprise me again. I certainly won't forget meeting you."

"That's all right," Molly answered with an equally large grin. "There are far more of us where I came from."

Just then, they both heard the click of the doors being unlocked from the inside and turned simultaneously toward them. Ruby pushed open one of the doors and gestured them inside.

"Come on in. We're running a bit late today, so please give me a minute while I get the rooms unlocked," Ruby said, sounding a bit rushed.

"Well, I had better go," Molly said with a final smile. "Ann is the one who prefers to be the voice for group sessions. She feels she is less intimidating than most of the rest of us." Molly paused for a moment glancing at Garrett with a grin. "Or less distracting." With a wink, she closed her eyes and her body began to flow down into the familiar shape of his dearest friend. Ann opened her eyes, wiped her mouth with her hand and smiled at him.

"Good morning," Ann said.

"Morning, Ann," Garrett replied with a smile, reaching out to give her a big hug. She returned it enthusiastically before pulling back to look up at him.

"So, what did you think of Molly?" she asked with a

voice that was far too bland. Garrett just laughed.

"You know perfectly well I have a weakness for redheads," Garrett replied, still chuckling. "And accents, for that matter." Ann grinned at him.

"I know, and Molly is a sweetheart too. I figured you'd hit it off when you finally met," Ann said turning them both toward the conference room.

"You know, you really do have me at a disadvantage," Garrett said as they sat down.

"Oh? Why is that?" Ann replied.

"You know all four of my alters extremely well. But I've met over fifty of yours, and I still haven't even met half of them yet. I'm having a hard time keeping everyone apart," Garrett said with mock seriousness. Ann just laughed again.

"It's not easy, being we," she answered in a singsong tone that Garrett recognized from a frog puppet he used to watch on TV when he was a kid. Garrett simply chuckled again and shook his head.

They waited a couple more minutes before Ruby came bustling into the room again, both Phil and Katie in tow.

"All right, are we all here?" Ruby asked, looking around. "Where's Susan?"

"Sorry for late!" a familiar voice said from the doorway.

"Ah, good!" Ruby said, taking her seat at one end of the conference table. "So, the last time we talked I believe Phil was sharing about his fifth birthday party?"

"Actually Ruby, if I could have a moment," Garrett spoke up quickly.

"Certainly Garrett," Ruby replied surprised. "I am so glad you decided to volunteer to speak first!"

"Actually I have a bit of a story and then a request." Garrett answered, fully aware that she meant she didn't think he would ever voluntarily speak up in a group session. "So, I killed a few more people last week," he began.

"GARRETT!" Ruby shouted. "I told you not to joke about that!"

"Ruby, I'm not joking, and it is important that you all know what happened before I make my request," Garrett said seriously.

"No! Absolutely not! I will not be a party to stories of killing without doing something about it!" Ruby exclaimed vehemently.

Garrett opened his mouth to start yelling when he felt a hand on his arm. He glanced over at Ann to see her shake her head, then reach up and pluck at an incisor tooth with her thumbnail. Garrett froze for a moment, figuring out what she meant.

When he did, he raised an eyebrow in a perfect imitation of Sean. Ann simply nodded and sat back in her chair. Garrett, however, was already shifting, black evening attire sheathing his body as he turned toward Ruby again.

Derrick immediately locked eyes with Ruby, reaching out with his mind to mesmerize her. Her breath caught, like a small animal when faced with a predator.

"Ruby," his thick accent rolling off of his tongue as he pulled her deeper under his power, "you are distressed. Do not worry, there is nothing here to distress you. You have not heard anything distressing today, nor will you hear anything that worries you for the rest of the day. In fact, you have just conducted such a successful therapy session that you have decided to go home early." Derrick smiled, the tiniest hint of fang peeking through as he continued his instructions.

"You will return home, and spend the day doing something productive around your house. This will give you a feeling of accomplishment and you will retire early tonight with a good book, a glass of wine, and soft music." Derrick said in a low gentle tone, as if whispering endearments to a lover. The group watched as Ruby smiled distantly then stood and walked slowly out of the room. The others turned to Derrick, all but Ann with shocked looks on their faces.

"Why did you do that to Miss Ruby?" Phil's deep rumbling voice asked with a hint of anger.

"It was necessary," Derrick replied, his soft voice confident.

"Why was it necessary for you to do that to Ruby?" Katie asked, obviously concerned.

"She was not ready to hear what we needed to tell you," Derrick answered with a smile.

"And why that part about going to bed with a book and some wine?" Phil chimed in again.

"Ah, that, my dear boy, was to bring her pleasure," Derrick answered, his lips spreading in a wide smile. "I find that people usually respond to me best when I give them instructions that are pleasurable." Phil's brow furrowed for a moment as he thought about this.

"So, what is news?" Susan asked, staring hard at Derrick, her eyes unusually sharp as though she understood far more of what was going on than any of them would have expected. Derrick glanced at Ann for a moment before closing his eyes again.

Garrett opened his eyes and looked around the room before reaching into his jacket and pulling out the cloth-wrapped bundle.

"My friends, what I have to tell you is not happy or pleasant, and what I have to ask you is not easy. But you are the only ones I trust. The only ones I know who can understand the implications of my story. Will you hear it?" Garrett looked around the room and saw each of his friends nod. "Thank you," he replied softly, and then launched into his story.

CHAPTER TEN

"It began early last week when the first of the clown-masked gunman appeared. I was in the subway when one pulled out a machine gun and started shooting at everyone. Well, you've all met Peter, so you know he couldn't stand by for that. He really did kill the shooter in the subway. Then in the grocery store, there was a shooter there as well. Greybeard really did take that one out with a fireball. And then Derrick and Sean teamed up to incapacitate the one in the police station. I hadn't realized at the time that Derrick had found something on the body of the one in the grocery store. A small knife with the face of a clown etched on the blade." Garrett paused for a moment to gather his thoughts. He glanced up to see his friends watching him, waiting for him to continue. Taking a deep breath, he launched into the next piece.

"The part that you may not know is that I was involved in one of the gang fights as well. Or rather Peter was, and then Derrick…" Garrett paused again, closing his eyes. "Peter tried to save a woman from one of the gangs. He failed. Derrick lost it, went completely berserk. Slaughtered the entire group, save one. During the fight though, Peter noticed that one of them had the same clown face etched knife, and I've heard from others that the other groups may have had the knives as well."

"So what you are telling us," Phil began slowly, "is that you have been killing these murderers and have found a clue that no one else has found?"

"No," Garrett replied, "I'm sure others have found it as well. The FBI would not miss such an obvious clue. I just know that I've found it, and I have to do something to stop it!"

"So, you are thinking you are better than police?" Susan asked sharply.

"Yes! No, I don't know…" Garrett replied. "I just know that I can do things they can't. Go places they can't, and if necessary fight in ways they can't… And so can you."

"That is request?" Susan's Slavic accent growing thicker with emotion. "That we fight with you? Against that?"

"If necessary, yes. But first I need to know where this came from," Garrett answered as he unfolded the cloth to reveal the blade. Everyone leaned over to take a closer look at the blade.

"It looks evil," Katie said softly. Phil looked up at her, concerned.

"Delicate work," Susan noted. "Much skill."

"Right," Garrett said, starting to get excited. "Not something that just anyone could do, right? It would take someone special to make this, but all I could find were advertisements. I don't know which of them made this one." Garrett paused for a moment, then sighed, "If it even was one of them. It may not have been any of them. That's why I need your help." Phil took another long look at the knife.

"This is good work. Too good for your average artist. This guy is special. A guy like this will be known by other artists. Let me ask around and see what I can find." Phil said, his deep voice rumbling. Katie looked up quickly at him, her worry evident on her face. Phil noticed and smiled at her. "Don't worry Katie, I'm just going to go talk to some friends of mine. I'll be just fine." Katie just nodded and looked down at the table again.

"Searching we can do," Susan said her voice still sharp. "Fighting, no can do. Only two of you." She gestured to Garrett and Ann. "Me shadow, Katie bunny, Phil pixie. No can fight." Garrett saw Phil starting to bristle at the comment, and jumped in quickly.

"I know that. Ann and I are the fighters, or have fighters at least. But can you think of a better infiltration team than a shadow, a bunny, and a pixie? No one would ever suspect any of you!" Susan looked thoughtful, digesting that idea, when Ann spoke up.

"So it sounds like what we need right now is more eyes looking for the maker of this blade. Once we find him, and get the information out of him, then we can talk about what to do next," Ann said firmly. "So, who's with us?"

Garrett smiled slightly and whispered, "With us?" Ann just elbowed him in the ribs while she stared around the table at the other three.

"I help," Susan said firmly.

"I already offered to start asking," rumbled Phil, "so I'm already in." Katie was quiet for a long moment, fighting back her obvious fear.

"Okay, I'll do it." she said at practically a whisper.

"Good!" Ann proclaimed loudly, "So where do we start?" she asked, turning to Garrett.

"Well, I've got the listings for the metal etching shops. We could call and see which of them would do knives." Garrett said slowly.

"Perfect!" Ann replied. "Let's divide up the list." With a rueful chuckle, Garrett pulled out the printout of the shops and handed it over to Ann. Ann quickly split the list up into five parts and handed one to each of the friends.

"Now, everyone knows what they're doing?" Garrett asked. "All we need is to find out who did the etchings, or even who could do the etchings. I'll let you figure out how to whittle the list down."

"Well," Katie said softly, "we could start by saying we were looking to see which of them etched swords, because we were starting a club."

"That's good, Katie!" Garrett replied. "That should help weed out some of them, since I'm sure not everyone wants to work on a sword."

"Then tell 'em we already have a picture of what we want. Face of King Arthur or something like that." Phil added.

"Great!" Ann replied. "Then we can see who thinks they have the skill to do a face on a sword, so we know which ones to tackle in person!"

"That's awesome," Garrett said with a smile. "Thank you guys so much for helping me."

"That's what friends are for," Phil replied, giving him a hearty slap on the back. Garrett tried not to wince at the sting of the large man's hand.

The friends filed out of the room with promises to get together in two days with their results. As they left the building, Ann came up to Garrett and slid an arm around his, as though they were a lady and her gentleman.

"Share a cab with me?" Ann asked with a smile.

"Sure," Garrett said, smiling back. Garrett flagged down a cab and the two got in, waiving to their other friends. "Okay, what's up?" Garrett asked, turning to Ann. "You were a little too innocent back there, my friend." Ann laughed softly and shook her head.

"We really can't get much past the other, can we?" she asked rhetorically. "Susan's right you know," she said, a bit more somber. "If it comes to a fight, and it probably will, you and I are the only ones who can fight back. And only you have immortals, I think."

"I don't know how immortal they are, since there is only one way to test that," Garrett replied, trying to lighten the mood. "Besides, you have an angel, don't you?"

"Tammarion hasn't been seen for a long time now," Ann replied softly. "I don't know if she will join this fight."

"Well, I don't expect it to come to violence. I just want to find out who's doing this and get that information to the proper authorities," Garrett said firmly.

"You can't fool me, remember?" Ann said with a soft smile. "There's more to it than that."

"All right, fine," Garrett replied more somberly. "There's something else there. Something I can't explain. I've been involved in four incidents now. That's more than anyone else is reporting. There's some connection, some link between me and these attacks. I just don't know what it is. But I don't think they are going to stop until I figure it out."

"Now that sounds more like my Garrett," Ann said, leaning over to rest her head on his shoulder. "Peter is not the only Knight of the Tower, defender of the realm, you know." Ann said seriously. "You have the same protective nature he does. You're just not as flamboyant as he is." Garrett chuckled at the thought.

"I have parts of all of them in me. They are each created to be personifications of an aspect of my personality. Designed to take away the hardest edges, the greatest extremes of those aspects. The aspects themselves though are still with me. I am all of them, and together they are all me." Garrett paused for a moment. "That's how we maintain the balance. Each of their extremes has another physical opposite, but since I don't have an opposite I have to balance each of them inside myself."

"And you are all about balance," Ann replied. "You work for that in everything you do. Everything has an equal, every part of you has an opposite. I don't know how you do it. It's taken me over twenty years to get my inner ones to the point where they will work together as a community. To not fight amongst each other, and to put things in place to try to meet everyone's needs. How did yours split so evenly? So that there were balances and controls so quickly?"

"Like I said, it was designed that way from the beginning," Garrett replied. "Most people with DID split early, like toddler or early childhood. Their splits are chaotic, with no purpose or guide other than to give the pain of their abuse to someone else." Garrett paused for a moment, thinking. "Mine came later. I had seen the violent extremes of those around me. The anger, the rage at the pain of it all. I saw children commit acts of violence that most adults would never dream of, and I was old enough that I could recognize the seeds of that same violence inside of me. So when I split, I knew that the only way for me to be safe, for everyone around me to be safe, was to create a safety measure in each split. Two splits at a time, each with the opposite extreme, each with the power to contain the other if necessary. They were designed to do that."

"I've never heard of anything like that before," Ann said after a moment. "I've known a lot of people with multiple personalities, and I've attended a lot of therapy and group therapy sessions. But I have never heard of anyone designing how a split would occur. At least outside of some of the more extreme cases of ritualistic abuse, and never when splitting themselves. You are a very unusual man, Garrett Castlemain."

"Thank you, Ann," Garrett replied with a smile. "Coming from you, I'll take that as a compliment." Ann just laughed, her head resting on his shoulder until they reached their destinations.

That afternoon, Garrett tried to work for a bit on a writing assignment for a small, local paper, but his mind kept straying back to the thought that there was something he had missed. Some connection he hadn't seen. It nagged at him, and worried at his thoughts until he realized that he hadn't written a single word in over twenty minutes.

With a sigh, he stood up from his desk and stretched. He glanced around his bedroom briefly, trying in vain to find something to re-center himself. Looking for some minor distraction that would help him regain his focus.

Garrett laughed a bit at that. Most people looked at

him funny when he told them he had to distract himself enough to concentrate, but it was true.

If he tried too hard to force his concentration on any one thing, his mind rebelled and he couldn't focus on anything. If he gave himself a tiny bit of distraction however, something else for his mind to do, then it would sit back happily distracted and let him concentrate. Garrett laughed again, realizing he had just described the relationship between a parent and a young child. And speaking of young children…

Garrett closed his eyes, and looked around. The cave was the same every time, but it still felt like a bit of a surprise every time he looked at it. The thought of closing his eyes in one place and opening them in another sounded like it was straight out of the fantasy novels he enjoyed. Rising from the stone chair, he walked over to Justin's door and knocked.

"Hang on!" a young voice yelled.

"Okay." Garrett yelled back with a smile. Within a few moments, the door had flung open to reveal a very dirty little boy. "Justin, what happened?!"

"Umm," Justin looked down at himself as though he were surprised, "I got dirty."

"What were you doing in there?" Garrett asked.

"Making mud pies!" Just exclaimed happily, turning and running back into his room.

Garrett shook his head as he followed down the short hallway and into the large room. He saw immediately what Justin was talking about. His sandbox had been turned into a giant mud pit. There was dirt everywhere, and somehow the boy had acquired pie tins and was happily filling them with mud.

"So, I was wondering," Garrett began, "if you might

be interested in going to the zoo today?"

"The zoo!" Justin exclaimed even louder than before. "I love the zoo!"

"I know," Garrett chuckled. "That's why I wanted to invite you. I thought we might give Ann a call, and see if she would like to go too."

"Yippee!" Justin yelled. "Can we go now?!"

"Well, we have to clean up first," Garrett said warily.

"Oh, that's no problem," Justin said with a smile. "I'll be right back!" And with that, Justin raced out of the room. In a few moments he came running back in with a strange-looking device. "I got Sean to let me use his cleaner-upper," Justin explained proudly.

The device was white, about eighteen inches long and about six inches wide. It was cylindrical, with a handle running along what Garrett assumed was the top. Justin raced over to the sand and mud and pushed a button on the handle.

Immediately, the device began to emit a soft humming sound and as Justin waved it over the dirty spots Garrett was amazed to see the dirt particles rising up from the ground and moving into the device. Just as he began to wonder how much the device could hold before needing to be emptied, Justin turned to grin at him.

"See!" Justin bragged. "It's much better than a vacuum 'cause it only picks up dirt. Sean said it was something about 'nization. And look, you don't have to change it 'cause the dirt gets zapped when it goes inside." Justin was happy to explain, as he continued to wave the device over the dirty floor and walls. He even waved it over the toys that had suffered the grim fate of a mud bath, and sure enough, in a few moments they were clean too.

"And what about you?" Garrett asked with a smile.

"Oh, right!" Justin said and began waving the device over himself. As the boy had claimed, the dirt lifted right off and into the device, and within moments the boy was clean again. Garrett chuckled.

"Okay, let me go call Ann and see if she is up for the trip. Otherwise we will have to find someone else to go with us," Garrett said, moving back down the short hallway.

"How come?" Justin asked innocently.

"Because you are not allowed to be in public on your own," Garrett said.

"But I don't want to go with anyone else," Justin whined.

"Justin, what have I told you about whining?" Garrett asked sternly.

"That if I whine I won't get what I want," Justin replied softly.

"Right, so don't forget that when you ask for things. I will call Ann right now and see if she is available," Garrett said firmly.

"Okay," Justin said in a subdued voice.

Opening his eyes, Garrett looked around the room again before grabbing his cell phone. He really wished he was allowed to paint his apartment. The off white, yellowish walls were really ugly, Garrett thought to himself. Dialing Ann's number, he smiled as she picked up quickly.

"What's wrong?" Ann asked immediately.

"Nothing is wrong," Garrett replied. "I was just calling to see if you were busy this afternoon."

"Not really," Ann replied. "Just making some calls

on this list of ours."

"Wow, you really are into solving this mystery," Garrett chuckled.

"Well, I don't really have much else to do at the moment," Ann replied ruefully.

"Well, now you do if you want it," Garrett said, grinning. "What do you say to escorting Justin around the zoo today?" Garrett asked.

"I would love to hang out with the little guy!" Ann said happily. "That's a lot more fun than calling around to try to get prices for knife etching. I can be there in about an hour, if that's okay with you?"

"Sounds good to us!" Garrett replied. "We'll meet you at the zoo in about an hour. Thank you!" With a grin, he closed his eyes and looked over at Justin. "She's in."

"Yippee!" Justin yelled, his voice echoing in the large cavern.

"Now, let's get ready to go," Garrett said.

"I am ready," Justin replied confused.

"But I'm not," Garrett said with a smile. "We're going to meet her there in about an hour. So until then, you go play, but don't get too dirty."

"Okay, I won't. Thank you, Garrett!" Justin exclaimed, jumping into Garrett's lap and giving him a big hug. Hugging the five-year-old back, Garrett grinned.

"You're welcome, Small Fry," Garrett replied.

An hour later, Garrett arrived at the zoo, and looked around for Ann.

"You're just not good at this whole spotting thing, are you?" came a familiar voice from behind him. Garrett laughed.

"Apparently not," he replied, turning around with a smile. "Thanks for coming. I really needed to get out of that apartment today. I needed to do something normal after the last few days."

"I completely understand," Ann replied, giving him a quick hug.

"Okay, I'm going to go change. I'll be right back," Garrett said with a grin. "Oh, and here's ticket money for both of you," he said, pulling some cash out of his pocket.

Walking over to one of the displays, he wandered around to the backside of the billboard that showed all of the advertisements for the various zoo events in the next few months. Glancing around quickly and seeing that no one else was there, he closed his eyes. Looking around the cave, he saw Justin practically jumping up and down next to the stone chair.

"All right Justin, it's your turn," Garrett said with a smile.

"Yippee!" Justin cheered. Garrett quickly stood and moved back as the compact bundle of energy jumped up over the arm of the stone chair and sat down.

Justin opened his eyes and looked around. Leaning down a little, he peeked under the billboard and saw a familiar pair of legs. Scrambling under the billboard he raced over to Nana Ann with a laugh. Anticipating the charge, Ann had already crouched down to wrap him in a big hug. Justin loved Nana Ann, she always gave the best hugs!

"Are you ready?" Ann asked, smiling at him.

"I sure am!" Justin replied. "It's been ages since I've been to the zoo!" Ann just laughed and held out a hand for him to take as they walked over to the ticket counter.

Soon they were both inside and Justin was trying to point out everything he saw to Nana Ann. That was the other thing he loved about her. She was always interested in everything he was interested in. She never ignored him or said she was too busy to listen. And Justin couldn't wait to tell her all of the things he had learned about all of the animals in the zoo.

Justin barely seemed to take a breath as his unending dialogue continued. He told Ann about each of the animals, where they were from, what they liked to eat, and what liked to eat them. He insisted on reading every single plaque, and only had to have Ann help him with the words once or twice. For her part, Ann just laughed and enjoyed the enthusiasm of her young companion.

They had just entered the wolf exhibit and Justin had begun to explain the difference between a grey wolf and a red wolf, when Ann noticed that there were no other people in the exhibit. In fact, she realized, she had not noticed any other people in the last few minutes.

She had just opened her mouth to ask Justin if he had seen anyone in the last few minutes, when suddenly black-clad men were running into the exhibit from every direction. Their garish clown-painted faces covering the entire spectrum of colors and emotions, but each of them with a manic look in their eyes that promised mayhem when they were unleashed.

Before either of them had time to react, the pair was surrounded. One of the men laughed as he reached out and grabbed Justin by the shirt and picked him up.

"Well boys, what do we have here? A little bit of fun,

it looks like," said a gruff voice. "We don't need the kid to have fun with the woman, let the wolves have him." The man laughed, and with a powerful swing of his arm, he threw Justin over the railing and into the exhibit. Still laughing, he turned back to Ann. "And now for you grandm…"

The man's words froze in his throat as Ann's eyes flashed with yellow fire. The entire group moved back a step as the sweet, grandmotherly lady began to transform. Rising up to an impressive six-foot height, she held her arms out as golden plate mail began to cover her now lean frame. In her right hand, a two-handed great-sword formed, sheathed in yellow flames, and wings made of pure golden light erupted from her shoulder blades.

The man barely had time to gasp before golden eyes snapped open from under a winged helm to stare directly at him. In an instant, the great-sword had thrust forward impaling him on its glowing edge. Flicking him off to the side like a rag doll, the warrior angel turned to the rest of the group. Uttering a fierce battle cry, she charged into them.

Justin looked up from where he had landed in time to see Nana Ann turn into the beautiful, golden-haired angel. At least he thought it was an angel. Though she fought more like the Valkyries in the stories Peter sometimes read to him.

Suddenly, he heard a noise behind him. Turning slowly, he came face to face with the biggest wolf he had ever seen. Its long fur was black with bits of grey. The piercing amber eyes seemed to stare right through him as the pointed ears twitched slightly. The wolf approached him slowly, his hot breath ruffling Justin's hair as he sniffed the boy.

"Let's get out of here!" shouted a voice from above.

Justin spun around just in time to see three of the men jump over the railing, a flaming sword barely missing as it swung over their heads. Landing at the bottom, the three men scrambled out of the water in the ditch surrounding the enclosure and started making their way toward him. The trio slowed when they saw how close the great wolf was to the child.

"Nice puppy, good puppy," one of the men said in a soothing tone as they continued to approach slowly. The wolf braced his feet and started a low growl.

Justin made a small noise and began backing away from the three men. The old wolf turned at the sound and looked directly into the boy's eyes. Justin froze and stared back.

As he looked at the canine face he saw that the wolf's face didn't look angry, just curious. Impulsively he reached up with one small hand toward the massive wolf. The wolf paused for a moment, then reached up and touched the boy's hand with his nose.

"Hey!" shouted another one of the trio. "No making friends with the animals!" The man pulled a handgun from a holster behind his back and pointed it at the boy and wolf.

The wolf turned again at the shout, and seeing the man's aggressive stance went immediately into a fighting posture. His lip curling into a snarl the wolf growled, loud and threatening. The trio froze in their tracks. The great wolf's ears laid back and he took a step forward, the deep rumbling growl getting even louder. The one with the handgun grabbed his gun hand to steady himself.

"To hell with this!" he yelled squeezing off a shot.

The shot slammed into the wolf's shoulder, stumbling him back a bit. The massive wolf turned his head to look at the wound and Justin could almost see in his eyes the moment when the powerful predator lost control and went into full attack mode. With another snarl of rage the one-hundred-and-fifty-pound beast charged the trio.

Eyes wide with fear, the first man fired another shot that went wide before the wolf leapt into the air, slamming into his chest and knocking him down. He barely had time to scream before massive canine teeth bit deep into his shoulder and began to tear.

Justin turned away from the bloody display and began to run toward one of the trees. As he approached, one of the other wolves stepped out and growled softly at him. Justin froze, looking back the way he came.

He glanced back just in time to see the huge wolf bite the arm of a second man, and saw what looked like a tiny knife go flying off into the grass. The wolf then released the arm and jumped, knocking the second man to the ground as well.

Stumbling backwards under the weight of the wolf, the man fell, striking his head against a large rock so hard that Justin could hear the crack of his skull breaking. The final attacker had been able to draw a gun of his own and fired two shots, which both struck the wolf in the side.

The mighty wolf didn't seem to notice however as he charged the last man. The wolf went straight for his legs, biting deeply into his thigh. A great rush of blood gushed from the wound as the wolf started shaking his head, savaging the leg.

Desperately, the man tried to aim his gun at the fierce animal, but the wolf saw it coming. Releasing the leg, it lunged forward to bite the arm with the gun. Powerful jaws clamped down so hard that the bite shattered bone, and the gun fell from his nerveless fingers.

Justin was frozen, he didn't know which way he should run. He was vaguely aware of the others yelling inside for him to get out of the chair, but he was so scared he couldn't move, inside or out. As the enraged wolf finished off the last attacker he turned toward Justin, rage still in his eyes. With a snarl, the wolf began to charge when a voice rang out.

"Stop!" boomed the powerful, feminine voice.

Justin looked up to see the golden angel floating down into the enclosure on her wings of light. Holding her sword in one hand she extended the other, palm up, toward the raging beast.

"Calm," she ordered in a softer voice. The wolf shook his head, and clawed the ground with his paws trying to deny the command. "Peace," the woman said in a tone that was almost down to a normal volume.

Justin watched in awe as the eyes of the huge wolf began to calm, and he sat back on his haunches, staring at the golden-haired angel. Lifting her sword up and over her shoulder the flame died as she dropped it into a series of fastening loops on the back of her armor between her wings. Reaching up, she removed her winged helmet and turned to Justin.

"Are you all right?" she asked kindly. Justin just nodded as he stared at her. A warm smile spread across her lips as she reached out her hand toward him. "Good, I'm glad you are unhurt." Cautiously Justin made his way over to the beautiful woman and took her hand.

"Who are you?" Justin asked. "Is Nana Ann okay? Did you kill all of the bad men? How did you stop the wolf? Can I see your sword? Can you really fly? What's your name?" The angel smiled at the barrage of questions and held up her other hand to interrupt.

"I am Tammarion, and yes Ann is just fine, I am one of her alters. I did kill all of the bad men that were up there, but your friend has killed the three who came down here. I will show you my sword some other time." She paused to take a breath, but continued again before Justin was able to ask more questions. "Yes, I can fly, and as I said, my name is Tammarion." She smiled again at Justin, who was impressed she remembered all of his questions and actually answered all of them.

"What are you? Are you an angel? You look like an angel, but your helmet looks like the pictures of the Valkyrie, and your sword is big like theirs too. Do you know Peter? He has a really big sword too. Can I fly with…" Justin froze again, his words cutting off abruptly. Tammarion turned to see the alpha wolf walking slowly up beside her.

"It's okay, Justin, he has calmed down now. I think he wants to be your friend," she said with a smile.

Justin's eyes were wide as the huge wolf came up to him again sniffing. He started trembling in fear as the now bloody muzzle came up toward his face and he closed his eyes tightly. Suddenly he felt a gentle touch on his cheek and his eyes snapped open.

Looking into the great beast's eyes, he saw that there was no anger there any longer. Only the same curiosity he had seen earlier. Looking into their deep, amber depths, he stopped being afraid and let the great wolf gently lick his cheek.

"You see, nothing to worry about." Tammarion said with a smile.

Justin reached up his hand and gently touched the soft fur on the wolf's neck. The wolf looked down at the boy's tiny hand gently petting his neck and sneezed so hard that it ruffled the boy's hair. Justin giggled before pulling his hand away and turning back to the angel.

"Can we go home now? I think I'm finished with the zoo today," Justin said, starting to feel unsteady again from what he just witnessed.

"Of course. Come over here," Tammarion said, holding out her arms. Justin quickly moved over to give her a hug.

As she stood, she kept her arms wrapped around him, and he giggled as he saw over her shoulder the great wings of light snap open. With a single flap of the mystical wings, they were aloft and in moments were landing, not in the visitor area like Justin expected, but over the fence in the parking lot. Dozens more questions filled his mind as she set him down, but he realized that the others were yelling in his head and that he should probably go.

"I've got to go now. Everyone is mad," Justin said sadly.

"I do not believe they are mad at you little one, just scared for you," Tammarion said with a gentle smile.

"Can I see Nana Ann before I have to go? I want to make sure she's all right," Justin pleaded.

"All right," Tammarion answered. "I'll go get her."

"Thank you," Justin said, but she was already changing.

The lithe, armor clad form shifting as golden plates melted away and Justin could see the face of his favorite person in the whole outside world. He grinned as she gently wiped her mouth and opened her eyes.

"Nana Ann!" he yelled, flinging himself into her arms. She clutched him tightly to her for a few moments before she spoke.

"I'm so glad you are all right, Justin!" she said, the tears obvious in her voice.

"It's okay Nana Ann, I'm all right," Justin answered, pulling back so he could see her face.

"I'm so glad!" she said again, hugging him tightly. After another minute, he pulled back again, his brow furrowing as he saw tears rolling down her face.

"What's wrong?" Justin asked, concerned.

"I'm just so happy you're okay," Ann replied, wiping the tears away with her hand.

"If you're happy, why are you crying?" Justin asked. "I thought it wasn't good to cry?"

"Oh, no," Ann answered with a smile. "It's okay to cry if you are sad, or hurt. But you can also cry to show when you are happy. Tears are a way to show how you feel. So when you see someone crying, you know they are feeling something very strongly. Then, you can talk to them about what they are feeling, and help cheer them up if they are sad."

"Oh," Justin replied. "So it is okay to cry if you have a strong feeling? But it's okay to cheer someone up when they are crying too?"

"That's right," Ann replied, giving him another big hug. Justin hugged her back tightly before pulling away again.

"I have to go now. Everyone is upset, and Peter says it might still be dangerous," Justin said sadly.

"That's okay, he's right," Ann replied. "It's all right,

we will see each other again soon."

Justin just nodded as he closed his eyes and looked around the cave. Derrick and Peter were arguing again, yelling at each other, like always. Though they seemed madder this time than usual. Sean was discussing something with Garrett as he hopped down from the stone chair.

"Are you okay, Small Fry?" Garrett asked, stopping his conversation and walking over to Justin.

"Yeah, I'm okay. The angel saved me, and so did the wolf," Justin said matter-of-factly.

"I'm glad they were there to help. Why didn't you let one of us take over control?" Garrett asked, concerned.

"I didn't think about it," Justin said sheepishly.

"And you didn't hear us yelling at you?" Peter asked, breaking off his conversation with Derrick.

"No, I didn't. I was too scared to listen," Justin admitted. Peter turned to Garrett.

"That is something we need to work on," the knight said firmly to Garrett.

"I know. We will figure something out. I was just surprised we couldn't move him. I didn't think he had that kind of willpower to shut all of us out at the same time," Garrett said resignedly. He walked over and sat down on the stone chair. "We'll figure it out later, but for now I need to do some damage control." Opening his eyes, he looked around to see a very concerned Ann staring at him.

"You're right," Ann said without preamble, "they are targeting you."

CHAPTER ELEVEN

"What do you mean they are targeting me?" Garrett asked, shocked.

"This wasn't just some random group of thugs out for a day of bloodshed," Ann replied sternly. "There was no reason for them to be in the zoo, today of all days. It doesn't make any sense. Unless you take your whereabouts into account for each incident."

"But there were lots of groups and lots of single shooters, not all of them were around me!" Garrett protested, though when he thought about it he realized that in a city this large, the odds of him randomly encountering this many incidents was highly unlikely.

"True, so perhaps whomever it is doesn't know where you will be. They are just trying to guess where you might be and sending groups there just in case." Ann replied quickly.

"Yeah, that's possible," Garrett replied resignedly. "So now what?" he asked, dejected.

"What do you mean 'so now what'?" Ann replied, sounding a little irritated. "You know what, you already started it this morning with the others. We find out who is etching the knives, get them to talk, figure out who is behind this, and then take him out!" Ann said, sounding more angry and aggressive than Garrett had ever heard her before.

"Are you okay Ann?" Garrett asked softly, his voice full of concern.

"Yeah, I'm okay," Ann replied, deflating a little bit. "That just really scared me. They were on us before I could react and had Justin before I could stop them. If that wolf had been any less friendly, Justin could have been seriously hurt."

"I know, it's okay," Garrett answered, reaching out and wrapping her in a tight hug. "But he was, and Justin is okay." Ann let out a gusty sigh, squeezing him tightly.

"I know. I'm just glad that Tammarion showed up as quickly as she did," Ann replied softly, "It was probably a child in danger that brought her out of her solitude so quickly, and I'm glad it did. Things could have been much worse."

"I know. I felt the same way." Garrett replied softly. "We couldn't get Justin out of the chair so that someone else could take over."

"Chair?" Ann asked, pulling back a bit.

"Yeah, the control chair," Garrett replied. "The one you sit in to take control of the body?" Ann laughed, sharp and quick.

"I don't have a control chair," she replied with a grin. "That actually sounds a bit more organized than what I see."

"What? If you don't have a control chair, what do you have?" Garrett asked, perplexed.

"I have a doorway," Ann replied with a grin. "The doorway between worlds. If I face inside the doorway I can see my inner world, and if I face outside the doorway

I can see and interact with the outside world."

"But what happens when more than one person tries to fit into the doorway?" Garrett asked, still confused.

"And that question, my dear friend, explains a large number of my problems," Ann replied with a laugh. "If more than one person is in the doorway, more than one person is in control."

"Oh wow, that must get really confusing, especially if it's more than two at a time!" Garrett replied in shock.

"It does indeed," Ann said, pulling back a bit. "That's why we are more of a community. My alters and I have to work together to do things, even basic things like control of the body."

"But wait," Garrett said, "I'm still confused. If more than one person is in control, why do you still look the same?"

"I don't know," Ann replied. "That's one of the mysteries of the Dreaming I suppose. I would guess there is some sort of hierarchy depending on which ones are trying to control together. That if there are two in the doorway, then only one can hold the shape, so the hierarchy picks who gets it." Ann sighed again. "At least that's my guess."

"Wow, I had no idea it was so different for you," Garrett said. "It's pretty clear for us. If you are sitting in the chair, you are in control."

"Well," Ann continued, "what happens when more than one person is sitting in the chair?"

"Like on a lap?" Garrett asked, "The chair isn't big enough for more than one person to sit in it at a time. Though if others touch it, they can see and hear what is going on outside."

"What about Justin?" Ann asked. "He could

probably fit with one of you." Garrett thought for a moment.

"I'm honestly not sure," he answered. "We've never tried it before."

Ann just smiled at him, knowing the question itself would make him want an answer. Garrett never seemed to stop looking for answers. He rarely found them, but he never stopped looking.

The pair made their way back to the bus stop and caught the next bus home. They didn't say much on the trip, both of them lost in their own thoughts. When Ann's stop came, Garrett gave her a quick hug before she left the bus, and warned her to be careful with her calls. He rode the rest of the trip in silence, wondering where and when they, whoever they were, would strike again; and if they were out there right now, looking for him.

Failure. More failure. These dimwitted idiots couldn't succeed if their lives depended on it. Which they did! How many had He killed now? A dozen? Two dozen? He didn't know, and didn't care. Their lives were his to spend. And spend them he would; as many as it took to finish the job.

He ran his hand through his slick purple hair in frustration. He thought the zoo would be the perfect place for an ambush. He knew that the soft-hearted fool would want to spoil the child in order to calm his mind. It was either the zoo or the bumper car track. But his men who went to the bumper cars were killed by police, not by Him.

The zoo was different though… the zoo was strange. The news had said that the wounds looked like they had been made by a sword, so naturally the stupid knight had been involved. But they also said the wounds had been cauterized. Cauterized as they were made. He only knew of one fictional character type with a laser sword that could do that.

But no, He didn't have anyone from that world in His head. No one with telekinesis and a laser sword. Then who… what? What could have happened there?

With a cry of rage, he grabbed a knife from the arm of his chair and threw it at a helpless lackey that was loitering about. The man dropped something, weapons it looked like, to clutch at the blade protruding from the lackey's throat. Idiot! He should know better than to treat weapons that way! The man would no doubt have had to be executed if the fool wasn't already dying.

Something else was going on. Something different. Something unexpected. Well then, he would just have to ramp up his game then. Eventually one of them would succeed. One of the tired fools would kill Him. And if not… he grinned evilly. And if not, then the next phase of his plan would bring Him here. And then, if necessary, he would kill Him himself.

The clown-faced albino threw his head back and laughed. And as his crazed laughter echoed through the halls, black-clad men looked up from what they were doing, their eyes white with fear.

The next morning, Garrett woke early. Forgoing his run again he sat down at his computer to see if he could whittle down his portion of the list of engravers, while he waited for their stores to open. He had ten names on his part of the list, he figured he could get through that fairly quickly.

Sitting down at his computer Garrett pulled up websites for each of the companies who did metal etching. After browsing each of the sites, he was able to eliminate two based on the quality of work alone that was displayed on their website. Neither of them showed anything like the detail and artistry that went into these demonic-looking clown-head knives.

By nine o'clock, he was tired and ready for some breakfast. Grabbing a frozen breakfast sandwich from the fridge, he popped it into the microwave and set the timer. Pouring himself a glass of milk, he took the hot sandwich into the living room and turned on the TV.

It was set to a news station that was playing gory scenes of the zoo and apparently an attack at a bumper car rink. Garrett wished the news would keep that level of graphic detail to the evening broadcasts. Kids didn't need to see that kind of thing.

Although, he thought to himself, Justin hadn't been too badly off after seeing what happened to the men who attacked him and Ann. Though he could hardly be objective about that considering what Justin had been through in their childhood, and what he had seen since they had grown up. Especially in the last week.

Flipping channels, he found one showing one of his favorite comic book based TV shows, and sat back to relax for a bit. As he was enjoying his show he realized that there was yelling in his head, again. He closed his eyes for a moment to see what was going on. It was Peter and Sean this time.

Of course all of the yelling was coming from Peter, but Sean made no moves to leave the conversation, which meant he thought he had a point to make.

"I say we should go after him now!" Peter yelled, "Full frontal attack!"

"Of course you do," Sean calmly replied. "You fail to understand the most basic tactics, so naturally everything is a full attack to you."

"Look, elf," Peter shouted, getting right into Sean's face, "I understand tactics just fine, but when it's time to attack, then it's time to attack!"

"First, I am not an elf," Sean replied calmly to the giant warrior yelling in his face. "Second, it is not logical to assume that now is the time for a direct assault. We don't even know where we would be assaulting yet." That seemed to take a bit of the wind out of Peter's sails, but he was not out of the fight yet.

"Well, if we don't know where to go to fight, then we should bring the fight to us!" Peter exclaimed. "Make a big scene where whoever it is can see it and challenge him to come out and fight us."

"Also illogical," Sean replied smoothly. "It would be impossible to predict when our mystery nemesis would be observing local transmissions. Also, it is far more likely that a large man in plate mail waving a sword around would attract the attention of the police much more quickly than a mysterious enemy."

"Bah! I can handle a few city guards," Peter boasted,

"And that is exactly what would attract the attention of more 'city guards', as you put it," Sean answered, his voice carefully not showing his disdain. "And if you do a good enough job, you would attract military attention as well, which might be a more difficult challenge."

"Surely they would recognize my quest and leave me unhindered," Peter replied confidently.

"No, they wouldn't," Garrett answered, rising and walking over to the pair. "They would try to take you alive to be questioned and imprisoned for disturbing the peace. Though since we both know that wouldn't work, they would then be forced to kill you as a threat to the public."

"But I am not a threat to the public!" Peter said in outrage.

"Doesn't matter," Garrett answered. "That's how they would see you and how they would react to you. Whether it was true or not." Peter's shoulders slumped and he was silent for a long moment.

"Indeed, if that is truly how they would perceive me, then you are correct. I cannot give challenge in public and expect him to come to me." Peter growled under his breath. "Very well then, we shall do it your way and seek out our enemy." Sean raised a single pointed eyebrow at the surprising admission.

"Thank you," Garrett replied, clapping the tall man on an armored shoulder.

Sitting back down on the stone chair, he opened his eyes again to see that his program had ended. It was now playing a cartoon version of another comic book hero. Garrett grabbed for the remote when suddenly a maniacal laughter echoed from the television set. Garrett froze, staring at the screen as he watched a familiar clown-faced supervillain battle with the costumed hero.

That was it! It wasn't a comic book he had remembered seeing the story in, it was a cartoon version of the comic book! Leaping up off of his couch he raced into the bedroom and turned on his computer. Logging quickly into a streaming video site he looked up the cartoon in question, only to drop his shoulders in frustration as he realized that there were nine seasons available to be viewed. Watching through them all would take days, he realized.

Garrett closed his eyes in frustration, grinding the heels of his hands against his eyeballs he tried to think about how he could watch through nine seasons of the cartoon in just a day or two.

Suddenly it occurred to him, this was a problem with mathematics. Time spent versus time available. And if anyone could figure out how to bend time it would be Sean. Opening his inner eyes, he looked around the cave. Not seeing anyone nearby, he jumped up and went over to knock on Sean's door. It opened in moments to reveal the utilitarian grey garb of the pointy-eared alien.

"May I assist you?" Sean inquired politely.

"Yes, you can!" Garrett answered excitedly.

"Indeed?" Sean responded. "How may I assist you?"

"I need to figure out how to find a single television episode in a nine season cartoon in as little time as possible." Garrett answered quickly. Sean raised his expressive eyebrow.

"Indeed. Then what you need is a list of the episodes referenced with appropriate keywords so that you can reduce the number of possibilities." Sean replied calmly. "I am certain you can locate such a list. Perhaps with the descriptions of each episode to aid in your search?"

"Perfect, thank you!" Garrett answered, already turning back to the stone chair.

"I am pleased to be of assistance," Sean replied before closing his door again.

Garrett practically flung himself into the stone chair and opened his eyes. His fingers flew across the keyboard as he searched the fan forums for a list of all of the episodes with descriptions. After a half hour of searching, he finally found one that had each one listed and indexed by description. It even had connections showing which episodes contained which characters or story arcs.

Quickly downloading the list, he started filtering out the ones that didn't match what he was looking for. The costumed hero apparently had quite the roster of super villains set against him. Many of whom conformed to animal archetypes such as penguins, cats, crocodiles, moths, and bats. He quickly sorted all of them out of his list, as well as the ninjas, supernatural mud, plants, insane psychiatrists and cosmic villains.

When he felt he had narrowed down the list to only the clown-faced villain, he looked at the remaining list. Thirty-six episodes that featured the clown-faced bad guy. Okay, that was only eighteen hours of show. He could do that in a day if necessary.

As he queued up the cartoon on his streaming video, he suddenly had another thought. Closing his eyes again, he looked around the cave toward Justin's room. Standing with a smile, he walked over and knocked on the little guy's door.

"Just a sec!" called the young voice. In a few moments, the door opened and Justin grinned up at him. "Hey!" he said happily.

"Hey, Small Fry," Garrett answered, smiling back, "I was doing some research that involves watching a lot of cartoons and I thought you might want to help me."

"Help you?!" Justin said excitedly. "Sure! How can I

help?"

"Well, I thought we might try an experiment," Garrett said, crouching down to Justin's level. "I was wondering if it would be possible for more than one of us to sit in the stone chair at the same time. So I thought, if it were possible, you could help me watch the cartoons and look for the things I am trying to find. How does that sound?" Justin looked thoughtful for a moment before answering.

"You're trying to find stuff about the bad guys, aren't you?" Justin answered seriously.

"Yes I am," Garrett replied candidly.

"Will it be scary?" Justin asked.

"The cartoon won't be scary, but it might remind you of things that are scary," Garrett answered. "Do you still want to help me?" Justin thought for a long moment before nodding.

"Yes, I want to help," Justin said, lifting his chin.

"Good!" Garrett said with a grin. "Come on." The two of them walked over to the stone chair and tried to figure out how they could both sit down at once. After a bit of wiggling Garrett managed to sit in the chair with Justin wedged beside him. It wasn't particularly comfortable, but it was worth a try as they both opened their eyes.

Garrett blinked rapidly as his vision blurred in and out. He felt disoriented, like things weren't where they were supposed to be. He jumped in his seat as his right arm lifted, seemingly on its own. As his head turned he happened to see his reflection in the bathroom mirror and froze. He was Justin. He still had his own thoughts but the body looked like Justin.

Garrett was confused. After talking with Ann, he

figured that he would be dominant and the body would take his shape. That way Justin would just see through his eyes.

"Garrett," Justin's young voice emerged from his lips, "this feels funny."

"Yeah, it really does," Garrett replied, his own deeper voice echoing from the same mouth.

Garrett tried to shake his head, but it wouldn't move. He experienced a moment of panic before the head did move, only to look up at the computer screen. That was not what he had wanted to do, but apparently Justin was in control of the body.

"Garrett, I don't think I like this," Justin said, sounding worried. "Nothing feels right, like I'm covered in marshmallow sauce." Garrett tried to nod, but was again unable to control the head.

"Okay, we can stop now," he answered as the eyes closed and they looked around the cave with their own eyes before looking at each other. "All righty then, that didn't work so well," Garrett said, trying to sound jovial.

"No, I didn't like that at all," Justin said, squirming out of the chair.

"Well, I know if you are touching the chair without sitting on it then you can see and hear, but won't be in control." Garrett suggested.

"Yeah, but won't I get tired standing that long?" Justin asked sadly.

"Probably, yeah," Garrett answered. "So what if you weren't sitting on the seat? What if you sat in my lap? Should we see how that works?"

"Okay," Justin replied amiably. In a moment, he had scrambled up into Garrett's lap and closed his eyes. Garrett chuckled softly at his enthusiasm before closing his own eyes and opening them again in the outside world. He quickly glanced over at the mirror to see his own lean face looking back at him.

"Much better," he said, happy that his own voice came out of his mouth.

"Yeah, this isn't so bad," Justin's small voice answered, also from his own mouth. Garrett started for a moment, then relaxed as he realized that Justin was in the same position he was a few moments ago.

"Will you be okay like this?" Garrett asked, concerned.

"Yeah, it's kind of like when I am standing next to the chair," Justin replied.

"Good!" Garrett answered. "Okay, here's our task. I am trying to find episodes of this cartoon where the clown guy sends a bunch of other guys in clown masks to shoot at people. Then, he sends bigger groups of guys to do more damage. I want to find out what happens at the end of that episode."

"You got it!" Justin said enthusiastically. Garrett chuckled again as he printed out the list of which episodes they would be watching.

"Okay, so here are the ones we want to watch," Garrett said, placing the list next to the keyboard. "Don't waste any time with the ones that are not on this list."

"Okay," Justin answered, "I won't." And with that, the pair settled in to watch cartoons.

Hour after hour they watched. Garrett suggested to Justin that he might want to take a break, but Justin was adamant that he wanted to help and he could help by watching cartoons. Garrett had laughed at that, marveling on how unlikely that sentence was before settling down to watch more episodes.

More hours crawled, by when all of a sudden Garrett felt a shoving at his shoulder. Startled, he blinked and shook himself, realizing he had fallen asleep while watching the cartoons.

"I found it, I found it!" Justin exclaimed happily.

"What? How? What happened?" Garrett answered, only semi-coherently.

"I told you, I found it!" Justin shouted happily. "You fell asleep but I kept watching, and I found the one you were looking for!"

"Wait, what? How did you keep watching if I fell asleep?" Garrett asked, still in a bit of a fog.

"Well, when you went to sleep, your body got kind of limp. But you wouldn't wake up when I talked to you, so I tried pushing you. Except the arm moved. Your arm, the big one!" Justin explained. "That's when I figured out that if you are asleep but I am with you, I can control the body when it looks like you!"

"Wow, that's… wow." Garrett replied, intelligently.

"But look, look, I found it!" Justin exclaimed again.

Garrett turned to the screen in time to see the costumed hero taking out a man in a clown mask with a boomerang. As the masked man fell, a large gun fell from his hand and Garrett shot up in his chair, suddenly very alert.

"Justin, that's amazing!" Garrett said. "Thank you for keeping watch for me, and finding this!"

"You're welcome," Justin said, the ear-to-ear grin evident in his voice.

Garrett's focus narrowed down to just what was playing on the screen. Sure enough there were clown-masked shooters that the costumed hero had to take out one by one. They were in the subways, the grocery stores, police stations, schools, churches, everywhere there was a large gathering of people. The police did manage to catch some of them, but most were captured by the hero and his gadgets.

As the episode finished, he realized it was a three-part story as a season finale. Muttering under his breath, he queued up the next episode. Sure enough the violence had escalated, and now large gangs were patrolling the streets, forcing the hero into bigger and bigger fights.

And as he fought, the battles began to wear on him. He started having a harder and harder time winning the fights, and took more and more damage from the ever-growing gangs of thugs. The episode ended with a scene of the clown-faced villain talking about the final step in his masterful plan to get rid of the hero.

Growling in frustration, Garrett queued up the next episode just as his phone rang. Glancing down, he saw it was Ann, and grumbled as he paused the show to pick up the phone.

"Hello," Garrett said sharply into the phone.

"Good morning, grumpy," Ann's pleasant voice came back.

"I'm not…" Garrett paused for a moment realizing he had snapped at her. "I'm sorry, good morning. I didn't get a lot of sleep last night, so I apologize for being grouchy."

"Why didn't you get any sleep?" Ann asked, concerned.

"I figured out where I remembered the story from," Garrett replied, starting to get excited again. "It wasn't from a comic book. It was from a cartoon based on a comic book."

"Oh!" Ann replied, sounding excited herself. "Well what did you find out?"

"Nothing yet, I am still watching it," Garrett answered, a bit of exasperation in his voice.

"Well, that's unfortunate," Ann said, "because I was calling to let you know that you are late for the meeting with the group today."

"What?!" Garrett exclaimed, glancing at the clock. "Shoot! Okay, I'll be right there. Bye!" Hanging up the phone, he debated whether he wanted to watch the final episode before he left or if he should go now. Grabbing up the bus schedule he saw that he had just enough time to catch the next bus, but if he missed that one, it would be an hour until the next.

With a sigh of exasperation, he started to stand, but felt something funny around his midsection. Glancing down he didn't see anything, but then it occurred to him that the feeling wasn't external. Closing his eyes, he saw that Justin had fallen asleep in his lap.

With a small smile Garrett stood up from the stone chair, walked over into Justin's room, and gently placed him into his bed. Pulling up the covers, he kissed the sleeping boy lightly on the forehead.

"Thanks, Small Fry," Garrett whispered. "You are a life saver."

Returning quickly to the stone chair, he opened his eyes, and stood up from his computer. Glancing quickly at his watch to see how much time he had left, he slipped on his shoes and raced out the door, not noticing his rumpled clothes and hair in his haste to catch his bus. He would just have to watch the last episode when he got home again.

CHAPTER TWELVE

Garrett got off the bus in front of the local coffee shop where they had agreed to meet. Garrett didn't particularly like coffee, but Phil and Katie did, so they suggested one of their favorite hangouts. Walking quickly, he opened the doors to the strong smell of fresh coffee grounds. He paused for a moment to get used to the scent and walked in.

Glancing around, he quickly saw the other four sitting at one of the larger tables in the shop. With a raised hand to show he had seen them, he made his way through the maze of tables over to where they were gathered. Garrett let out a gusty sigh as he sat down heavily.

"You okay?" Ann asked with concern.

"Yeah, I'm fine," Garrett replied. "I was just up too late last night doing research."

"How can do research in middle of night?" Susan asked, her Slavic accent thicker than usual.

"I wasn't researching the knives; I was researching a story," Garrett replied. "I think I found out where these guys are coming from. Or at least what story whomever is sending them is following."

"You think someone is playing out a scene in a book?" Phil asked, surprised.

"Not a book, a comic book," Garrett answered, shaking his head. "They are using a cartoon version of a comic book to come up with their plans."

"Who would do something like that?" Katie asked.

"I'm not sure about that yet," Garrett said, shrugging. "I just know that what has happened in the last week matches the storyline I found."

"So what happens next?" Phil asked as he leaned forward.

"I'm not sure yet," Garrett replied, sighing again. "I was just getting to that part when I realized I was late coming here, and that if I waited, the next bus didn't come for another hour." The group nodded. Most of them understood trying to fit a life around an inconvenient bus schedule.

"So, we are watching story then?" Susan asked after a moment.

"Sure," Garrett answered, surprised. "If you guys want to come over to my place, you are welcome to watch it with me." Katie gave a small smile as Susan nodded her head decisively.

"Thanks guys," Garrett said a little embarrassed. "I didn't think you would want to be involved past the point of finding the etching place."

"You're a good man," Phil said, looking at him with an intense gaze. "You may smart off in therapy when it's your turn, but you are always supportive of us when it's our turn to speak. And even when it's not you." Phil paused for a moment. "We've all talked to the little guy, and heard his stories about you, all of you. We've seen the knight bluster about righting the wrongs done to all of us, and we've seen your wannabe vampire go out of his way to be kind when he thinks no one is looking." Garrett chuckled slightly.

"I think Derrick might take exception to the term 'wannabe'," Garrett said with a grin.

"Yeah," Phil answered, "but I've read the books you based him on, and he's not like the selfish, conceited creatures described in the books. He pretends to be, but when no one is looking he does nice things for people. Even when they are looking, he does them anyway, and tries to play it off as a selfish act. And you know Sean has offered his assistance to all of us, any time we need him. That's not just participating in group therapy, that is being a friend."

Garrett sat back in his chair, stunned at the speech. He glanced over at Ann, who was just grinning as she sat back in her chair watching.

"Thank you," Garrett said to Phil. "Thank all of you. I truly appreciate that." Garrett shook his head slightly. "You know, Ruby would be very impressed with us right now. She would tell us we've made a big breakthrough today." The group laughed together for a moment at the comparison before settling down to business.

"Okay," Ann chimed in, "what did everyone find?" Garrett looked sheepish for a moment.

"Umm, not much. After eliminating two of my ten, I got caught up trying to find the story and didn't call any of mine," Garrett said guiltily.

"Garrett!" Ann exclaimed in exasperation. "After all that and you didn't even do your part of the work you had asked our help with?"

"No," Garrett answered, "I'm sorry." Ann let out a gusty sigh.

"Okay, fine, we'll come back to yours later," Ann said turning in her chair. "Katie, how did yours go?"

"Not much luck," Katie said softly. "Most of them said they wouldn't want to do anything that detailed. I only have two who said they would try it."

"Excellent," Ann said with a grin. "Susan?"

"Five said can do job," Susan replied. "I think maybe one is lying. Trying to swindle."

"Okay," Ann said matter-of-factly. "We'll leave that one out unless we don't have any luck with the others. Phil?" The big biker grinned as he turned to her.

"I think I got something. Maybe not the one who did the blades, but perhaps the one who did the design." Phil answered still grinning.

"Oh?" Ann asked excited.

"Yeah, I mentioned to my tattoo artist that I was looking for a new tattoo. That I wanted to get a demonic clown, to really scare people," Phil said, looking proud of himself. "Told him with all the clown killers on the loose, that would really scare people away when they saw it."

"Phil, wasn't that dangerous?" Garrett asked. "Aren't you afraid he will tell someone what you're looking into?"

"Nah," Phil replied with a wave of his hand. "He's been my tattoo guy for almost fifteen years now. He knows I sometimes do stuff that's scary, to keep people away. This will look like just another attempt to push the world away again."

"So what did he say?" Ann asked.

"He said that one of the artists he buys designs from came out with a bunch of evil clown designs about six months ago," Phil answered. "Said none of them were what he was looking for, but maybe my tattoo guy could use them. Sold them to him in a pack of about two dozen. I looked through them, and didn't find the one that is on the blades, but I saw a couple that could have been close."

"That's fantastic," Garrett exclaimed. "So how do we get in touch with the artist?"

"Way ahead of ya," Phil answered with a grin. "I asked if this guy does commission work. That I wanted something really unique. He told me the artist does do commissions and that if I bought a new design, that he'd give me half off the tattoo if I sold him the design afterwards. Then he gave me the guy's name and number." Phil grinned even wider as he held up a scrap of paper with the artist's information on it and handed it over to Garrett.

"Phil, you are the best!" Garrett said, grinning from ear to ear. Phil just sat back in his chair, looking extremely proud of himself. "Okay guys, I think I need to do the questioning by myself." A chorus of angry exclamations met his statement and he held up his hands. "Hey, I'm not trying to keep you out of this one, but Derrick can go places no one else can, and he can question people in such a way that they have to tell him the truth. Also, he can erase their memories of the questions afterward. It's safer if he does it alone." Garrett looked at each one of them as they grumbled their assent.

"So are you going to question all of the metal workers yourself as well?" Ann asked, still sounding frustrated.

"I think I have to, Ann," Garrett replied sadly. "We can't afford to have them tell anyone what we are looking for." Ann nodded briefly.

"All right, but I'm coming with you to the locations at least," Ann said firmly.

"Ann, I don't think…" Garrett began.

"Let me finish," Ann said, holding up a hand. "I won't go inside, but I should be there in case things go badly." Garrett sighed as he realized she was right.

"Okay, fine. But you have to stay out of sight unless I need you," Garrett said firmly.

"I can do that," Ann replied, pulling out her bus schedule. "We should plan our route though, to hit as many as we can today."

"Guys," Phil chimed in. "I don't think traveling by bus is going to work. It will take you all day just to hit three places." He turned in his chair to Katie. "Miss Katie, if you would be willing to loan them your car, it would be my pleasure to escort you wherever you need to go today." Katie looked surprised for a moment then blushed a deep crimson.

"Of course you can use my car," Katie said softly. "If Phil can take me on my errands today, I won't need it." she smiled softly up at Phil, who was looking proud as punch again.

"Thank you Katie, Phil," Garrett said sincerely. "I really appreciate your help." Katie dug in her purse for a bit before pulling out a large wad of keys and keychains, and handing them over to Ann.

The group stood to leave, and with lots of hugs and entreaties of caution, they made their way to the parking lot. Susan waved as she went to her car and got in. The rest of them walked over to where Katie and Phil's vehicles were parked.

Garrett took a moment to admire the custom paint

job on Phil's cycle. It looked like a cross between black flame and dark smoke as it both curled and flowed over the well-loved bike. Katie's car, on the other hand, was more of a baby blue-green that had obviously seen better days.

Phil went to his motorcycle and lifted a seat to pull out a spare helmet, handing it over to Katie. Katie looked at it nervously before putting it on her head and fastening the chin strap. Garrett held out his hand to Ann for the keys but Ann just shook her head.

"Nope, I'm driving the getaway car," she said with a grin. "You get to go inside and get the goods." Garrett laughed.

"All right, have it your way," he said holding up both hands in surrender. Ann smiled smugly as she went around to the driver's door and opened it.

"I know I've already said this," Phil began, "but be careful, all right?"

"Don't worry, we will," Garrett replied, clapping the big biker on the shoulder.

With a nod, he swung his leg over the bike and sat down. Katie, still looking nervous, climbed onto the bike behind him and wrapped her arms tightly around his midsection. Her head rested against his back, with her face turned toward Garrett and Ann.

"Good luck," she said, right before Phil started the engine with a roar, and she squeezed her eyes shut.

"That is one brave girl," Garrett said as the roaring bike took off down the street. Ann just laughed.

"That's not bravery," Ann said with a grin, "that's love."

"What?" Garrett said, looking over at her.

"Haven't you see her making googly eyes at him

when she thinks he isn't looking?" Ann asked, surprised. "Or how he always looks at her whenever he does something he's proud of? They are head over heels for each other, even though neither of them has said it out loud yet." Ann continued. Garrett shook his head that he hadn't noticed.

"I didn't know that," Garrett admitted, opening the passenger door and getting inside. Ann just chuckled again and got in the driver's seat. "I suppose we should talk to the artist first," Garrett suggested. "He's the one most likely to have had direct contact with the one who commissioned him to draw the evil clown face."

The pair rode in silence as they traveled downtown to a tall apartment building. Ann parked the car along the curb, and looked over at Garrett.

Garrett took a deep breath, and got out of the car. He walked over to the payment meter and selected thirty minutes. Swiping his card, he waited for a moment for the parking sticker to print out before walking it back over to Ann.

"Good luck," Ann said, taking the parking sticker to put in the window.

"Thanks." Garrett smiled far more confidently than he felt. Closing his eyes briefly, he looked into his inner world. "You ready, Derrick?" he asked the elegant vampire standing next to the stone chair. Derrick just grinned, showing only a hint of fang. Garrett shook his head as he opened his eyes again.

Walking over to the doors, he saw an old-style call-box, and quickly skimmed the names until he found the one he wanted, C4. Pushing the button for the correct apartment, he waited patiently for a response.

"Yeah, what do you want?" came an irritated voice

from the call-box.

"Is this Vincent? Vincent Govan?" Garrett asked politely.

"Oh good, you can read," came the sarcastic reply. "I didn't ask you to ask my name, I asked you what you wanted." Garrett cleared his throat and tried to sound confident.

"I am here to talk to you about a commission," Garrett replied.

"I don't talk about my clients," returned the voice angrily.

"No, no," Garrett stammered, "I want to commission you to draw something for me." Garrett heard a heavy sigh from the call-box.

"Fine," the voice replied, sounding resigned. "Come on up and we'll talk about your little project."

Garrett heard the familiar sound of a door buzzer sounding to indicate the main door was unlocked. He opened the door quickly and looked around. It was a fairly basic-looking apartment building. Four apartments on the bottom floor with a staircase leading up to the other units.

Garrett stumbled back as three people burst from one of the apartment doors on his right. There were two adults and one child, all wearing some kind of robe and cloak. The two adults were dressed in black and were holding red laser swords in a ready position. The third was a boy of about twelve reigniting his own green laser sword before charging at the two adults. Blinking rapidly, he realized that the boy was probably having a daydream about the show he was watching.

Garrett smiled and moved toward the staircase, when something caught his attention. The illusionary boy doing battle with the two adults was moving with a level of skill and grace that surprised him.

Not many people had that level of detail and precision in their daydreams. The boy had some skill, not just with a sword, but also with his ability to control his thoughts and direct them where he wanted them to go.

Garrett again marveled at how rapidly the younger generation was becoming accustomed to the Dreaming. They were able to use it in ways that most adults could only dream of. Garrett chuckled to himself at the pun. It was true though. For them, the Dreaming was not some terrible event that shattered their world. For them, it was just another part of life, to be learned, explored, and used.

Idly, he wondered what the world would be like in a generation or two, when there was no one left who remembered a time without the Dreaming. How much would the world change when the children who were learning to use the Dreaming grew up and took charge of everything?

He watched the battle play out for a few more moments. The adults seemed to have the advantage, of both numbers and reach. But the boy showed greater agility, and was able to use his smaller size to evade most of their attacks rather than trying to block them.

Just then, he heard a voice from behind the door the three figures had emerged from. He couldn't tell what the voice was saying, but it sounded like they were calling a name. Instantly the three figures winked out of existence. Probably the boy's mother calling him, Garrett thought to himself.

Taking another deep breath to settle himself, Garrett

began climbing up the stairwell to the fourth floor. He paused for a moment as he felt a mental tap on his shoulder. Closing his eyes, he looked over at Derrick standing next to the stone chair.

"We are indoors, I believe it is my turn to take over," Derrick said, his Romanian accent causing the words to roll off of his tongue.

"I thought that I would go in first, and talk about the commission," Garrett replied, "then you would come up when we started questioning him."

"No," Derrick said firmly. "It is better if he does not see you at all. I can wipe all traces of me from his mind, but wiping you from his mind, especially if he has been told to watch for you, is more difficult."

"Hmm, I didn't realize that," Garrett said, pondering the implications. "Okay, go ahead." The pair quickly switched places and Derrick opened his eyes.

A quick glance around showed him that there was no one else in the stairwell, and that the windows were all on one side. Grinning in a way that could only be described as predatory, Derrick began thinning into mist and drifting up the center of the stairwell.

When he had reached the fourth floor, the mist paused and began to coalesce into the darkly elegant form of the vampire again. Moving quickly over to apartment C, he knocked gently on the door. Within moments, a ragged-looking man answered.

"What..." the man began, but Derrick was already making eye contact and pushing at the much weaker mind with his own. The man's mind was indeed weak, making it simplicity itself to mesmerize him. Taking the man by the shoulder, he guided him deeper into the apartment, closing the door behind them.

"Sit, my young friend," Derrick instructed, gently pushing the man toward a chair. The man sat with a limp grace that was common to those under deep hypnosis. "Now then, I have some questions for you. And you will answer all of them, truthfully. Do you understand?" The man nodded, his eyes starting to droop slightly. "Excellent. My first question is this; did you draw the face that has been etched onto this blade?" Derrick pulled out the cloth-wrapped blade, showing the etched clown face to the man.

"Yes," the man mumbled.

"Excellent," Derrick said, smiling just enough for his fangs to peek out. "And was this the only one?"

"No," the man said, still mumbling. "Lots of drafts, not good enough."

"I see," Derrick looked at him hard. "And who said they were not good enough?"

"Buyer," the man replied.

"Who is this buyer?" Derrick asked pointedly.

"Don't know," the man answered.

"What do you mean you don't know?" Derrick growled. "If you did not meet with him, then how did he disapprove of your work?"

"Someone else." The man seemed to be struggling for answers. "Someone else came. Took the drawings away. They came back, not good enough."

"I see," Derrick said calming slightly. "Just how long ago was this?"

"Six months ago," the man replied, starting to get more agitated.

"That long," Derrick said under his breath. "And what was the name of this mystery employer?" he said forcefully.

"Don't know," the man said, shifting in his seat.

"Why don't you know?" Derrick said, becoming angry again. "Don't you see the names of those you sign contracts with?"

"No contract," the man replied. "Just called him boss. No contract, money up front." The man was visibly agitated now. Derrick frowned.

"Why are you moving around like that?" Derrick asked. "You're supposed to be sitting still, answering my questions."

"I… I…" the man started to stutter, when suddenly there was a crack, and the sound of breaking glass behind them. The man's head snapped back as though he had been hit by a baseball bat.

Derrick whirled to see where the attack had come from. He noted the broken window and looked out just in time to see the barrel of a gun being pulled back from the curtains of the building next door.

Derrick's head snapped back to look at the shabby man, but it was too late. The shot had taken him right in the forehead. He was dead. Derrick began to feel the anger rising in him again, and briefly considered leaping out of the window over to the other building, but it was still daylight. He could not change form in the sunlight and would fall to the ground before he made it to the other building.

Another crack resounded and a line of fiery pain traced its way across his left arm. Derrick cursed in a language older than any now spoken, and dove to the side out of the line of sight of the windows, landing in a dirty kitchen.

The cursed devils were using silver shot! Most wounds he could heal in moments but although he could touch silver without harm, any wounds he suffered would heal very slowly. Closing his eyes briefly, he looked over to his mental companions arrayed around the stone chair.

"They are using silver shot," Derrick growled. "I will make it to the door, then Garrett you must again take over.

"No!" Peter demanded. "Their projectiles cannot pierce my armor. I must go forth to do battle with them!"

"Simple-minded fool," Derrick snarled. "And what if they are ready for that? You can hardly get out unnoticed, and if they have something bigger than a gun, you would be in trouble." Peter bristled, but Garrett waved him to silence.

"Derrick's right, I have to go," Garrett announced. "I am the one most likely to be able to get out of the building without being detected."

Derrick just nodded and opened his eyes again. In a burst of vampiric speed he dove out across the room. Seeming to fly over the floor he made it through the door before touching down again. In an instant, he closed his eyes and traded places with Garrett.

Garrett raced down the stairs, trying to think of what would make him look different enough he could make it out the door unseen. He removed his jacket and left it on one of the landings, but didn't think that would make enough of a difference. As he reached the bottom of the stairs he froze in surprise.

The door, where he had seen the three figures from the dream a few minutes ago was open. As he watched, a young mother pushed her son out of the door in a wheelchair. The boy's body was rigid, and twisted from some unknown birth disorder.

The boy's face, however, was unmistakable. It was the same boy he had seen with the laser sword, leaping and dashing gracefully around the room. Doing battle with his foes. Garrett's breath caught in his throat. This was it, this was the silver lining in all of the madness. The useful, happy side of the Dreaming amidst all of the pain and sorrow it had caused. A mind unfettered by the restrictions of a broken body. A mind free to be and explore and express itself in any way it wanted.

His face broke into a grin as he finished coming down the stairs. He nodded politely to the mother, then whispered under his breath as he passed, "Well fought, young one." He wasn't sure, but he thought he saw the twisted mouth curve upwards in response.

Garrett moved swiftly through the doors and out onto the street. He glanced briefly at Ann, still sitting in the car as he passed and shook his head slightly. Moving quickly, he strode into the alley that separated the two buildings. He mentally whispered to everyone else to be ready as he put his back against the wall, and waited to see what would be coming after him, and who would be best to meet it.

CHAPTER THIRTEEN

Garrett didn't have long to wait. A pair of men moving with the lithe gracefulness of professional martial artists entered the alley from the other side. Their faces were painted, not in the gaudy image of a clown, but with the dangerous-looking ferocity of a tribal warrior. Each was well armed with both guns and blades scattered around their bodies.

Peter it was, then. Closing his eyes for an instant, he signaled the massive knight and quickly traded places with him.

Peter was eager for the challenge. He wished to redeem himself after the failure with the mob, and this was the perfect place to do it. He jostled his shield on his arm to make sure it was secure. It always was. Drawing his massive sword, he stepped out into the alleyway.

"I cry challenge!" Peter roared at the pair of dangerous-looking men. The men didn't blink, they each simply drew an Asian-style sword and started forward.

There were no words expressed, and Peter was surprised to find himself hard-pressed in the first moments of the fight. The pair worked in concert, one drawing his attack so that the other could test his defense.

The first attacker moved to Peter's left, his sword working in and around, trying to find a way around Peter's shield. Meanwhile the second attacker had shifted to a two-handed stance and was striking as quickly as he could, with a great deal more power than Peter had expected from a normal human. Fortunately, his strength was great enough to move his massive broadsword in time to parry each of the blows.

All of a sudden the top of Peter's shield shot inward, ringing against his helm. Peter stepped back in surprise, noting the projectile weapon in the hand of his left opponent. He nodded to himself as he quickly stepped back into the fray. The left opponent had fired his projectile at the top of the shield, hoping to distract him. He must be more careful, the projectile weapons of this day were far more powerful than the ones from his era.

Deciding it was time to go on the offensive, Peter took a wide step forward while simultaneously swinging his arms out to the sides. As he had hoped, the opponent on the left was knocked back by the shield bash, though the one on the right had managed to block his sword strike, though Peter was gratified to see that the block had pushed the warrior back several steps.

In a maneuver he had seen on Garrett's picture box, Peter continued his forward stride, angling to the left. Two steps later he was turning sharply toward the wall on the left side. Leaping up, he planted his left foot against the wall to give himself the leverage to pivot his body around. He used his momentum to twist his torso around and plant his right foot higher against the wall. Pushing off with his right foot he twisted the rest of the way around, leaping from the wall toward the left attacker who had recovered from the shield bash and was moving forward again.

Eyes widening as he realized his peril, the first attacker brought his sword up in a vain attempt to block the strike. As four hundred pounds of combined knight and armor crashed down from almost five feet in the air, the downward swinging broad sword had the force of a jackhammer. The man's sword shattered an instant before his skull did the same.

Landing with surprising ease for such a large man, Peter used the impact to crouch down and leap forward again, his shield leading. Unfortunately, he had not yet moved two steps when something struck his helmet like the hind kick of a draft horse.

The force of the blow stopped him dead in his tracks and the well-armored knight looked up to see two more assailants in the mouth of the alley. One of whom had one of the larger projectile weapons and who was obviously taking aim at his head again.

Peter brought up his shield to block the impact but the force was so strong it knocked his shield back into his helmet, ringing it like a gong. Peter staggered back momentarily, his ears ringing. The second attacker took that opportunity to slide around to the right, and with a flick of his sword, to cut the chin strap on Peter's helmet.

The man spun as he crossed around to Peter's right, his left arm coming up with another projectile weapon, firing it at an upward angle at Peter's helm. Before Peter could react, his helmet had flown up off of his head to crash to the pavement ahead.

Peter knew he was in trouble. He no longer had a helmet and the man at the end of the alley was too far away to reach before he fired another shot. Lifting his shield to the level of his eyes, the knight charged forward anyway.

The man raised the weapon to his shoulder again, taking aim, when all of a sudden a flaming sword erupted from the man's chest. His partner looked over in shock for a moment before drawing his own blade. With an almost negligent flip, the impaled attacker was flung off of the blade and into the wall of the alley. And there before him was a golden warrior. A woman armored in gold plate mail and glowing like the dawning sun.

Peter was momentarily dumbfounded. Who was this goddess of battle, and where did she come from? He slid to a halt as she turned to engage the other attacker. Peter blinked as he saw the shimmering wings of golden light coming from her shoulder blades.

But before he could marvel any longer, instinct took over and he pivoted on his right foot, sweeping his sword around to parry the blow aimed at him by the second attacker coming up from behind. Their exchange didn't last long. Without his partner to keep Peter's shield occupied, the man was unable to land a single blow anywhere but the shield. Peter on the other hand was able to use his sword to full effect, and in a final, powerful swing, removed the man's left arm at the shoulder.

The man screamed in pain and dropped the sword as his legs gave out. Crumpling to the ground on his back, he still had enough presence of mind to draw his projectile weapon and fire off two shots. The first glanced off of Peter's shield harmlessly, but the second grazed up his cheek, barely missing his eye. With a cry of rage Peter took a single step forward and brought the bottom edge of his shield down onto the man's neck with a crunch of finality.

Remembering the final attacker, Peter spun around just in time to see the golden-haired warrior rising from a crouch, ducking under a swing aimed at her head. Her sword swept upwards in a familiar strike. Pivoting as she rose, her blade bit deeply into the man's left hip, continuing up through the ribcage and out again at the shoulder. However, her movement did not stop there, as she used her momentum to leap upwards in a spin.

As she came back down from her spin, her two-handed great-sword struck again, this time biting into the man's left shoulder and continuing through his right hip. The golden goddess landed lightly on her feet, her sword snapping down to the side to stop precisely at her side, the point a fraction of an inch from the ground.

The remains of the man tumbled to the ground as they stood there motionless, listening for any other sounds in the alley. After a moment, she turned and walked toward him. He stayed frozen at her approach, not knowing the proper form of address for a goddess. Sheathing her sword at her back, she extended an arm.

"Well met," the angelic voice said, "I am Tammarion." Peter quickly wiped his sword clean on his cloak and sheathed it. Reaching out to clasp her arm in a traditional greeting he smiled.

"I am Peter, Knight of the Tower," he proclaimed. Peter was taken aback however, when a single delicate eyebrow raised in an all too familiar gesture.

"You are wounded, knight of the tower," the warrior maid stated, glancing at his face. Before he could react, her hand raised to touch his face with the gentleness of a butterfly alighting on a leaf. Peter felt a warmth in his face and looked at her in awe. "There, a healing, so that you are fit for battle again."

"I thank thee, milady…" Peter began, but she interrupted.

"I have healed the wound only," she said her voice cooling, "but I have left the scar." Peter was confused.

"Why then did you not complete the healing?" he asked.

"To remind you," she replied, her eyebrow arching again. "I observed your fight, Knight of the Tower, before I intervened. You were arrogant, and cocky. You fought like you believed yourself invincible. And yet, as we have observed, you are not." Tammarion looked sternly into his eyes. "You are not the only one in that body. There are others you are oath-bound to protect. Others who have no ability to protect themselves. How then will you protect them, Knight of the Tower, if you are dead of your own arrogance?"

Breaking his gaze, she walked over toward his fallen helmet. Peter stood there as though he had been poleaxed. She was right. He had been arrogant; too confident in his own skills to take the proper precautions. She returned, holding something in each hand. She lifted one hand which held the weapon that had wounded him.

"What is this?" she asked, her voice cold and firm as an instructor teaching younglings.

"A projectile weapon of this age," Peter began, but she was already shaking her head.

"It is a gun," she stated simply. "Do you no longer learn the weapons of your enemies? Are you that far gone into conceit that you believe their weapons to be beneath you?"

Spinning the weapon in her hand, she glared at him. In an instant, the spinning weapon had frozen and she had discharged eight shots into his breastplate in the space of a heartbeat. Glancing down in shock, he saw each had left a tiny dent. He blinked for a moment as he realized that the dents formed the image of a smiling face. He looked back up to see her face relaxed, almost smiling, though still stern.

"Yes, your armor is proof against a weaker gun like this one," she assured him. "However, it is not proof against the larger, more powerful guns." Reaching out, she handed him the now empty weapon. "Learn it, use it," she advised him. "You can only defend against things you know, and you are not more powerful than all of them, Knight of the Tower." Peter looked down, abashed. Suddenly he felt her feather light touch on his cheek again, and lifted his head. The golden goddess was smiling at him.

"Do not despair," she said to him with a smile. "Remember that humility is a virtue as well. And remember that all good can be distilled down to a single phrase. Be kind."

With that, she opened her arms and began to transform back down to the sweet grandmother with the sparkling eyes. In an instant, his head was ringing again. Peter stumbled back a step as he realized the sweet little grandmother had slapped him!

"What the hell do you think you were doing?!" Ann yelled at him. "Tammarion may be all sweetness and light and forgiveness, but I am the momma bear!" Peter took another step back in the face of her wrath. "I said, what do you think you were doing?! You could have been hurt; you were hurt. You could have been killed! Don't you understand?" Peter was again shocked when suddenly her arms were around his neck and she was crying into his shoulder.

"You're like my sons and grandson all rolled into one," Ann sobbed. "I don't think I could survive it if you died! I've never had a real family before. You are my family, you big lummox!"

Finally, Peter understood. He had not known that Ann had no other family. And he had not realized she saw them as her son. With more gentleness than he had ever shown another, the powerful knight wrapped his arms gently around her and held her, allowing the sadness and fear to be washed away with her tears. After several minutes, her tears slowed and she pulled back to look at him.

"Dear lady, I am deeply sorrowful for the recklessness of my actions. I do indeed have a charge to protect, and I have served him ill as well." Peter looked into her reddened eyes. "Can you forgive me my mistakes with the promise that I shall mend them?"

"Of course," Ann smiled, still a bit sad. "I love you like my own son. How could I not forgive you?"

"I know that you love Garrett, and I shall work harder to protect him," Peter said gently. Ann laughed softly.

"Not just Garrett," she said with a smile. "All of you. I feel that way about each of you."

"Even Derrick?" Peter said surprised. Ann slapped him on his armored shoulder. "Yes, even Derrick. I don't care that the two of you fight like cats and dogs. I agree with everything Phil said about all of you earlier.

Even Derrick is essentially good at heart." Peter smiled.

"I will ensure that he does not know you said that," Peter replied. Ann just shook her head at him and gave him another hug. "Garrett would like to return now," Peter said after a moment. Ann nodded and pulled back.

Closing his eyes, Peter looked around for Garrett and quickly switched places with him.

Garrett opened his eyes to see Ann, tears still on her face, smiling at him. Wrapping her up in a fierce hug, he whispered. "I love you too, Ann." She just hugged him even tighter.

After a few more minutes, and some nervous laughter, the pair made their way back to the car and pulled out. As they started down the street, they were both surprised to see several police cars racing past them, to screech to a stop near the alley.

"The guns," Garrett said, trying to remain calm. "Someone reported the gunfire."

"It's okay," Ann replied, once again calm and in control. "They don't know it was us, and we got out before they blocked everything off." Garrett nodded.

"Okay, you're right," he said with a sigh. "Next time though, we might not be so lucky. We also don't know if there was anyone else watching that didn't show themselves. I don't think there's anything I can do to disguise myself, but perhaps you should change into someone less noticeable." Ann nodded.

"You're right," she sighed. "As much as I hate it, you are right. Okay, hang on." Turning the car, she pulled into a nearby parking lot and parked in a stall at the far end of the lot. Closing her eyes briefly, her body began to shift. Garrett knew the moment he saw the shock of red hair who it was.

"There," Molly said with a grin, her Irish brogue in full swing. "How's that for a disguise?"

"Actually, I said someone less noticeable," Garrett replied with a chuckle. "Which description, I might point out, you do not fit."

"You don't think I can blend in?" Molly asked archly.

"No," Garrett said frankly, "I think you attract attention, no matter where you go." Molly just laughed.

"Och, perhaps you're right," she admitted. "But if we switch at each stop that might help, so it won't be that bad if I'm seen at the next one."

Garrett wasn't sure how accurate that was, since they were driving the same car to each location, but he was willing to give it a try. The next couple of stops went quickly. So quickly in fact that Molly didn't bother to change when they left each stop.

"You know," Garrett began, "I don't know if we're going to find the person we're looking for this way."

"Oh?" Molly replied, "Why do ya' say that?"

"Just a feeling," Garrett replied pulling out the blade. "This etching has a level of detail one would expect from a master artist, however it seems like it was mass produced. There are far more of them than a six-month timeframe could account for if they were etching them by hand." Molly nodded.

"That make sense," she said. "So what could mass produce etched blades with that level of precision?"

"I'm not sure," Garrett answered, "but probably something high-tech. Like a scanned image in the computer where a machine does all the work."

"Where would we find someone who has that kind of equipment?" Molly asked.

"I would have to look it up," Garrett replied. "A larger corporation probably. I don't think any of these small artistic shops would have the capacity to purchase that kind of equipment." Molly nodded again and turned the car down a side street.

"Where to now?" Garrett asked.

"Library," Molly answered with a smile. "That was the closest computer I could think of."

Within a few minutes, the pair had pulled up to the library and headed into the computer lab. Garrett had a library card, so they were able to reserve a computer quickly.

"So what do you think?" Garrett asked. "Industrial etching?"

"No," Molly replied, her brogue softening a bit, "I don't think they call it etching when it's done by a machine." she paused for a moment, thinking. Suddenly she snapped her fingers. "I know! Greybeard knows a lot about crafting and chemicals, he might know what it's called."

Without waiting for a response, she closed her eyes. Garrett quickly looked around to make sure no one was watching. Thankfully, the computer lab was completely empty. Within a few moments, she had transformed again into a spindly old man in grey robes. He tugged on his long beard as he opened his eyes.

"Now what?" he demanded imperiously.

"Good afternoon, Greybeard," Garrett said, trying to be polite.

"Yes, yes, dispense with the pleasantries." The old man waved a hand dismissively. "The girl said you had a question." Garrett nodded in acknowledgment.

"Yes, I do," Garrett replied. "I wanted to know about industrial etching. Or the ability to mass produce an image on a steel blade."

"Right, right," Greybeard said quickly, "The term you are looking for is chemical milling. They use acids to burn the image into the metal."

"That's it!" Garrett exclaimed excitedly. "Thank you!"

Garrett turned quickly back to the computer and began typing in his search terms. He barely noticed that Greybeard did not leave after answering the question, but watched his actions on the computer with interest. In moments he had the names of two local companies that did chemical milling. Grinning, he turned to Greybeard.

"So, are you coming?" Garrett asked.

"Of course not!" Greybeard said in a huff. "I have far better things to do!" And with that, he blinked and Ann was again sitting in the chair.

"Wow, that shift was fast," Garrett remarked.

"He does seem to be able to switch faster than the others," Ann replied. "I think he does some kind of teleportation switch to swap places with someone in the doorway. So it doesn't take the time to physically move, the other person is just there, in the doorway."

"That sounds very disorienting," Garrett said sympathetically.

"It certainly can be," Ann answered, shaking her head. "Especially if you were in the middle of doing something else. So, what did you find?" Garrett grinned again.

"I found two companies who do the chemical milling

that Greybeard talked about," Garrett said, pointing at the screen.

"Great!" Ann replied enthusiastically. "Let's get going!" Garrett grabbed a piece of scratch paper and wrote down the two addresses. The pair quickly exited the library and got back into the car, ready to start the next step of their search.

The first company was located just outside the city limits, which took them almost an hour to reach. The pair rode in comfortable silence, each lost in their own thoughts. Garrett kept thinking back to what Ann had said; that he was her only family. He had been touching the stone chair both during the fight and after it, so he had seen and heard everything.

He knew that he loved her dearly, she was his best friend. A friend whom he told literally everything since they attended group therapy together. He didn't know if he thought of her like a mother or not though.

His own mother had died in childbirth. His father had been largely absent, unable to deal with being a single parent. So, he really didn't know what having a father felt like either, for that matter. He had been fairly certain his father had blamed him for his mother's death. However, his father had died in a car accident over ten years ago, so he never had the chance to ask.

Glancing over at her, he smiled at her perpetually happy face. He almost never saw her angry or upset. She really was always looking for that silver lining. Garrett nodded to himself as he looked out the windshield again. Even if she wasn't an actual mother to him, Garrett thought, she acted enough like one to make little difference. Leaning over in the seat he bumped her shoulder with his, causing her to look over at him.

"Hey," Garrett said with a smile, "I just wanted to say thanks. I really appreciate how much you've done to help me, and are still doing to help me." Ann smiled, glancing back at the road. "I heard what you said to Peter," he continued, "and I may not know what a mother is supposed to be like, but you are my best friend, and I can't imagine doing this without you. Thank you."

"Of course," Ann replied with a smile. "I couldn't let you do this alone. You are my best friend too. I never had kids of my own, but I do have a sister, and I saw how she was with her kids. I got to see how much she loved them, and did everything in her power to care for them. I hope you don't mind that I sometimes think of you like a son. Like all of you are my sons." Ann stared at the road, blinking rapidly.

"I don't mind a bit," Garrett answered, wrapping an arm around her shoulders and giving her an awkward side hug from the passenger seat. They both laughed at that before settling back into the drive.

"Justin, however," Ann continued after a moment. "Justin, I want to spoil like a grandchild." Garrett laughed.

"And he loves his Nana Ann too!" Garrett said grinning at her. Ann laughed happily.

"So in that case," Ann said firmly, "we need to promise that both of us will do everything in our considerable powers to stay safe." Garrett nodded, sobering up at that.

"I promise," Garrett said seriously.

"Me too," said Ann. They rode in companionable silence for a few more minutes before pulling up in the parking lot of the first company. "Hey," Ann said turning to him, "be careful." Reaching out, she pulled him into a hug, squeezing tightly.

"I will," Garrett answered, hugging her back. "Promise."

After a few moments, he pulled back and got out of the car. Walking quickly in the front doors he looked around at the vaulted glass ceilings of the lobby before going up to the greeter's desk.

"May I help you?" the older gentleman sitting behind the desk asked.

"Yes, I wanted to talk to someone about an order," Garrett replied. "I needed to do some detailed work but in somewhat larger quantities.

"Well, you've come to the right place," the man said perking up a bit in his seat. "We do that kind of work all the time here."

"Great!" Garrett replied enthusiastically.

"Give me just a moment," he said, picking up a phone. "Mr. Jamison, you have a customer who would like to talk about an order." The man paused for a few moments listening. "Yes, sir. I'll send him right up." The man turned to Garrett and pointed back down the hallway. "Go down the hallway on my left and you'll see the elevators. Go on up to the third floor, Mr. Jamison will meet you there."

"Thank you very much," Garrett replied with a wave.

Walking over to the elevators he pushed the up button, trying to calm his nervousness. In less than a minute the doors opened and he headed up to the third floor. He was greeted at the door by a tall, slender man in a grey business suit, who held out his hand.

"Hello," the man said with a friendly smile. "I am Mr. Jamison, Director of Project Management."

"Garrett," he replied, realizing as he said it that he should have used a fake name. Oh well, in for a penny, in for a pound. "Garrett Castlemain."

"Good to meet you Mr. Castlemain," Jamison said amiably, taking Garrett's hand in a firm handshake. "Shall we go to my office to discuss your project?"

"Of course," Garrett said, making sure to note the location of the elevator as they went down the hall toward Mr. Jamison's office.

"Please sit down," Jamison said, gesturing to a leather chair on the near side of the room. Jamison walked around to sit behind a desk, glanced at his computer briefly, punched a few keys, and then turned back to Garrett. "So, Mr. Castlemain, what can we do for you?" Garrett froze, realizing he had not worked out his cover story beforehand. He blinked a few times, then shook his head.

"My apologies," Garrett said with a rueful smile. "My allergies sometimes make it a bit hard to hear clearly." Jamison smiled and nodded acceptingly. "So I'm am, uh, an instructor," Garrett said, thinking quickly. "I, uh, teach kendo." Garrett started to relax as a good cover story started to come to him. "And for my students, I wanted to gift them with a sword when they graduate out of the student ranks."

"Ah, yes!" Jamison said enthusiastically. "We can absolutely help you with that." Garrett hesitated at the man's unexpected enthusiasm before continuing.

"Yeah, uh," Garrett continued, "and I wanted to make it personal, you know? So I thought if the swords had something on them, like a face or something? Or a mask?"

"Of course," Jamison said his eyes wide with

excitement. "We have done masks before. I don't know about a face, but if you have a picture I can scan it in and take a look."

"Oh, um, right," Garrett fumbled again, "I, uh, forgot to bring the picture." Jamison calmed slightly, losing a bit of his enthusiasm.

"That's no problem," he said, still more enthusiastic than Garrett expected. "We can work with the photo and get you pricing when you come in again."

"Right, sure," Garrett replied, trying to pick up his train of thought. "So all you need is a photo, or a picture and you can scan it into your computer to be etched into something?"

"Of course!" Jamison replied perking up again, "It's that simple, and we can work on as many items as you like."

"Oh, good," Garrett said, trying to think of a fast way out of the building. "So, yeah. I'm going to go and get the photo, and uh, I will be back." Jamison frowned slightly.

"Of course, though I have to tell you," Jamison said leaning forward, "I will be out of the office for the rest of the afternoon. You may want to call my secretary and set up an appointment for tomorrow."

"Oh! Right! Of course," Garrett said, reaching out to take the business card that Jamison offered. "Thank you."

"And thank you, sir," Jamison said, a smile back on his face as he extended his hand again. Garrett shook it firmly as he stood. Turning, he went back to the elevator, wondering the entire way if Jamison had suspected he was lying.

Garrett made his way to the bottom floor without

incident. He raised a hand in farewell to the older gentleman behind the greeter desk and made his way out of the building and over to the car. Getting in quickly, he buckled up as Ann started the car and pulled out.

"Well?" Ann asked as they got back on the road.

"Umm, I don't know," Garrett answered sheepishly. "I forgot to think of a cover story and fumbled a lot when I talked to their project director." Ann shook her head, glancing over at him briefly.

"But can they do that kind of work?" Ann asked, getting right to the point.

"Yeah, they can," Garrett answered, "and he was very excited to do it." Ann just nodded.

"Okay, so now we check the other one," she said matter-of-factly.

Thankfully, the second shop was only a few miles away from the first. As they pulled up, Garrett noticed that this building was quite a bit more run down than the first one. The parking lot had grass and other weeds growing from the asphalt, the paint on the building was worn and chipping off, and the fence was badly in need of repair.

"Garrett," Ann said looking around. "I don't like the looks of this place."

"Neither do I," Garrett replied, "but we have to try, just in case." Ann nodded and parked in one of the nearby spots.

"I know I said this before," Ann said, "but this time I really mean it. Be careful."

"I will," Garrett said, giving her a smile.

As he exited the car, he looked around cautiously. Not seeing any immediate danger, he walked through the front doors and into the lobby. Immediately, he could tell that this building had been abandoned. The furniture was torn and dusty, the floor was covered in random papers, and one of the windows in the back of the lobby had been broken out. As he turned around to leave, he heard the sound that was starting to haunt his nightmares. The sound of a machine gun bolt being drawn back.

CHAPTER FOURTEEN

It was time.

The final stage of his glorious plan was about to be set into motion. And he was so excited he could almost kill someone. All his plans, all his traps, all his preparation had finally led to this moment. It was time to throw down the final bread crumb.

Standing quickly, he walked over to the door and flung it open. Outside were two of his regular men standing on either side of the doorway, and four dozen more standing in neat rows, two by two in the huge, cavernous room.

The men were deadly silent and still. Barely a flicker of breath emanated from them. They were perfect. His own mindless killing machines. It had taken months to program them properly. But he knew the way. Oh yes, he knew.

He knew how to break the body, so that the mind had no defense. How to go from one extreme to the other, so that both the body and mind were spinning and unable to focus. Hot, cold, pain, pleasure, gentle, hard, big, and small, each and every sensation carefully calculated to be disorienting, radically different than the last, until finally the mind broke under the strain.

And then, once it was clean and ready for programming, he trained them. He trained each of them to be killers. Merciless, without a hint of compassion to slow them down. Unstoppable killers, who would each give their own lives if it meant the kill would be successful.

Despite all of this, he had little hope of their success. The failures of the first two phases had shown him, had taught him, just how much he had underestimated Him. Not because of His own power, but he had underestimated His little friends. That was the answer. That was the key. It was the only thing that explained what he had learned. No one in His head could burn a body to ash. No one in His head could tame wild beasts. No one in His head could heal anyone other than themselves. No, it had to be His little friends. That was His hidden strength… and His gaping weakness.

"Each of you," he yelled, in a tone that was almost screeching, "Each of you has been trained, honed, perfected into my killing machines! You know what you've been trained for. You know who you've been trained for." He paused for a moment then, for dramatic effect. "But you are no longer going after that one!"

What was that?! A twitch! A movement?! How dare one of his great killers move at a dramatic time like this! With a scream of rage, he lunged at one of the pairs in front, grabbing a blade from the hip of the one on his right, and in an instant, slicing it across the neck of the man's partner on the left. So intent was he on his victim that he almost didn't notice the movement of the killer that he had just stolen a blade from.

A flicker out of the corner of his eye was all the

warning he had. Bringing his right arm up, still holding the bloody blade he managed to deflect the long knife of the still-living partner with his forearm. Pain erupted as the knife bit deeply into the muscle on its way across.

The entire room seemed to freeze, almost holding its breath in expectation. He looked down at the deep wound inflicted by the traitorous man. Looking back slowly at the man, he was gratified to see the shock of fear cross the man's face before the next pulse of pain hit him. A cry erupted from the pale lips; part pain, part rage, and completely insane.

Dropping the knife, the albino thrust his bare hands forward, fingertips first, into the chest of the man who had wounded him. The powerful strike pierced the skin, and the demented maniac wrapped each hand around a rib. With another cry of rage, he pulled his hands apart with superhuman strength. A crack echoed through the vast chamber, then another, then the unspeakable tearing sound of a body being ripped in two.

The crazed albino held his kill aloft, allowing the rain of blood to soak his purple hair before throwing the pieces in opposite directions. His eyes were wild, as if waiting, wanting the barest excuse to repeat the grizzly display.

The killers, however, did not move. Each of them stood stock still. Not even the flicker of an eyelash betrayed their reaction to two of their number being slaughtered before their eyes.

After several deep breaths to remind himself that if he killed all of them, there would be no one left to kill Him, he was able to continue with his instructions.

"I am not sending you after the freak you have been trained to kill," he yelled into the echoing chamber.

"You will first complete a different mission for me. You will target His friends. Each of them, one by one. Capture them if you can, kill them if you can't, but I want all of His allies eliminated before the next dawn!" Breathing heavily, the purple haired albino looked into each and every face in his kill squads. His burning eyes looking for any sign of weakness that must be culled out.

Raising his still bloody arms over his head he screamed. "KILL!"

"KILL!" Echoed from each pair of lips in the chamber.

He just threw back his head and laughed, a long, drawn-out, maniacal laughter. Oh no, these pliable idiots would never succeed in killing Him. But His friends were another matter entirely.

Garrett froze at the sound of the sliding bolt, but glanced with just his eyes down to the floor. Silently, he swore under his breath. He was still standing in the sunlight of the entryway. Derrick was not going to be able to help on this one. A quick blink showed him that everyone was nearby and ready to help. Slowly, he raised his hands and turned toward the sound of the bolt.

Garrett was surprised to see four men with various firearms and blades strapped all over their bodies. Each face painted in a different warrior mask from a different culture. They appeared to be in pairs, each pair standing a bit apart from the others.

The four men said nothing, though one nodded as though confirming something. All four of them brought their rifles up to their shoulders as Garrett thought furiously. Watching the fingers of the one who nodded he waited for the tell-tale twitching of the tendons in his hand. An instant before they pulled the trigger, Garrett blinked.

In that instant he shifted down to the much smaller form of Justin as all four shots went over his now much lower head. Justin crouched down as the body shifted again. The powerfully armored form of Peter completed the crouch raising his large shield in front of him to intercept the next volley of bullets.

Grinning ferociously, Peter came out of the crouch in a leap to his right side. Using his shield to intercept the bullets from the pair on the left he surprised all of them by not striking the pair to the right but instead diving between them as he twisted in midair to hit the ground on his back.

As his back slapped the ground with a metallic clang, he shifted again. Sean's arms were already up with his laser pistol in hand. Two quick shots eliminated the two attackers on the right as he slid out of the light from the front windows. Another quick shift, as a moment later bullets riddled the ground he had been laying on, but Derrick had already thinned out to a mist and moved deeper into the shadows.

Suddenly, the building was rocked by what sounded like an explosion outside. Glass shards peppered the two remaining attackers and they raised their arms to shield their faces. That instant was all that Derrick needed. Grabbing a dusty old couch by the leg in one hand and a torn chair in the other he hurled them at the attackers.

The pair looked back just in time to see the furniture before it impacted, lifting them both off of their feet as they were knocked backwards out of the light of the front windows. In less than a second, Derrick had moved with vampiric speed around the room and dispatched the last two attackers. Another explosion rocked the building and Derrick shifted again into the armored warrior.

Peter raced outside, not bothering with opening the front door as he smashed his way through with almost no resistance. He looked around just in time to see Greybeard diving with surprising agility behind a wall as a hail of bullets rained down where he was an instant before.

Looking around quickly, Peter noticed four piles of ash, which he assumed were former attackers, knowing Greybeard's penchant for fireballs. He counted six more, however, behind various forms of cover, opening fire in rounds to keep the spry old wizard pinned down.

Peter's first thought was to charge them. Make them attack him so that Greybeard could counterattack. However, he remembered what Tammarion had said regarding not underestimating his opponents.

Eyes quickly scanning the area, he spied a sapling nearby, still held up by being lashed to wooden poles. Moving quickly, he stepped over to the tree and with a mighty heave, ripped it from the ground. Grinning to himself, he leaned back and hurled the tree at one pair of attackers like a javelin.

Peter didn't stop to see if it landed, however, before he was charging toward Greybeard. He rounded the corner just as another spray of bullets riddled the ground behind him.

Greybeard was muttering and fumbling for something in his robes. Peter arrived just as he pulled out a small flask with an exclamation.

"Got it!" Greybeard said, pleased.

"What do you have there?" Peter asked.

"Potions!" Greybeard said sharply. Peter tried not to get angry with the crotchety old man.

"I can see that," Peter said with a bit of a growl in his voice. "What potions?" Greybeard looked closely at the one in his hand.

"Levitation," he replied, then he held up another hand, "and this one is invisibility."

"Excellent!" Peter exclaimed. "Then you can go invisible and fly over their heads to attack!"

"No, you fool!" Greybeard snapped, "I can only take one at a time, and I am trying to decide which one would be best."

"Do your potions work on other people?" Peter asked.

"No," Greybeard replied irritably, "they don't."

"Not even those like yourself?" Peter pressed. Greybeard paused for a moment.

"I don't know," he said reluctantly. "I've never tried."

"Well then," Peter replied with a grin. "I believe it is high time we make the attempt." Closing his eyes momentarily, he proposed his idea to the others.

"A highly logical and well thought out plan," Scan remarked in his perpetually calm tone. Peter was about to snap back at him, but again remembered Tammarion.

"Thank you," he said, trying to be polite. Sean raised an eyebrow, then nodded in acceptance.

"However," Sean continued, "I think that I would be better suited to use of the invisibility potion, since I am the only one with ranged weapon." Again, Peter started to snap at him, then paused for a moment to think. Even as agile as he was, with his well-made armor, he still made noise. And that nose would be heard even if he were invisible.

"Very well," Peter said reluctantly. "But do not hesitate to switch if you get into trouble." Sean again nodded as they switched places on the stone chair.

Sean opened his eyes to see Greybeard again digging around in the pockets of his robes.

"I am prepared," Sean started. "I believe that I should take the invisibility potion and move around behind them. I will lay down a distraction while you, having taken the levitation potion, can attack unexpectedly from above."

"Fine," Greybeard nodded. "That might actually work."

"And what is the precise duration of the potion's effects?" Sean inquired.

"It's not that precise, son," Greybeard advised him. "Magic is an art, not a science." Sean simply raised a single eyebrow, then extended his hand for the potion. "And what happens if this doesn't work, and you don't go invisible?" Greybeard asked.

"Then we will devise a new strategy," Sean replied calmly. Greybeard muttered under his breath at that, but handed over the potion anyway. "Now, to see if it works." Sean said calmly, removing the cap from the flask and drinking the potion in one long swig.

Handing the empty flask back to Greybeard, he waited calmly to see what the effects would be. After a few moments, he detected an oddly cool sensation flowing across his skin. Simultaneously, he noticed Greybeard's eyes widening.

"Well I'll be," Greybeard exclaimed excitedly. "It worked on you!"

"Indeed," Sean said in his usual calm tone. "I did not detect any difference in my own light refraction, however your reaction indicates you are detecting a difference. I would like to study this in more depth at some other time." Sean paused, getting back to the matter at hand. "I will now traverse the exterior of the building to approach the gunmen from behind. When you hear the sounds of the attack, you should partake of your potion, and join in when you are ready."

"Fine," Greybeard said. "With one slight change." Greybeard quickly uncapped the other flask and drank it down. "Don't know how long it's going to take to work, so I should be ready when you are."

Sean simply nodded and took off at a ground-eating pace around the building. Even with his current rate of speed, he calculated it would take him fifty-six point two seconds to circle the exterior of the building. He hoped the invisibility potion would last that long.

At precisely the fifty-five second mark, he slowed his pace to a careful creeping walk. Three point seven seconds later, he had taken up an advantageous position behind a large hardwood tree, and taken aim at two of the assailants.

Two quick shots eliminated their threat, however it

also attracted the attention of the other four, who turned and began firing in the vicinity of his shots.

Taking a quick glance around, Sean did not see any additional cover sufficient to his needs. Looking up he also determined that the branches were higher than the four point nine six meters of his maximum high-jump.

Taking out his scanner, he opened the display and determined that two of the four attackers were moving toward him as the other two laid down cover fire. Sean angled himself against the tree so as to give himself as much time as possible to react should the invisibility potion wear off suddenly.

Just then, his scanner lit up with a bright flash, indicating a sizeable discharge of electricity. Sean wondered if a power line had been hit, and after a glance at the screen to determine none of the attackers were vertical any longer, peeked around the tree.

What he saw before him was a very satisfied-looking wizard, hovering approximately fourteen point three meters in the air. His fingertips still crackling with electrical discharge. Sean raised an eyebrow as he stepped around the trunk.

"Fascinating," Sean said, approaching. In an instant, the old man's hands lifted at a strange angle and Sean stopped moving.

"Oh, right," Greybeard said, his arms lowering. "It's just you. The effects haven't worn off yet and you startled me!" he accused, but without much anger to back it.

"My apologies," Sean said, making no effort to hide the noise as he continued to walk forward. "I believe however, we have located our objective."

"What?" Greybeard asked, starting to float

downwards slowly.

"This location is well guarded," Sean explained. "That would tend to indicate a desire to remove or eliminate anyone else from ascertaining what activities are taking place here."

"You're probably right about that," Greybeard said, tugging gently on his long beard.

"However," Sean continued, "it is also obvious to me that our abilities are not conducive to clandestine activities. We will need to enlist some assistance to continue this line of investigation." Greybeard frowned.

"What did you have in mind?" he asked suspiciously.

"It occurred to me," Sean responded, "that our other three companions each have abilities that would make a clandestine entrance more feasible." Now Greybeard looked concerned.

"You want to involve the others in this war?" he asked softly.

"I see no other alternative," Sean replied, his voice as calm and collected as ever. "They have requested the right to participate, they possess skills that we do not, and they are the only ones either Garrett or Ann trust to tell what is going on. I think we must utilize their skills if we wish to succeed in this mission." Greybeard nodded, but his face was unhappy.

"All right," he said slowly, "but we have to find a way to keep them safe while they do this."

"I do not know how much aid we can give to that endeavor," Sean replied, "however, I am certainly willing to make the attempt."

"That's all we can do," Greybeard said sadly. "Though I would have wished we didn't have to involve them." Sean looked closely at him for a moment.

"Your compassion does you credit," Sean said, pleased with what he saw. "You do well at concealing it with your gruff demeanor." Greybeard's face screwed up as though he had swallowed something bitter.

"I don't mean to be such a grouch," he admitted. "It just hurts less if you don't let people too close."

"I understand your sentiment, though I do not agree with it," Sean answered. "I have observed that the reciprocation of affection has an overall enhancing effect on people. Whereas a lack thereof, has a profoundly opposite effect."

"Bah!" Greybeard said. "You keep your opinion, pointy-ears, and I'll keep mine." Sean nodded in acceptance, but noted the softening of the old man's features.

"Shall we return to report our progress?" Sean inquired.

"Return where?" Greybeard asked, starting to move toward the miraculously undamaged car.

"Garrett's house," Sean answered. "In order to invite the others over to plan our next steps." Sean paused for a moment, taking in the undamaged vehicle. "Inquiry; how did you manage to engage that many armed opponents and not damage Katie's vehicle?" Greybeard laughed.

"Molly," he answered. "She didn't like sitting in the car and waiting, so she got out and started to follow Garrett to the door. That's when they attacked. Winged her in the arm, too, before I managed to teleport her out. She's all right, it is barely more than a scratch."

"Indeed," Sean replied. "I am pleased that she is not seriously hurt."

"Well, once I got her out I cast a shield spell to

deflect the bullets. Then I started shooting back," Greybeard said smugly. "Of course, what I shoot has a bit more of a bang than little bullets." Greybeard grinned fiercely. "Didn't take them long to go for cover and call in reinforcements."

"So we observed," Sean replied. "Your assistance has been appreciated. If it is acceptable to you, I shall drive the vehicle while one of you makes contact with the others."

Greybeard nodded again before disappearing. In his place stood Ann, who wiped her mouth before looking around quickly.

"I heard," she said, pulling out the keys and handing them to Sean. "I'll call, you drive."

CHAPTER FIFTEEN

An hour later, the five friends had all crowded around the television in Garrett's tiny living room. As he queued up the appropriate episode, he also tried to explain what had happened to them as they went searching for the origin of the clown-faced blades.

The group was silent as he told them about the artist, the sniper attack and the assassins. He quickly glossed over the part where Peter had been chewed out by an angel, and instead jumped quickly to their encounter at the abandoned building.

"How did you trade places so fast?" Katie asked as he finished the story.

"Well, we all stood around the stone chair and just jumped in and out as quickly as we could. Peter and Derrick helped a lot in moving people faster." Garrett said, finally finding the season he was looking for.

"Stone chair?" Asked Phil.

"Yeah, the control chair," Garrett began. "Wait, you don't have a chair either, do you?"

"Nope," said Phil. "I've got a control stick, though. Kind of like a joystick from one of the old Atari games."

"Wow," Garrett replied, "that must make things

interesting when you switch."

"Not really," said Phil, shrugging. "Since most of my alters are so small, I often don't see them come up. I just know one minute I am holding the joystick and the next I'm opening my eyes on the ground and the joystick is just sitting there on the table, waiting for me to take it again."

"I used to have that a lot," Ann chimed in. "I would go to an empty place when someone else took control. I would have no memory of the passage of time or what had happened while someone else was up. One minute I would be one place, then I would blink and be somewhere else, anywhere from five minutes to five years later."

"Five years?" asked Katie in surprise. Ann just nodded.

"There was a period in my early twenties where there was a five-year gap in my memory. I had no idea what I did during those five years, and I had to fake my way through conversations until I could get the gist of what had happened and what they were talking about," Ann said, her voice calm.

"That sounds terrifying," Katie said.

"It was," Ann agreed, "but I was familiar with losing time by then, so I was pretty good at faking my way through conversations while I figured things out."

"Still happen now?" Susan asked, her thick Slavic accent giving everyone pause to make sure they understood.

"No," Ann answered with a smile. "Now we work together as a community, and I don't get pushed to the empty place when someone else wants control for a bit. Which also means I can usually watch from the doorway to see what is going on. It makes it much easier to keep up when I switch back again."

"Ah, yes," Susan replied. "Same for me. I have window. Someone want control, they come to window. I can see through them though, to see through window."

"See through them?" Garrett asked, intrigued. Susan nodded.

"Yes, all ghosts," she replied. "Can see through them, like shadows."

"You know, I don't think I've ever seen you switch," Garrett said musingly. "Not since the Dreaming hit anyway."

"Of course," Susan replied with a grin. "No one can see them. All ghosts." The group laughed for a minute, each of them feeling greater camaraderie in this band of misfits than most of them had ever felt in their lives.

"What about you, Katie?" Ann asked. "What does your inner world look like?"

"It's a spotlight," Katie said softly. "Whoever has the spotlight gets the attention and has control."

"That makes sense," Garrett said. "Especially with most of your alters being small animals, they would tend to want to avoid attention, and hence the spotlight." Katie nodded with a smile.

"Well, are we all ready to see what these lunatics have in store for us next?" Garrett asked flippantly. The group just nodded and crowded in around the couch and armchair. Ann and Garrett sat on the floor, with the rest taking the seats.

"Now remember, this is the third episode in the story arc," Garrett said as the television queued up the streaming video service. "We have all seen what happened in the first two. First lone gunmen shoot up public places, forcing the hero to try to be everywhere at once. Then mobs of thugs roam the streets, forcing the hero to fight groups of them to exhaust him. Then he gets this." With that Garrett pushed play.

The episode opened quickly enough, with the villain laughing about his master plan. Garrett's eyes widened in recognition as the villain sent out pairs of assassins to try to kill or wound the hero. He quickly realized that's where the pairs of well-armed fighters were coming from.

As the scene blinked briefly indicating where a commercial break would have been when this showed on a regular television station, Garrett wondered where the story would end given that only ten minutes remained of the episode. He frowned at the thought and watched with even greater intensity.

"Fine!" the cartoon villain yelled. "If you morons can't kill him, then you'll just have to kill his friends!" Garrett's eyes widened in horror as he quickly glanced around at his own friends sitting in his living room.

Just then, he heard a crash coming from his kitchen. Garrett surged to his feet as the knight quickly took over.

Peter didn't bother running around the couch, but in a standing broad jump that would have been impressive even without the full suit of armor, he leapt over the couch, occupants and all. As he landed on the other side, he jostled his shield on his arm making sure it was secure. It always was.

In three steps, he had entered the kitchen in time to

see two of the black-clad, painted assassins rise, guns pointed his way.

With a roar, he angled his shield in front of him and charged the pair. He slammed into them as their bullets ricocheted off of his shield, driving them back against the wall. He was gratified to hear one scream as the attacker on his right fell back out of the window and down to the ground below. The one on the left grunted to the cracking of ribs as he hit the wall, his back slamming against the window frame.

Whipping his shield back, he grabbed the slumping form with his right hand and flung him back out of the window so hard, he flew across the alley to slam against the wall of the neighboring apartment building. Just then, another crash sounded from what Peter thought was the bedroom. Whirling, he charged back out of the kitchen, wondering if he would be in time.

With a smile, he saw that he had little to fear. Tammarion had already moved to intercept the two attackers coming from the bedroom. Peter grinned at their lack of tactical expertise. The pair had attempted to charge through the door one right after the other, which of course lined them up perfectly for Tammarion's forward thrust. She had easily spitted them both on the blade of her great-sword, and was pushing them off with an armor-clad boot.

Peter looked around to make sure he didn't lose track of where the civilians were this time, and froze in shock. All three of the non-combatants were gone. He didn't see any of them. He was just about to ask Tammarion about it when the front door of the apartment burst open in a shower of splintered remains.

Peter instinctively raised his shield to deflect the tiny

projectiles. As he lowered his shield again, he noted a couple of tiny cuts on Tammarion's face from the blast, since she had no shield to protect her. Thankfully, her armor was in perfect condition, so there was little risk of harm from the door shards.

One of the attackers had already made it through the doorway and was moving into the living room, with the second coming close on his heels. With a quick nod to Tammarion to indicate she should take the one in the doorway, Peter took three great strides toward the attacker, making his way around the couches.

Remembering one of the cartoons that Justin liked so much, Peter pulled his shield off of his arm. The attacker froze for a moment in confusion, giving Peter all the time he needed to fling his shield edgewise at the stunned man. The resounding clang of the edge of the steel shield striking the man in the forehead was almost as satisfying as watching the bone crumple around the impact and the sight of the man flying backwards to strike the far wall.

Peter frowned for a moment as his shield simply dropped to the floor after the impact, rather than bouncing back to him. That was not what he remembered from Justin's show.

He glanced back to Tammarion in time to see her deflecting projectiles with the bracers on her wrists. In two more strides she had come within range of her attacker. The man swung his rifle at her like a bat, but the angel blocked the strike on her left bracer. A resounding clang echoed through the room and the weapon itself broke into three pieces.

Stepping back, Tammarion lifted her leg, and with a snap, slammed her foot into the man's chest. The push-kick knocked him back out of the doorway and into the hallway beyond. Following the man out with a grim expression, Tammarion left no doubt as to the man's eventual fate. Faintly, the knight heard a voice in his head commenting about how her usage of her bracers was reminiscent of another warrior from popular fiction.

Moving quickly around the couch, he picked up and moved a dining chair to the side in order to get to his shield, swatting absently at a moth. As he reached down, he paused for a moment. There was a small, white and brown rabbit standing on his shield. He quickly shooed the animal off and rose, strapping his shield back on his arm.

No sooner had he secured it then a hail of projectiles punched through the thin outer wall of the apartment, and rang against his shield and armor. The tiny missiles were entering wildly, indicating that the shooter did not know where they were, but was trying to cover the entire room. He risked a glance back over to Tammarion again, only to see she had remained in the air, but moved her body into a horizontal position so as to remain above the hail of bullets.

Suddenly the bullets stopped, and Peter lowered his shield, turning to the doorway. He jumped back in alarm however as a strange figure hovered in front of him. It looked like some kind of shadow, but was floating in the air independently of any person to generate it. Muttering a curse about dark magics, Peter drew his sword preparing to do battle with the shade.

Just then, he felt something striking his helm, almost like knocking. Glancing to the side, he realized it was internal, not external and closed his eyes. Sean stood by the chair, pulling his hand back from his knocking on the knight's helm.

"My apologies for the method of garnering your attention," Sean began. "However, it was imperative that you discontinue your attack."

"Why?" Peter asked angrily.

"Because the entity you were preparing to attack is actually Susan," Sean replied calmly. "Or rather, one of Susan's alters."

Peter paused for a moment, remembering the conversation they had about the various alters of Garrett's friends. Peter hadn't paid a great deal of attention to those who did not have some form of combat capability. He realized, however, that Tammarion's advice had included this knowledge as well. He had not remembered that the other three friends had non-combat forms that were excellent at keeping concealed. He grunted at Sean to hide his irritation at himself before opening his eyes again.

Nodding briefly to the shade, he quickly stepped around it and made his way to the door. However, his brief moment of distraction had been enough time for Greybeard to have taken over for Tammarion. Peter caught a glimpse of grey robes flapping out of the doorway, and heard a shouted word in some other language as he strode forward.

Suddenly, his skin began to tingle and his muscles started twitching. Upon hearing the screams of the men out in the hallway, Peter allowed himself another grim smile. Greybeard had used his lightning on them.

Quickly poking his head out of the doorway, he saw the smoldering bodies of two more attackers and Greybeard standing near the stairs with a triumphant grin on his face. His joy was short-lived, however, as more small missiles riddled the stairwell, one of them striking the old man in the leg. Greybeard cried out in pain, stumbling backwards toward the doorway.

"Get back inside," Peter roared, striding forward to protect the mage with his shield. Hearing another voice in his mind, Peter nodded. Stepping back, he changed again.

Derrick was angry. It was enough that these inconsequential mortals had threatened him, but now they had injured one of the few that they could call friend. He needed to feed, and in a rare moment of rage, he did not want to feed on blood sweetened by the rush of pleasure, but on blood soured by fear. It was time to make them afraid.

Striding purposefully out of the apartment, he glanced down the hallway as the image of a steel wall transforming out of nothing covered the door and front wall of the apartment at the end of the hall. Derrick shook his head grimly. It would take more than the illusion of a steel wall to stop these fanatics.

With two quick strides, he leapt up and over the guardrail that surrounded the stairwell. As he cleared the rail, he shifted his shape into that of a very large bat and began circling downward. There, one floor down, he could see the men with the machine guns. Tucking his wings in, he dove toward them.

The hail of bullets that struck him were little more than an inconvenience. Apparently they had not planned on facing him, since the bullets were all made of lead, and not silver. Angling toward one of the men, he shifted shape again an instant before impact. Riding the man down to the floor, he bit savagely into the man's unprotected throat.

This was no gentle bloodletting; this was a frenzied feeding. Derrick drank deeply as the blood pumped out of the ragged tear in the man's neck. He allowed himself a few more moments to feed before lifting his gore-drenched face toward the other shooter.

The man, who had just started to overcome his surprise and lift his weapon froze in place. Confronted with a demonic visage that looked like death itself had come to claim them, he was frozen in his tracks. Derrick wasted no time leaping up, and with a quick wrench, breaking the man's neck. Biting deeply, he took a long draught of the precious life-giving fluid before dropping the limp body to the ground.

As the fresh blood rushed through his body, his senses heightened and the vampire paused to listen. Voices, a lot of voices coming from just outside the apartment building. Moving over to one of the windows, he looked down at the street below.

Just outside the door was a large mob of people, dressed in black with painted faces and looking like they were ready for trouble. The size of the group gave him pause, however. It was easily twice as large as the gang that had met their end on this very street.

Leaping back over the bannister, he shifted form again into a large bat and flew back up to his own floor. Shifting back into his vampiric form as he landed, Derrick strode back through the doorway only to freeze in his tracks, the tip of a very sharp-looking great-sword at his throat.

"Are you under control?" Tammarion asked curtly,

her sword never wavering.

Realizing he still had a great deal of the vampire face showing, he nodded and took a deep breath. Willing himself to calm down, he felt his face resume a more human appearance.

"I am," he replied smoothly. With a brisk nod, Tammarion sheathed her sword along her back again.

"When your behavior became more bestial, I grew concerned you had lost control again and would pose a threat." Tammarion answered his unasked question.

Derrick simply nodded and entered the apartment. His sharp eyes noted the fluffy rabbit hiding behind the couch, the moth-winged fairy in the corner, and the shadow moving on its own along the wall. Good, he thought to himself; no casualties.

"There is a large group of men, whom I believe intend us harm, gathering outside the building." Derrick informed the unusual group.

"How many?" Tammarion asked.

"At least three dozen, perhaps four," Derrick replied, his accent thick with frustration.

"Too many for us to battle," Tammarion thought out loud.

"Not and come out unscathed," Derrick replied to the rhetorical statement. Glancing back over to the angelic warrior, his eyes narrowed briefly. "How much can those wings of yours carry?" he asked. Tammarion shook her head.

"Not much more than my weight," she replied.

"How about the weight of a bunny, fairy, and ghost?" he asked nodding to the corner.

"Of course," she replied, "but where will you be?"

"Creating a distraction," Derrick replied, his face

shifting back into its more feral form. Tammarion looked at him for a moment then nodded again. She quickly reached down and picked up the fluffy rabbit, and gestured to the fairy.

"Come, you will be safe in my gauntlet," she stated, shifting the golden glove on her arm to allow enough space for the tiny body to fit inside. Once the moth-winged man had settled in, she turned to the ghost. "I don't know how the wind from my wings will affect you. Can you grasp around my neck from behind? On my back you will experience the least amount of wind from my wings." The shade seemed to detach itself from the wall and drift over to the golden-haired angel. Tammarion gasped softly as the shadowy arms wrapped around her.

"Is there a problem?" Derrick asked at her reaction.

"No," Tammarion replied, "it's just cold where the shadow touches."

"Well then," Derrick said with an aggressive-looking grin, "time for me to make a distraction." Tammarion again gave him a long look.

"Be careful," she said.

"My dear lady," Derrick responded, "careful is the last thing I intend to be." Throwing her one last wolfish grin, he dashed out the door and into the stairwell. Trusting that the angel would get the rest of them out safely, Derrick dove for the window and crashed through.

Allowing himself to slip into the darkest parts of his bloodlust, Derrick was pleased to see the looks of shock and fear on the faces of the men below him. Shifting into the form of a wolf, he struck the center of the group, claws and teeth flashing.

Reaching deeply into his mind, he tapped into the swirling tornado of anger and rage he called the maelstrom. A red haze covered his vision as his world narrowed down to a single word. Kill.

To an outsider, it would have appeared as though an entire pack of wolves had struck the mob. The wolf was everywhere, teeth tearing at throats, claws raking at the soft tissue of the belly. There was no hesitation, no pause to devour, the wolf went from one kill to another without slowing. The raging animal had dropped a half dozen before the rest of the crowd had even been able to react.

Angrily, they attempted to restrain the best, but to little avail. As soon as one hand had grasped a leg, the hand was abruptly severed by the unnaturally sharp teeth of the beast. As another grabbed at the muzzle to contain the deadly fangs, claws far sharper than nature had ever created raked bloody furrows in the grasping arms. The wolf twisted and wrenched its body around, attempting to strike as many of the attackers as possible. Red eyes blazed as the wolf fought with a savage fury that surpassed anything found in reality.

Six more had fallen before they realized that they would not be able to restrain the raging animal. Drawing their guns, they began to open fire. The wolf shrugged off the impact of the lead bullets without slowing. Their companions, however, were not as fortunate, and several more men dropped, riddled with bullets as each shooter tried to zero in on the rapidly moving form of the wolf. Realizing their danger, several individuals started to break away from the group, trying to escape.

Everyone froze, however, when the crack of a rifle shot echoed in the street as one of the deserters dropped in his tracks. A second black-clad individual took a step away from the crowd, but he too dropped to the sound of another rifle shot.

Reluctantly, the others who had tried to run turned back to the raging form of the dusky wolf, only to see more of their companions bleeding on the ground. The wolf still twisting and spinning, looking for a target.

"Tackle him!" a strong voice rang out across the empty street.

With a quick glance at each other and a shrug, several of the men dove for the beast. His lupine body twisting, the dark grey form of the wolf managed to lock his jaws on the first of the men who leapt at him. Unfortunately, the group already had momentum, and the body of their now dead companion shielded them from the claws and teeth of the wolf. Snapping and writhing, the wolf tried to find something to bite, thrashing under the pile of men trying to break free.

"Hold him still!" the voice rang out again.

The crowd parted to reveal another pair of painted assassins, rifles held in front of them. The wolf thrashed even harder, his sensitive nose picking up the scent of silver as the men approached. Lifting his head, the wolf howled into the sky. The haunting sound echoing against the tall buildings of the deserted street.

The men froze in surprise as the faint image of huge, ancient trees began to appear all over the street. Everyone looked around for the source of the dream that was creating the trees.

Unable to locate the dreamer that was causing the trees to appear, the two men continued to approach the pile of men on top of the now calm wolf. As the man in front chambered another round into his rifle, the wolf just snarled up at him. The man's eyes narrowed grimly as he brought the rifle up to his shoulder, ready to end the threat once and for all. He looked up quickly, however, at the sound of a car engine revving.

That one glance was all he saw as a blue-green car with a shock of red hair flying out of the window came racing out of the alleyway and slammed into both riflemen and several of the other attackers as it sped down the street. The shock of watching the bodies of their comrades spinning into the air was just the distraction that Derrick needed.

Twisting his body around, he managed to get his paws under him and heaved. The pile of men shifted just enough for him to slip out from under them, and in the confusion of bodies raining down, he raced to follow the speeding car.

CHAPTER SIXTEEN

A short time later, the five friends again sat at the coffee shop to talk about what they were going to do next. The group, however, was unusually silent, each of them looking more at their drinks than each other. Each of them had seen the video and knew that all of their lives were in danger.

"You should all get out of the city," Ann finally said, breaking the silence.

"We can't do that," replied Phil. "We won't leave you to face this alone."

"But Phil, all of your lives are in danger," Ann said emphatically.

"So are yours," he replied firmly.

"Yes, but we are able to fight back," Ann said sadly. "None of you have any alters that can fight them."

"Then perhaps we need to do something other than fight," Katie spoke up softly.

"Like what?" Garrett asked. Katie was quiet for a moment as she gathered her thoughts.

"Like doing what we talked about," she answered. "Like sneaking in and finding out who is behind all of this."

"But that puts you at even more risk!" Ann said in frustration.

"We know risk," Susan spoke up. "We're all at risk, anyway. This way, we can help."

"By getting killed?!" Ann answered, her voice raising.

"No," Phil replied, trying to calm her, "by not being where they want us to be. By being quiet, and sneaky, and hiding where they would never expect us to be." Garrett looked over at Ann.

"He does have a point," he said with a shrug. "If the bulk of their people are out looking for us, then their own headquarters may actually have fewer people inside." Ann crossed her arms and scowled.

"Possibly," she said grumpily, "but I still think it's too much risk."

"Don't worry," Susan said, putting a hand on Ann's arm. "We protect each other."

"Fine, but one of us should go with you!" Ann said firmly.

"You don't have a stealth form," Phil said with a small smile.

"Garrett does!" Ann replied. "Derrick can shift into animals, or even mist."

"That's true," Garrett replied. "I should go with you, in case there are problems." The group nodded reluctantly.

"But you are the one they are after," Phil said after a moment.

"They're after all of us now," Garrett said, shaking his head.

"Well, what about me?" Ann said, folding her arms and sitting back.

"You get to drive the getaway car," Garrett answered

with a smile. "Molly really likes to do that, apparently." The friends shared a brief laugh at that. The memory of the fiery-haired woman driving Katie's little car like some kind of violent NASCAR driver making all of them smile.

"Fine," Ann grumped, "but if I hear anything that makes me think you guys are in trouble, I'm coming in guns blazing!"

"I didn't think you had any alters with guns," Garrett teased. Ann just stuck her tongue out at him, causing the group to laugh again.

"All right, but we should wait till morning before we go in," Ann said, trying to calm her frustration. "These guys seem to be more active at night."

"Agreed," Garrett replied, "but I don't think we should split up. We could be picked off too easily one by one. Together we will be able to hold off any other attackers." The group nodded, then fell into silence as they tried to think of a place they could all go. After a moment Ann spoke up.

"You can all stay at my place," she said with a small smile. The group turned to her in surprise. "I have a small house near the edge of town. You'd all be on couches and air mattresses but I think you would all fit."

With murmurs of thanks, the friends finished off their drinks and stood up, heading for the door. They all waved at the barista behind the counter, but none of them were surprised when she didn't take her eyes off of the shirtless Latin guitarist playing a love song for her from one of the tables. It looked like too good a dream to interrupt.

The friends slowed a bit, however, as they approached Katie's car. The deep dents in the front fender reminding them of just how dangerous this was. They had been able to get the blood off of it at a self-serve car wash, but the dents would be harder to repair. It was a tight squeeze, but they all managed to fit into the small car. No one said anything as they headed out to Ann's place, each of them wondering if there was anywhere they would be safe.

The group began to relax as they turned in to Ann's neighborhood a short time later. It was a quiet little suburb, with lots of family houses and small children playing in the yards. People were smiling and laughing, playing and working in what seemed like the most normal-looking neighborhood most of the friends had ever seen.

As they pulled up in front of Ann's house, the friends couldn't help but smile. Every inch of the one-story cottage exuded a warm, welcoming air. The lawn was well kept, and there was a large flower garden under the windows facing the street. Even the happy lawn gnome in the front yard seemed to fit the warm, welcoming air of the place.

Ann smiled as she bustled up to the front door and unlocked it, gesturing them all inside. They slowly made their way into the house, still rubbernecking around to take in this unexpected oasis of peace and calm.

The interior was no different, from the flower print couch, to the brick fireplace along the side wall. Between the sofa and the fireplace was a triangular curio cabinet filled with what looked like tiny porcelain and glass lady bugs. A small upright piano stood along the opposite wall, a thin book of music lying open on the stand. As they all made their way inside, Phil started looking around in confusion.

"What's wrong?" Ann asked.

"Where's your TV?" Phil replied, curious. Ann simply laughed.

"Oh, I have one, I just don't keep it in the living room." she replied with a twinkle in her eye. "The TV is in my room. This room is for spending time with people."

"Oh!" Phil answered, surprised. "Well, that makes sense."

His voice trailed off as he tried to think of things people could do together other than watch television. Katie smiled and slid her arm around Phil's. Phil smiled as he looked down at her, patting her hand where it rested on his right arm. Katie leaned her head against his arm and sighed softly in contentment. Ann grinned as she turned to show the group the rest of the house.

"Over here is the kitchen," she said, passing by it on the way to the hall. Susan looked intrigued when she saw an aebleskiver pan hanging over the stove.

"You make aebleskivers?" Susan asked with a grin.

"What?" Ann asked. "Oh! Yes, I love them. And they're always a fun treat for guests who don't know what they are. In fact, I'll make some for breakfast tomorrow."

"What's an evil-skever?" Garrett asked confused.

"No e-bul-ski-ver," Susan enunciated.

"It's like a pancake," Ann said turning to Garrett with a grin. "A spherical pancake."

"Cool!" Garrett replied, poking his head into the kitchen to get a look at the pan. It looked like a cast iron skillet with seven divots in it, a little bigger than golf balls. Garrett grinned back at Ann. "I can't wait!" Continuing down the hall, Ann quickly pointed out the bathroom, her bedroom, and the sewing room.

"I have an air mattress that will fit in here," she said, looking into the room. "I can put most of the cloth away so there is room to set it up." Katie smiled when she saw the piles of cloth and the two sewing machines on a table along the wall.

"What do you sew?" Katie asked.

"Oh, this and that," Ann replied. "I make quilts and blankets, I crochet scarves and mittens, and I do a little bit of tatting as well."

"What is tatting?" Phil asked. "I've never heard that term before."

"A dying art, sadly," Ann replied. "You use thread tied in knots to make patterns, essentially. A kind of lace-making."

"You make lace by hand?" Phil said surprised. "I thought you needed a machine to do that."

"Well, machines do most of it now." Ann replied with a small smile, "but before machines, people used to make it by hand. My mother taught me how, and I like to use it to make new and interesting designs out of the lace."

"Like what?" Katie asked, also interested in the brief lesson.

"Oh, like this." Ann said reaching in and grabbing one of the delicate looking bits of lace on the table. "It's not done yet, but when it's finished it will be a reindeer." Katie looked closely at the unfinished piece.

"It's beautiful," she said in awe.

"Thank you!" Ann beamed. "It's a labor of love, really. It takes hundreds of hours to make. And since machines can do more intricate work in a fraction of the time, you could never sell it for what it's worth in labor alone. But I like to give them as gifts. Because to me, that means I have spent all of those hours thinking about that person and working to create something unique just for them."

"That's lovely!" Katie exclaimed, grinning like a schoolgirl. Ann continued to beam as she turned in to her room.

"I have a large bunch of blankets and pillows that someone could use to sleep on the floor in here," Ann said, gesturing, "and we can fit one on the sofa and one in the recliner. Which gives everyone somewhere to sleep tonight." Ann smiled bravely, trying not to think of the reason they were all trying to cram into her little house.

"Thanks, Ann," Garrett said, coming over to give her a hug. "We all appreciate it." Ann squeezed him back tight enough to let him know how upset she really was, then quickly let him go.

"My pleasure," she replied, turning to the rest of the group. "I don't think I have enough food for everyone to make dinner, so how about ordering pizza?" she asked. Everyone grinned and nodded in agreement. "Then after dinner, we can play some card games," Ann said, starting to grin for real. "I can teach you all how to play Hand and Foot!"

"Hand and Foot?" Garrett asked. "What's that?"

"Oh, it's complicated, you'll like it." Ann said with a twinkle in her eye. "Just remember, all the rules are real, even if they sound made up." Then she laughed and walked over to her computer to order the pizza.

Finally, finally it was all coming together. They had almost won. Almost snatched victory out of his hands. But in the end, he would triumph. The albino swept his purple hair back and out of his eyes. They had finally made one critical mistake, and that would cost them all. One by one, it would cost each of them their lives. Each death more painful than the last. Each scream of agony, music to his ears. And the purest torture for Him.

The fool had tied himself to weaklings. Pitiful dregs who could barely even defend themselves, and yet somehow kept eluding him. But that was all over now. They could no longer escape. Could no longer plan and plot his demise while he raged, helpless to stop them.

Now was the time for his revenge. The time where he brought the wretches together and used them one by one to extract every ounce of pain possible from Him. To make Him beg, plead, and abase Himself all to try and save His friends. Only to fail. Time and time again He would fail. Until the end, when His begging would be for His own death.

And then, only then, would death be granted to Him. He would have to earn it, the albino thought to himself. Earn it by begging, earn it by pleading, earn it by kissing the very ground beneath his feet. But earn it He would, and when He had begged and pleaded until there was nothing left, He would finally feel the sweet kiss of death.

The crazed clown laughed to himself at the thought. One of his men looked back at him to see what he was laughing at. The murderous albino whipped out a knife as long as his forearm and slammed it into the man's back, reveling in the rush of blood that washed over his hand and down his arm.

Idiots. When would they learn to mind their own business? At least until he ordered them to do otherwise. Yanking the knife back out, he barely noticed as the man slumped to the ground, nearly dropping the object the man was helping to carry.

So inconsiderate, he thought. Butting into other people's business like that. Didn't that man's mother raise the man right? Apparently not. He should probably have the mother killed as well for doing such a poor job at raising a son. He waved to one of his assassins, gesturing the pair over. The pair locked to attention in front of him without a word.

"Do you know this man?" the albino asked, gesturing to the body on the floor. "You may answer."

"No!" One of the pair barked, remaining ramrod stiff.

"Find out who that was, find out where the mother lives and kill the woman for doing such a poor job as a mother." A pale hand waved the pair away almost before he had finished speaking.

Yes, yes we cannot have a poor excuse for a mother continue to live and continue to pump out babies who would also be badly raised. It would be a menace to society, that's what a mother like that would be. Yes, a menace to society, and the albino couldn't stand the competition.

There was one small snag in his plan, however. The old woman. The old crone was too powerful, too versatile for him to capture alive. And the old woman would come with Him when He tried to rescue His friends. It would have to be a trap for the crone then, he thought. Something lethal, but not instantaneous. Fast enough that the old woman couldn't be saved, but slow enough that He could watch the woman suffer before death.

Another peal of vicious laughter echoed in the night air. He had just the thing! Oh what a tangled web… but yes, the perfect thing. Not too fast, not too slow, but unstoppably lethal. Slow enough for there to be pain. Slow enough for suffering. Slow enough that He would begin His journey with the greatest agony of them all. Throwing his head back, he laughed again, long and loud, and not a single head turned his way as they carried their burdens past him.

Garrett woke the next morning with a start. He looked around quickly, momentarily confused, then he remembered. He was at Ann's and had slept on her recliner last night. He did not see Phil, who had spent the night on the couch, so he got up and made his way to the bathroom.

Garrett was surprised to find the bathroom door open with no one inside. The other doors were closed though, so perhaps Phil had decided to join Katie sometime in the night. Garrett shrugged, he hadn't even known they liked each other without Ann telling him, let alone how far their relationship had gone.

Finishing quickly, he made his way groggily into the kitchen. Surprised that it was also empty he glanced at the clock. It was after ten o'clock and no one else was out of bed? Garrett frowned, thinking. Perhaps he should go and knock on the doors. It was getting late in the morning and they had a busy day ahead, storming a manufacturing plant full of bad guys.

Garrett chuckled to himself as he remembered an incident a few months back when he and Phil had stopped to get a Slurpee after group therapy one day. A mother and her young son were walking the aisles when they rounded the corner. The young boy's eyes got wide and he pointed at the pair excitedly.

"Look, ma! Bad guys!" the boy exclaimed loudly. The poor, embarrassed mother had turned bright red, scooped up the child, and raced out of the convenience store. Garrett had turned at the sound of Phil's evil-sounding chuckle.

"Smart kid," he said with a grin. Garrett just laughed.

He supposed they had looked like bad guys. Phil was a giant biker with a shaved head, tattoos, and a black leather vest. And Garrett was wearing black shoes, and black jeans, with a black t-shirt that read 'The last thing I want to do is hurt you - but it's still on the list'. So, he could understand why the kid might think they were bad guys. Still chuckling at the memory, he knocked on Ann's bedroom door.

"Rise and shine," Garrett said cheerfully. "Time to storm the castle." Garrett heard a rustling movement from inside, and after a few moments the door cracked open to reveal Ann's haggard face. "Are you okay?" Garrett asked.

"No, I didn't sleep very well," Ann replied. "Where is Susan? Is she up already? I didn't even hear her leave." Garrett frowned.

"No, she's not out here." Garrett replied, beginning to grow concerned. Ann opened the door the rest of the way to reveal an empty pile of blankets on the floor. As she did so, she stumbled slightly, catching herself on the door. Garrett reached out in case she fell.

"Ann! Are you okay?" Garrett asked concerned.

"No, I don't feel very well," Ann replied, still holding onto the door for support. "I usually do pretty well in the mornings, but I can't seem to get the room to stop spinning." Now Garrett was getting really worried.

"Try to sit down so you don't fall, I'm going to look for the others," Garrett said, reaching out to help her sit on the floor. Once she was safely seated, he turned quickly and knocked hard on the door to the sewing room. He only waited a few moments before opening the door. As it swung open, he froze at the sight of the empty air mattress.

"They're not here," Garrett called out, looking around the room.

He froze dead in his tracks again as he took the first step into the room and felt the carpet squelch beneath his bare feet. Looking down slowly, he lifted his foot, his eyes wide at the sight of the red liquid dripping off of it.

Looking around in a panic, he almost missed the piece of paper on the table next to him, with a tiny knife stuck through and embedded into the wood of the table. Garrett got a good look at the knife and felt the blood draining from his face as he recognized the clown face etched into the blade.

Reaching out, he grabbed a hold of the paper and pulled, tearing it through the edge of the knife. Leaving the knife stuck in the table, he started reading.

"You thought you had won, but now you have lost,
The lives of your friends will then be your cost,
So come down and play, there's no other way,
A roll of the dice has been tossed."

"Ann!" Garrett yelled racing back over to her room holding out the paper. "He's got them! Whoever is behind all of this, he's got them."

Ann read the page with the same growing horror. She looked up at Garrett, panic in her eyes as well. Seeing his fear however seemed to have a stabilizing effect on her. Quickly she calmed, squared her chin and nodded decisively.

"Well then, let's go get them!" she announced firmly. "Help me to my feet so I can get dressed. And don't worry, we'll get them back." Reaching out to help Ann to her feet, Garrett looked down at her, panic still on his face.

"How are we going to do that?" Garrett asked, starting to sound more like the child Justin than the adult Garrett.

"Magic!" Ann grinned, yanking clothes out of her dresser and heading for the bathroom.

CHAPTER SEVENTEEN

A few short minutes later, the pair of them were back in Katie's car and racing down the quiet suburban streets. Garrett drove quickly, while Greybeard muttered to himself, pulling vial after vial out of a large satchel.

"So, how's it coming?" Garrett asked nervously.

"Great, wonderful, perfect," Greybeard groused. "You just focus on your job and let me focus on mine."

"Okay fine, I'm sorry," Garrett replied, not sounding sorry at all. He couldn't help but stare, however, at the ever-growing and impressive pile of vials stacking up around the aged wizard.

"You just remember that you can't take two at once, they will cancel each other out," Greybeard said, looking closely at one of the vials. "And I don't know if the effects will last through switches, so if someone else comes out, expect that the potion has worn off."

"Got it," Garrett replied, trying to keep his eyes on the road.

Greybeard went back to muttering as he continued to pull vials out of the satchel. Garrett tried not to think about what might be happening to his friends as he raced down the streets, heading for the freeway.

Unfortunately, his imagination had other ideas. Faintly, he heard a voice in his head, observing that perhaps he shouldn't have watched all those horror movies. They finally reached the freeway, and Garrett put the pedal to the floor.

"Hey, watch it!" Greybeard yelled as Garrett swerved in and out of traffic.

"Sorry!" Garrett replied without taking his eyes off the road.

After what seemed like an eternity, they finally took the exit that would lead them to the machining shop where they thought their friends were being held. Garrett stopped the car about a half mile away from the fenced parking area. Greybeard looked up with a frown.

"What are you stopping for?" he asked querulously.

"I figured there would likely be guards watching the area around the building," Garrett replied. "If we want to sneak in we're going to have to make sure we're not seen just parking the car." Greybeard only grunted in response, his attention back on the large pile of flasks on his lap. "So what have you got for me?" Garrett asked, impatient to get going.

"Hold your horses," Greybeard snapped. Garrett frowned at him.

"Hey, we probably don't have much time," he began, "so if you could finish up that would be great." Greybeard again only grunted in reply. Garrett sat there staring at him, fuming. He knew there was nothing he could do to speed up the old mage however, so he simply sat there glaring at him.

Greybeard continued muttering and pulling vials out of the satchel, seemingly unconcerned by the increasingly hostile glare directed his way. After several more agonizing minutes, he looked up at Garrett.

"Okay, I think I found them all." Greybeard said, still ignoring the glare.

"All right," Garrett replied, "what have you got?"

Greybeard reached into the satchel and pulled out a thin leather belt with six loops along one side. Picking up one vial at a time, he gently slipped them into each of the loops until they were snug.

"Levitation," he said, sliding the first vial in. "Invisibility." In went the second vial. "Strength, Stone Skin, Speed," he continued, sliding the vials smoothly into the loops. Finally, he held up the last vial. "And this one, this one is special," Greybeard said almost reverently sliding the last vial into the loop.

"Special? How?" Garrett asked, looking closely at the vial.

"This is a Time Stop potion," Greybeard replied, still in a reverent tone.

"That's not possible," Garrett said. "How can a potion I drink stop time for everyone else?"

"I don't know, all right?" Greybeard said, getting angry. "All I know is that it works. Drink this and time will stop for everyone except you." Garrett looked back at the vial in surprise. "And be careful with it!" Greybeard snapped again. "I've never been able to duplicate it. I managed one batch decades ago, and this is the last of it."

"Thank you," Garrett said softly as Greybeard's head snapped up in surprise. "Thank you for everything. I am more scared than I have ever been in my entire life, and you have given me a chance to get them back. It means more to me than I could ever tell you." Greybeard grunted again.

"I understand," Greybeard replied. "Don't worry, we'll get them back. After all, who could possibly stop our combined crew?" he asked with a wicked smile.

"Well, there is that," Garrett chuckled. "Okay, let's go."

"Hey," Greybeard said as he opened his door, "shouldn't you slip into someone more comfortable with this kind of mission?" Garrett chuckled again at the reference.

"Yeah, thanks again," Garrett answered as he closed his eyes.

Looking around, Garrett saw everyone clustered around the stone chair, their eyes eager with anticipation. Nodding, he stood and looked closely at each of them, noticing little details that would ordinarily pass right by him.

Derrick's eyes gleamed in the torchlight of the cave, a thin ring of gold circling his iris. Peter stood rock steady except for an almost imperceptible clenching and unclenching of his left hand. Sean had no twitches or odd behavior to distinguish him. In fact, he was standing so still Garrett could not even see him breathing. If it wasn't for his eyes blinking, he could have been mistaken for a statue.

Justin, however, was the exact opposite. He didn't stop moving. Walking around and around in-between the others and clutching an old ratty-looking teddy bear, he looked like he was on the verge of tears.

"All right, we're ready," Garrett announced. "Greybeard has given us a belt with six of his potions. We can only use each one once, and not at the same time."

"What are they?" Peter asked.

"Levitation, Invisibility, Strength, Stone Skin, Speed, and Time Stop." Garrett replied. Sean's eyebrow raised in inquiry.

"How can the mage capture Time Stop in a potion?" Sean inquired. "That would seem to affect those outside of this body."

"I don't know, and neither does he," Garrett answered. "He just said it works."

"Fascinating," Sean replied. "I look forward to being able to study its effects." Garrett nodded, turning to the others.

"Derrick, you are on point for entry." Garrett began.

"I should be the one going in," Peter interrupted. Garrett looked at him with a glare.

"Peter, we do this together or not at all," Garrett said angrily. "We don't have much time, and we need to work together if we're going to be able to save them, all right?" Peter stared hard into Garrett's eyes before finally nodding.

"You have become more," Peter said cryptically. "I will follow your instructions." Garrett frowned, trying to understand what Peter was talking about. After a moment, he shook his head and continued.

"Derrick is on point for entry. Peter, you are the heavy in case he gets into trouble. Sean, you are operations. Coordinate movements and switches, to optimal effect. And Justin, you need to keep back and out of the way. This is going to be dangerous and I don't want you to get hurt." Garrett paused for a breath, but Justin didn't wait.

"Garrett, I want to help too!" he cried out.

"I know you do, Small Fry," Garrett said soothingly, "but this is going to be really dangerous and I need you to be safe."

"I helped before!" Justin exclaimed. "Last time, I helped! I got small enough so they missed us. I helped!"

"I know you did, little man," Garrett replied consoling, "but now that they have seen you do that, they would be ready. And you don't have thick armor like Peter." Garrett knocked his fist against Peter's breastplate, causing the metal to ring. "Or the ability to heal like Derrick." Garrett continued, gesturing to the vampire.

"I just want to help," Justin said again, his lip quivering as though he was about to cry.

"I know, me too," Garrett answered, "but I have to stay back just like you do. I don't have armor or healing, either." He leaned down and picked Justin up. "So, I have to stay out of the way too."

Justin's lip continued to quiver, but he didn't break down into tears. He just nodded and leaned his head over to rest it on Garrett's shoulders. Garrett hugged the child tightly for a moment before looking back at the other three. Derrick stepped up and sat down in the stone chair.

Opening his eyes, Derrick looked up at the sun with a scowl, silently wishing they were doing this at night. Looking over to the other side of the car, he saw Greybeard muttering and slipping vials into another belt with the same small loops in it.

He gave the old mage an evil grin and grabbed the already full belt as he stepped out of the small car. Flipping his cloak up, he slid the belt around his waist and fastened it. Then paused with a frown as he heard Sean's voice in his head.

"If the belt with the potions is secured to one of us, it will not be available to the others." Sean said calmly, his voice loud and clear in Derrick's head.

"Good point," Derrick replied aloud. "Greybeard, what will happen to the belt when we switch? Will they not stay with me, and travel inside?" Derrick asked patting the vials in the belt.

"What? Oh, right." Greybeard answered, looking up from his work. "No, the belt should stay here no matter who's up. I think I got the enchantment right on that one."

"I certainly hope so," Derrick said sardonically, "or this is going to be a very brief rescue attempt." He looked around quickly, scanning for anyone who may have seen them. "Are you ready?" he asked, glancing at the old mage again.

"Ready," Greybeard said, fastening the belt around his waist and tucking the satchel behind his cloak.

"Then we go," Derrick said with an evil smile. "My speed."

"What…" Greybeard began, but cut off with a yelp as Derrick swept him up in a fireman's carry across his shoulders and began to run.

Terrain flashed by as Derrick ran at full speed, for although he could not change while in direct sunlight, he could still use his inhuman strength to run. Within a minute, they had reached the fence around the perimeter of the facility.

Derrick stopped almost instantaneously and dropped down into the bushes that lined the property. Greybeard slid off of his shoulders, looking a little greyer in the face than he had when the ride had started.

"Hey, warn me next time you're going to do something like that, huh?" Greybeard asked, his voice still a bit shaky from the unexpected run.

"I didn't think you would agree if I had told you," Derrick said with another evil smile.

"I most certainly would not!" Greybeard replied angrily. "That was completely undignified!"

"Well," Derrick responded, "it's a good thing I didn't ask." Greybeard grunted in irritated acknowledgment before turning back to look at the building.

"I don't see anyone," Greybeard said cautiously.

"You won't," Derrick replied. "They're not out in the sunlight. None of them are visible to you from here. Fortunately, they are visible to me."

"How's that?" Greybeard asked.

"The blood," Derrick replied. "I can see the heat of their bodies. Even when they are in the shadows, or behind a reflective window."

"Well, that's convenient." Greybeard said wryly.

"Isn't it?" Derrick said, turning to the wizard with a fang-baring smile.

"Glad you're on our side," Greybeard muttered under his breath. "Can you get to them without them seeing you?"

"No," Derrick replied, shaking his head. "Not in the sunlight."

"Then we're going to have to use the Invisibility," Greybeard said, grabbing at a vial from his belt.

"Only one of us should use it," Derrick said, placing a hand on Greybeard's arm. "Take out the guards, then the other can follow." Greybeard nodded, slipping the vial back into his belt.

Derrick grinned again and grabbed the second vial from his own belt. Downing the potion quickly, he waited for the signal from Greybeard that it was working before quietly leaping over the fence. Still moving with inhuman swiftness he scrambled up the wall to the second floor of the building.

Glancing around quickly, he found a window that did not have anyone behind it. Extending his nails into long, sharp points, he dug them into the frame of the window itself, got a good grip, and pulled gently.

The sound of the wooden frame tearing out sounded impossibly loud to the vampire, though admittedly a great deal quieter than the breaking glass would have been had he decided to simply jump through. After a few moments, the rest of the frame broke free, and Derrick was able to gently place it inside the room before entering himself.

Once inside, he moved to the door and listened carefully. He could hear the heavy footfalls of the guards pacing the hall, and after a moment, the heartbeats of the guards in the adjacent rooms keeping watch. Timing his movements for after the patrolling guard had turned a corner, Derrick slipped out of the room and into the hallway. Once out of the sunlight, he dissipated into his mist form and floated up to the ceiling.

He had almost reached the first door with guards in it when the patrolling guard came around the corner. In a flash, Derrick had shifted back to his vampiric form and charged the surprised guard. His movements were so fast that the guard didn't have time to raise his weapon before Derrick had reached him and, with a powerful, wrenching twist, had broken the man's neck.

Easing the dead guard down to the floor, Derrick

quickly made his way back to the first room. Dissipating back into mist, he silently slipped under the door and into the room. He noticed two guards near the window, with the same setup they had seen earlier. Derrick assumed by the face paint that they were another one of the assassin pairs, and that their guns would be loaded with silver just for him. Briefly, he turned his mental focus inward.

"Two guards, fully loaded," Derrick said, opening his eyes and looking up from the stone chair at Sean. "Would you like to try the same trick we pulled at the police station?" Derrick asked. Sean simply nodded and readied himself for the switch.

Refocusing on the outside world again, Derrick, still in mist form, silently floated up behind the pair. Waiting for both of them to be within arm's reach, he shifted quickly back to his vampiric form.

Before the pair realized he was behind them, the body had switched again, the tall pointy-eared alien reaching out almost before the shift was complete. In less than a heartbeat he had grasped the nerve bundles in each of their necks and pinched down hard.

They each had a moment to register shocked surprise before they slipped into unconsciousness and Sean lowered them down onto the floor. Rising quickly, they shifted again, the elegant vampire once more in control. Derrick glanced down at the two unconscious guards, and without missing a beat reached down and tore both of their throats out. Growling softly at the outcry in his head, Derrick closed his eyes.

"That was cold-blooded murder!" Peter cried, his face drawn in anger.

"Was it necessary to kill them?" Sean inquired. "I had

rendered them harmless."

"Was it necessary?!" Derrick snarled at them. "Of course it was necessary! Sean, how long does that pinch thing of yours last?"

"Approximately five to ten minutes depending on the constitution of the recipient," Sean replied calmly.

"Exactly," Derrick said angrily, "and in ten minutes they would have awoken and used whatever alarm system they have to call down the entire place on us."

"But was it necessary to murder them?" Peter shouted again. "Could you not have bound them instead?" Derrick glared at the knight.

"No, I could not have bound them," Derrick answered. "First, it would take too much time, and second, do you really think they would stay bound very long?" Peter paused, thinking the comment through tactically for a minute before shaking his head.

"No, you are correct," Peter replied in a subdued voice. "They would not have remained bound for long. Either through their own actions or the actions of their allies, they would have escaped and continued to be a threat to us and our friends." Derrick blinked to hide his surprise at Peter's agreement.

"Exactly," Derrick replied. "Like the angel said, we do whatever we must to protect those in our charge."

Peter nodded gravely, his eyes unfocused and his thoughts distant. Derrick looked over at Sean again in challenge. Sean simply raised an eyebrow at him. With another small snarl of irritation, Derrick opened his eyes. One room down, two to go, he thought to himself.

Shifting again into mist form, he slipped under the door and back into the hall. Pausing for a moment, he listened again for heartbeats. One in the next room, and two in the room after that, Derrick thought. No other guards in the hallway yet, so I had better be quick.

Slipping silently under the next door, he quickly took stock of the room. Despite the fact that there was only a single guard in this room, Derrick decided that this was the most dangerous of the three rooms.

The guard stood behind a very large gun mounted on a three-legged stand. The odd part about the gun however, was that it didn't have a trigger. Instead it had two handles on the back side of it, with what looked like a large button in between them. Coupled with the fact that Derrick could see a long belt of very large ammunition coming from the side of the weapon, he suspected that this was their answer to Peter's thick armor.

Briefly relaying that information inside, he moved up behind the guard. This guard was more alert than his fellows, and turned around at the first touch of cool mist. His alertness did not save him as Derrick shifted back into his vampiric form and in the blink of an eye had darted forward to bite savagely at the man's throat.

Feeding quickly, Derrick shivered at the rush of power that came with the bright crimson fluid. It was over in moments, the guard growing limp in his arms as Derrick drained him dry. He had turned to leave the second room when he felt a tapping on his mental shoulder, and closed his eyes.

"A moment," Peter said, looking down at him, the visor of his helm raised.

"What?" Derrick replied, suspiciously.

"That weapon you saw," Peter said, still being unexpectedly polite. "That is one of those 'guns' that Tammarion spoke of?"

"Yes, it is," Derrick said, unsure if he could trust Peter's new polite attitude.

"How does it work?" Peter asked, still calm.

"Usually there's a trigger, but I don't know about this one," Derrick replied, becoming frustrated. "I know enough to stay safe in this world, but my memories are of a much older time." Peter nodded and turned to Sean.

"Could you teach me how to use it?" Peter asked, still being unusually polite. Sean raised an eyebrow.

"Indeed," Sean replied. "Though from Derrick's description, this is not an ordinary gun. It is a rapid-fire weapon with larger than usual ammunition. Hence the tripod mount. It is far too heavy to be carried around like a typical firearm. And then there's the problem with the ammunition. Because it is so large, and the gun fires so rapidly, it takes an enormous amount of ammunition, which in itself is extremely heavy."

Derrick then remembered the bag that Greybeard pulled all of the potions out of and sighed.

"Hey, bucket-head," Derrick said grumpily, "I may have an answer to the ammunition problem, but we've got to get Greybeard in the building first." And wonder of wonders, Peter actually smiled at him. Derrick tried to remember the last time he had seen Peter smile at him, but could not think of a single instance.

"Thank you," Peter replied. "I shall await his arrival." Derrick started at the knight for another moment, then closed his eyes again.

Derrick moved to the door and listened intently. He could still only hear the sound of the two heartbeats in the last room. Briefly, he wondered where the other guard patrols had gone and why none of them had been by yet. Then he remembered that time worked differently inside and decided that their conversations had not taken as long as he thought they did.

Shifting again into mist form, he moved back into the hallway and toward the third door on that side of the hallway. Just before he slipped under the last door, however, he paused. The heartbeat, the two heartbeats were not in the right place. One was near the window, but the other sounded like it was right on the other side of the door.

Derrick wondered briefly if they had triggered some kind of silent alarm, or if the guards he had already dispatched had been checking in with each other. That would explain why the two guards in the last room were not watching the window. One may have been assigned to watch the door when they didn't hear from the other guards on the floor. And if that was the case, they would be watching for him to mist under the door. With a mental grumble, he again focused his attention inward.

"We have a problem," Derrick said, looking up from the stone chair. "One of the guards in this room is not where he belongs."

"What do you mean?" Peter asked.

"I mean one of them is standing by the door," Derrick growled. "I think they are watching for me."

"If they are watching for you," Sean replied, "then perhaps we should give them someone else."

Derrick glanced at the scanning device and pistol at Sean's hip and grinned, baring his fangs. Rising from the stone chair, he gestured for Sean to take his place with a bow. Raising an eyebrow, Sean sat in the chair and closed his eyes.

Sean opened his eyes, and glanced up and down the hallway. He did not detect any other individuals in the immediate area. Taking out his scanner he opened the case and watched as various readouts displayed the results of the scan.

Making some minor adjustments, he narrowed the scanning focus to detect structural layout and lifeforms within close proximity. His eyebrow raised at the results. Derrick had been correct. The two individuals on the other side of the door were no longer watching externally. While one was still near the window, the second was in fact in a position to immediately see and act against anyone who entered the doorway. In fact, he was also in a crouched position making him difficult to detect or retaliate against should someone decide to enter the door using brute force. Sean was fortunate that he did not require use of the door in order to eliminate the current threat.

Taking a position in the hallway immediately adjacent to the individual watching the door he checked his scanner one last time to confirm position of both individuals. Raising the laser pistol he fired two precise shots through the wall. After a brief moment, he then heard the thumps which indicated that his stratagem had been successful.

Two strides brought him back to the door, which he opened, but did not go through. He allowed the door to impact the far wall lightly, then moved through the doorway at a crouch, wary of incoming attacks. Thankfully, his caution was unwarranted and both individuals had indeed been dispatched.

With long strides he made his way back into the room where Derrick had made his entry. Looking out of the window toward the bushes where they had left Greybeard, he waved his arm, gesturing for Greybeard to come in.

He was unsurprised to see that it was Tammarion who made her way out of the bushes, flying easily up and over the fence toward the open window. Stepping back, Sean made room for the angel to land and then shifted back into the eagerly awaiting vampire.

Derrick opened his eyes just as Tammarion landed in the small room. For the briefest of moments, he wondered what angelic blood tasted like. Then shook his head to clear the thought and stepped over to her.

"Welcome to the hunt," Derrick said, his rich, Romanian accent thick with anticipation. "I have a question for Greybeard."

Tammarion looked at him for a moment, and Derrick could swear that she could see every thought in his head. He shivered uncomfortably as she nodded and closed her eyes. The shift was rapid, though surprisingly not instantaneous, and Derrick was able to watch the transformation with interest.

The long, blond hair lightened until it was white, the winged helm contracted and moved into a conical point before a wide brim sprouted out of it. The golden wings wrapped around her torso and darkened into the grey robes he was familiar with. And the lovely face aged rapidly, wrinkling before his very eyes. He was so intent on watching the aging process that he almost missed the delicate nose thickening and elongating into the much larger hawk nose of the old man.

"What do you want?" Greybeard grumped.

"That satchel you use to keep all of your potions in," Derrick began, "can it carry other things as well?" Greybeard's eyes narrowed.

"Possibly," he replied, "but it gets difficult to find what you want the more you put in there."

"Would you consider loaning it to Peter?" Derrick asked, trying to sound polite.

"What would that tin-plated powerhouse want with my dimensional bag?" Greybeard asked, his surprise causing him to be even grumpier than usual.

"He would like to use it to contain ammunition for a weapon," Derrick answered, his smile coming close to showing his fangs again.

"Ammo?!" Greybeard said, exasperated. "Why doesn't he get a bloody quiver if he wants to carry ammo?"

"Come," Derrick replied, "let me show you." He led the old mage out into the hallway and over to the second room. The old wizard froze at the door, gazing in on the weapon.

"He wants to carry the ammunition for that?" Greybeard asked, shocked. "And what good will that do him? That thing is mounted, for heaven's sake!"

"Perhaps I should allow him to demonstrate," Derrick replied, closing his eyes.

"All right, you're up!" Derrick said to Peter as he rose from the stone chair. Peter again smiled as he sat down, leaving Derrick wondering again if he had somehow entered the wrong mind.

Peter opened his eyes and looked down at the mage with a smile. Greybeard nodded his head, not yet trusting himself to speak.

"I would like to be able to use that weapon," Peter said, gesturing toward the large gun, "but I will need to be able to carry enough ammunition to use it properly. I have been told that you might have a way I can do that?"

"Probably," Greybeard said, back to his old grumpy self again. "But if you put all of that in my bag," he said, gesturing to the boxes beside the gun, "you're going to break my potions, and that would turn out badly for all of us." Peter nodded.

"Is there somewhere else you can store the potions?" he asked with genuine concern. Greybeard stared at him for a long time before giving a gusty sigh.

"Yeah, there is," Greybeard said resignedly. "Hang on." And with that, the old man closed his eyes, his body shifting into the fiery red-head. Peter frowned as they finished the change.

"Why are you here?" Peter asked, concerned.

"I volunteered," she said, as though daring him to dispute it.

"It is not safe here," Peter replied, not rising to the bait.

"I know, which is why I came up to tell you about this gun," Molly answered with a bright grin.

"You know what this is?" Peter asked, shocked.

"Sure," she replied, her Irish brogue lilting with humor. "I was friendly with a soldier back in Ireland and he loved to talk about his guns." The beautiful woman chuckled deep in her throat. "In fact, they were the only things he loved more than me." Peter looked at her with concern.

"That must have been painful," Peter replied.

"Och, it wasn't that bad," Molly said, her grin returning. "I knew what he was going into it, and when he was shipped off to another duty station, we stayed friends for a while. But, back to the topic at hand!" she declared. "This is a Browning M2A1 .50 caliber machine gun, with both semi-auto and fully automatic firing capabilities. It is belt fed, with a quick-change barrel to help keep it cool and a fixed headspace and timing." Pausing to take a breath she noticed the blank stare on the knight.

"My apologies, milady," Peter said. "I do not know what any of that means."

"Och! Of course you don't!" Molly said, unfazed. "So let me put it in your terms. You can set the gun so it shoots one bullet at a time, or set it so that it will keep shooting as long as you hold down the trigger." she began, pointing at the large button in between the two vertical handles. "You see the belt coming out of the side? That's the ammunition. If you shoot it too often or too fast though, the gun gets unbelievably hot, so you can switch out the barrel, that's the front part, for one that is still cool. And the headspace and timing means that even you can use it without having to know how it works on the inside." Molly beamed at the knight, excited to see what he made of the explanation.

"So I hold the handle, push that right there," Peter began, pointing at the trigger, "and it will keep firing until either I stop or I run out of ammunition?"

"Right!" Molly said happily. "Now let me show you how to use it." She walked over to the gun and lifted the top up. "See here, where the bullets are?" she asked. Peter just nodded, taking it all in. "Well, when you run out, all you have to do is grab a new belt, lay it in here and close the lid." Molly demonstrated the belt change procedure and looked back up to see Peter still nodding. "Then, you pull back on this handle." she began, tugging on the handle sticking out of the right side of the large gun. After several attempts, Peter leaned over.

"May I?" he inquired. Molly shrugged with a grin and moved out of the way. Peter pulled gently and slid the charging handle all the way back before releasing it.

"And now it's ready to fire." Molly said brightly. "Just don't do it here! It makes a huge racket when it fires!" Peter nodded again, lifting the massive gun in one hand, tripod and all. Molly's eyes widened. "Wait, you're going to try and shoot that thing standing up?"

"It would be more effective that way, don't you think?" Peter asked with a smile of his own as he grasped the firing handle in one hand and the carry handle with the other.

"No good," Molly said shaking her head. "That handle in the front, it's attached to the barrel which goes back and forth when you shoot it." At Peter's blank stare she rephrased, "That one moves," she said pointing to the handle coming off of the barrel. Peter nodded again and switched hands, with one on the back and one hand on the charging handle on the side. "Nope," Molly said again, "same problem."

Peter frowned as he looked at the gun closely, not seeing any other places to hold it. Suddenly, he grinned again and reached over his shoulder to pull off his shield. Securing it to his arm, he lowered it to chest height, then braced the gun on top of the shield.

"There," he replied. "That should solve the aiming problem." Molly grinned at him.

"Remind me not to get on your bad side," she said, shaking her head.

"I thank you, milady," Peter said to her with a small bow. "I had not expected such a lovely instructor in the arts of modern warfare." Molly blushed, but kept eye contact with him.

"My pleasure, big guy," she said, tossing her long mass of curly red hair to the side with a wink. Suddenly, she straightened and looked off to the side. "Hey, Greybeard says he's ready, so I had better go." Peter nodded again, then set the gun down and reached out to take her hand. Gently, he lifted it to his lips kissing the back of her hand lightly.

"Again, thank you, milady," Peter said solemnly. Molly just grinned happily.

"Och, any time," she replied, her brogue thick as she tried not to blush. Pulling her hand back, she nodded once, then closed her eyes, shifting again into the old grey robed man.

"Are you quite finished?" Greybeard snapped at the knight.

"Indeed," Peter said, hefting his new weapon again. "Molly was quite helpful."

"Good," Greybeard replied. "I freed up the bag for you, now let's get you some ammo."

The pair went over to the large boxes piled to the right of where the gun was previously stationed and began opening them. Three of the boxes yielded the .50 caliber ammunition the gun required, while the rest held other forms of ammunition, presumably for all of the other weapons they had seen. One box even contained silver ammunition, mostly for the rifles.

Shaking his head, Peter picked up two of the three

boxes of .50 caliber ammo and moved them to the side. Greybeard attempted to pick up the third, but was unable to move it more than a few inches. Grumbling, he yielded when Peter came back over to pick it up.

"Okay," Greybeard said, lifting the satchel up and over his head, "This is a dimensional bag, which means you can put just about anything you want inside and the bag won't fill up and it won't get any heavier. Allow me to demonstrate." Greybeard opened the top of the satchel and pointed at one of the boxes. "Okay, go ahead and put one of those cans inside." he said. Peter opened the box and pulled out a large, rectangular ammo can. Greybeard nodded to the open satchel and Peter gently lowered the can inside.

His eyes widened in surprise, despite what Greybeard's explanation, when the can went into the bag and kept going. Glancing at the underside of the bag, Peter was amazed that he could not see any bulge or tug when the can, which was far deeper than the bag, went completely inside.

"See?" Greybeard said triumphantly. "No problem."

"How much can it hold?" Peter inquired.

"I'm not sure," Greybeard said evasively. "It just keeps taking as much as I can put in." He shook his head as he waved a hand. "Now, I know it must have a limit somewhere, I just don't know what that limit is yet. So, just keep loading," Greybeard finished with a growl.

Peter nodded in acknowledgment and continued to load ammo cans into the bag. When they had finished, Greybeard handed the satchel to the knight.

"Okay, here you go," he said. Peter was again surprised to feel that the bag weighed no more than the scrap of cloth used to make it.

"Thank you, my friend," Peter said, clapping the old man on the shoulder.

"Don't mention it," Greybeard said, startled.

"Now, to battle!" Peter announced with an unmistakable gleam in his eye.

CHAPTER EIGHTEEN

"Hang on," Greybeard said, holding up a hand to halt the knight before he had taken more than two steps. "We're still on covert status, right?" Peter froze for a moment, then nodded sadly.

"Indeed we are," Peter replied. "I shall fetch Derrick." Closing his eyes, he looked up at the waiting vampire. "Call me, if you are in need," the knight stated, hefting the large gun onto his shoulder. Derrick just nodded as he sat back down in the stone chair.

"You rang?" Derrick asked, with a fang-baring grin. Greybeard just humphed at him impatiently. Derrick bowed mockingly and glided out the door with inhuman grace.

Once he reached the hallway, however, he was all business again. Turning to Greybeard, he spoke in low, soft tones. "It is entirely possible that if these two were aware of our entrance, that the entire compound is now aware of us. Greybeard humphed again.

"Then we deal with them," he said confidently.

Derrick just nodded at him and continued forward, listening intently.

The pair reached the end of the hallway and carefully moved into the large entryway. The domed room was filled with comfortable furniture and coffee tables arranged in small groupings. The exterior wall held a pair of elevators and a door labeled 'Stairwell', with a second hallway on the far side of the room.

"We should probably take the stairs," Derrick said, after a moment to ensure the room was empty.

"Well, if they know we're here, should we set up a distraction?" Greybeard asked, gesturing toward the elevators. Derrick nodded and moved to the one on the right and pushed the button going down.

"We should set them both up," Greybeard suggested. "You hit all of the buttons in one of them, then we'll hit just the bottom floor on the other one, so they arrive at different times. Meanwhile, we'll be taking the stairs."

Derrick nodded and waited for the elevator to arrive. After a few moments, they heard the ding announcing the doors opening. Derrick stepped forward toward the open door and froze.

Machine gun fire erupted from the open elevator, slamming into the vampire and knocking him backward. Crying out in pain, Derrick rolled to the side to get out of their line of fire. It was a momentary reprieve, however, as the two black-clad men stepped out of the elevator and continued firing, riddling the vampire with bullets.

In a flash of green light, a pale green arrow lanced into the head of one of the shooters, dropping him instantly. Startled, the other shooter turned to see

Greybeard muttering and waving his hands again. Reacting quickly, the black-clad man spun around and began firing at the wizard. With a cry, Greybeard leapt to the side, landing hard. The shooter's distraction, however, proved his undoing as twin fangs lanced into his neck from behind.

Derrick drank long and deep, using the strength of the man's blood to heal the dozens of bullet wounds covering his body. After draining as much as he could in the first few moments, he let the body drop to the floor. Striding rapidly over to the fallen wizard, he drew back in surprise when the old man cried out in fear and raised his hands as if warding himself.

"What?" Derrick asked, confused at the reaction.

"Sorry," Greybeard replied, lowering his hands. "I saw your eyes glowing gold and your face enraged and I feared you had lost control" Derrick growled in irritation.

"If I lose control enough to be hunting you," Derrick replied, his voice darkening, "trust that you would have no warning or opportunity to cast any of your protections. I know what you're capable of, wizard." An instant of fear flashed across the old mage's face before he calmed.

"You're right," Greybeard admitted. "That's part of what scares me about you. If you were to ever lose the battle to your bloodlust, no one I know could stop you." Derrick sighed heavily, trying to relax again.

"Which is why I have a watchdog," Derrick replied unhappily. "That tin plated powerhouse was designed to stop me if I ever go too far. So, you have nothing to worry about." Greybeard frowned, digesting the implications of that when the elevator doors dinged again.

"Did you call the elevator again?" Greybeard asked, his eyes wide.

"No," Derrick replied curtly.

In an instant, the vampire had shifted into his wolf form and started charging toward the opening door. The shooters, however, didn't wait for the doors to finish opening before they opened fire. Derrick was again riddled with bullets as he attempted to dodge to the side. Greybeard cried out in pain behind him as Derrick tried to duck back into the elevator room.

He was stopped by another spray of bullets, however, and quickly retreated. Glancing back at Greybeard, he could see the old mage trying to crawl away, a dark bloodstain blossoming on his left side.

Derrick again tried to dart into the elevator, but the attackers were too alert to give him the opportunity. Another spray of bullets slammed into the walls and floor as he darted back out of the line of fire.

The angry wolf howled in frustration, his rich voice ringing in the confines of the room. The howl was long and throaty, resonating with anger and pain. A muffled curse came from the elevator, and Greybeard gasped in surprise.

There, in the middle of the room was the image of a giant elm tree. Its long, upright branches reaching through the top of the dome. Unlike most of the illusions caused by the Dreaming, however, this tree was slightly transparent, and the faint image of walls and windows could be seen through its large trunk.

Derrick howled again, giving voice to his anger and frustration. And as he howled, more trees began to slowly fade into view. These trees also seemed to have a transparent, almost unfinished quality to them. For Derrick, however, they were just the distraction he needed as one large tree formed right in front of the doorway to the elevator.

Derrick charged, still howling, hoping that the tree would shield him from view long enough to get inside the elevator. The two black-clad men cursed and tried to aim their weapons down as the vampiric wolf came charging into the tiny compartment, but it was already too late.

Savagely, Derrick tore at the calf muscle of one shooter as he raced around behind them. Leaping into the air he slammed against the second, tearing viciously at his throat. The dead man's body had not even had time to hit the floor before the enraged wolf leapt again, this time at the wall just past the falling shooter.

Rebounding off of the wall, his body twisting in mid-air, he used its firm surface to launch himself at the second shooter, who was just beginning to rise from the crouch he had dropped into when the wolf had ravaged his leg.

Massive jaws clamped onto either side of the wounded man's head, and with a strength unattainable by any ordinary wolf, the jaws flexed, crushing the skull of the second shooter. Shifting back into vampire form, Derrick blinked as the forest disappeared. In an instant, he was kneeling next to Greybeard, and looking at the large bloodstain on his robe.

"Can Doran heal you?" Derrick immediately asked. Greybeard nodded, wincing in pain.

"Yeah, by taking the wound into himself and then healing it," Greybeard answered.

"You have lost too much blood," Derrick stated.

"You must be healed or you will die."

Greybeard just nodded again and closed his eyes. The shift was not instantaneous. Unlike most of Greybeard's shifts, it was slow and drawn out, as he continued to wince in pain. Derrick noticed, however, that during this shift not everything changed. The bullet wounds that Greybeard had suffered, Derrick could now see there were two of them on his left side, remained even as the grey robes faded and the body sprouted long, brown fur.

After several moments, the change was complete, and the nine-foot sasquatch was laying on the bloody carpet with two bullet wounds in his chest.

Derrick nodded his encouragement to the beast as Doran slowly blinked his large, brown eyes. Looking down at the wounds, Doran narrowed his eyes, as though sizing up an opponent. After a few more moments, the great, soulful eyes closed, and the furry healer brought his hand up.

Slowly, he passed his hands over the wounds, and Derrick heard the faint clink of the bullets falling to the floor after being pushed out of the wounds. The huge sasquatch took a deep breath, then nodded and smiled as he opened his eyes again to look at the concerned vampire.

"I am glad you are feeling better," Derrick said with a smile. "I wasn't sure you could heal one of your own alters." The furry head nodded as Doran sat up again. He held up a long fingered hand and extended his index finger upwards.

"Ah, you have had to heal them once before," Derrick answered, guessing at his meaning. Doran nodded again. "Let me guess, Greybeard that time as well?" Again Doran nodded. "Potion go wrong?" Derrick asked.

Doran smiled again, wide enough that Derrick could see his impressive set of teeth. Set much like a gorilla or chimpanzee, he had the same four large, pronounced canine teeth with the flat incisors in the front and large molars in the back.

"Well, I think our attempts at distraction have failed," Derrick said, looking over at the bodies in both elevators. "The stairs it is then."

Doran rose slowly, his full nine-foot height towering over everything in the room. Gently he reached out and touched Derrick's arm. Derrick turned and looked back questioningly. Doran moved over to the center of the room, and gestured to the floor, then brought his hands up over his head in a shape that looked like a vase.

"The tree?" Derrick asked, and Doran nodded. "I'm not sure," he replied. "I didn't think those of us who were not alone in our heads could manifest our dreams. Though this is the second time it has happened to me." Doran looked questioningly at the fallen attackers, and Derrick followed his gaze. "Them?" Derrick asked. "I suppose it's possible. I was in wolf form both times, so it may have been those around me thinking of a forest when they saw me as a wolf. Though come to think of it, I don't think I've seen any dreams manifesting when any of these shooters were attacking us either." Derrick's voice faded away at the implication. Doran shook his great head and placed his hands under his tilting head like a pillow. "No dreams?" Derrick nodded, following his thought. "Possibly. If they aren't able to dream, then none would manifest around them." He shook his head again. "No wonder they're so angry."

Doran's lips twitched in a smile as he nodded in agreement.

The pair moved toward the stairs, not wanting to stay in their exposed position any longer. Suddenly, Doran stopped and turned around. Derrick watched curiously as Doran reached down and grabbed the backs of two couches. Lifting them with apparent ease, the nine-foot sasquatch carried them over to the elevators and placed one in the doorway of each of them. Derrick nodded, finally understanding his large friend's actions.

"To keep them from being able to recall the elevators and using them to surround us," Derrick stated. "Good thinking."

Doran smiled again and made his way to the stairwell door and stepped through. Derrick followed quickly, and was surprised to see Doran vaulting over the rail of the stairwell.

Just as he was about to ask why the gentle giant had not used the stairs, he noticed the ease with which the sasquatch swung from rail to rail making his way straight down the stairwell shaft. With a flicker of amusement in his eyes, Derrick considered shifting into his large bat form in order to fly down, but decided against it, noting how narrow the stairwell was. Instead, he raced down the stairs at inhuman speed.

The vampire was moving so quickly that he almost didn't see the stairwell door open right in front of him. Throwing up his arms crosswise in front of himself, he hit the opening door with the force of a charging rhino.

The door slammed closed, but not before striking whomever had opened it with enough force to knock them back into the room they came out of. In an instant, Derrick had turned and grabbed one of the handrails bolted to the wall.

With a powerful tug, he yanked the steel handrail off of the wall and turned back to the door. Turning to the railing next to the center opening of the stairwell he stuck one end of the rod through the metal rails, then moved to brace the other end against the door.

Finding a good place to brace it, he turned back to the railing only to see that Doran had made his way down to that floor and had bent the handrail around the thick outer frame of the stairwell railing. Derrick looked at the sasquatch in surprise.

"I wasn't aware you had supernatural strength." Derrick said, a hint of wariness in his tone.

Doran shrugged with a smile before continuing to swing his way down the center of the stairwell. Derrick frowned for a moment before continuing his run down the stairs.

Reaching the lowest floor, the pair stood in front of the steel door to the second level basement. Doran looked down at Derrick to ensure he was ready, then grabbed the doorknob and pulled. His furry brows furrowed as the knob refused to turn.

Taking a firmer grip, Doran twisted the doorknob hard. Derrick looked up in surprise at the breathy whuff of frustration that sounded, oddly enough, like that of a horse. Doran noticed his look and shrugged again, removing his hand from the knob to reveal deep indents on the rounded knob from the sasquatch's grip.

"Allow me," Derrick said to his large friend as he took a step back, preparing to kick the door.

Doran, however, placed a hand on the vampire's arm, his gaze peering into another place. After a moment he nodded and the body changed to that of the fiery redhead.

"Miss me?" Molly asked with a wink.

"But of course," Derrick replied, his thickly accented voice sounding silky smooth as he addressed the lovely woman. Molly just laughed and reached into her hair for a hairpin. Derrick looked at her in confusion. "You surprise me, my dear," he said, some of the smoothness falling away as he addressed her. "With that lovely mass of curly locks I had not expected you to use hairpins." She laughed again as she knelt down to inspect the lock.

"Och, I like to keep a few handy, just in case," Molly said, peering intently at the keyhole, her Irish brogue lilting with amusement at the vampire's confusion.

"In case of a need for breaking and entering?" Derrick inquired, incredulous.

"No," Molly answered, bending the hairpin and sticking it into the locking mechanism, "in case of a need for a hairpin."

Derrick just stared at her for a moment, then shook his head and let her continue with her work. After a minute or so, she gave a tiny little laugh of triumph and reached up to turn the knob on the door.

"Good luck," she said as she rose. "Strong enough to stop even Doran, but thankfully, good enough to have a very smooth action as well."

"And where, if I may ask," Derrick began, "did you learn such an unusual skill?"

"Oh, I was friendly with a locksmith a few years back," Molly answered with a grin. "He wanted to show off by teaching me how to open locks. Sadly, he couldn't keep his skills to himself, and ended up opening a lock that belonged to someone else without their permission." Derrick's lips quirked up in a half-smile.

"Judge let him off easy though, only three years in minimum security. The barrister wanted him for fifteen, for high flight risk, he said." Molly shook her head, her mass of curls dancing about her shoulders. "He was still in his devilling though, so it's no wonder the judge didn't take him seriously." The ancient vampire frowned at her for a moment.

"I am not familiar with the term devilling," Derrick replied with a hint of suspicion in his voice.

"Devilling?" Molly asked. "You've not heard the term? Now that does surprise me, coming from one as experienced as you." She grinned and winked at him before continuing. "Devilling is like an apprenticeship for barristers, or lawyers, as you call them here in the States. Or perhaps internship would be more appropriate, since they don't get paid."

"Indeed," Derrick prompted, intrigued. "How then do they earn enough money to live on?"

"Search me," Molly replied with a shrug. "I was never very friendly with any barristers." Derrick chuckled deep in his chest.

"I see." The vampire swept her hand up in a grand gesture, kissing her knuckles lightly. "I thank you for the education." Molly just laughed, her eyes twinkling.

"Och, you're quite welcome." she replied pulling her hand back after a moment. "But I'm being told I must be going now. Good luck to ye!" And with another great smile, her twinkling eyes closed and she began to shift again, this time into the golden-haired angel.

"Are you quite finished with your flirting?" Tammarion asked, looking down at the slightly shorter vampire.

"Never, dear lady," Derrick replied with a roguish

grin. Tammarion simply shook her head and gestured toward the now unlocked door. Still smiling at her Derrick opened the door and slipped through.

He found himself in a long, concrete corridor that stretched some distance before a door on the left side broke the monotony of the whitewashed walls. Looking farther down, the vampire could see additional doors, but none save the last were marked.

Derrick paused for a moment to look at the signs on the far door, and relay descriptions of them inside. He then frowned and nodded as Sean informed him that they were the danger signs for toxic, flammable chemicals.

"And how do we know they are being held on this level?" Tammarion inquired coming up behind him.

"We don't, dear lady," Derrick replied, turning back toward the slightly glowing angel. "However, this is the lowest level, and Sean felt it was logical to start at the bottom and work our way up as we searched for them." Tammarion nodded then gestured toward the door. Derrick frowned and turned to face her more fully.

"And why, may I ask," he inquired, his voice darkening, "am I the one in the vanguard of our search? Would it not be better for us to split up to look more quickly?" Tammarion paused and looked closely at the vampire.

"No, it is too dangerous to split up," she answered, "And you are in the vanguard because you are immune to most damage. So, should we be surprised, you would be largely unaffected by any attack."

"And why do I feel that is not the only reason?" Derrick pressed, still frowning at the angel.

"Because it is not," the angel replied calmly. "I can

feel your hunger, creature of the darkness, and I am loathe to trust it." Derrick's eyes flashed golden with anger.

"Then I shall tell you the same thing I told the old mage," Derrick answered, his voice stiff with suppressed rage. "If I wanted to cause you harm, there is little you could to do stop me!" Tammarion stared at him for a few more moments before nodding.

"While the encounter may end up surprising you, I fear you are likely correct." Tammarion admitted. "My apologies, Derrick. This is neither the time nor the place for this conversation. Please know it is not your heart I distrust. You have shown yourself to be honorable and caring. It is your thirst, and how much control it has over you that I distrust." Derrick's anger cooled quickly at the startling apology, and after a moment he nodded.

"It is forgiven," he replied, his voice once again smooth and cultured without, a trace of anger. "You are correct; the thirst can drive me to acts I would not ordinarily take. However, I am well sated at the moment. And I do not believe that my own armored gaoler would permit me to harm any of you, even by accident." The golden-haired angel nodded her understanding.

"I think you may find that Peter is not so much your jailer as he is your protector," Tammarion said, her tone softening. Derrick, however, raised his hands to forestall her next words.

"As you said, this is neither the time nor the place for this conversation," Derrick said shortly. "We have friends to find."

"Agreed," Tammarion replied, reaching for the door, but paused at the feel of a touch on her arm.

"Allow me," Derrick said, his voice again rich and

smooth. "As you said, I am more durable than any of you in that body." Tammarion smiled at the vampire and took a step back.

In a movement almost too quick to see, the ancient vampire had flung open the door and raced inside. Because of the swiftness of his actions, it was almost a full three seconds before the sound of gunfire erupted in the room beyond.

Derrick had already reached the far side of the room to break the neck of one shooter before the angel with her glowing golden sword swept into the room, taking the head of another shooter less than a heartbeat later.

The pair charged toward the other two men in the room, each of them moving faster than the human's eyes could track. Tammarion's sword bit deep as she thrust it into the chest of the third man in the room. An almost immeasurable instant later, Derrick reached the last of the men, his hand slamming into his chest as though he was going to tear the man's heart right out of his chest.

However, the vampire stopped before delivering the killing blow. The shooter's eyes were wide with fear and questions as he looked up at the demonic visage of the enraged vampire. Derrick, however, looked over at Tammarion.

"Sean thinks it will take too long to search every room on every floor," Derrick said, his accent distorted slightly by his elongated fangs. "He suggested a guide might be able to help us."

Tammarion's face brightened with excitement as Derrick turned back to his opponent, staring deeply into his eyes. After a few moments, the man began to relax, all traces of fear or strain washing out of his body. "Now, my new friend," Derrick said, his voice changing with his appearance again. "Where can I find the three friends kidnapped from the old woman's house last night?" The man smiled vaguely as he gestured toward the door.

"In the last room," the black-clad man replied. "Boss thought you wouldn't want to go in, since it was filled with toxic chemicals."

"Did he now?" Derrick said with amused malice. "Well then, it is good that we have you to show us the way, isn't it my friend?"

The man nodded vaguely again as Derrick stood him back on his feet. The man started slightly as though he hadn't realized he had been knocked off of his feet to begin with. With a fanged smile of encouragement, Derrick gestured the man toward the door. In a daze, the man walked out of the room and started down the hallway.

The pair followed him to the last door, glancing briefly at the warning signs before looking back at the door again. The man reached into his pocket and pulled out a small set of keys, moving to unlock the door. The instant Derrick heard the click of the lock, he pulled the enthralled man back and out of the way.

"Stay here," the vampire commanded, before turning and opening the door.

Inside was a moderately-sized room with several banks of computers and chairs along most of the walls. Along one wall, in front of the largest row of computers, was a large bay window. Derrick stepped over to it and looked down.

The window opened up into a huge room filled with giant vats of liquid connected to each other through various tubes running throughout the room. Tammarion stepped up to him, taking in the scene at a glance.

"We must keep going," she said gently, nodding toward another door on the far side of the room.

Derrick turned and made his way over to the far door, the sounds of Sean discussing the various instruments and what they meant echoing in his head. Moving through the door, he found himself on a catwalk spanning one side of the room he had seen through the glass. Aware of how exposed they were, he moved quickly and steadily across the bridge, reaching the door on the far side in moments.

Suddenly wary, the vampire stopped before opening the door. Concentrating on his hearing, he closed his eyes momentarily. After a moment, he was able to discern two large strong heartbeats, one tiny heartbeat, one heartbeat that sounded more like the buzz of an insect and a humming sound he did not recognize. He turned as Tammarion approached.

"What can you sense?" she asked quietly.

"Two large males, what sounds like a small animal, an insect, and a strange humming noise," Derrick replied, just as softly. Tammarion nodded decisively.

"It is them," she replied. "Each of them has shifted into an alter and has been captured that way." Derrick frowned.

"How could they capture the shadow?" he asked. "A ghost can travel through objects."

"I do not know," Tammarion said. "The humming noise, perhaps?" Derrick shook his head.

"I am not certain I can get into the room and kill both of the men before they can harm the others." Derrick admitted with a scowl. Tammarion smiled.

"Thank you for your candor," she replied. "Perhaps

another would serve better here?" Derrick sighed and nodded, closing his eyes.

"We have need of your precision," Derrick said with a scowl, opening his eyes in the cave and looking around for Sean.

"Of course," Sean replied calmly. Derrick rose from the stone chair, still reluctant to allow anyone else to control the body while they were still in danger.

Sean sat quickly in the stone chair and opened his eyes to see Tammarion watching with interest. Sean raised an eyebrow, then opened his scanner without a word.

Taking a quick measurement of its readings and calculating the proper vectors, taking into account the thickness of the door, the motion of the enemies, the proximity to the large electro-magnetic device, and probable follow-through trajectory, he drew his laser pistol and pointed it at a precise angle toward the door.

Two shots were discharged in rapid succession, and a quick glance at his scanner indicated that both guards had been dispatched. Without a word, Sean reached out and opened the door, taking a half of a step inside before freezing in place at the scene before him.

CHAPTER NINETEEN

It was quite an elaborate trap, Sean had to admit. Very cleverly worked and potentially unstoppable by someone moving rapidly through the doorway. He could detect three independent triggers, though it was the physical tripwire touching his ankle that alerted him to the potential danger.

A quick glance around the room revealed a laser tripwire near chest height, and if he was correct, a pressure plate one point five meters from the doorway. Which, he calculated, was approximately how far Derrick traveled in a single stride when he was moving at top speed.

The trap itself was overly elaborate, bordering on the dramatic, by Sean's estimation. However, it appeared to be effective. Any one of the three triggers would initiate a computerized response.

The computer would release a mechanical grip on a tiny three-centimeter by three-centimeter by three-centimeter cage suspended near the ceiling, containing their tiny pixie friend. The cage would swing down on a wire connected to a different point in the ceiling resulting in a pendulum-like arc when it reached its terminus. The cage would then swing until it impacted the depressor of a large syringe.

That syringe was mounted three quarters of the way inside of another cage, this one six centimeters by four centimeters by eight centimeters, and containing a small brown and white rabbit. The impact would not only push the depressor in order to move the plunger, it would also move the syringe the additional one quarter of its length necessary to puncture the thin hide of their rodent friend.

Calculating the probability that the syringe was filled with some form of lethal substance, Sean decided the odds were ninety-nine point eight nine four seven three two to one for the substance being lethal.

The tiny cage would then rebound against its pivot until it impacted what appeared to be the coils of a large electromagnet. This would doubtless cause an electrical surge through the metal bars of the tiny cage, resulting in an effect similar to that of the 'bug zapper' device commonly used to deter small, flying insects.

This would, of course, kill their second friend instantly. Additionally, the impact of the metal cage against two of the coils would likely cause a short circuit of the electrical system.

Looking closely at the device, Sean noticed a secondary device on the underside. It appeared to be a small explosive charge attached to another magnet with an opposing polarity.

Sean deduced that a disruption in the current electromagnetic field would cause that magnet to suddenly attract toward the coils of the first device, likely triggering some form of blasting cap. That, in turn, would initiate a larger explosion that would, in all probability, destroy the entire room and everyone in it. Sean wondered if the two guards were aware of the end result of the final device, or if whomever led them simply didn't care if two of his guards were sacrificed in the attempt to destroy any intruder.

Sean confirmed his initial assessment. An overly dramatic and complicated trap that, if not calculated precisely, would fail at one or more points of its implementation. It was particularly redundant since the final explosion would eliminate everything in the room regardless of what else occurred.

However, Sean knew, whomever had designed the trap had indeed calculated precisely, and Sean was confident it would behave as intended. In total, Sean's observations and calculations had taken precisely two point zero one three seconds, which meant he could expect a response to his lack of movement approximately…

"What's wrong?" Tammarion asked, seeing Sean freeze.

"A trap," Sean replied succinctly. "However, it is a trap that can be circumvented by interrupting its initial impetus." At Tammarion's silence he continued. "If you observe over my left shoulder you will notice a tiny cage suspended near the ceiling four point three meters into the room at a fifty-two-degree angle from this doorway. Upon breaching the doorway, a laser tripwire will cause that cage to fall and initiate a series of triggers that will result in an explosion capable of destroying everyone and everything in this room."

Sean decided that it would be extraneous to recount the details of every stage of the trap and decided to formulate his instructions in as succinct a form as possible.

"What I require is that when I lower my body into a crouch, that you will fly into the room as quickly as you are capable, and arrest the descent of that small cage. Once that is complete, I will be able to enter the room and dismantle the remainder of the devices." Tammarion simply nodded and braced herself for a literal flying leap. "Now," Sean announced, dropping into a low crouch.

In a burst of speed, Tammarion dove over the top of the pointy-eared alien, snapping her golden wings of light out as soon as she had cleared the doorway. As predicted, the tiny cage began to fall the moment she crossed the threshold. Fortunately, as Sean had calculated, her momentum was sufficient for her to reach the tiny cage before it hit the terminus of its descent and begin its pendulum swing.

The angel hovered there, turning to look back at Sean as he rose smoothly and stepped over the tripwire and into the room. Sean noted that he did not have to step over the wire, as the cage had already been removed from the equation, however it could still pose a hazard, so he chose not to risk it.

With practiced efficiency, he removed the syringe from the small cage to ensure that the animal did not brush against it when leaving the cage before opening the door in the front. The rabbit hopped out, seemingly happy to be free. Sean noted that Tammarion had done the same for the tiny cage in her hands, releasing the pixie to fly itself around the room.

Unfortunately, she then released the cage, not realizing that there was still a danger should the cage continue its pendulum trajectory and impact the electromagnet.

Sean's hand shot out as he leaned forward to halt the cage's descent a scant quarter of a centimeter from its terminus. Tammarion looked startled, then her eyes widened as she realized the likely cause of his rapid movement.

Taking the wire suspending the cage in both hands, Sean pulled with ninety-eight point two kilograms of force, causing the wire to snap and releasing the cage. Sean placed the cage on the floor, so that it was no longer a risk even by accident before turning back to the electromagnet.

After taking a few minutes to study the final step of the intended trap, Sean concluded that there were no secondary traps to disarm before removing the explosives. Gently, he pulled the device out from under the electromagnet and examined it more closely. After another minute's study, he was able to remove the primary magnet from the explosive device, as well as the blasting cap, rendering the explosive mostly harmless.

"Well, that's two of them," Tammarion said, returning to the ground. "Where's Susan?"

"I suspect she is still in her phantasmal form and has been suspended within the electromagnetic field surrounding this machine," Sean replied, continuing to study the machine without touching it.

After several minutes of intense study, Sean determined that there was a capsule suspended inside of the magnet, and that this capsule most likely contained their third friend.

"I will require the use of the Stone Skin potion," Sean said, looking over at Tammarion. "I will also require you to hold me suspended over the machine for approximately four minutes." Tammarion frowned.

"Does that potion change your weight?" she asked warily.

"I do not know," Sean replied calmly. "However, I will need to remain suspended over the top of the machine so that I can extract the capsule inside it. The Stone Skin potion should allow me to come into contact with the electricity without harm, as stone is typically non-conductive."

"I don't think I will be able to hold your body weight suspended over that device." Tammarion admitted reluctantly.

"Indeed, which is why you shall ingest your Levitation potion. Ordinarily that would disrupt your flight capabilities. In this case, I believe that my own weight should provide the necessary ballast to allow you to control your flight with little difficulty."

"Very well," Tammarion replied, still sounding unconvinced.

Sean nodded at Tammarion to proceed. He then removed the fourth potion from the belt that was still wrapped around his waist, and in one smooth movement had uncorked the vessel and ingested the contents. After a few moments Sean took one of the wires that had held the magnet to the explosive and attempted to poke his arm with it.

"I feel nothing," Sean stated. "It is logical to assume the potion is having its desired effect. If you please?" Sean asked, looking over at the angel.

Putting her doubts aside, Tammarion rose into the air, taking a moment to become accustomed to her lighter weight. She then reached down to grasp Sean's arms, and lift him off of the ground. Sean considered reminding her that he would require the use of his arms, but decided against it. The angel had proven herself capable in the past, and Sean had no cause to doubt her memory or cognitive capabilities at this time. As he had calculated, Tammarion released his arm so that she could grasp his belt with first one hand then the other.

"Ready?" she asked, rising higher into the air.

"Ready," he replied.

At that, she released her hands one at a time again, this time to grasp his ankles in quick succession. This had the result of flipping him over in midair so that he was upside down. With a quick glance to ensure he was where he needed to be, Tammarion flew up and over the top of the electromagnetic device.

Gingerly, she lowered him down toward the coils, wincing as his arms made accidental contact with the electrically charged coils. Sean, however, exhibited no discomfort, so she continued to lower him. After a few minutes, he looked up at her.

"Up," Sean instructed. "I have the canister."

Quickly, Tammarion drew him up and flew him over to an unoccupied corner of the room before lowering him to the ground. Sean held the canister tightly in one hand, while reaching out to the floor with the other.

"You may release me," Sean said calmly.

Tammarion released his ankles and backed away. Sean held the one-armed handstand for a few seconds to ensure his balance, then in one smooth motion, he bent his body at the waist to lower his legs until they touched the floor, then lifted his torso until he was vertical again.

Sean looked down at the canister, noting the tiny seam that indicated a lid. Detecting no hinge, he surmised that it was likely screwed on. Grasping it tightly, he twisted, and in one sharp movement removed the lid.

Immediately, a dark grey form emerged from the canister, floating over to a wall as though it were trying to blend in. Sean looked inside the canister and nodded to himself. Magnets on the inside as well, just as he expected. Placing the canister on the floor next to the tiny cage, he looked at the companions.

"And now to make our exit," Sean said, acting on the assumption that all of them could understand and follow his directions. "Tammarion, please take point, the three non-combatants follow immediately behind, and Peter will take up the rear guard position. A moment." Sean closed his eyes, focusing inward. Opening his eyes in the cave, he gestured to the knight as he rose quickly from the stone chair. Peter sat down and opened his eyes.

Jostling his shield on his arm to make sure it was secure he looked around the room. It always was. Seeing that everyone was ready, he simply nodded to Tammarion. Tammarion nodded back, then strode quickly out of the room and onto the catwalk.

Seeing the rabbit wandering around aimlessly, the tiny pixie flew down and landed astride the furry animal. Grabbing its ears in his tiny hands, the pixie directed the rabbit to the door to follow the angel. Peter was grateful when the shadow followed the other two out of the room. With one last glance around to ensure they had not forgotten anything, Peter followed the group out onto the catwalk.

Peter looked around warily as they made their way across the long, open expanse. Despite his caution however, the first rattling hail of bullets took the entire group by surprise. Spinning rapidly, he attempted to identify where the shots were coming from.

"Run!" he yelled, his deep voice booming in the large room.

Tammarion spread her wings and flew the rest of the way forward to ensure that the room ahead was clear. Peter turned to where the shots were coming from and moved quickly to keep pace with their friends.

Another hail of bullets ricocheted off of his shield as he rapidly sidestepped to keep himself between his friends and the shooter. All of a sudden, a new hail of bullets strafed the small group from the opposite direction. Peter cursed soundly, they had been flanked!

A high-pitched, squealing cry caused him to spin around, his mind already processing what he did not want to believe. As he spun, he saw the tiny form of the pixie spinning off into the air and the broken body of the rabbit falling back from where the bullet's impact had knocked it into the air.

For a moment, time froze and everyone stared in horror at the sight of the blood pouring from the wound in the rabbit's side. Peter was aware of a large body slamming into reality next to him, as a heart-wrenching cry echoed in the suddenly silent chamber.

"KATIE!" Phil cried, dropping to his knees to cradle the tiny rabbit. Another sharp rattle of bullets, however, reminded Peter that they were still under attack.

"GO!" he yelled at Phil. "I've got her!" Phil did not respond, his eyes distant, tears falling from his unseeing eyes. "GO!" Peter yelled again, reaching down to scoop the rabbit out of his arms and tucking it against his body behind his shield.

The knight looked down in surprise as he realized the tiny creature was still breathing. He was just about to push the grieving man toward the door to get him off of the catwalk when Phil's eyes snapped up, and ignited in red flame.

Peter took a step back as he watched Phil's mouth spread wide, his teeth sharpening to appear almost shark-like. As he watched, black smoke began to seep from the large biker's back, and Peter knew it was not a shark that was coming.

With a start, Peter realized that he was witnessing the splitting of a new personality in his large friend. As the smoke continued to pour out of Phil's back, his now triangular teeth silvered with a metallic sheen. In a matter of moments, the dark smoke had completely surrounded the man until all that could be seen was the burning flame of his eyes and the silver glint of his triangular teeth.

With a final swirl, the smoke cleared to reveal a tall, broad shouldered creature in an ankle-length hooded black duster. The cowl of the duster was pulled up and over its head, and Peter could see only darkness under the hood save for the burning eyes and razor sharp teeth.

It appeared to be wearing a charcoal grey shirt with black pants and black leather biker boots. Its forearms were wrapped in thick leather bracers, with steel spikes glinting in the fluorescent light. Black leather gloves completed the covering so that not an inch of the creature's actual body could be seen. Its body was crisscrossed with thick chains, and Peter could not decide if they were intended to be weapons or armor.

The most unusual thing about its appearance, however, was the darkness surrounding its form. It appeared to be a cross between inky black flames and coal dark smoke, flickering and flashing like fire, while simultaneously billowing and rolling like smoke.

The creature turned to look at Peter, and Peter could feel the utter cold, the total lack of compassion coming from the creature. He knew in that moment that this creature was built of pain and rage for a single purpose. And that much like the raven in Poe's epic poem, who poured his soul into his name of Nevermore, so too did this creature have a single name and defining purpose.

"Vengeance," Peter whispered almost unwillingly.

At that word, the creature gave him a small nod, then turned back toward the room, which had grown ominously silent. Reaching down into his duster, the creature drew two long barreled pistols, holding them upright, pointing at the ceiling as though he were about to begin a duel. Peter watched in fascination as the creature caused the black flames encasing his body to spread outward and cover the two firearms before lowering them to point at the room.

The tension broke suddenly as bullets exploded from three different directions all focused on the creature. For his part, Vengeance quickly sidestepped his previous position and began returning fire. Each bullet also wreathed in the same black flame that encased his pistols.

Shaking himself out of his reverie, Peter charged forward again, spinning to avoid the creature as he passed him on the catwalk. The creature seemed to intuitively sense the movement as it, too, spun in counterpoint, both allowing Peter to slip by without difficulty as well as positioning itself for another round of gunfire at the now four different shooters who were trying to eliminate this new threat.

Looking ahead, Peter saw that Tammarion had shaken herself out of her surprise at the same time he had and had finally reached the door on the far side. Peter heard screams and the sound of more gunfire from the room ahead, and a moment later the body of a black-clad man smashed through the huge window looking out into the main room and tumbled to the floor below. By the time Peter and their ghostly companion had reached the door, Tammarion had cleared out all of the men from the intended ambush.

Turning back, Peter started to call out to Vengeance that he could follow only to see the creature vault over the catwalk railing to the floor thirty feet below. Shaking his head in futility, Peter went back into the room just as a thick steel door slammed down in front of their only remaining exit.

Peter hesitated for only a moment before placing the wounded rabbit on top of one of the banks of computers. Just as he had taken a step back, more machine gun fire slammed through the open doorway. Peter's shield snapped up to block the deadly hail, taking a step forward into the doorway.

"Tammarion! Cover the door! Sean says that it is an automatic fire door, whatever that means! I will switch so he can…" Peter's words cut off abruptly as the angel's face registered an instant of shocked surprise before the body shifted again to reveal the fiery red-head.

"Yer the one with the shield, you big lummox!"

Molly shouted at him, her brogue becoming more evident with her distress. "You cover that door. I'll open this one."

Peter acknowledged the wisdom of her words with a nod before turning back toward the open doorway, and not a moment too soon. Another burst of deadly bullets slammed against his raised shield, nearly pushing him back.

Setting his jaw with a growl, Peter braced himself in the doorway, preventing any stray bullets from passing him to threaten the friends still behind him. After another couple of minutes blocking the attacks from outside the room, Peter risked a glance back. Molly was staring intently at the screen, her fingers flying across the keyboard.

"Where did you learn that?" Peter asked, surprised again by this versatile young woman.

"My first job after graduating from my senior cycle was as a medical receptionist," Molly replied, still typing furiously. "I learned how to type very quickly. I also worked at an internet service provider, and they taught me how computers worked. I picked up the rest on my own." Peter shook his head in amazement before turning back to the doorway.

"And I've just about got it… There!" Molly cried, "Ouch!" Peter spun in time to see her shaking her hand, and a tiny, green spider flying off to land on the computer console and scurry away. "Bloody thing bit me," Molly said indignantly, before hitting one final key on her keyboard.

With that, the large steel door rose again revealing the sturdy door they had entered the first time. With a grin, Molly stood, took two steps toward him, then slumped to the floor, her eyes rolling back in her head.

"Molly!" Peter yelled, turning to race over to her and dropping to one knee beside her. Looking up again, he muttered, "Damn you, Sean! Fine, do what you must," and closed his eyes.

Sean opened his eyes to make a quick examination of the fallen woman. He was reassured by her moan, and double checked to ensure that her eyes were not dilated, indicating a concussion.

Thankfully, they were not dilated, however there was a small red mark on her hand, where Sean assumed she had suffered the spider bite. He gently patted her face to encourage her to wake, when he saw the foaming spittle starting to leak from the corner of her mouth.

"Molly!" Sean said with a note of urgency in his voice, still patting her face. "Molly, can you hear me?"

Slowly, almost groggily, Molly opened her eyes. Sean noted the lines of pain on her face as he continued to examine her.

"Are you all right? Can you hear me?"

Molly nodded, then winced in pain again.

"How do you feel?" Sean asked, touching the back of his hand to her forehead.

Molly made an unpleasant face, then tried to smile. Sean could see the haze of pain in her eyes.

"Can you speak?"

Molly looked at him for a moment before her eyes widened in panic. Her hands slapped against his arms as she fought to try to form words.

"It is all right," Sean attempted to reassure her. As

her head turned back and forth in fear, he looked again at the growing foam at the corner of her mouth, his concern rising.

"Molly, it looks as though you have been poisoned from that spider bite. Can you summon Doran to heal you?"

Molly looked away, as if someone else were speaking to her. Suddenly, her eyes snapped back to look at Sean and she shook her head in refusal.

"Why can you not summon your healer?" Sean inquired.

Molly simply shook her head, her hands clenching into fists then relaxing again.

"I believe that your symptoms are more significant than you may realize. It would be best if you were under the care of a healer."

Molly seemed to steel herself before shaking her head again.

"Molly, your symptoms are increasing." Sean stated, as her body began to tremble. "You must change into your healer."

Again, Molly shook her head, her fists clenching tightly. Sean grew more and more concerned as her body trembles increased as though she were freezing.

"Doran," Sean said sternly, "your assistance is required!"

As Sean watched, he saw the faint outline of a large, furry form over the top of her now convulsing body. The image lasted only a moment though, before Molly clenched her fists even tighter, the rest of her body thrashing in what had quickly become a full seizure. Sean felt himself being yanked backwards mentally as he was pulled forcibly out of the stone chair.

Garrett snapped opened his eyes, looking down at the fiery red-head in a panic. Grabbing her clenched fist in his hands, he began to plead with her.

"Molly what are you doing?" Garrett asked, panic evident in his voice. "Molly, let Doran come up! Let him heal you!" He couldn't tell if the stubborn Irish woman could even hear him any longer as her body shook, her head rapping on the concrete floor.

Garrett leaned forward, slipping one arm under her shoulders and pulling her half into his lap as her seizure continued to grow stronger.

"Molly! Molly!" Garrett implored, his voice rising into a yell. "Don't do this Molly!"

He wrapped his arms around her, clutching her tightly against his chest as he tried to contain the worst of her convulsions. Realizing he wasn't getting anywhere calling for her, he tried calling others.

"DORAN!" Garrett yelled. "We need you!" After a few moments, he tried again. "Tammarion! Where are you?" As before, with the image of Doran, a ghost of the great wings of light surrounded her before fading away again.

"Molly, what are you doing?!" Garrett yelled, becoming more and more agitated. "Why won't you switch?!"

For an instant, Garrett thought he saw her face pause, and give him a tiny smile before wincing again in pain. Then, as though that one small act had drained the last of her strength, her body began shaking and convulsing in earnest.

"MOLLY!" Garrett yelled, his voice taking on a wild, panicked tone. "Ann, Greybeard, somebody! You've got to get her out of there! You have to let Doran heal her!"

Her petite body thrashed so violently in his arms that he almost couldn't hold on to her. Finally, her shuddering frame convulsed one last time as a loud crack echoed in the small room before her body went suddenly limp in his arms.

"NO, MOLLY!" Garrett screamed into the now silent room. Horrified shock stabbed through his chest like a blade as he realized what her limp form meant. "ANN!" he screamed, his head flung backward with a primal scream of anguish before bursting into heart-wrenching sobs.

CHAPTER TWENTY

Garrett had no idea how long he sat there sobbing, clutching the still form against his chest. He barely noticed when a gentle arm wrapped around his shoulders, enfolding both of them. Nor did he hear the much quieter tears of the woman who held him close, grieving with him.

It wasn't until he heard the gentle, broken song in a Slavic language he did not recognize that he realized that Susan was rocking them back and forth in her arms. Her voice catching with tears as she sang what sounded like a lullaby.

Slowly he regained his senses, and his own sobs lessened. Tears continued to stream down his face as his body relaxed into the same gentle, quiet crying. Soon, the only sounds that could be heard were the soft tears of two friends who had lost someone dear to both of them. The two friends looked up with shocked surprise, however, as another pair of arms wrapped around them, and a third set of tears joined their own.

"Katie!" Garrett said in surprise, his voice harsh and rough with grief. "You're okay?" Katie nodded, still unable to speak herself through the tears. "What?

How?" Garrett pressed, still in shock. Katie struggled to compose herself enough to talk. Finally, she managed to reply in a harsh whisper.

"Muffins wasn't dead," she said sadly. "She was just hurt badly. Once I was able to get one of my other inner ones to take care of her, I was able to switch back again."

"But your wounds!" Garrett said emphatically, "Didn't the wounds shift with you?"

"No," Katie frowned. "Why would they do that? It was Muffins that was shot, not me."

"But when Greybeard was shot and Doran came out, he still had the gunshot wounds!" Garrett exclaimed.

"Oh," Katie answered, surprised. "I don't know why that happened. It's never been like that for me. If one of us is hurt, they keep the hurt even when they go inside."

"But how…" Garrett began, but stopped as a tall figure darkened the open doorway.

The three friends looked up at the face of the creature Vengeance. Susan shuddered visibly at the sight, but Katie didn't seem to be afraid of him in the slightest.

The creature's flaming eyes widened slightly, then the flickering smoke rose to envelop his body. After a moment the smoke dissipated and Phil stood there looking down at the friends, his face a mixture of joy at seeing Katie alive and well, and grief at seeing Molly's body.

"Oh, Phil!" Katie sobbed, standing quickly and wrapping her arms around the burly biker before breaking down into deep, wracking sobs of her own.

Wrapping his arms around her, Phil slowly dropped to his knees beside their other friends, pulling Katie gently down with him. Tears fell silently from his eyes as he held Katie tightly in his arms, holding her through her grief. The tough-looking man locked eyes with Garrett, his face lined with concern and shared sorrow. Garrett felt his own eyes start to well up with tears again as he nodded in acknowledgment to his friend.

After a few more minutes, the four remaining friends pulled back, three of them rising on shaky legs. Garrett, however, could not seem to muster the strength to rise.

"We can't stay," Phil said softly. "We still have to get out of here."

Garrett nodded, and looked down at Molly's face. He could almost imagine she was sleeping, which made him smile a bit at the thought. Tenderly, he leaned down to place a kiss on her forehead.

"I love you, Ann." Garrett said softly, his voice still thick with grief.

"Love always to you," Susan said softly, reaching out to touch Molly's cheek. Katie let go of Phil and knelt down next to Garrett.

"We love you," Katie said, her fingertips gently reaching out to touch Molly's other cheek. Phil knelt down on one knee next to Katie.

"You will be in our hearts, always," Phil said, taking one of Molly's small hands in his own massive ones.

After a moment, the four of them rose again, Garrett gently laying the body down on the floor before rising. The group turned to the door making their way out of the room when they heard a familiar voice behind them.

"And I love all of you!" said the sweet, motherly voice. As one, the four friends whirled around to see Ann sitting up, a warm smile on her face.

"ANN!" Garrett yelled, racing back to her, sweeping the grandmotherly lady up in his arms with a cry of joy and spinning her around. Ann laughed and returned the hug tightly before pulling back and tapping him on the shoulder.

"Could you put me down please?" she asked with a grin. "I'm starting to get a touch of vertigo."

"Of course! Sorry!" Garrett said, lowering her back down until her feet touched the ground again.

Instantly they were mobbed by the other three friends who wrapped all of them up in a giant group hug, alternately laughing and crying with joy to see their friend alive and well. After a few minutes the group pulled back, their eyes filled with questions for their friend.

"What happened?" Garrett asked, confused. "I thought you were dead!" Ann smiled at him, but her smile was laced with sadness.

"No," Ann replied, "I didn't die." Ann paused for a moment, collecting herself. "Molly did," she finished softly.

"What?!" the group exclaimed in unison. Ann held up a hand to forestall their questions.

"Whatever that spider was, it caused some kind of severe anaphylactic reaction." Ann explained. "Without some sort of immediate treatment, like an epinephrine injector, there was nothing that anyone could do to stop it."

"Couldn't Doran heal it?" Garrett asked, his voice deep with sorrow. Ann shook her head.

"He tried to come up to heal it, but it wasn't going to be enough," Ann replied. "Molly almost let him come up, but she must have seen in his eyes that he knew he would fail. Which means that if he came up and then failed to heal the body, he would have been the one who died." Ann's voice broke as she continued. "When Molly saw that, she refused to allow him to switch. She grabbed the doorway and held on so tightly that even Doran couldn't move her."

"She gave self as sacrifice?" Susan asked, her voice hushed with awe. Ann nodded.

"She did. She saw in Doran's eyes that this was a death sentence, so she gave her life to save his," Ann replied. "She held on till the last, so that he couldn't switch with her at the last moment. Even in death she was strong, which is why it took us so long to be able to allow me to come up again."

"But, how are the rest of you alive?" Garrett asked, confused.

"I don't know," Ann replied with a shrug. "Doran thinks it's because of the Dreaming; that we all became completely separate entities instead of just different personalities. So when one of us dies, it is that one entity who dies, not the body itself." Phil let out a gusty breath causing everyone to turn to him.

"Sorry," Phil said, still looking relieved. "Muffins is still hurt and I don't know if she will make it. So the thought that if she dies, she won't take Katie with her…" His voice trailed off, not needing to finish the thought.

Katie turned to him and wrapped her arms around his neck, pulling him down for a long kiss. The three friends just smiled as they watched the pair happily. Finally coming up for air, Katie snuggled into Phil's arms, her head on his chest.

"So, can we get out of here?" Katie asked worriedly.

"Absolutely!" Garrett replied. "Though Ann and I should probably change." Ann nodded as the two of them stepped back and closed their eyes.

Peter opened his eyes to see Tammarion standing next to him, her eyes blazing in challenge. Peter recognized the look, the need to find an outlet for all of the hurt and anger they felt. With a nod of acknowledgment to the angelic warrior, he turned to the three friends.

"Phil," Peter started, "your new alter. Can you summon him? We may need the help."

"I don't know," Phil replied looking distant. "I don't think so, he's so new I don't even know how to talk to him." Phil paused a moment. "Actually, I think he may only come out to avenge someone." Peter nodded.

"I thought that might be the case." Peter said grimly. "Very well then. Tammarion, if you would take the lead?"

The angel nodded as she drew her sword and started toward the door. The group exited out into the hallway, braced for an all-out attack, so they were surprised to discover the hallway was empty. Not wanting to question their good fortune, the band made their way to the end of the hall to start up the stairwell. As Tammarion swung open the stairway door however, they were all forced to back up rapidly as large chunks of concrete poured out of the doorway.

"They've blown the stairwell," Tammarion said, coughing softly at all of the dust that now blew out of the open door. "Which begs the question, where is your guide?" she asked looking around.

"Then we find another way," Peter replied grimly, jostling his shield arm again. "I do not know where Derrick's thrall has gone. Though if they have sealed our exit, he has likely been recaptured or killed."

Tammarion nodded, and turned to go back down the hallway. She passed the first door, knowing it contained a single room that had already been cleared of enemies. Moving quickly to the second door, she motioned the group back before shearing through the lock and latching mechanism with a single downward swipe of her glowing great-sword.

Quickly, she spun to the far side of the door as machine gun fire riddled the door itself, knocking it open to slam against the wall with a resounding bang. Tammarion ducked her head around the open doorway, then flung herself backwards as more machine gun fire riddled the wall where she had been standing a moment earlier.

With an easy tuck and roll, she landed in a crouch, her eyes flashing as she gestured to Peter that there were nine in the room. Peter gave a quick nod in response, then readied himself against the wall opposite the doorway.

With a roar like a charging bull Peter brought his shield up and charged the wall next to the door. Machine gun fire tore through the open doorway as those inside mistakenly thought he was going to charge into the room from there. Much to their surprise, the heavily armored knight blasted through the wall itself like a wrecking ball, his powerful legs pumping rapidly.

The first shooter was unlucky enough to be near the wall when Peter slammed through, and took several flying bricks to the head, dropping him instantly.

The second fared little better when three hundred pounds of fully armored knight shield-slammed him, blowing him ten feet back to strike a third shooter, tumbling them both to the floor.

Peter didn't slow, however, and continued to charge, his massive, booted feet slamming down onto the fallen men with bone-crushing force as he raced by.

The fourth man on that side of the room had time to turn his weapon, leveling it at the knight and releasing a short burst before Peter reached him. Once again, thankfully, Peter's shield proved to be bulletproof and the shots rang against it in a sharp staccato. Unluckily for the fourth shooter, Peter was close enough that one of the bullets managed to ricochet straight back from his shield and strike the shooter in the forehead, killing him instantly.

The final shooter on that side of the room turned and managed to take more careful aim as Peter dealt with the first four. Peter, however, was ready for him, and rather than continuing his charge as he passed the fourth shooter, he dropped down into what looked like a baseball player's slide into home base.

Bullets flew over his head as he slid, the full force of his massive body striking the last man at the ankles and flipping him forward. As he slid, Peter had drawn his sword, and had it perfectly positioned to intercept the man's falling body, impaling him through the chest right up to the cross guard.

Finally, impacting the far wall of the room, Peter absorbed the force of the slide by flexing his legs and then pushing away again. Tucking into a shoulder roll, he managed to come up onto one knee. Snapping his right arm out, he flung the impaled man off of his sword, then crouched down low behind his shield.

As he had hoped, the four shooters on the far side of the room were distracted by his display and had turned toward him. Bullets slammed into his shield from four different angles, the sheer force of the impact causing him to slide backwards against the concrete floor. Peter grinned fiercely at the success of his plan, knowing that Tammarion would take full advantage of their distraction.

Punctual as always, Tammarion dove into the room, her wings holding her aloft so that she would be above any stray bullets that came through the doorway. Thankfully, she had little to worry about as the shooters were more concerned with blasting a hole in Peter's shield than any flying menace from above.

This oversight was to prove their end as well as Tammarion's mighty blade, swinging down to the right, sheared through the back of the skull of the first shooter, and her backswing from right to left cleaving through the top of the head of the second.

Angling her flight downward, the third stroke of the great blade stabbed downward into the junction of the third man's head and shoulder, driving deeply into his body until it pierced his heart. Spinning in mid-air she swung her sword around, the man still impaled upon it.

Tammarion used his body as both a shield and a battering ram to slam into the fourth shooter, knocking him backwards like a golf ball struck by a man-shaped club. Following through on her "golf swing" caused the impaled man to fly off of the blade and strike the far wall.

Turning back to the man she had just clubbed

backward, the beautiful angel drove her sword downward through his chest, pinning the stunned man to the wall.

Feeling the bullets cease, Peter glanced over the top of his shield to see Tammarion pull her sword out of the last man, wiping it clean on his shirt before he slumped to the floor. Peter grabbed the edge of his cloak to wipe his own blade clean as he scanned the room.

"Dead end," he said, shaking his head.

"Why are each of these dead end rooms filled with attackers then?" Tammarion asked, her brow furrowing with concern.

"Each of them must be a trap to attempt to finish us off," Peter replied with a shrug.

"No, that's too simple," the angel replied, "They must have known that in groups of less than twelve, the odds were hopelessly stacked against them." Peter shrugged again and moved toward the hallway door.

The third door was considerably farther down the hallway, closer to the toxic room than the stairwell. As they approached it, Peter stepped up, braced his shield and kicked hard, blowing the door off of its hinges and into the room.

He had only that instant to freeze and yell, "BACK!" before a torrent of bullets slammed through the doorway and walls. The group flung themselves backwards, hoping they were out of range of the storm of lead that peppered the hallway.

Susan cried out as one bullet struck her in the arm, and Phil barely managed to escape with a graze against his cheek as he tried to protect Katie with his body. Tammarion had immediately taken to the air, flying higher than the bullets were impacting.

Peter, however, was in the center of the onslaught, and was struck several times as he dove to his right, trying to pass their field of fire. After hitting the ground in his dive, he rolled several times until the bullets were no longer passing over his head.

Rising to a knee, the group on the other end of the hallway could see where several bullets had found gaps in his armor and where blood now stained his steel plating. Peter lifted his visor and looked up at the still flying angel.

"There are too many!" Peter shouted at Tammarion, trying to be heard over the still-flowing tide of bullets. His face becoming grim and resolute he stood and turned back toward the wall that was still being peppered with gunfire.

Reaching into the bottomless satchel, he pulled out the massive .50 caliber machine gun and flipped the top up to load it. Sliding the belt into the correct position and flipping the top back down, Peter pulled back the charging handle and lifted the mighty weapon with his right hand so that it rested on the top of his massive shield. Snapping his head down in a sharp nod of determination, he gripped the handle of the weapon.

The rain of bullets, however, had not abated, causing the group to wonder how many Peter had meant when he said too many. As a section of the wall collapsed under the withering fire, the group finally saw the inside of the room with horror.

There were dozens of men in the room, and like a well-coordinated fire team, they were rotating forward in waves, shooting until their ammo was gone, then stepping back to reload while another wave stepped forward and continued shooting.

It was a brilliant strategy, frequently used on ancient battlefields after crossbows had become popular. And as long as the bullets lasted, there was no way to penetrate their field of fire. Understanding this, Peter had not chosen to attempt to penetrate their field of fire but to walk into it.

Depressing the trigger of the mighty gun, the hallway was rocked by the deafening roar of the .50 caliber on full automatic fire. Peter strode into the storm of bullets, sending back a monsoon of his own. The sound of the booming gun mingled with the screams of the men in the room was almost too much to bear.

The friends watched in horror as Peter took round after round. Although most of them struck his broad shield with little effect, many of them slipped past to strike his legs and the top of his helmet that were not covered by the shield.

The knight never hesitated, continuing to shoot round after round into the room as he walked slowly back down the hallway, strafing his shots back and forth, trying to eliminate as many enemies as he could. Under the devastating power of the .50 caliber weapon, the friends watched as walls crumbled and fell. They could see through the crumbled walls, rank after rank of the attackers being mowed down like wheat.

Katie turned her head to hide her face in Phil's chest, as the sight became too much for her. Phil continued to watch, though his face turned slightly green as a real life scene from a bloody horror flick played out before his eyes. Susan's eyes were wide with shock and horror as she just kept shaking her head in disbelief, and Tammarion simply looked grim and a bit sad as she watched the devastation.

After what seemed like an eternity, the giant gun in the knight's hands went silent, its ammunition spent. As Peter took the final steps toward the group he stumbled and dropped to a knee.

The group could see blood pouring from his legs, one of the greaves was missing from his left shin, and his helm was covered in deep dents. Tammarion swooped down, preparing herself to shift into the sasquatch when Peter held up a hand.

"Not yet," he said. "There are more of them. I saw several escape through the back of the room. You need to stay in armor until they are no longer a threat." Tammarion's gaze was angry as she landed in front of him.

"You need to be healed," she stated flatly.

"Yes," Peter replied, "and I will be. Just as soon as the area is secured." Peter lifted his visor and gave the angel a small, pain-filled smile. "Do not worry. None of these wounds is life threatening. I will keep until we are safe."

"Very well," Tammarion replied reluctantly. "Then you must retreat from battle to tend your wounds. Let another take your place." Peter grimaced, but nodded. He closed his eyes, and looked around the cave in his mind.

"Your injuries are considerable," Sean said, his voice impassive as always.

Peter simply grunted and tried to stand. He managed to rise a couple of inches before the pain exploded through his legs and he dropped back down into the stone chair. Sean raised an eyebrow before turning to Derrick.

"I will tend his wounds," Sean informed him. "You may take control."

Derrick was surprised that he felt no elation or joy at seeing the knight finally laid low. After all their years of conflict, he had expected to be more pleased at Peter's distress.

In fact, he was shocked to discover he was actually concerned about the big oaf. He did his best not to show it however, as Sean leaned over to lift the three-hundred-pound knight easily from the chair. Faintly, Derrick heard a voice in his head saying something about there being far too many people with super strength in this mind. Derrick shook his head, as he sat down in the stone chair, and closed his eyes.

Opening his eyes, as he rose gracefully to his feet, Derrick looked at the four friends. Tammarion looked grim but resolute, but the other three were a mixture of horror, fear, disgust, and shock. The vampire risked one quick glance into the room before turning away again. It was a charnel house, with nothing left in it but the dead and quickly dying. He turned a stern look at the four friends.

"We're not out of this yet," Derrick said, his voice firm and commanding. "I know none of you are fighters," Derrick continued as Phil bristled a bit, "But I want each of you to take a weapon, just in case."

"I can't," Katie sobbed, her face still buried in Phil's chest. "I can't look at it, I can't!" Derrick scowled, but understood that forcing her to confront the butchery that had just occurred would not be helpful either.

"Fine," Derrick said after a moment, "I shall retrieve a weapon for you."

Turning, he strode quickly into the gore-soaked room, looking for a body that was less bloody than the others. After a bit of searching, he located one, and removed his rifle and two of his handguns before returning to the hallway. "Here," the vampire said, "Phil can show you how to use them. Now let's go!"

Phil's eyes brightened in appreciation as he took the weapons and began explaining safety and handling tips to the girls. Gently herding the group into the room, Tammarion and Derrick kept a close lookout for any shooters still alive enough to pose a threat. After a few moments, Tammarion looked over at Derrick with a small smile.

"Nice distraction," she said nodding to the group who was walking around the edge of the room, completely focused on the guns in Phil's hands rather than the gore of the room they were walking around. Derrick smiled wide enough to show fang.

"Thank you," he replied. "I thought they might need the confidence." The angel nodded in agreement as the group reached the door at the far end of the room. "Allow me," Derrick said with a bow as he moved up to the door itself.

Slamming the door with a single palm strike, the powerful vampire blasted it off of its hinges and into the hallway beyond. Crouching low, he readied himself for whatever attack would meet them on the other side, only to see an empty hallway with a single door at the far end.

Moving quickly down the hall, he gestured for the rest of the group to stay close. As he reached the far door, he again slammed a palm forward to strike the door. The ancient vampire stepped back in shock however, as the door did not budge. The only result of his strike was a great booming sound that echoed in the narrow hallway.

"Now that we've announced ourselves," Tammarion said moving forward and lifting her great-sword.

Derrick growled softly, but gave way to the angel and her flaming sword. The sword flashed twice and the group watched as crisscrossing cuts caused the door to fall away in four triangular pieces.

In an instant, he was through the empty doorway and halfway into the room, scanning quickly for threats. His eyes widened as he heard heartbeats all around him and he turned to warn his friends.

"Wait! Don't…" Derrick began, but the group had already followed him into the room.

Before even he could move, several large men with painted faces had stepped up behind the three friends not in armor, placing large blades against their throats. Tammarion cried out and raised her sword, but froze at the cold, dead-eyed looks in the men's faces, knowing full well that she could not kill all three before one of them struck. In the silence of the standoff, the sound of a single pair of hands clapping caused Derrick to turn slowly.

There, on a large stone chair in the far end of the room, sat a clown. Not a happy, brightly- colored clown like one would see at a circus, but a purple-haired albino in a dark green suit, his eyes black and cruel under a large brow. Slowly, the albino clapped his hands together in salute.

"Well done," the clown said sarcastically. "You've reached the boss level. But unfortunately, you've lost all of your extra lives." The sadistic face smiled as he gestured to the three captured friends. "Looks like you've only got one left, tisk, tisk." The evil clown chuckled as he smiled at the vampire. "So, what's the boss strategy for this level?" Throwing his head back, the sadistic clown laughed maniacally at his own joke, then looked back down at Derrick, eagerly awaiting the answer.

CHAPTER TWENTY-ONE

Derrick glared back at the clown, drawing himself up into the disdainfully arrogant posture favored by the aristocracy for centuries. The albino grinned at him before turning deadly serious.

"And if your plan is to have angel cakes there do something flashy, then you need a Plan B," the clown said with a growl. "Tell her to shift. The grandmother would work fine I think." Sensing Derrick's hesitation, he got angrier. "Tell her to shift, or the other three die, right here, right now!" A manic tone entered his voice as he sat straighter in his chair.

"Do it," Derrick ordered Tammarion, his voice harsh with anger.

"Do what?" Tammarion replied, looking confused.

"Do as he says!" Derrick barked, thinking furiously.

"What who says?!" Tammarion shouted back, trying to get through to the vampire. It worked, and Derrick looked back at her in surprise.

"What the clown from hell sitting on that stone chair says," Derrick answered, puzzled.

"Derrick, I don't see a stone chair, and I don't see any clown," Tammarion replied calmly.

"What?" Derrick exclaimed, spinning back to the purple haired albino clearly sitting in a large stone chair at one end of the room. The evil-looking man just giggled viciously, clapping his hands like a toddler.

"Ooh! The plot thickens!" he exclaimed gleefully.

"What are you talking about?" Derrick asked, looking back at Tammarion's confused face.

"She can't see me," the clown answered, his voice dropping into a harsh whisper. "Only you can see me."

"Then how do you give orders to your men?" the vampire asked cagily.

"Oh, I gave them instructions beforehand." The clown waved away the question with his hand, slumping casually back into the chair again.

"Then how can I see you?" Derrick asked, desperate for more information. The clown began to answer, then frowned staring at the angel again.

"WHAT DID I TELL YOU?!" he screamed, his eyes wild and demented. "CHANGE TO THE GRANNY!" Tammarion jumped backwards as if struck.

"Derrick, what was that?!" she asked, her blade now pointed at him.

"Did you hear him?" Derrick asked, encouraged.

"Hear him?!" Tammarion replied, her eyes wide. "I heard you! You turned to me, and your face morphed like you were shifting. It turned into an evil-looking clown's face with dead black eyes and yelled 'change to the granny' before shifting back into your face!" Derrick's eyes widened in horror as he looked back to the clown, still sitting in the suddenly familiar-looking stone chair.

"Are you possessing me somehow?" Derrick asked, already knowing the answer.

"Possessing you? I AM YOU!" The pale face lifted again with a maniacal laugh that chilled even the cold blood of the vampire.

"But how…" Derrick began, but the demonic clown pointed a finger at him dramatically.

"Order the granny out now, or one of them dies." the albino said, his voice icy cold. Derrick turned back to Tammarion.

"You're going to have to switch back to Ann," he said reluctantly. "If you don't, one of the others will be killed."

Tammarion looked for a moment as though she would protest, but something in the vampire's eyes told her that this was more serious than all of the other dangers they had encountered so far. The angel simply nodded and closed her eyes.

The body shifted quickly, and Ann managed to raise her hand to wipe at her mouth before a fourth man stepped up behind her and placed a blade against her neck as well. Ann just stood stock still, no doubt very aware of the situation before she came up.

"Happy?" Derrick snapped at the clown.

"Oh, always!" the clown replied with an evil giggle. "But even more so now that it's down to just you and me. The way it was meant to be."

"How did you do it?" Derrick asked, "How did you come up without any of us seeing you?"

"Now, now," the clown giggled again. "That's not much of a strategy, now is it?" The tall albino stood, walking slowly toward the vampire. "Getting me to start monologuing while the oh-so-smart Sean figures out my weakness?" His stride was slow and lazy, almost seductive had it not been for the maniacal grin plastered on his face, or the crazed look in his dark eyes. "Though I do understand the allure," he said, his eyes widening. "The chance to preen and gloat at how brilliant you are. The opportunity to tell the 'hero' once and for all that he's a zero!" He giggled again softly, almost within arm's reach now. "The answer is simple, of course. I stayed in my room, where you couldn't see me." The clown stopped, holding up a hand, palm facing the vampire. "I know what you're going to ask, so don't bother. How did I take control if I stayed in my room, right?" With another grin, he continued, lowering his hand again. "Simplicity itself. I just made a control chair in my own room." The albino laughed at the joke, gesturing back toward the stone chair at the far end of the room.

"Derrick, what's he saying?" Ann asked, trying to remain calm. The vampire looked back at the clown, who gestured to her in ascent.

"He is divulging his entire plan to me," Derrick said in a conspiratorial whisper. "Just like in Justin's cartoons." The clown laughed uproariously.

"Oh, well done, sir!" he roared in approval. "Raise troop morale, by making them think you have it all under control!" The clown continued laughing so hard he had to bend over, his hands on his knees. "Classic strategy! Our erstwhile knight must be advising you!"

The clown continued to laugh, his hands on his knees, face downward. Derrick took the chance and lunged for him, his hands forming into claws and going for the albino's throat.

Faster than the vampire would have thought possible, his opponent was again standing straight, with a pistol pointed right between the vampire's eyes. Derrick froze, his eyes locked with the albino. Once again, a shock of cold malice raced through the vampire's body, and he knew without a shadow of a doubt that the gun was loaded with silver shot, and the clown would kill him without blinking an eye. Derrick relaxed with an easy smile of his own.

"Surely you knew I had to try," the vampire said, his accent smooth as he raised his hands and took a step back.

"Of course I did!" the clown shouted, seemingly angry at the vampire's calm tone. "I planned it that way! Why did you think I bent over?" Derrick nodded sagely.

"Of course, you wanted to test me. Test my mettle, my reflexes, my speed." Derrick acknowledged.

"Naturally!" the clown said, his tone rising again. "I wanted to prove I was better, faster than you!" Derrick just nodded again.

"You certainly got the drop on me," he conceded. Strangely, this seemed to send the albino into a tiny fit. He yelled and stomped, waving his arms wildly.

"Of course I did!" the clown screeched. "I planned it all!" The vampire's eyes narrowed dangerously.

"All?" Derrick asked, the menace evident in his voice. "You planted that spider didn't you? You set it as a trap to kill Molly." With startling suddenness, the clown was again calm and composed.

"Of course," the mad albino answered with a small bow. As he rose, he pulled a small, clear vial from a back pocket. Derrick saw a dozen of the tiny green spiders as the clown continued. "Though I had intended to kill all of them. I was hoping the venom would be enough to transfer, or that the stupid, furry monster would try to heal it." Derrick frowned.

"Why would you want him to heal it?" the vampire

asked, confused. The clown scowled at him.

"Because if she had gone back inside with that bite, it might have spread to all of them." the albino pouted. "I wanted the poison to spread, to replicate inside of her mind." Derrick again looked at the mad clown in confusion.

"Nothing like that exists on this world, you can't have designed them react to our shifts." Derrick said slowly.

"Of course not!" the clown replied angrily. "But I can get a spider with a hallucinogen in its venom that would make all of them think they had the spiders on the inside. I just needed her to go inside and the poison in her body would kill them just as dead!" Practically screaming at the end, he stalked back over to the throne and slammed the vial down. Derrick was surprised when it didn't break with the force of the blow.

Glancing side to side as the clown's back was turned, he caught several of their enemies trying to follow the one-sided conversation. Several of them looked confused, but not enough to slack in their duties. However, they all jumped as though they could hear him as the purple haired albino threw his head back and screamed in frustrated rage.

Derrick took his opportunity to dash forward as quickly as he could run, claws out, fingers rigid as he prepared to slam them into the tall man's back.

With a laugh, the clown spun, his own inhuman speed matching that of the vampire. A drawn blade in his right hand came around to parry the clawed strike, and Derrick leapt backwards in pain. He looked down at his hand to see a long cut along the palm and thumb, a wisp of smoke rising from the wound.

"Silver," Derrick said with disgust. "Of course." The clown just bowed elaborately then raised his dagger in a classic guard position.

"Are we done with the talking part now?" the clown said gleefully. "Is it time for the fighting part?" Derrick felt a tap on his mental shoulder.

"It is indeed." he answered the clown, "and here is your opponent." In a blink, Derrick threw himself off of the stone chair allowing Peter to slide into control.

Peter jostled the shield on his arm to make sure it was secure. It always was. Looking at his opponent he took a quick appraisal. The clown was tall, just inches shorter than Peter himself, but with long arms and legs. The clown face was similar to the men he had first killed, with what he had thought were demonic masks.

However, this man wasn't wearing a mask, his own face maintained that complexion naturally. The purple hair shook as the albino trembled in anticipation. Peter was not fooled by the twitches and antics, however. He noted the perfect guard position, down to the placement and angle of the feet.

This man was a duelist, and had experience facing a longer blade with his shorter one. Peter wondered where he had received such training, before drawing his sword slowly and raising it in salute.

"I am Peter!" he announced, "Knight of the Tower! And I come to challenge you to battle!" The clown's posture sagged for a moment before straightening again.

"Oh, goody! A playmate!" he squealed. "And I am the Jester! The man of a thousand laughs, and a thousand and one deadly jokes!" The clown started to bounce on his toes, apparently eager to begin. "And I accept your challenge. Round one, FIGHT!"

With a double feint right then left, the clown came in hard and fast. Faster than Peter had thought possible by anyone other than Derrick. The dagger glinted in the light as it cut sharply inwards, toward a seam between his breastplate and his back plate under the left arm.

It was only the broadness of Peter's shield that saved him from being killed in the first blow as he swept his arm down, causing the shield to rotate and cover the exposed area.

The dagger scraped against shield, then back plate as the albino darted around behind the knight. Peter was ready for the maneuver though and pivoted smartly to the right to parry a thrust that would have scored the back of his neck at the juncture of his back plate and helm. Trying to switch to the offensive, Peter twisted his wrist so that his blade's edge was downward and swept his sword out and down at the clown's head. The Jester unfortunately danced back with a laugh, then darted in again.

This time, Peter met him face to face, his great shield blocking the dagger stroke as his sword stabbed forward. Peter was shocked when the Jester twisted just enough for the blade to pass by his stomach, while raising his arm that held the dagger over the top of Peter's shield.

Peter gasped as the dagger suddenly began to lengthen, spearing downward toward the slit in his visor. Wrenching himself backwards Peter managed to backbend under the blow and come back up hard with a shield slam.

Peter gasped in pain as he lifted back up again, the

wounds in his legs reopening as he slammed his shield outward. Peter was surprised again when the gangly man executed the same technique he had witnessed in his battle with the gang. Leaping into the air, the clown took the blow on his feet and used it to flip himself backwards, landing on his feet nimbly.

A second blade joined the first in the Jester's hands, both blades now full-sized swords whirling in the hands of a man who knew full well how to use them. The match devolved into a flurry of blows, strikes, and parries, with neither side gaining an advantage.

Peter heard a gasp behind him, but did not dare look around. The sound unfortunately did cause a hitch in his rhythm and a serpent-quick strike of the blade slipped under his guard to stab deeply into his knee. Peter cried out in pain again, disengaging and stumbling backwards. He managed to retain his feet, and seeing his attacker not pressing the pursuit, he risked a glance at the friends.

"I could see him!" Katie said in what was almost a whisper. "I could see you fighting."

Peter looked in shock at the others who simply nodded. Peter frowned, but nodded his acknowledgment of her words before turning back to the fight. The albino grinned as he approached, appearing supremely confident as he parried each of Peter's blows easily. Peter frowned again.

This had been easier a moment ago. He had been able to keep pace with the Jester earlier, but now it felt as though he was barely capable of matching him blow for blow. Peter realized in shock that he was slowing down! But why?

A tiny slip of one boot gave him his answer. As he parried and shield blocked simultaneously he managed to sidestep and buy him a moment's reprieve. As he did so, he looked down at the floor. The floor which was now spread liberally with his blood. Peter again lost his momentum for a moment in shock.

He was bleeding out! The concept took a second to register. He was a Knight of the Tower! He could not lose! Peter would not fail for so simple a thing as blood! He decided that he must finish this conflict quickly, and charged the grinning clown.

Executing the same double right left feint the Jester had tried earlier, Peter dashed forward, slamming his shield outward as he passed the Jester on the left side. Unfortunately for the knight, the crazed clown had seen this coming as well, and as Peter slammed left with his shield the Jester spun counter-clockwise to roll with the strike and slashed down with both blades as Peter passed him. His silver blades cut deeply into Peter's hamstrings. Peter dropped to his knees with a cry, expecting the next blow to take his head.

After several long moments without a blow, Peter turned to see the clown just standing there, beaming at him. Peter struggled to try and stand but dropped to his knees again, the tendons in his legs cleanly severed.

"Well that was fun!" the clown giggled, clapping again. "Round two?" Peter tried again to rise, knowing he would be helpless now against the duelist's skill. "No, no, NO!" the albino roared. "You were round one! I beat you! Now it's time for round two!" the Jester announced crossly, stamping his feet. "Send in your next challenger!" Peter closed his eyes in defeat, and allowed Sean to take control.

Sean rose easily from his knees and turned to face the self-proclaimed fool. His posture was relaxed, though both of them knew he would be able to react at a moment's notice.

Examining his opponent critically, he could see that the Jester was not experiencing any quickness of breath despite his duel with the knight. The twin swords glistened red with blood as the albino held them pointed down and outward. The clown seemed to be eyeing him as well, and just as intently.

"I believe you requested another opponent?" Sean said calmly.

"Oh goody!" the clown giggled. "Another playmate to abuse!" Sean raised an eyebrow.

"I will not permit you to commit acts of abuse upon myself or any of my companions," Sean replied.

"Permit, PERMIT!" the Jester screamed at him. "Who said anything about permitting?! I am going to abuse you, whether you want it or not!"

"That would be illogical. Most abuse takes place in a situation where there is a disparity of power between the two parties," Sean stated, launching into lecture mode. "When there is no disparity or perceived disparity of power between the individuals, then abuse is unlikely to occur. What you are proposing would fall more broadly into the category of torture. This intent was evident in your actions toward Peter. You had ample opportunity to take his life once you had removed his ability to walk, however you did not do so. Instead you gloated over him, rubbing in the fact that you had won. This would fall under the category of psychological torture. Your intent was obviously to humiliate him, not kill him."

The clown just stood there staring at the pointy-eared man, with his mouth open and his eyes glazed over. As soon as Sean stopped talking the albino shook his head and glared at him.

"That was the most inane piece of drivel I've ever heard!" the crazed clown exclaimed. Sean shook his head.

"I do not believe so," he stated calmly. "If it had been inane drivel you would have become bored and interrupted. You did not, which indicates that you were listening intently, seeking to examine my intellect and evaluate it. Did I give you a sufficient sample of my intelligence?" Sean inquired.

"Oh yes," the Jester replied, grinning evilly. "You have indeed shown me you are not as intelligent as you would like people to believe. In fact, you are nothing…"

The clown's words cut off in an instant as Sean drew his laser pistol and shot both of the albino's blades, knocking them out of his hands. The clown's eyes widened in surprise as he dove to the side.

"Fight time! Yippee!" he screamed happily. "Round two, FIGHT!" Landing in a shoulder roll, the Jester came up with twin automatic pistols, firing each of them in successive bursts at the now running alien.

Sean calculated quickly as he ran, dodging to the side an instant before another spray of bullets slammed into the wall where he would have been. Sean fired quickly at seemingly random points around the room. However, it was time for the clown to jump and dodge as each shot reflected off of a mirrored surface of some type and angled back toward the Jester.

Dropping the empty pistols, the Jester grabbed two submachine guns from behind his back and pulled the triggers. Bullets flew around the room, causing at least one casualty among the guards as Sean ducked and dodged around walls, pillars, and guards in an attempt to evade the assault.

Sean noted that the Jester did not intentionally fire at his own troops, however, he did not seem to hesitate to kill one of them if they were in his way. Sean also noted the eyes of his companions starting to track not only his movements but also apparently the movements of the albino, indicating that they were able to see him intermittently.

He found this to be a fascinating development as the Jester had indicated that they shared the same physical body. In fact, he noted as he grabbed one of the guards and threw him in the direction of the clown, their eyes always snapped back to his opponent just before his actions killed someone, or almost killed someone.

The Jester, seeming to grow tired of this game, tossed his weapons down and pulled a new set of firearms from behind his back. This time, it was a pair of short-barreled shotguns with ammo drums attached to them. With a roar of maddened rage, the clown charged toward Sean, firing rapid shots from each shotgun, and decimating the walls and concrete pillars in the room.

As he ducked, dodged, and rolled to avoid each new blast, Sean also noted that none of the guards were acting hostile or aggressive toward him, even when he used them as shields. This would tend to indicate they had been given explicit instructions not to touch him, but rather to leave that to their master.

Sean took a chance and stopped his ducking and dodging long enough to turn face the Jester directly. He fired three rapid, calculated shots, one at the center of mass on his opponent, the second at head height to the Jester's right, the third waist height on the Jester's left.

As Sean expected, the clown suddenly moved significantly faster, dodging to his right then ducking down and shifting left. Sean had anticipated this, guessing that the Jester might be right-handed, based on his primary shot as he attacked. What he had not anticipated was the half-backbend the Jester enacted to get out of the way of the third, lower shot.

Though he would never admit it outwardly, Sean was unsettled to see the Jester move in a similar manner to a popular movie that featured sentient computer programs who were capable of moving so quickly they could dodge bullets. Spinning to his left, Sean ducked behind a concrete pillar to analyze this new information.

Sean understood now that his opponent was merely toying with him and was in no danger from any physical attack that Sean could use. He also understood why the unstoppable knight had failed. Peter had truly no chance of succeeding against this opponent. The Jester was too fast for Peter to ever keep up with him. In fact, Sean surmised that only Derrick could potentially move fast enough to stand a chance in a physical fight, and even that was uncertain.

As he continued to dodge sprays from the shotguns, Sean also began to understand that he himself was in no danger from the manic attacks. The Jester moved so rapidly Sean knew that he would also be more than capable of laying down fire in a wide enough arc that despite Sean's physical prowess, he would be incapable of dodging. He was truly being toyed with.

Rather than being upset however, he became curious as to why his opponent would put on such as show of attacking him without any real intent to harm him.

Replaying the Jester's movements in his mind, Sean also realized something else. Whenever the Jester moved beyond the bounds of human capabilities, he also became visible to the others in the room. He had noted Ann's piercing gaze as the clown had dodged Sean's triple shot a moment ago.

This could indicate that a source of power or energy was being tapped by his opponent, but that using that energy pushed him a little more into the outside world. Sean decided that the only way to be sure was to test his theory, and holstered his laser pistol.

Sean calmly stepped around the concrete pillar he had been standing behind and walked slowly toward the crazed clown. He did not flinch or pull away as shots blasted all around him, tearing chunks out of the floor and walls. Sean continued to walk forward slowly, his hands at his sides, obviously weaponless.

The albino seemed to become even more crazed, screaming wordlessly and pulling both triggers on his shotguns. Blast after blast reported from the barrels of both automatic shotguns. Sean just kept walking forward with full confidence that he would not be injured by any physical attacks. After another two point seven five seconds of screaming and shooting, the Jester abruptly stopped both, looking straight into Sean's eyes.

"So, you finally figured it out?" the clown asked, his voice cheerful. "It took you long enough! You really are far less intelligent than those simpletons give you credit for." the clown mocked with a grin. Sean accepted the comment with aplomb.

"I am curious as to why you continued your assault when you had no intention of actually harming me?"

Sean inquired.

"You see!" the Jester screeched. "Stupid, stupid, stupid!" Sean simply stood there, staring at him. "You started it!" the Jester said, in a whining voice meant to emulate and mock a schoolchild.

"Indeed," Sean acknowledged, recalling that he had fired the first shot. "What then was intended to be our battleground?" he inquired. The clown sneered at him disdainfully.

"What do you think?" he asked, still in a mocking tone of voice. Sean nodded briefly.

"A contest of the mind," Sean stated, knowing that the Jester would mock him for so obvious a statement, yet wanting to ensure that his friends knew what was occurring.

"Of course a contest of the mind, you dolt!" the Jester screamed, moving to within a quarter of an inch from Sean's face. "You are useless physically! You couldn't dominate a housefly! And in a moment, I will prove you couldn't outthink one either!"

Sean again nodded, and reached up a hand toward the Jester's face. The albino sneered at him, but surprisingly allowed the contact. As Sean made contact with his fingertips on various nerve points in his opponent's face, he sent his mind out and into that of the crazed clown.

Just before making contact, the irony of joining minds with someone who was already in his mind occurred to Sean. He had no more opportunity to think after that, as his mind touched that of the mad albino.

The first thing he saw was a rainbow of swirling color. It was almost like looking down the eye of a tornado from above, only swirling with strong primary colors. In the center of the colors, standing in the eye of the color storm was the Jester, grinning up at him like a maniac. Sean felt himself being drawn downward, toward the gruesome visage. Faster and faster he fell, pulled like a magnet toward his opponent.

Realizing his danger, Sean attempted to rise up again, but he was pulled inexorably downward. As he neared the chaotic clown at near-terminal velocity, he realized he did not occupy a corporeal form. He registered an instant of surprise before being drawn into the dead black eyes of the maniac.

The second thing he saw was a dark and shadowy plain. It seemed as though he was standing in the center of a savannah, but with dark, swirling, black smoke all around him. Although Sean felt no need to cough with all of the smoke, it did restrict his field of vision to less than three meters in any direction.

For a moment, he attempted to calculate the distance more precisely, but discontinued the attempt when he realized the swirling smoke was making it a non-static distance. Intrigued, he began walking forward into the smoke. While the smoke itself did not clear, neither did it worsen, ensuring that Sean would continue to be able to see approximately three meters in any direction.

After walking for what he calculated to be seven point seven six minutes, he began to hear sounds. They started as indistinguishable whispers in the smoky darkness, but soon became a chorus of voices echoing from every direction. Each one was different and distinct, though many of them sounded like they were from youths rather than adults.

"You're stupid!", "You stink!", "Weakling!", "I'm very disappointed in you.", "Why couldn't you be more like Tommy?", "Mr. Castlemain, your behavior is unacceptable.", "Hey Casper!", "Douchebag!", "Coward!", "Nerd!", "Don't make me beat you!", "I'm going to pummel you after school, dork-wad!", "Can't you do anything right?", "Failure.", "Idiot.", "Loser!", "What's the matter, can't get a real girl?", "Ew! I wouldn't touch you with a ten-foot pole!", "As if!", "Gross! Why would you even talk to me?", "Do I need to teach you a lesson shorty?", "I don't think so!", "I just don't think of you that way.", "You're such a dork!", "Just a big, fat loser!", "Why don't you stay with your own kind?!"

The voices continued, growing louder, each of them jumbling against each other until they started to become indistinguishable again. Sean recognized the sentiment behind them, though. They were the voices that Garrett had heard throughout his young life.

All of the ridicule and bullying he had experienced had come here to rest, growing and festering until they became the dark smoke. Toxic and caustic, burning at his mind, his self-image, his self-worth, until he began to believe the voices and turn them into his reality.

In fact, it was these very whispers that had resulted in Sean's creation. He had split as a logical, unemotional, alien based on a television show that Garrett's parents had watched, precisely because he was unemotional and would not be affected by the words of Garrett's peers.

Nodding to himself, he continued to walk, unaffected by the voices which grew louder and louder. He did note, however, that the insults being thrown were starting to sound crueler and crueler, incorporating profanity and offensive language.

As he continued to walk, Sean also realized that the

variability of the voices was declining and more and more of the insults were coming from a single voice. Sean stopped as he finally recognized the single voice. It was Garrett's voice.

The bullies had won and Garrett himself was now the one hurtling insults. They had convinced him that all of the evil, cruel things they said were true, and he had begun saying them to himself, reinforcing their cruelty a hundred-fold.

Sean nodded to himself in acknowledgment again, and continued walking. As he walked, the dark smoke of negativity began to clear, the now singular voice growing quieter and quieter until it faded into nothing. In that instant, Sean found himself inside of a building.

A quick glance around showed him to be in a school, likely an upper grade-level school since there were lockers lining every wall. A blink, and he was outside again, this time on a running track. He watched as a scrawny youth walked slowly around the track, a book in his hand, reading as he walked.

As he watched, he saw a small group of larger youths coming up fast behind the first, and shoving him. The book went flying out of the smaller child's hands and he struck the ground hard. The group of bullies didn't slow as they passed him, though one of them hesitated long enough to slam a kick into the fallen boy's ribs.

Glancing up to ensure he had not been observed, the abusive youth laughed and ran to catch up to his friends. Slowly, the thin boy picked himself up and went over to retrieve his book. The relief on his face when he saw the book was undamaged was palpable.

Another blink, and Sean was in what appeared to be a locker room. He again witnessed the thin boy, now standing in front of a small locker. He began to get undressed, but moved very slowly, casting furtive glances at the shower room every few seconds.

Glancing over, Sean could see the shower room was nothing more than a tiled room with four columns centered in the room. Each column had a half-dozen shower heads coming out of it, and groups of boys laughed and pushed each other as they showered.

With a final look at the door to the locker room to see the coach inspecting each boy as they left to ensure they did actually take a shower, the thin boy sighed heavily before straightening. Slowly, he walked into the shower room.

As he crossed the threshold, the young boy winced visibly as all of the other boys began to laugh and point at him. As Sean observed, he could see nothing wrong with the youth. No visible deformity that would provoke the ridicule. Yet almost as one, the entire group of boys laughed and taunted the youth as he began to shower.

Sean blinked again and was now in a crowded hallway of the school, the thin boy walking nearby. He watched as a different group of youths came up to the boy and knocked his books and papers to the floor with a laugh.

Another blink and he was in a cafeteria, watching the boy speaking awkwardly to a girl who was sitting at another table. As he watched he could hear her cry out in disgust before slapping him, to the great amusement of the other girls at her table. The boy looked both crestfallen and humiliated as he turned away.

Another blink and he was on the street; the boy was walking down the sidewalk away from the school. Without warning, another, much larger boy stepped out from behind a bush. Sean estimated that he must be several grades higher, since he towered over the young boy. With a meaningless insult, the older boy began to strike the youth. Blow after blow landed until the boy fell to the ground, desperately trying to protect himself from the kicks the larger boy was now throwing his way.

Yet another blink and Sean found himself in what looked like a bedroom. And although there was nothing wrong with the room itself, Sean began to feel a sense of foreboding. Realizing that he was designed not to be able to feel emotions, he looked around the room in confusion. After a moment, he saw the boy from before, only much younger.

He was huddled in the corner staring at the door to the room, his eyes wide with terror. Looking into the boy's eyes he could feel the fear radiating out from him. Sean looked quickly back and forth between the door and the boy, fear rising in his chest. No! He should not be able to feel fear. And yet the terror grew.

His eyes snapping back to the boy, Sean realized that this was a trap. The boy was a projective empath, and was reliving one of the most terrifying moments in his life. In desperation, Sean tried to shield his mind. Using every telepathic technique he knew, Sean attempted to block the raw terror radiating from the boy.

It took only moments, however, for the logical, unemotional man to realize the futility of his actions. The boy's terror was growing to the breaking point, and for the first time, Sean felt true, undiluted fear.

Stark, raw terror ripped through his mind as the boy's own fear continued to mount. A cry ripped itself from Sean's throat as his legs gave out and he collapsed to the floor, his whole body trembling and shaking with the force of the horror that the boy knew was coming.

Slowly, the door to the bedroom began to open. In that instant, Sean knew that he had lost the battle of the mind against the Jester. Helpless, the pointy-eared alien began to cry, screams of raw fear tearing at his throat, his body shaking violently with the force of the emotion. He had lost.

CHAPTER TWENTY-TWO

Garrett opened his eyes and looked around. A cry of surprised joy brought his head whipping around. He looked over to see Ann, her eyes wide with fear and relief as she took a step toward him. Her guard grunted as he grabbed her arm and tightened his grip on his knife, pressing it against her throat.

"Ann," Garrett started. "What happened?" Ann seemed almost not to notice the blade at her throat or the strong grip of the guard as she spoke rapidly.

"It was Sean!" Ann said with tears in her voice. "He walked forward and reached up with his hand. Then he went stiff for a while, and after a few minutes he began to fade! It was like he was disappearing right in front of us! And as he faded away, we saw that evil clown start to fade in. And just as the evil clown started to become more solid than Sean, Sean collapsed to the ground crying and screaming and shaking!" Ann finished. "I've never seen anything like that happen before! I thought he didn't feel any emotions! Then the clown laughed hysterically, and blinked out at the same time you blinked in over where Sean had fallen."

The sound of slow clapping brought Garrett's head

around again, and he saw the Jester sitting in the stone chair again, just like he had been when they first came into the room. Garrett started to open his mouth but the crazed albino beat him too it.

"NO!" he screeched. "NOT YOU! NOT YET!" The clown's eyes rolled wildly as he practically fell out of the stone chair. "Your time will come! But not yet! Send me the vampire, or they all die!"

Garrett opened his mouth to retort, but hesitated at the wild look in the Jester's eyes. He closed his mouth again and then closed his eyes to let Derrick know he was up again.

Derrick opened his eyes and stared straight up at the Jester, his eyes narrowing in hatred. A growl built in his throat and he could feel his claws lengthen on his thin fingers. He bared his fangs in a snarl which seemed to delight the clown to no end.

Remembering the Jester's earlier speed, however, Derrick reached down and removed the last vial from his belt, the Time Stop potion. In one quick motion, he flipped the top and drank it down.

As he tossed the empty vial away, Derrick noticed that the guards all appeared frozen in place, along with his friends. Staring for a moment, he realized that Greybeard was wrong. It wasn't a Time Stop potion at all. With his heightened senses, Derrick could see that everyone was still moving. They were just moving so slowly that it looked like they were frozen. Then, the sound of his most hated voice brought his head whipping back around in a snarl of surprise.

"Wonderful!" the albino exclaimed with delight. "You're already ready to fight!" Realizing that with the Jester sharing the same physical body he had just wasted the Time Stop potion, Derrick's only response was a deeper growl. "Round three! FIGHT!" the clown yelled.

Derrick exploded into motion. Faster than the eye could see, he slashed at the deranged clown with his now lethal claws. A lightning fast right, left, right combination of horizontal slashes had the Jester backpedaling to stay out of reach.

Derrick lunged forward, fingers rigid, aiming for the albino's belly. But the Jester was on his toes, his own hands locked in a rigid form of Hapkido as he blocked outward with his right hand, his left darting in like a spear toward the vampire's throat.

Derrick was ready for the movement, though, and lowered his chin, opening his jaws to reveal the impressively sharp edges of his teeth as his face morphed into something resembling a demon rather than a man. His head snapped forward like a canine, biting at the white fingers. With a cry, the Jester pulled his hand back before the blow landed, losing only the top bit of skin to the razor sharp teeth of the angry vampire.

"Not fast enough!" the Jester taunted. "And now it's gone!" The clown gestured around the room, emphasizing the fact that the potion had run out and everyone had come back up to full speed.

Derrick just snarled again as his hands hooked upwards, driving his claws in toward the Jester's belly. The clown blocked with both hands down and outward, but the vampire lunged forward, teeth going for the unprotected throat. The Jester's eyes flashed with anger as he turned his head toward the incoming vampire and slammed his head forward in a forehead strike that knocked the vampire backwards.

Derrick was barely able to keep his feet after the blow, but did not slow his relentless assault. Charging back in again, he struck high with his right claws, then low with his left. As the Jester blocked both blows Derrick launched a round kick with his left foot trying to drive his claws past the block and into flesh.

The Jester unfortunately did not attempt to block the powerful kick, but danced backwards laughing, taunting the angry vampire. Derrick felt his rage rising, growing out of control. In an effort to stay in control, he tried focusing on his friends, trying to do something to keep himself from going over the edge.

"I can see them!" Katie said softly, though Derrick's ears picked up her voice easily. "Barely though," she continued.

"I know," Phil assured her. "It's not that you can't see them, they are moving too fast to follow."

The guards as well seemed to have lost their focus on their prisoners and instead were watching the fight avidly, now that both combatants had become fully visible.

Derrick snarled again even more bestially as he flew at the Jester's face, claws extended. Giggling like a schoolgirl the Jester caught his wrists and spun, trying to flip the airborne vampire over and down into the ground.

Derrick had anticipated this move as well, and bent at the waist so that his feet were pointed toward his hands, so that when the Jester pulled forward and down trying to pull Derrick off balance, he ended up accelerating the kick as well. Derrick's feet slammed into the clown, knocking him off of his feet to fly several feet through the air before striking one of the concrete pillars.

The crazed clown was back up in an instant, but Derrick had moved in to press his advantage. Claws slashed and bloody ribbons flew from the Jester's shirt. Stumbling back, the clown raised a bloody hand up to his face. The awed fascination the clown displayed at the sight caused even the enraged vampire to pause.

Almost reverently, the albino brought the hand forward and in a gesture that caused the four friends to recoil, he licked the blood on his hand in one long stroke.

"Ah!" the Jester said looking up at Derrick. "I see why you like it so much!" Derrick snarled again, gathering himself for another lunge. "I wonder how your blood tastes!" the Jester screamed as they both charged simultaneously.

In a fury, Derrick slashed again and again, no longer caring what strikes landed. A red haze began to descend over his vision as he moved faster and faster. Arms whipping back and forth, claws raking anything they could touch, Derrick felt himself begin to slip out of control.

All of a sudden, the maniacal laugher of the homicidal clown broke him out of his all-consuming rage for an instant. In that instant, pain exploded all over Derrick's body. Looking down in shock he saw over a dozen cuts on his own hands, arms, and body. Each of them smoking slightly, and not closing as his wounds typically did.

Looking up, he saw the glint of another silver blade

in the Jester's hands. Derrick felt a flash of satisfaction as he saw an equal number of bloody gashes all over the Jester's body, but as the clown brought out a second silver blade for his other hand Derrick felt his spirits fall.

"Is it time?" the Jester asked gloatingly. "Is it time for the end?"

Rage building again, along with a determination that if he fell he would take the lunatic with him, Derrick lunged back into battle. This time, however, he transformed into his wolf form as he leapt at the clown. The Jester's eyes widened an instant before the enraged wolf struck, knocking him to the ground.

Hind claws raked at the pale white belly as sharpened teeth snapped at the pale face over and over again. The Jester flailed wildly, trying to keep those massive jaws away from his throat. Finally, the albino thrust an arm forward, accepting the crippling bite from the powerful jaws, but freeing his other hand to plunge the silver blade deep into the wolf's side.

Releasing the bite with a yelp of pain, the vampiric wolf scrambled backwards, but not before another strike from the glinting blade plunged deep into his chest. Derrick let out another yelp of pain as he tried to back away, but his legs gave out under him and he collapsed to the floor.

Red blood stained the floor in a quickly spreading pool as Derrick tried to rise again. His feet could not seem to gain purchase, however, as his claws scrabbled against the concrete before his legs gave out again and he fell to the floor with a whimper.

The Jester giggled again, then laughed, then threw his head back with a maniacal belly laugh that seemed to unnerve even his own guards. Taking a step forward, he raised the silver blade high, obviously intending to finish off the dangerous wolf. Derrick, seeing his end approaching, lifted his head with a mournful howl of defeat.

The guards all jumped at the sound, their eyes flicking back and forth between the fallen wolf and their crazed master. Every eye in the room widened a moment later as the faint image of giant trees began to form in the room. The Jester froze, homicidal rage playing across his face.

Derrick howled again, long and low. The guards began to murmur in surprise as the trees began to appear more solid, until they were as realistic looking as that of any dreamer. The Jester few into a fit of screaming.

"WHOSE DREAM IS THAT?!" he screamed, head whipping around wildly. "WHOSE DREAM IS THAT?!" Racing around the room, his head snapping back and forth, trying to identify who was manifesting their dream in his room. "It can't be!" he continued to scream. "You can't dream! I took your dreams! None of you can dream!" Moving even more erratically, he finally reached one of his guards, his eyes wild with crazed rage. "NO DREAMING!" he cried as his blade flashed out, slicing the throat of the unfortunate guard. In an instant, he had moved to the next guard, and torn his throat as well. "Who's dreaming?" he cried out again, "I took your dreams from you! Who's left to dream?"

In that instant, Phil's eyes flashed red and a dark flickering smoke rose to quickly surround him. In less than a heartbeat, he had transformed into the demonic Vengeance.

Using the guard's momentary distraction, Vengeance drew his two massive pistols, black flames igniting around them as he lifted his arms. With a single simultaneous trigger pull, the heads of the guards restraining Katie and Susan exploded in a wash of gore.

With a cry of outrage, the guard behind Vengeance yanked his blade backwards attempting to take the head off of the flaming black demon. The man cried out again in fear when his blade found no purchase and simply slid into the blackness under the hood without coming into contact with flesh.

Turning rapidly, Vengeance fired again up into the guard's body, his flaming red eyes flashing. His own guard dispatched, he turned to look over to Ann, only to see that she had apparently witnessed his transformation and had also changed into a more durable form.

Tammarion's mighty blade flashed forward to block the large knife at her throat and her golden wings of light had buffeted backwards to knock her guard back and away from her. Spinning quickly, her flaming great-sword separated the guard's head from his body. Locking eyes with the dark visage of Vengeance, they both stared for a moment, then nodded and turned in opposite directions to start taking out more of the guards.

Susan, realizing they were a liability, grabbed Katie's arm and pulled her backwards and out the door. Tammarion and Vengeance noted the movement but didn't have time to follow as they worked their way around the room, killing as many of the guards as they could.

The Jester finally broke out of his rage, realizing that two of his captives had begun slaughtering his guards, and the other two had escaped. With a snarl of his own, he dashed back toward the still fallen vampiric wolf, determined that if he was going to fail, he would at least kill the vampire first.

Raising his silver knife as he ran, he stopped short just before he reached the wolf. There in front of him was a small towheaded boy, around five years old, standing between him and his prize. With a tiny hand raised like a traffic cop the small boy glared at the killer clown.

"Stop!" Justin yelled at the clown. "You can't kill my friend!" The entire room seemed to freeze in shock. The silence was so absolute that one could hear a pin drop. After a moment of shock, the Jester threw back his head and laughed loudly at the boy.

"Stop?!" he cackled. "And who is going to stop me?"

"I am!" Justin replied firmly.

"You?!" The clown's black eyes glaring at the child. "How can you stop me? I am big, you're small, I have a knife, and you have nothing!" A truly evil grin split his white face. "In fact, I think I'll kill you first, and then kill the wolf!" And with that he started forward again.

"Justin!" Tammarion screamed, seeing the killer clown moving forward and knowing she was too far away to get there in time.

Justin just closed his eyes and placed his hand on Derrick's furry neck. Derrick howled again, long and lingering. In that instant, something around them seemed to snap, and both guards and the pair of warriors drew back in surprise as bullets began slamming into trees instead of going right through them.

In fact, one running guard slammed face first into a tree that was suddenly solid, instead of the illusion he expected it to be. The Jester froze again, his eyes wide in amazement.

"What did you do?" The clown asked in a hushed voice, as he looked around. "You made them real?!" Frantically, he looked at a tree right next to him and reached out to touch its rough bark. "How did you make them real?!" The boy just opened his eyes and smiled up at the bewildered albino.

"I believed in them," Justin said simply.

"What!" the Jester shouted turning back to the boy. "What do you mean you…"

His angry voice trailed off as a second, deeper howl echoed from the trees. The albino's black eyes widened again as the forest thickened around him. Bushes and grass sprouted from the concrete ground, and smaller trees interspersed themselves between the larger ones.

One of the guards cried out in amazement as he reached down to brush one of the ferns and found it was as solid as the trees. The howl echoed again in the new forest and everyone, with the exception of the boy and the vampiric wolf started looking around, trying to find where the sound was coming from.

Everyone seemed to notice at the same time when the massive form stepped out of a clump of tall bushes. It had the appearance of a wolf, the massive muzzle filled with sharp teeth, the pointed ears twisting as it listened to the forest. The hind legs were lifted up to their toes just like those of a wolf, with only the paw touching the ground.

This wolf, however, did not walk on four legs. Striding upright on his powerful hind legs, the grey, furry body stretched over seven feet in the air before reaching the tips of the pointed ears. The yellow eyes flashed with intelligence above the fanged jaws. A massive shoulder span stretched into long, well-muscled arms that ended in viciously clawed hands that flexed almost involuntarily at the sight of the deranged clown.

The massive werewolf threw back his head and howled. His deep voice reverberated through the trees, causing a shock of primal fear to lance through each of the stunned guards. The clattering of guns hitting the ground was all the proof the giant wolf needed that the guards had all surrendered. With a scream of rage, the Jester charged the werewolf, silver blade flashing.

The wolf's eyes flashed as well as he intercepted the silver blade by grabbing the flat of the blade between two claws and stopping its movement cold. The Jester looked up in fear as he gave one tug on the blade and realized he would not be able to pull it free.

Releasing the knife, the clown lunged forward, his hand snapping forward in a spear like strike. The werewolf, unfazed by the movement, simply reached down and caught the striking hand in a clawed grip stronger than forged steel.

His eyes now wild with fear, the Jester pulled another silver knife and tried to strike again. The werewolf tossed the first knife away, leaned down and roared into the white face of the attacking clown. His roar blew the albino backwards, only the clawed grip on the Jester's hand keeping him from flying back into a tree. The werewolf snapped his jaws forward as the roar ended, his massive fangs slamming together a fraction of an inch from the Jester's nose.

The Jester just stared up into the eyes of the wolf, his dagger dropping from nerveless fingers as he realized this was one creature he could not beat. The wolf reached around with his left hand and gripped the back of the Jester's neck in his massive, clawed hand, lifting him off of the ground.

"NO!" the Jester cried out as it dawned on him who the werewolf actually was. "NO! You can't be my opposite!" His voice rose an octave as he screeched in outrage. "I don't have an opposite! I was the first! You can't be here to stop me!"

"Yes, he can," Justin's quiet voice seemed to cut through the wailing outrage of the trapped clown.

"No! I was first!" the Jester cried again.

"What do you mean you were first?" the familiar voice of Garrett said as he rose from the ground where Derrick had been a moment earlier. "I am the core personality. I was first." The Jester sneered at him.

"You were first huh?" the clown said disdainfully. "And how do you know that?" Garrett frowned.

"I am the one with the name we were born with." Garrett replied, suspiciously. The angry clown started to laugh before the clawed hand tightened around the back of his neck.

"A rose by any other name?" the clown said mockingly. "What's in a name? I tell you I was first!"

"Impossible!" Garrett exclaimed. "You have powers that didn't exist before the Dreaming. You can't have been first!" The Jester spat at Garrett's feet.

"Fool! Imbecile! Idiot!" the albino screamed. "Tell me, have you tried to co-control the body yet?"

"What?" Garrett replied, confused. "Well yes, once."

"And how did that work out for you, pudding?" the Jester asked looking amused.

"It was a bit awkward." Garrett answered, his curiosity getting the better of his anger for the moment. "When Justin and I shared control, everything looked different, including me in the mirror."

"OF COURSE IT DID!" the Jester screamed before being cut off by the squeezing claw. He glared up at the werewolf for a moment before replying again. "That's because the meddlesome boy is older than you are! He came before you did!"

"That's not possible!" Garrett exclaimed again.

"HA!" the clown said the irony thick in his voice. "And how do you think I was able to keep taking control of the body without you knowing? It was mine first!"

"I don't see how…" Garrett started.

"I WAS FIRST!" the clown screamed again, ignoring the claws around his neck. "I was Garrett Castlemain! The stupid boy split from me! Then that pointy-eared freak, then the wool-headed knight, then the weakling vampire!"

"But how…" Garrett started again.

"But nothing!" the Jester continued. "I was Garrett! I am Garrett! They created you to replace me! To shut me out! To keep me away from control! Idiot! Can't you see you were a clone, a fake, a simulacrum? You were designed to take my place! Except you would be able to function in society. You wouldn't break because you didn't have my memories!" Garrett frowned up at him.

"I do have memories of my childhood." Garrett said puzzled.

"Only the good ones," the Jester answered calming slightly. "The bad ones were kept away from you. Why do you think you did so poorly in group therapy?" he mocked. "You didn't have the memory of what caused the splits, so you couldn't talk about them in group. I did! I held them all! So when I had my chance, I created my own control chair. Then I figured out how to change myself. I was the core personality after all. I could do whatever I wanted with my mind and body! I gave myself the power to beat you! To beat all of you! I watched and I waited until I knew how to defeat each and every one of you! And so I have!" the Jester exclaimed triumphantly.

"But I can't have been created later!" Garrett exclaimed. "I don't have an opposite! And everyone in my head has an opposite!"

"Imbecile!" the Jester screeched again. "Of course you have an opposite! You utter moron! Don't you know? Don't you see?! It's the voice! That voice that talks about everything you do, everything you say. The one that analyzes and explains everything that happens in your life, your thoughts, your dreams, everything that happens inside of your mind. Your opposite is the Narrator!" Garrett blinked rapidly, digesting this information.

"But..." Garrett started. "But I..." But as he thought about it he realized that it was true. There was a voice that was always going, talking, analyzing everything that happened to him. An endless running monologue that talked about everything that happened to him. "But that's not a personality!" Garrett exclaimed. The Jester made a rude sound.

"It's personality enough!" he mocked. "You're not much of a personality either! You were crafted, designed, molded to be completely and utterly boring! There is nothing unique or original about you. Other than the fact that you stole my identity! You kept me from being myself again, from being Garrett! You are why I had to become the Jester!" Garrett stepped forward to look into the mad eyes of the clown.

"It looks like you did too good a job of it," Garrett said quietly. "You changed yourself so much that you became an alter. And as soon as you did that, another had to be created to match you, to beat you, contain you. That's the way this mind works. There is no way to escape it."

"Then if I kill you, we will have an odd number again, and this wolf will disappear!" With a snarl of renewed rage, the Jester flicked his wrist producing another silver dagger and stabbing forward with it.

In a move too quick for anyone to see, the seven-foot werewolf reached out and caught the Jester's arm before the blow landed that would have killed Garrett. The beast bent the arm upwards to stop the blow, and Garrett winced at the loud snap as the Jester's blade hand pointed upwards again, bent not at the wrist, but in the middle of the forearm. The knife fell to the ground as the werewolf leaned forward and growled into the mad clown's ear. Screaming and crying in pain and rage, the Jester just thrashed in the wolf's strong grip.

"Thank you," Garrett said, looking up into the suddenly kind eyes of the werewolf. The mighty head nodded once. "What is your name?" The werewolf stared at him intently for a moment, not saying a word.

"I think his name is Gaheris!" Justin exclaimed, coming up to the wolf and hugging one furry leg tightly. Garrett looked down at the boy in surprise.

"The brother of Sir Gawain? From the Knights of the Round Table?" Garrett asked.

"Uh-huh!" Justin replied happily.

"That works for me, how about you?" Garrett asked, looking up at the big wolf. He chose to interpret the curling back of the wolf's lips to reveal a massive row of sharp teeth to be a smile of ascent and smiled back.

"Now how about you, Small Fry?" Garrett asked. "How did you do this?" Garrett asked, knocking on a now solid tree.

"I believed it," Justin answered simply.

"You believed it?" Garrett asked. "What do you mean?" Justin shrugged.

"Derrick dreamed it, and I believed it," Justin replied.

"I don't understand," Garrett said, confused.

"That's okay!" Justin said racing over to hug him as well. "You don't have to!" Garrett looked up as Tammarion and Vengeance walked over to them, all of the remaining guards now tied to trees.

"You've been busy while we were talking." Garrett said with a smile. Tammarion grinned at him.

"You were occupied," she said. Her gaze shifted down to Justin, then up to Jester and Gaheris. "But how are all of you here?" she asked. Garrett shrugged.

"I don't know. I don't understand it either," he replied. "Justin?" he asked, looking down at the boy who just shrugged at him.

"I don't know," Justin mimicked with a grin.

"Justin!" Garrett said exasperated.

"Nope!" Justin said suddenly serious. "Ask Sean!" And with one last giggle, he closed his eyes, and his small body morphed into the pointy-eared alien. Garrett saw with relief that the unemotional man seemed no worse for wear after his own ordeal.

"Hey!" Garrett exclaimed. "You're all right!"

"Indeed," Sean replied with a raised eyebrow. "Once our furry friend here took hold of the clown, his power cut off as well."

"His power?" Garrett asked. "Which one?"

"His strongest power," Sean answered. "He is a projective empath. He can force emotions on others and cause them to feel what he wants them to feel. The opposite of the receptive empath most people are familiar with from various sci-fi programs." Garrett's eyes widened at the implication. "Many people know about the receptive empath who can read others emotions, can tell when others are lying, or what their true intent is. This is the reverse. Instead of feeling the emotions of others, the projective empath makes others feel his emotions. That is how he controlled his followers and why we never saw their dreams. He pushed out their ability to dream by flooding them with primal emotions that overwhelmed rational thought." Garrett whistled slowly.

"Wow," he said after a moment, "And he could do that to anyone? And keep it up even when he wasn't in control?"

"Yes, he could keep projecting even if he was not in control of the body," Sean answered. "Though I expect he needed to come up regularly to refresh his hold on them. But no, not to anyone. He would be most effective on those who were weak-willed, or had a particular emotion or vice he could exploit." Garrett nodded.

"Such as sorrow, depression, anger," Garrett guessed.

"Indeed. Those would be powerful emotions he could play on and enhance until his victim was under his control," Sean concluded. "However, he could not take over those whose minds were too complex, or who experienced too many emotions. People like us with more than one mind inside of our head were far too complex and difficult for him to control, he could only influence." Garrett nodded again in understanding before turning to the tall werewolf.

"So what now?" Garrett asked. The wolf tossed his head to the side indicating he was going to go. "You will take him with you?" Garrett asked with concern. The wolf only nodded, squeezing the still thrashing clown a bit tighter until the man stopped thrashing. "And you will make sure he can never get out again? Never hurt anyone again?" The great head again nodded before looking down at Garrett with surprisingly kind eyes. "Thank you," Garrett said softly, reaching out to place a hand on Gaheris' furry arm.

The wolf smiled again, baring his teeth before turning and loping back into the forest, a much subdued clown dangling from one arm. After a moment, Garrett was hit in the side by a flying body.

"I thought you were going to die!" Ann said, squeezing Garrett tightly. He smiled and wrapped his arms around her and hugged her back.

"Nope," Garrett replied. "Not with the help of my friends." Ann nodded, then tensed in his arms.

"Where did they go?" she asked, looking around. "Sean and Justin?" Garrett looked around for a moment, then closed his eyes.

Looking up from the stone chair he was surrounded by his mental companions. Sean, still watching with a raised eyebrow, nodded in reassurance. Derrick was once again in his impeccable eveningwear. Peter limped slightly, but slowly walked up to the chair and saluted him with a fist to his armor-plated chest. Justin, however, leapt up onto his lap and gave him a great big hug before climbing back down again. As Garrett looked around the room, he noticed the door to one of the previously locked rooms closing, a wolf-like hind paw stepping inside just before it closed. With a smile, he opened his eyes again.

"They're back up here," he said, tapping his head. "They're all back up here."

"Oh!" Ann replied happily. Then she looked around again. "But if they're gone, why is the forest still here?" Garrett's eyes widened as he reached out and knocked on a very solid oak tree growing from the basement floor of an enclosed factory building.

EPILOGUE

Garrett sighed heavily as he stood in front of the social services building again, debating whether he wanted to go in or not. With a shake of his head, he realized he didn't really have a choice; all of his friends were in there. Friends that had seen him through thick and thin. Friends who had literally seen the very worst parts of him.

Garrett had been terrified that they would want to have nothing to do with him after they found out that he had been the cause of all of their grief. That he had almost gotten all of them killed, and in fact did get Molly killed.

His friends, however, had been more understanding than he had any right to expect. They all declared that the trouble was caused by the Jester, not by Garrett, and wouldn't hear any of his protests that the Jester was the first Garrett.

"But you're Garrett now," Katie had said with a smile, "and you are our friend." She'd given him a big hug after that, Garrett remembered with a smile. So had Susan, though she didn't try to express her feelings in words. The hug was enough. They were friends.

Garrett and Phil had talked for a long time about

Phil's new alter, Vengeance. Phil hadn't brought him up in group yet. He wasn't sure if Ruby was ready for that kind of a shock.

Garrett grinned at the thought. Not that he was able to force Vengeance to come up anyway, since it seemed that he only appeared when Katie was in danger. Garrett's grin widened. Phil and Katie had finally come out and declared their love. Not that it was a surprise to anyone at that point, other than Ruby, of course.

Garrett laughed at that. Their first group session after the incident with the Jester, they had walked in together holding hands, sat down next to each other and left together, their hands never coming unclasped the entire time. Garrett wondered how they got into the car that way.

He was happy that his friends had found someone to love. And they were deliriously happy together, but it was a happiness that spread to include all of them. Whenever the gang was together now, it didn't feel like people in a group therapy session any more. It felt like family.

Still, he really didn't like the therapy part any more than he did before. Which is why he was still standing here on the steps like a dope. He shook his head at his own foolishness. He had faced down the very worst parts of his psyche. The darkest, most terrible things he could imagine, personified, and he had come out alive. Not just alive, but renewed. With a new sense of himself, and a new respect for his fellow alters.

That had been a challenge to work out though, that he was an alter. He'd kind of been focusing on that in group, which is why he didn't want to go in. It was still a very uncomfortable topic for him, despite all the progress he made. But at least he knew who he was now, mostly. He still hadn't been able to get Justin to tell him how he had created the forest though. Justin just kept saying he didn't create it. That Derrick had dreamed it and he had just believed it.

That one had really baffled the police, he read on the newspaper website. An old-growth forest suddenly sprouting out of a perfectly solid building. Police were confused, biologists were confused, and engineers were confused. The only ones not confused were the religious nuts. They all thought it was a sign. Some secret message from a mysterious deity that wanted them to get back to nature again. Garrett chuckled.

None of their gang had talked to the police, of course. The five of them had gotten out as quickly as they could and reported the tied-up guards anonymously. The police naturally had mounted a search for the anonymous tipper, but it was hard to get DNA traces from a forest.

So now there was a forest at the edge of town. Lots of people came to look and pray at the site. Garrett hadn't been able to go back, though. Too many memories.

He blinked quickly to keep the tears out of his eyes. It still made him angry, of course. He missed the fiery redhead and her fast-driving, gun-toting, computer-hacking, smart-mouthed self. He blinked again, shaking his head. He hadn't brought that up in group yet either. He wasn't sure how to explain that one of Ann's alters had died, but she was still alive. Not a bridge she was ready to cross yet either, fortunately.

Garrett looked up at the social services building and sighed again. He really didn't want to talk about his feelings again. Shrugging his shoulders inside his jacket, he shook his head at his own reluctance. He was just about to start up the steps when a familiar head poked out from between the double doors.

"Hey, slowpoke!" Ann said with a grin. "Get in here! Ruby is waiting for you." Garrett just laughed as he started up the steps.

"All right, fine!" Garrett said, reaching the top and wrapping his friend in a big hug. "But this time you get to go first at sharing time!"

COMING SOON

THE

AWAKENING

LEGENDS OF THE MAKERS: BOOK TWO

BY

JEFFREY BAILEY

OCTOBER 2017

ABOUT THE AUTHOR

A self-described voracious reader, Jeffrey Bailey loves nothing more than to curl up with a good story. Instilled with a love of reading at a very young age, his first passion was for tales of King Arthur and the Knights of the Round Table, and it wasn't long before he began writing short stories of his own.

Publishing many of his stories in school magazines and newsletters throughout grade school, he continued to write stories and poetry while serving in the U.S. Army, though wisely he refrained from showing any of his poetry to his drill sergeant.

His interest in psychological disorders began as a young man working extensively with people suffering from Dissociative Identity Disorder, and culminated in an assignment for his psychology degree where he was asked to act out that very behavioral disorder in public and record the results. The reactions he recorded were so profound that he started to ask the question; "What if everyone outside could see what they see inside?"

Jeffrey currently resides in western Washington where he remained after leaving military service. His hobbies include comparative theology, ancient mythologies, and reading to his son to instill in him the same love of literature that Jeffrey himself enjoys.